Rhapsody of Blood

Volume Three – Resurrections

Books by Roz Kaveney

Author

Fiction

Rhapsody of Blood: Volume One – Rituals
Rhapsody of Blood: Volume Two – Reflections

Poetry

Dialectic of the Flesh

What if What's Imagined Were All True

Non-Fiction

From Alien to The Matrix: Reading Science Fiction Film

Teen Dreams:
Reading Teen Film and Television from "Heathers" to "Veronica Mars"

Superheroes!:
Capes and Crusaders in Comics and Films

(with Jennifer Stoy)

Battlestar Galactica: Investigating Flesh, Spirit, and Steel

Nip/Tuck: Television That Gets Under Your Skin

Editor

Tales From the Forbidden Planet

More Tales from the Forbidden Planet

Reading the Vampire Slayer:
The Complete, Unofficial Companion to "Buffy" and "Angel"

with Mary Gentle

Villains!

with Neil Gaiman, Mary Gentle & Alex Stewart

The Weerde Book One

The Weerde Book Two: Book of the Ancients

Rhapsody of Blood

Volume Three – Resurrections

A Novel of the Fantastic

Roz Kaveney

Plus One Press
San Francisco

This is a work of fiction. All of the characters, organizations and events portrayed in this novel are either the products of the author's imagination or are used fictitiously.

Plus One Press

RHAPSODY OF BLOOD, VOLUME THREE – RESURRECTIONS. Copyright © 2014 by Roz Kaveney. All rights reserved. Printed in the United States of America and the United Kingdom. For information, address Plus One Press, 2885 Golden Gate Avenue, San Francisco, California, 94118.

www.plusonepress.com

Book Design by Plus One Press

Cover artwork by Graham Higgins, copyright © 2014 by Plus One Press

Publisher's Cataloging-in-Publication Data available on request

ISBN-13: 978-0-9860085-9-7
ISBN-10: 0-9860085-9-1

2012946881

First Edition: November, 2014

10 9 8 7 6 5 4 3 2 1

To Laurie Penny

Acknowledgements

My thanks are, as usual, due to Deb and Jacqueline, my patient and diligent editors.

A team of my friends either listened to me read this or read sections of it. Among these are Simon Field, Lesley Arnold, Zoe Stavri, Cel West, Angelica Tatam, Radhika Holmstrom, Pat Cadigan and Charles Stross – my thanks to you all.

Robert Irwin gave me access to his extensive library on Alchemy and earlier forms of The Work. My thanks to him and Helen for their hospitality.

And Paule, as ever.

Resurrections

"It is the heart of the heartless world:
it is the opiate of the people"
— *Marx*

"Jesus died for somebody's sins but not mine"
— *Smith*

Sorrow's Friend

Egypt, the East, Judaea 16 – 20 BCE

"You're just a big tease," Crowley said. "Typical feminine nonsense, for all you are a Power."

I really had no idea what he meant.

"You keep talking about the one you refer to as Josh—but you also keep saying that I am not worthy of hearing his story."

"No more you are."

"But it is clear that he's the only man or god you've ever loved. Were you lovers?"

"Of course not."

"But you loved him—and there's something more, isn't there?" This annoying man was far too good at reading faces—some of his magic was real, but most of it was mere conjuring and knowing people well. "Your spear—it's not what my friends in Germany call the Spear of Destiny, is it? That that terrible old bore Wagner wrote an opera about?"

This was far too good a guess.

"You killed him." He looked smug and impressed and appalled.

"Not exactly—it was complicated." And also a story whose end I did not know, which meant, I realized, that I would tell him.

It would amuse me to leave him as frustrated and uncertain as I have been for two thousand years.

You would say the boat was shaped like a lute, long and narrow at the prow and deep-bellied as a pregnant woman. No one had built a lute then, and the first time I saw one centuries later, it reminded me of that ship, trim and yare and smelling of pine-resin, pitch and the incense that was its usual cargo. The ship, though. I loved it at first sight.

I was on my way home to my sister, who was alive in those years, and was minded to hurry to her side. I had waited so many decades for this rebirth that perhaps, I thought, I was too eager, too little mindful of the Great Work in which she was engaged. Although I missed her mightily when away from our home, I was less nostalgic for the fumes and bubbling of her workroom. Perhaps I should take my time and savour the wait of a slow and human journey, and the anticipation of a homecoming that was not merely a matter of slipping in and out of shadow.

I thought on this and sat on the docks at Caesarea, thinking of that stretch of coast in earlier days, when it smelled more of salt-grass and less of sweat and fried food.

Then I saw the ship and decided that I was minded to travel on it.

Using a little glamour to distract the boatswain, to prevent him thinking too closely on who I might be, I hired myself on to it as a guard, as I sometimes did, though not for the pay. Men were less inclined in those years to hire women for acts of violence, but even a casual and beglamoured glance showed him that my weapons had seen much use, and my mere survival in the world of arms served as my reference and guarantee.

As the ship pulled away from the quay, rowed by its free crew into the current, and then catching a fresh breeze in its sails, I sat on the deck quietly. I felt the newly scrubbed deck underneath me, so well-carpentered that it was like a caress.

Nearby two pretty Greek boys played dice for each other's favours, and two Judaean boys watched them with abhorrence and fascination. One of the Jews was stropping the blade of a knife against a leather belt, one end of which he held in his teeth and the other he pinned to the deck with his heel. I liked the look of determination on his face, and noticed the efficient movement of blade against leather. He struck me as a serious lad, with a mind that focussed like a burning glass on anything he set his mind to. I was not wrong about him, though over the centuries I have had cause to wish I had been.

Around us the crew and captain busied themselves with their own concerns, which were none of mine. I stretched a little, basking in the sunshine, and yet a sudden feeling of unease passed through my mind and was then, for the moment, gone. I noted it, though, for while I am often wrong about the specific meaning of such sensations, they are almost never entirely trivial.

One sailor passed a flask around the passengers—the two young Jews waved it away but one of the Greek lads swigged avidly, then poured it into the flirting open mouth of his companion. I saw, but did not notice, the sailor with the flask nod to his captain as he walked away, putting the flask aside without taking a swig himself.

It does me good sometimes to sit and watch and remember simple humanity, the weak lives that I defend against the strong and evil. Sometimes also, listening to chatter, I heard things that might interest me—travellers' tales or the gossip of street vendors and whores.

Few knew of the Rituals in those years—there had been too many decades of the letting of blood for entirely other purposes, and some crucial documents had met the fate of many more useful manuscripts, burned when Caesar burned a part of the Museion or when the First Emperor killed his scholars. People do not have to know their nightmares' names in full, though, to smell them on a hot wind or fear them in the watches of the night. I listen to their moans, and their jokes, and their bawdy; and once in a while evildoers meet their end before they have done all the harm they might have.

Mostly I travel by sea for the wind and the brisk sun of dawn and the sting of salt spray on my skin, simple pleasures I see no reason to deny myself. And sometimes the sea wind and the chatter of the birds that soar on it instruct me as much as the talk of sailors and fellow-passengers about things I need to know.

Again, there came that sense of unease, like that which prickles one's neck and shoulders when one is observed from behind. I stood up and looked out to sea and one of the Judaean lads came and stood by me trying to see what I saw, while his companion continued to work on the knife. I looked up at him—he was a thin, lanky youth—and noticed that he had the second prettiest eye-lashes I had ever seen on a man. I should have guessed who he was in that moment, though my failure is one of the few things in our friendship that caused no harm of any kind.

He addressed me without any doubt. "What do you seek, Huntress, that you stare so endlessly out into the empty sea?"

"I do not know. Something out of its proper place."

He did not answer, but peered out to sea with an intensity equal to his companion's focus on his knife. I had not advertised my name or work on the boat, but he was a clever lad, who shared with me a capacity to listen to those around us. So often, when people quote his words, I know that he was repeating something he had heard another say and was not too proud to appropriate.

"I watch," I continued, "to be sure that nothing seeks me. I have many enemies and some have names I do not know."

"But what could stand against you, who have cast down so many of the Mighty?"

"There is an adversary out there."

"Satan? Who was once the Lightbearer, the Son of the Morning?"

4

I smiled, for this young man, whoever he was, knew little of the world. "Another, and a worse…But there are other things I fear. I saw this sea once, when he rose from his bed to trample, and it is sensible to be wary as we travel across him, lest we become the night itch he wishes to scratch or the cramp that he needs to walk about to be rid of. The sea is a man who cannot be reasoned with, and to whom smart answers matter not at all."

"Yet what stories that man could tell," he said, in the slow longing voice of one to whom story was a taste dearer than honey.

"If you dare," I replied, "one day you should to talk to his least brother, the Lord of Salt, who lies at the borders of your homeland. He is a treacherous and cantankerous being, but he loves to talk. And these days, few remember him."

It was time I sought the Lord of Salt's counsel again myself, I thought. It had been too long, long enough that I had forgiven him, and more beside.

I reached over and clasped the young man's hand; I had thought him a scholar, and yet his hands had the calluses of hard work as well as the grooving of one who used a stylus a lot. "You know my name," I told him. "You may call me by it, rather than my title or my trade."

I looked back out to sea—I had no fear that He would rise again in this age, since He had slept fitfully for so many centuries, but something was not right. "I do not think this sea wakes, but something…"

He pulled me over to where his companion sat, looking vaguely disapproving. As I approached, he spat the belt end from his mouth, wrapped it around himself and slid the long knife into a sheath at his side. Alongside it, the belt had a loop through which it carried a small metal hammer.

"This is my brother, Judas son of Joseph," my new friend said, "and they call me Josh. And this is Mara, whom men and gods call Huntress."

His brother acknowledged me with a nod, but his attention was still on the knife, whose handle he stroked with his right hand.

5

I noticed that Josh said "my brother" and that he did not say "Josh, son of Joseph," and in that moment surmised whose son he was, and knew I should have known him instantly. Live long enough, and your own old mistakes come round a second time, and you try to avoid making them again, and you repeat half of them, and the rest of the time you make mistakes that are all new.

Still, I thought it harmless enough, and it probably was, that I sat and talked to the two youths of times gone by, though I did not wish to scandalize them by talk of matters that might concern them deeply. I talked of more recent things, scandals at the Court in Rome, and a creature made of living amber that I had shattered into pieces and strewn along the coasts of the Northland.

As boys will—and young women too—they thrilled to the tales, and so I talked of the virtue of my solitude, and how I hunt alone, and never talked of companions, still less of apprentices. And as I talked, the sun dipped down in the far West and they drowsed and it was time that I earned my passage by looking out to sea and back at the shore, and into the phosphorescent wake we left behind us and ahead, from a perch on the mizzen-mast.

In the years of the triumphs of Octavian who had taken the name Augustus, the years after Actium, pirates had been swept from the sea and some thought them gone forever. I knew otherwise but welcomed the pause, for pirates like bandits are men who have learned to think of other men and women as their prey, and such are willing bloody hands that set themselves to the Rituals more readily than the bloody hands of military men.

It is not that I take no care for the great slaughter of war, it is that only occasionally does it become something of which I need take direct note.

Word had come South, years earlier, that Augustus' great peace was done and that legions had died in the forests of Germany, and those who chafed under Rome stood up a little more, and desperate men who might have cowered or starved longer, thought they might take a chance. And then the emperor died and was called god, for all the good it did him, who did not blossom into anything of the kind for all that Romans burned incense to him, and for all the men who had died to make him great. Such things work often, but often do not.

His adopted son took his throne, but not as securely, and small mice nibbled at the ropes that held empire together. And ships needed to hire guardians again.

Thus it was that, that night, in the hour of the wolf—though he howls not at sea—I saw three small dark shadows pull away from an empty stretch of coast where they had been hugging the shore, and shouted out the alarm.

One of the crew reached out with a club to rap me senseless, as men will do sometimes who are both treacherous and ignorant of who I am. I was mild with him, and merely broke his wrist. I ceased to shout, though, because it was clear to me that the men coming aboard were expected.

The captain rushed across to me. "Be gentle with him, Huntress," he said. And then, in a tone that he presumably thought would ingratiate him with me, "After all, none of this is the sort of thing with which you concern yourself."

I let the crewman drop to the deck and seized the captain by the arm, gently but firmly, so that the bruises would not numb his arm for more than an hour or two. "I decide what concerns me, little man."

I stepped away from him to stand by Josh and Judas, who had awakened; Judas had his long knife drawn and was standing protectively by his brother.

The men who had come aboard while I was remonstrating with the captain, sun-burned muscular men old before their time, paid little attention to them, and had seized the young Greeks from where they lay entwined, still hardly awake. From where I stood, I could smell poppy on the breath of the Greeks; earlier the reek of pine resin in the wine had masked it.

The youngest and largest of the pirates stepped forward, meeting my hostile stare as few men care to, and put his arm on the captain's shoulder, ignoring his business partner's wince. "As my friend says,"—his voice was deep, dark and mellow and it occurred to me that this pirate, or, as I guessed, fisherman had missed his vocation—"this does not concern you. Why should you or your friends care what happens to these two?"

Josh spoke out; he reminded me of his father in his natural oratory, but where Jehovah dominated, this lad persuaded.

"She cares because it is the right thing to do. Those two paid their passage as much as we did, and have the same right to safe arrival at their destination."

His brother spoke up too. "My brother is right. If they are freeborn, you have no right to take them, nor if they are slaves, and belong to their master."

I should not have been surprised. Rich young men going to Alexandria—students of the law and the Law.

"But,"—there was, after all, no reason why the pirate chief should not be as fascinated by such matters as they were, and as keen on instruction—"what if one were servant and one master? As would be my guess."

Judas thought for a second, but his brother did not hesitate. "The same applies—you can take neither his freedom nor his property from the master. And their contract with the captain remains the same, as does the law of nations, which sets itself against piracy."

As Josh spoke, he twisted sideways, and suddenly had the captain by the throat. His brother stepped forward through the space he had created, and laid his knife gently against the big vein in the pirate's neck.

Prettily done, and obviously they had rehearsed such moves, but I could wish they had waited for me to deal with the matter.

The bodyguard, or some such, who had taught them had clearly not seriously expected them to have to deal with men of real violence. The pirate was equally quick and brought his right arm around, clubbing the knife away from his throat and felling Judas to the deck.

8

Where he reached up, dazed though he was, and stabbed the man through the foot, though without pinning him to the deck. With his other hand, he reached for his hammer, but before he could grab it, two of the other pirates grabbed the youth by the scruff of his neck and held him for their commander, who swore as he pulled the knife from his bleeding foot and considered where to stick it.

I coughed, loudly. And was gratified to see that every single person on that deck froze, as if in a children's game, and not through any making of mine, but through prudence alone.

"All four youths are under my protection. Now go away before I lose my temper."

Josh stepped away from the captain, walked over to the pirate chief, touched him once on the hand with his brother's knife and stepped away before anyone could move against him. The man's foot ceased to gush blood—it was as if nothing had ever happened to it.

Any doubt I had as to who this young man might be, disappeared.

The pirates released the young Greeks, but still stood rather close to them, as if they might choose to snatch their arms again.

"I have starving villagers to feed." The pirate chief had the aggrieved tone common to bullies who find someone prepared to fight back. "Sold to a man I know in the desert, those Greek sodomites would have fed us for a month."

I have little time for such excuses. "So ask that man for help, or sell him something else—do not turn to piracy."

He continued to try to stare me down. "He has no charity in him, that man, and we have nothing he wishes to buy save our own children."

I made a note to find this man, and talk to him severely. Such men often have those who would work the Rituals as their customers and need to be discouraged.

"So fish, since that is your proper trade."

"There are no fish." There was now actual desperation in his voice. "The sea has been empty for two months. My cousin here knows of this."

I looked at both men again, and at the pirate more intently. Both men had the same furrow between the brows, the same strong jaw. It was the pirate's size that had stopped me noticing these resemblances between him and the captain.

Then I knew what had made me uneasy earlier. If there were no fish in this part of the sea, where there had previously been enough for fishermen to rely on them, it was because something was eating them. Something was out there, and what I had sensed was the presence and wrath of something that was tracking us, and had been tracking us since Caesarea. Ever since Josh and Judas and I had come on board and stepped into the realms of the sea. And the creature had no grudge against me that I was aware of.

I could not say anything, yet, for the sailors and pirates might risk my anger and throw the two Judaean youths overboard to it. As if that would save them, any more than it had the men who threw Jehovah's reluctant prophet to it, all those years before.

And that was a story that ended less well than legend states.

Why it had swum out of shadow I could not guess, perhaps just following some shoal of idiot creatures that had darted out of their proper seas, but it was here now, and if I could sense it, it could sense Josh, and his father's scent upon him. A scent that would drive the creature to resentful fury.

It is all very well to pierce the tongue of Leviathan with a hook, and to ride the sea with it on the end of your cast rope for days until it tires and floats to the surface as if finished. Yet to be too tired at the end to use your harpoon, and your gaff, and gut the great beast for the hungry seabirds and busy sharks is merely to store up problems for another day.

I had told Jehovah this, the very first time he started to boast to me of his new-found prowess in such matters. His rivalry with the creature the idiot boy Dagon had become was strong in those years. He never listens to me; it survived and went back into shadow to lick its wounds and now was back again, enraged.

I glanced out to sea once more, knowing what to look for, and there in the distance it was, its great shining eyes peering at us, though my guess was that it had other, more acute senses.

And suddenly it dived, deep and deeper, and yet the sea into which it plunged was only partly the mundane sea around us. There was a tension in the air around us; great gouts of foam and torrents of water were boiling into the space in shadow that we occupied— we were not swept away by them, and yet we knew in our bones that they were there.

Bones that were not broken or battered, and yet could not but be touched.

And that force in the air was not just the waters of shadow, but the strength of angry hostile will.

A will that was an inarticulate roar and yet crisp and clear as an argument in court.

The nature of the Great Beasts is often mixed and mismatched— many of them are single creatures, but they have needs like other beasts, and the products of their unlikely unions are sometimes creatures of nightmare.

Leviathan was not Whale or Kraken or Crab or Serpent or Shark; it was child and grandchild to all of them and who knows what creatures besides? There are many beasts in shadow gone from the world before men walked it—great lizards and their cousins that swim or fly, jellyfish whose stinging trailers could empty whole mundane seas, scorpions whose lashing tails were like falling pines. The Chimera that Perseus killed was only one of these hodge-podge dangerous creatures, and far from the worst, because it was an animal merely, and had no thoughts in its head.

Most of them fear men, or the gods some men and women become. I have, without godhood, put fear into the hearts of many such beasts myself, and have killed others that would not learn to stay in their proper place in shadow.

Some creatures never learn fear and are hard to kill and intelligent enough to feel hatred. The Leviathan had at least enough intelligence to wish to play with us a while, as a kitten does with a butterfly that it watches and then smashes to painted dust. One of its stinging tassels whipped out of nowhere and flicked a man off the mast and onto the deck, where he writhed as one horribly burned with great blisters bubbling on his limbs.

Josh touched him, and this time I watched the youth carefully and saw that the sudden clearing of the man's skin, the ending of his pain, was not without cost to his healer, who went pale of a second.

"Easy lad,"—I had seen such healers before—"you will need all of your strength before this night is through."

He shrugged off the hand I had rested on his shoulder, but not in an unfriendly way, just that of one who had business to take care of. Business that was his and his alone.

His stepbrother had turned to the man he had stabbed moments before. "We should clear this ship as quickly as possible." His voice was that of someone telling a friend something the friend already knew but had not yet voiced.

The pirate chief looked at him with respect and clapped his hands as if giving a set signal. His men swung themselves over the side and into the small boats with rehearsed speed, and held out hands to catch the two young Greeks without any hint of further menace or plan against them. The boats had room to spare and at a nod from the captain, most of his men joined his cousin's.

I turned to the captain as well.

"This will go better if I don't have to worry about you,"—I looked at the two young Judaeans—"or you."

"This is my concern as much as yours." Josh turned to his stepbrother. "But you need to join the boats while you can because I must be about my father's business, and you have your father's business to take care of should I fail."

It was as if he had read my mind.

"No, Huntress, I can read faces, but not minds." He laughed. "And I can also read scripture, and know what we face and why."

I felt abashed.

"You must tell me what he is like." The youth looked wistful. "I have hardly met my father, past an inspection in my childhood and a clasp of my hand. If I am, as they tell me, well-studied in scripture beyond my years, it is because I have a selfish motive."

One of the stinging whips took off the mizzen and another missed Judas by inches. The captain looked sadly about him at his ship, then shrugged and swung himself down to his cousin.

"Go," Josh pleaded with his brother. "The Huntress will protect me better than you can. And I would rather not worry about you."

Judas looked reluctant, but reached out his hand to touch Josh's shoulder, and then swung down into the last boat, which pulled away.

Had the beast been a brute merely, the boats might have been heading into utter destruction, but its attacks had been meant to isolate. There might not be a mind in play here, but there was some aspects of one, at the least.

Together, Josh and I stepped towards the side of the ship that faced the open sea and waited for Leviathan to rise.

As rise it did, out of water into air, and, at the same time, out of shadow fully into the mundane. Coils and muscles and whipping barbs and ropes of flesh—so much contained energy and yet, around us, hardly a ripple, just that strength and malice and water that poured off it as it rose yet vanished back into shadow before it could put even a spray of dampness on our deck.

It was silent, and yet its intrusion into the world was like a bellow of wrongness.

If I had ever thought it a Great Beast merely, I had been wrong; it had rage in those great eyes, eyes the size of doorways, and pain too. I had never thought before what a tragedy it must be to be a creature almost capable of articulate thought yet utterly dumb, having no mouth with which to shape language.

This creature had a beak like an octopus, fringed with a beard of writhing tentacles, and behind that beak lay row upon row of teeth, so long and sharp that it could never close its mouth. It had eaten, not fish alone but some other great beast, because guts and loose flesh lay among both tentacles and teeth as if they had fallen there and would have to be washed away by the sea, for it could not rid itself of them. And beyond those teeth, a tongue and something glinting in it like silver in the depths of a mine.

"There lies my path." Josh pointed into that terrible maw. "And if things go ill, my grave. But what a fine one, don't you think?"

He laughed aloud and slight as he was, I saw his father's strength in those narrow shoulders and thin waist. Below us, the sea roiled and the ship juddered and shook. The youth had presence and will; it was not, in the end, the capacity to crush stone to gravel in the palm of his hand that had made his father the Hero Twin.

"I know that you are stronger than you look, Huntress. I would be obliged if you could throw me as far into that mouth as you can manage, and then do what you can to hold those teeth apart for a moment or two."

It was a plan that even I was inclined to think of as foolish, but I had to say, I liked the boy's style.

He hopped up on to the rail and stood like a diver—I did little more than boost the leap he made and then leaped myself into the creature's mouth, dancing my feet in among the gaps between teeth and pricking the roof of that mouth oh so gently with my spear as if I might do worse if I chose to.

Yet I knew the beast would only halt a second or two, might at any moment rage and try to crush me. I was confident that this beast would not and could not be the death of me, but I feared that I might not be able to protect the lad Josh.

Almost before that fear could form itself into a plan, he darted back past me, dancing on the points of those teeth as elegantly as I, or perhaps more so. It was as if his feet moved in and out of shadow.

He had in his right hand the cruelly barbed silver hook he had taken from the creature's tongue, which yet dripped blood and worse things, fluids that had stained his left hand where he had touched and healed.

Not relying on the creature's gratitude, I made haste to seize him again and leap with him to the deck of the ship.

14

Leviathan moaned and the noise was like the falling of trees in a high wind, but then it was silent as if the wind had dropped, or as if a sudden moment of increased pain had taken the slow path to its brain, followed by the realization that that pain, and the long festering which had preceded it for centuries, was gone.

One of the tentacles from the creature's lips reached out and wrapped itself around Josh's wrist. I readied myself to cut it and free him, but all it did was unwrap itself, feel its way up his arm and along his shoulder, and then stroke the contours of his face slow enough to memorize his features.

The tentacle touched his lips and he moved them, as if speaking, but I could not hear what he said. Then it withdrew.

There was a sudden suction that sent the boat rocking as Leviathan was suddenly not there—it had dived deep and fast and the water it displaced splashed onto the decks in great gouts. Josh reached down with the hook and washed it clean in the salt water that streamed down into the gunwales past his feet. Without blood and fluid on it, the hook gleamed almost white in the moonlight, but also with light of its own.

He passed it to me. "That should probably be returned to its owner."

"We are not on regular speaking terms," I shrugged, "but I will take care of it for the time being."

Jehovah's fish-hook is not, after all, the sort of thing which should be left lying around.

There was something I needed to be sure the boy knew.

"I don't know whether you realize that you can flick your feet in and out of shadow. I have only once seen anything like it. People can't usually do that—you danced on the points of that beast's teeth where most of us, even the Mighty, would have to sidle our feet through the gaps."

I'd once seen a horde of the dead and semi-dead dance their way across the sea, but they were asleep or mindless.

"Do I?" He looked guilty. "I've been wandering in and out of

15

shadow as long as I can remember. It's fun." He had a look of mischief in his eyes, and I realized how young he was and how recently he had been a child.

His brother was the first to leap up on the deck when the boats pulled out from the shore to us and he hugged Josh wordlessly in relief.

"You knew I'd be all right; I had the Huntress to help me."

I found myself not even slightly resenting this young man's talking as if he had been the leader. It was not presumption, just the simple truth.

The crew reassembled on deck alongside their friends the pirates, and set about making good the damage and cleaning away the last smears of slime and other things. I've always been impressed at how quickly human beings can rebuild their works when they have a mind to.

I took a moment to think which proved, in the event, a very short time indeed, because hardly had I taken breath when a white bird, with eyes that appeared gentle but a beak as cruel as that of its progenitor, fluttered down and perched on the rail beside us.

"I have nothing to say to you," I said, because I try to have as little as possible to do with the children of the Bird.

The white bird spoke to me, nonetheless, in a whispering version of the chant Jehovah's angels use. Like its flame-coloured sibling who accompanies Lucifer, its voice was sweet, though not as sweet as its parent's, and far less resonant.

"The Lord God Jehovah/ whose place is on high/ thanks you, Huntress/for your care for his son." Then, in a more normal voice, "I will take back that fish-hook now. He has a use for it."

I wordlessly pulled the hook from my quiver, where I had stowed it, and it reached up a talon and took it, keeping its other claw firmly attached to the rail.

Josh walked across. Clearly he and the White Bird were old friends, because he reached out and patted its head and it stroked his arm with its beak, its head on one side. Judas came over and stroked it too, more tentatively.

I looked askance at this, and Josh shrugged.

"We have known Ghost since our childhood," Judas said. "We would be sent sweetmeats from the Lord's throne and Ghost would wake us in the night and pop them in our mouths."

"The Lord watches over all his children/ but his son, and his son's brother most of all," the White Bird whispered.

I determined then and there that I would take an especial interest in these two young men, just because it pleased me to and because I distrusted the influence the White Bird might have on them.

Against my better judgement, I spoke to it directly. "Will you be accompanying us to Alexandria, or returning to perch on his throne?"

It looked at me with its sly beady eyes. "The boys are in good hands, I see. No reason for me to delay. Between you and Philo, their education will be taken care of." It turned back to Josh and Judas. "Do not let the Huntress lead you to take stupid risks. The Leviathan might have killed you."

Josh stood up, skinny and proud. "That was my plan, that the Huntress helped me execute. You may tell my father that I have healed the brute he hurt and requested that it leave these seas and cease to trouble his people. I doubt I could have done it safely without the Huntress, but it needed doing."

Judas put his hand on his brother's shoulder. "Had she not been here, I would have helped Josh, even if it cost me my life."

"Ah, youth in its pride," the bird cooed. "It took me centuries to teach prudence to your father after he had spent a few months travelling with the Huntress. I will remind him, and perhaps he will forgive you your recklessness."

It looked at the pirate chief. "Simon, whom men call the Rock," it cawed officiously. "The Lord will not punish you, this time, for interfering in his son's travels, but he forbids you to be a pirate any longer, or to sail these seas. For a while."

The pirate gave it a bleak look. "How shall I feed my people?"

17

"For that I care not," cawed the White Bird with an uncharacteristic harshness that reminded me of its parent. "I have given you the Lord's word; see that you obey."

With that, it fluttered into the sky, with the Lord's fish-hook held firmly in its talons. The first light of dawn flashed from the steel as it rose, glimmered a second and then was gone with the bird into shadow and to Jehovah's high place.

We stood and watched it go; I was glad enough to be done with it that I watched longer than I needed, lest it return and cause more trouble.

Judas reached into the wallet at his belt and scribbled a few words on a fragment of parchment, which he passed to the man Simon. "My father owns a vessel which is not currently in use. It will serve you to fish. On Galilee, if you can travel there." He spoke as one with authority and easy arrogance.

Josh smiled at Simon.

"Go," he said. "And sin no more."

It was the evening of the second day when we came within sight and smell and earshot of Alexandria, late enough that the mirrors of the Pharos were reflecting the great fire at its heart and no longer the beams of the setting sun.

Your age has still little to compare with that lighthouse in size—there is nothing as tall in your London and little in Paris or New York. The ancients knew nothing of your electricity and little of steam, but they managed with water pressure and finely crafted mechanisms, that were beautiful as well as useful.

The trumpets of the Tritons that decorated the sides of the Pharos, when used to instruct ships in the direction they should take, were tuned—not mere harsh noise like the whistles of your steamboats. There was a glory to the world then, which went long ago and has not returned.

The two young Jews stared at it fixedly. Judas pointed at something—I knew not what—and Josh pulled out one of the small wax tablets he was never without, and scribbled notes and calculations there.

They caught me looking at this, and Judas explained. "Our father Joseph has some interests in the building trade. That is one of the reasons he has sent us here."

Josh smiled. "He values learning for its own sake, and for piety's sake, but Joseph has always got his eye on bricks and mortar and gold."

A fleet of small boats had come alongside us, at the point where the featureless mud and scrub of the Delta suddenly started to open out into the harbour. The captain was having nothing of their offers to unload his cargo or his passengers but let a pilot aboard whom he clearly knew well, and who looked like yet another of his cousins.

Together they put their hands to the tiller—the mouth of the harbour had a myriad little flourishes of white even in the twilight where the sea met the current coming from the city's waterways and it was all too easy to assume that every such flourish was that, when some were temporary spits of sand and silt on which it would be all too easy to run momentarily aground and spill oneself.

And there were small boats pulling at the hulk of a boat that had wrecked itself earlier—this was the great harbour of the East but only as safe as constant effort made it.

There was not a strong wind in our sails, from any direction, so that the rowers pulled and cursed, both in an even rhythm. But the breeze off the land blew the scent of mud and grilled meat and incense and shit, like any port but more so.

A beam from the mirrors shone on us, briefly, and we passed whatever inspection was purposed by those that directed it; then the trumpets sounded once and the beam led us across the water to our berth.

Our berth—and this said much of the value of the cargo Josh and I had saved when we saved the ship—was not on the southern side of Pharos island, or in the unfashionable West Harbour. It was next to the great warehouses on the north shore of the city itself, where the slummier areas of Rhakotis bordered on the great houses of Brucheion.

Warehouses of brick faced with marble that glimmered in the torchlight of the wharves, warehouses that mattered more to the city than its palaces, now that Egypt was ruled from Rome. This was a beautiful city, but it was a pragmatic one—a symbol of how the pride of Egypt had been humbled by Greece and then Rome, and by the Persians before them.

I had known Egypt and its gods in their pride, a pride that had lasted for thousands of years, firm as the Pyramids, and yet all things pass, save me and a few other immortals. I saw Alexandria built, its street grid laid out in white flour, and I have seen it pass—the one which bears its name is fine, but a shadow.

The wharves here were paved with neat cobbles and the ship was made fast to elaborate iron stanchions as we stepped ashore. I kept an eye on the two young Greeks lest there be some last minute treachery.

The captain caught my eye on him as he walked over to them and shook his head.

"You are under protection of a power to whom I owe much," he told them. "Know then, sir and miss, that I was paid to give you to my cousin to sell. You have powerful enemies, and one of them is your kin. You might yet be safer as slaves in Arabia than rich heirs in this city."

I looked again, and realized that I had been successfully misled— the taller of the two, the one I had thought master, was in fact the elder, taller sister of the boy I had thought catamite.

I noted their faces because there are few that can successfully fool me, and that without glamour, and wondered whether I would encounter them again—as I did, but that is another tale, a romance of treachery defeated by love, which has no place here.

"I knew it," Judas said.

"No," Josh said, "you did not, and neither did I. Let us see that as a warning not to jump to conclusions or condemn without knowing all the story."

He told it as a parable once, and I heard him, but somehow it was arranged that the tale did not find its way into that farrago of half-truths that Christians make so much of.

The brothers looked around them as they walked to the end of the quay and soon were greeting a man in his forties who hailed them by name from some way away. He held a lit lamp—the wharves were well lit with torches, but he was clearly not one to take chances. He had come from the dark streets and would soon return to them.

He had a longer beard than the Greeks of this city, even its Stoics, were wont to wear, and it was not oiled or curled; by his features, he was no Greek.

Josh waved me over, eager to introduce us. The man looked me up and down disapprovingly.

"Huntress, this is Philo, philosopher of this city, and the teacher Judas' father has chosen for us. Philo, Sir, this is Mara, the power known as the Huntress."

"You are mistaken, lad." The older man's voice was sonorous as an actor's, sharp as a prosecutor in a court of law. "This is the sort of woman I am supposed to encourage you to stay away from. Look how she is dressed. I would think her a mere slut were she not also some kind of woman of violence. Be warned, she is after your pocketbook or worse. The Huntress is but a myth, a symbol of justice and female rage, made up by poets and pagan priests."

It is never worth my while to pick quarrels with clever men who only hear their own words—I knew of this Philo, who sought to reconcile the thought of the man Plato with the theology of the Jews, and who doubtless had a sideline in carrying water in sieves.

Josh bowed his head in submission to his teacher, and did so with a smile in his eyes that was better than any verbal irony. I would see him again, soon, no doubt, and it was not worth arguing the toss with this philosopher.

I saw Judas move to protest and stayed him with a hand to his arm.

I made a low bow to both lads and their bearleader, who walked away as if he wished no further discussion. They smirked at each other, looked back at me and then followed him, off no doubt to the quarter of the city that people called Delta, after the letter rather than the river.

I turned to the ship's captain, who was bobbing around as if he wished to say something. "Yes?"

"Huntress, I owe you and that young man much."

"Your ship and all it contains."

"Indeed so. If there is ever…"

I thought it unlikely—he was not, after all, a man whose moral character inclined me to recommend his services a second time—but who knows?

"If I have need of you—though that day may never come—I will find you and ask you, you may be sure of that. In the meantime, I shall have my eye on your trading, lest you sell other children to those who would use them to work harm."

"I would never do that." He had the grace to look shocked at the idea.

"How do you know that you have not done so already? Great malefactors do not announce themselves as such, you know."

So many people commit crimes they think small and make themselves the accomplice of worse; I try only to punish the fully guilty, but my temper is unreliable at times. I nodded an admonition to him, and walked through the space between two torches and into shadow, and through that darker faster Alexandria to my own place.

Sof's Great Work, as I have said, had its smelly side and so we had established our home amid tanners and dyers at the side of one of the canals that took the outflow from Mareotis through to the West Harbour. Much of the worst of the byproducts of her work she disposed of in shadow, but there was enough else that we would have been uncomfortable neighbours in any place where other trades were carried out. As it was, no one liked to complain, and sometimes her work smelled so sweet and clean that it purified the

22

whole neighbourhood for days. She tried to explain to me that it was all a matter of balance, but I never, in those days, understood much of the Work. I wish that I had never had to acquire the knowledge.

Our home was never locked, for who would rob the Huntress or her sister-lover? Sof was no warrior, but she had her strengths and her ways of fighting, as many of those who live many lives have learned.

She was seated, when I entered, sipping broth from a large earthenware bowl, that she placed carefully down on the table before rising to her feet, and walking around the table and into my outstretched arms.

What do you mean, what did she look like? She looked like Sof, though in those days men called her Maria or Miriam, as they had some centuries earlier when she lived among the Jews who mourned their homeland in Babylon when she had first turned her mind to the Work. They had called her by that name again in a life a few decades before this one, when she had first sought the aid of the glass blowers of Alexandria and the work had moved from bud to flower, as retorts and other wares swelled and cooled at her command.

I always knew her when I found her—though sometimes I mistook others for her when anxious—but of course sometimes she was as brown and hawk-nosed as I myself have always been, and sometimes a Nubian, or one of the Silk people. She had at least once been one of the red-haired Celts of Britain, though I had not met her in that life.

So, let us say, that she was, in this life and in that year, a woman early in her third decade, but with silver in her hair that she let stand in a great streak among the henna she still generally affected. Some solvent had splashed her there, and the hair had, after a while, grown out white.

She was tall and had the wiry strength that comes from long hours pounding metals and other things for the Work, work which had given her a cough I did not like. Her mother was a merchant out of Tyre, her father a copper-beater from the Nubian kingdoms down the Nile—she was a daughter of Alexandria.

23

I noticed two men in armour seated quietly and sharing her meal, so our greeting was decorous—a kiss on each other's cheek and then on the mouth. After aeons without her, I was glad every time I saw her, but we had learned restraint in times when it was appropriate and now it seemed to have become the place where we lived. I have retained the appearance of youth, but not its abandon.

The two soldiers, one an officer, some kind of noble with that hungry look of ambition they all had and the other a common soldier, had the sort of impassive pale face that the Romans went in for—they were as passionate a people as any, but good at schooling their features. The officer was clearly a man of fashion—the crest on his helmet was excessively high and the red cloak slung across his shoulder of the very finest wool, in folds that he had clearly practiced renewing regularly in front of a mirror.

I glanced a query to Sof.

"They're here to ask you politely whether you will do the Prefect a favour." She smiled. "The handsome one is here to ask you and the other one is to get in your way if you decide to hit them."

I looked at the pair of them—at a closer examination they were less hard to read than I thought. Nervousness at having a job to do they had been told was difficult, and determination to persuade me, and an undercurrent of disgust—not with me, or with Sof, or with the smell of her Work, but at something they had seen recently.

"So, these bodies you want me to look at?"

That's usually why the authorities remember I exist. The less intelligent of the soldiers started to answer, and was nudged ungently by his superior.

I glared at them and they fell silent. "Whatever your mission, you can wait while I eat. I have come a long way to sit at my own table."

I sat down and Sof wordlessly passed me a bowl of soup she had ladled out when I was not paying attention—simple barley and peas and onions, but she had the talent at cookery you would expect of a great alchemist.

Why would you doubt that? Just because men do alchemy all

wrong? All the great alchemists were women and they were all amazing cooks as well. Not their fault if people misunderstood everything they said or wrote down.

When women had charge of alchemy, it was a matter of herbs and roots and flowers as well as of rocks and jewels and stars. It was the Great Work that had a place for all things, and if it has failed ever since, it is because men forgot that simple truth.

As I say, it was as delicious a soup as I have ever eaten—and I have dined in Olympus, Asgard, and Xanadu.

The handsome clever ambitious one cleared his throat. Oh dear, this was going to be a set speech.

He actually had it on a scroll.

"Gaius Valerius, prefect of Egypt and Alexandria, to Mara, the Huntress, greetings."

I waved him to silence. "I will come, of course," I said. I listen to the gossip of the streets, but sometimes my informants are the mighty of this world. I go wherever the trail of possible Rituals leads me, from shepherds' huts to the palaces of the great.

I kissed Sof briefly, though with quiet passion, and she stroked the back of my neck as she had done over the years, and we both thanked the two soldiers for waiting.

I could have abandoned them and made my own way through shadow to the palace of the Prefect, but I saw no especial urgency. We struck out of the small crowded streets of the quarter where Sof and I lived and up the street called Aspedia to the great Canopic boulevard. There was bustle in the slums where men and women work all night at trades that know no time—less traffic on the larger roads and none on the boulevard save the Roman troops that constantly patrolled it.

This was an occupied city and the hand of Rome lay heavy on it. Seeing me walk with soldiers caused some to curse, until shushed by those who knew me and knew that my mission has nothing to do with mayfly empires.

They brought me to the palace that had once been the Ptolemies'

25

and was now the residence, though not the property, of the Prefect, and down its golden corridors. I had not expected to be received in the great staterooms, but we walked into the quieter, shabbier meaner part of the palace, to where Gaius Valerius had set up his private audience chamber in a room that was almost snug.

He was a lean, though not meagre, man in middle life; the sort of Roman who made no concessions to his posting, but kept his toga heavy and his hair short. He was seated at a folding table, one that had the look of many campaigns and many baggage trains, and eating bread and boiled cabbage and a chicken wing, and drinking wine from a coarse red earthenware bowl. Beside the Prefect's chair was an open chest, containing a number of scrolls.

From a small stoppered flask, he poured dark reeking liquid over his food and smiled a thin-lipped smile when he saw me react.

"You have no taste for garum, then."

I was disinclined to give him the advantage, though I have never seen the point of ruining wholesome food with rotten fish juice. "After the black soup of Sparta, there is no food left that can terrify me. But I confess a mild distaste, yes."

The black soup of Sparta—there was something that could make a woman regret immortality. Or at least the vivid memory that goes with it; I will never get the taste of that broth from the back of my throat.

Gaius put down the bowl and made as if to offer me food and drink. I had been taken away from my own table and had no great wish to salve my irritation by partaking of any of another's. Besides, I found his ascetic airs irritating—he was eating the diet of a poor farmer in Italy, not that of the peasants over whom he ruled. He was making a point about his Roman virtue, and had had cabbages brought to him across the sea rather than eat dates and pounded chickpeas with his bread.

Still, he was the power in this land for the moment, and my work would be easier if I paid him what respect he deserved.

"Some water, perhaps," I said.

He gestured me to sit down at his table, and a slave so discreet she was almost invisible placed a glass of clear cold water beside me. Gaius ignored her, which meant that he was one of those Romans who regard slaves as pure instruments. I do not know which kind of slave-owner I dislike more—those, or the ones who glory in superiority and exploit it.

The Romans were no worse than any other empire and less imaginatively cruel than some. They could hardly be described as reluctant to shed blood, and yet the Rituals were something of which they were rarely guilty; the years when they were ruled by the Etruscans had taught them something, at least.

He took another sip of his wine and looked me searchingly in the eyes. I met his gaze, and noted that he had no trouble meeting mine, something few men arrogant enough to challenge me in this way could manage for long.

"So," he said, "you are the Huntress." He pulled one of the scrolls from the chest beside him, unrolled it, read a second and then refurled and replaced it. "My predecessors seem to have thought well of you, which is why you are still tolerated in this city now that it is ours."

I forbore to point out that no-one had made a serious effort to drive me out of a place where I chose to live since Qin Shi Hwang, who had accomplished most of his ambitious plans but not that. Nor, come to that, had he managed to live forever.

"I saw this city built"—I shrugged—"and doubtless one day I will see it topple into the sea like other cities before it. For the moment, I abide and watch. There were gods in this land once, who now are old and frail, many of them, or dust merely; and I abide."

I reached over and broke off a fragment of his bread, and rubbed it to crumbs between my hands.

"Your predecessors served their terms out, all save the first of whom you Romans do not speak, though his damned memory is green among the people of Alexandria…And they are one with the Pharaohs and the Ptolemies," and I blew the dust of his bread away to illustrate my point. "Your predecessors asked my opinion from time to time, and found it useful to do so, as did the Ptolemies, and many of the Pharaohs. And I find it useful to talk to the Prefect of Alexandria and Egypt, from time to time, as I did to the slaves that helped build the Sphinx, and the priests the Persians burned. But no-one tolerates me, Gaius Valerius. I am here."

I looked him back in the eyes and held him until he broke and looked away.

I have dealt with many men like him over the years. I know the little jibes and cynical sneers they expect me to put up with before they accept that my reputation is true and I am who I say I am. It saves time to look them in the eye and let them see how small they are in mine.

I had brought the silence, and now I broke it. "So, where are these bodies? And why should I be interested?"

"This was one of the palaces of the Witch Queen Cleopatra. There is a chamber below where there is ice, eternal ice." He shivered at the very thought. "One of my legates persuaded me—I care not to meddle with such things—that it would be a useful place to store those bodies that were not already decayed past usefulness, or that the Egyptians had not messed up with their damned spices and bandages."

I smiled. "The one you name the Witch Queen had little magic save her own wit and grace,"—I thought fondly of a dinner spent flirting—"and some few cantrips mostly to do with keeping moist the paint with which she decorated her eyes. Even those she had inherited from her aunt, of the same name, who was a wise woman but died young. That is why you have never heard of her. But yes, I can imagine that the Queen's aunt had a chamber of eternal ice. She was one of the prime devisers of the Work and was skilled in the Art as well."

We had, back in my beloved's workroom, not a chamber of such ice, but a small cabinet of it, that I had procured with great labour from the furthest reaches of shadow. I thought with mild horror of a royal woman so powerful she could have procured a room of the stuff, and brought it back.

Nor was the room some poky little closet. It was a cellar fit to store many vintages in, though they would not have been drinkable afterwards, and smelt less than any charnel house or morgue that I had seen before and have seen since, though there were many bodies there, and they had died in ways that normally empty the body of its filth and corrode it thereafter.

As Gaius and I entered it, he gave a little shudder, and not just from the cold. One of the nearest bodies had a head whose cranium had opened like a flower, and a small elderly Egyptian man was poking its nostrils with a small probe while he talked in Greek to the young officer who had brought me to the palace.

"See here?" He had only traces of the accent most Egyptians cannot break themselves of when talking Greek, and hardly lisped at all. "Dese nostrils are completely clean—not even traces of mucus left, but see, de sinuses are completely broken down. Such a messy way of clearing out a skull."

He and the young legate looked round. The legate waved an introductory hand. "I thought we could do with an expert, and one trained in discretion. Psametikos here is an embalmer—one who knows the good old ways and can do you up as neat as if you were a pharaoh of old. Psammei—these are my boss, the Prefect of Alexandria and Egypt, and the Huntress, of whom your legends speak."

Psametikos made obeisance, but bowed lower to me than to the highest in the land, which was gratifying. I had never especially got on with the Egyptian gods, but they had rarely been sources of trouble for me, save for bloody Sekhmet. Oh, and the first Sobekh— his replacement is charming enough.

I bowed my head back in respect, and then walked around the room in silence, showing a moment's respect to the dead men—and I noticed that all of the corpses were men, and all had died in their prime. No boys, and the only elderly men were the one Psametikos was examining and one other, whose skull was in similar condition.

29

All of them had burst open somewhere. A couple had chests that had opened, spreading their ribs out like victims of the torture the Northmen called the blood eagle, but with no loose lungs flapping, indeed no lungs visible at all in the cavity. In others, the explosion had taken place lower down; in each case, it was as if the crater had been scooped clean and then washed down.

I looked at the Egyptian and the two Romans. "Organs missing in each case then?"

They nodded—the Egyptian stood up straight and tucked his probe in a small wallet at his belt. "Dey all have something missing—a heart, or lungs, or a liver. With some of dem, I had to search for what is gone—dere are plenty of small organs in de human body, you know, and I for one do not know what dey are for. Nor did your Hippocrates nor your Aristotle. And with dese two old men—it is de brain."

I had never seen anything like this before, and I suspected a magic less than the Rituals of Blood, but kin to them. I turned to Gaius Valerius.

"These killings are not, I think, of direct interest to me, but nonetheless, you have my attention. Did anyone see these men attacked?"

The legate shook his head. "Most of them were found by their households, in the morning. Some died with wives or concubines beside them, who saw and heard nothing. The freeborn were most insistent and slaves had nothing to tell us—we even stopped torturing the last few batches because there was no point and the heirs were complaining."

It was as if the organs had left the bodies of their own accord, taking all the blood and all the shit with them. The mental image that struck me was appalling and I knew instantly that it must be correct.

"I wonder what he's doing with them," I thought aloud.

Gaius looked puzzled, the legate and Psametikos less so.

"The wizard ⸗" I thought a second longer. "Technically not a necromancer since his victims are not dead when he summons their organs, and what he does is not a death curse, just something that inevitably kills."

The legate furrowed his brow a little. "Building something?"

"I do not think so, because he has taken no bones and no skin that I can see. Just organs."

"How do we know the wizard is male?"

"Because a woman would not care to replace her organs with those of a man. Men are less particular."

Both Gaius and the Egyptian looked sick.

"People seeking long life," I sighed, "will do almost anything. But given a choice... And clearly this wizard can steal organs from whomever he chooses. He is a master of shadow as well."

I hand-waved impatiently at their blank looks. "Almost anyone who has power can pass fast and unseen through the realm adjacent to the mundane. Shadow is far more than that, a realm that extends vastly beyond the world you know, but that will do for now. This man can not only summon organs to burst from their proper place, but, since no one seems to have reported stomachs and lungs wandering around the night streets of Alexandria, he can make them gifted in this way."

I thought a little further.

"Perhaps he needs to be there, but in shadow, and plucks the organs as they burst into the air, and takes them away in a satchel, or perhaps one of those handy jars Psammetikos' colleagues use. Yet he is not such a master of shadow that he can merely reach in and extract from within without tearing the skin and the flesh."

Just because there are shadow skills I have never cared to master, it does not mean that, down the years, I have not had occasion to imagine, and sometimes see, what those of us with skill might do if they tried and cared to. I prefer my killing clean and done with bronze, steel or jade.

I asked the legate, "Can I have a list of the victims, their professions, their general state of health and what was taken from

31

them?" I am not systematic myself—patience has never been one of my virtues—but when I have access to a vast system of clerks and spies, I will make use of it.

He nodded, and I looked at the most recent victim, a frail man whose white hair, and the deep lines time had carved into what was left of his face, indicated that he had obviously been in the last days of his life even before his brain exploded from his skull. "Do we know who this one was?"

"Some sort of scholar," the legate said dismissively. "The colleague who found him tried to explain what exactly he studied but I could not understand him. A thick Judaean accent and some subject too obscure for a simple soldier like me."

"A Judaean?"

My thought remained unspoken because a slave was suddenly in the room whispering to the Prefect Gaius. He looked tired; indeed, it was very late. "Forgive me, but apparently a delegation are waiting to see me urgently."

He turned to go. "That will be his colleagues." I started to follow him from the room, having seen as much as I needed to, for the moment. "They will be asking for the release of his body. Judaeans are not unreasonable about these things, but they prefer funerals to happen as quickly as possible."

It occurred to me that the Judaean's colleagues would be the best people to ask what was in his brain that made it of interest to our wizard.

I followed the Prefect up a small and winding staircase, to emerge through a small door and from behind a large and mendacious tapestry of the first Ptolemy standing by the deathbed of Alexander, into a room I had last seen a few days before Actium, on an evening when Queen Cleopatra postured in full armour and Mark Anthony drank an amount unusual even for him. It was a room constructed for councils of war and epic orgies, and, as on the present occasion, for making delegations of unruly citizens who had to be tolerated feel very small.

It was not as magnificent as it had been three score years earlier—the Romans had let it become a little dusty, a little shabby, and there were moth-frays on the tapestry, golden threads hanging loose from its fringes. This was the sending of a message, too—we are Romans and we rule, but not with any damn nonsense about doing it with style.

Gaius climbed the steps to a chair that was not quite a throne and waved me to a smaller chair beside it. I preferred to stand at the foot of the steps, because while it was pleasing to receive his respect, I do not care to be seen as working for empires rather than with them.

Especially when dealing, as here, with a stiff-necked man on whom I had already made a bad impression—the delegation was headed by the sage Philo, as I had rather expected, and he was accompanied by a crowd of merchants and scholars, and by his pupils, among them my new friends Josh and Judas. The boys looked tired from their travelling, but were clearly fascinated to be here.

The delegation may have intended to shout and stamp, but a few minutes of being cowed by this room had left them merely muttering.

Philo was obviously perturbed to see me there, but where a less clever man might have blustered at the Prefect, he bided his time patiently. He had doubted me earlier, and was having to reassess— some men I break with my gaze and others I prefer to allow to recognize their own humiliation.

Gaius Valerius spoke from the Prefect's seat. "I am taking a personal interest in the deaths of which your colleague's was one. The power of Rome will avenge him, and all of the others—my seriousness in this matter is shown by the fact that I and Rome through me have asked the power known as the Huntress for her help."

I looked round at them: mostly Judaean scholars and merchants, but a variety of others who had come along with them, doubtless because of the tumult in the street, and the gossip value. Or possibly, in at least one case, to find out how much we knew.

33

I had to assume that the killer was in the room, as men who light fires for pleasure often come to see the ashes and sniff the burned flesh. If so, he might show himself by unhealthy excitement—but no, this was not some mere pervert but someone with steel and nerve and a capacity to wait for gratification.

Still, there were at least two people in the room I knew to be innocent because they had not been in Alexandria, and so, when I spoke, I looked at them. Josh and Judas were bright lads and might spot something I had so far missed. And their master could hardly object to my involving them in the official business of Rome—or if he did, he would have to put up with it. I am the Huntress, and I do normally hunt alone, but if these two lads were being trained up to be important in the affairs of gods and men, it would save me time later if it were done right now.

"We seek not only a murderer and a sorcerer, but a thief. He takes hearts and lungs and livers and guts—we think in an attempt to replace his own and become immortal—though the exact magical methods he plans to deploy are at present unknown to me." I shrugged. "Every so often the wickedness of men manages to come up with something even I have not seen before. And Alexandria is, among other things, the capital of cleverness."

I turned to Philo, who was leader here if anyone was, and a man to whom I wished to show the respect he had denied me. "Sage—who was your dead colleague and what were his studies? Because it would seem to me that you would steal a brain for what it contained rather than for itself."

Philo smiled, but not out of friendliness or pleasure. "Eleazar, as we tried to explain to your friend the legate over there, was a student of gematria. Of the hidden language of numbers contained in words and meaning conveyed by numbers. He also studied the writings of the Egyptians, because he believed that while we were slaves here, Moses and others learned much of how the heathen priests encoded ideas in symbols. He was a very learned man and I fail to see what use his work was to anyone."

I could see him preparing for a lengthy explanation of why gematria was wrong and his own Platonist speculations entirely different and far sounder. Which, interesting as it might be, was a distraction from the matter in hand. So I waved him politely to silence. "Perhaps the point would be to steal knowledge you did not already possess so that you could be certain that you had taken it and now had it."

The legate had entered and passed me a scroll; I glanced at it and saw that he had given me all the names I has asked for, along with a few salient facts about them, and the organs that had burst from them.

"Sixty," I noted, surprised. "I did not see that many."

"Some of the first were too badly shattered to be much use for examination, and, as I said, some were taken for preparation by Psammetikos and his colleagues. As the price of their advice."

I could see Philo bridling that the Egyptian undertakers had got bodies on request and nodded to Gaius.

"Citizens and Judaeans,"—he used his official voice—"you may have the bodies as soon as we are done with them, which in the case of Eleazar the scholar, I am determining is now."

His voice did not actively ask them to leave, but most of them did. I gestured to Philo to stay, less because I thought his likely approaches much help to me than because if he stayed, his pupils would. And after all, he might surprise me—he was an intelligent man, even if he was a Platonist and a snob.

As the rest of the delegation left, Gaius nodded to a couple of his slaves who, without being told what to do next, brought in stools. Philo sat down on one and made himself as at ease as if this were his lecture room. I preferred to continue standing, as did the lad Judas, though he paced, having not learned the gift of stillness. Josh sat cross-legged on the floor and looked as if he were the most comfortable of us—Gaius remained on his not-quite-a-throne, clearly not planning to speak, but interested to see what our discussions might reveal.

Gaius had looked askance at me a second when I gestured the three Judaeans to stay, and so I addressed him and the legate. "I have asked these three to stay because I know two of them to be guiltless in this matter and cannot imagine that the other would be."

"Youths hardly old enough to shave?" Gaius started.

"Prefect,"—I walked over and touched Josh's shoulder where he sat and his brother's where he paced—"I have faced down pirates with these two at my side, and dealt with one of the greatest among the monsters of the deep. And I knew this one's father when the world was new and Atlantis still, for the moment, stood. Believe me, there are few older men I would trust more."

I walked over to their tutor and reached out my hand to him, which, somewhat reluctantly, he clasped.

"As for their tutor, he is a learned man even for this city, as well as one whose worship makes it unlikely he is our wizard. Judaeans have a reluctance to consume blood, and Philo here has never had the reputation of a hypocrite." I spoke as true as I found him—he was a man who could not be influenced with most currencies, but honest praise he knew deserved, that would win him over a little.

The legate flicked his red cloak into an even more stylish drape before sitting at a table and making notes on another of the seemingly inexhaustible supply of scrolls he kept in the wallet at his belt.

I carried on where I had left off a few minutes earlier. Perhaps this group of men could solve my perplexity. "I am assuming he is stealing other men's organs in order to replace and improve his own—but why so many?"

Josh looked slightly sick, but rather pleased with himself. "Because though he knows what he is doing, he is not ready yet to do it to himself. He is proceeding by trial and error, and seeking out raw materials in order to refine his methods."

Philo was not to be outdone by one of his newest pupils. "But why, in that case, would you steal a brain for its knowledge? If he is not ready to implant Eleazar's knowledge into himself, why steal it?"

Judas had waited and now jumped in—these boys were far better than I at thinking this stuff through. I thought at the time, I should watch these two in case they ever turn to the dark side, but I grew too fond of both of them to think that all that likely, with results I fear I did not see coming.

Young Judas was, if anything, more rigorous and imaginative than his step-brother, and far too enthusiastic, positively bubbling with ideas. "It's very awful, sir," he said, "that he picked your friend to kill, but we should not assume that he was killed for the specifics of his knowledge—we are in Alexandria, where literate and knowledgeable men are to be found on every street corner." He grew even more intent. "What if, with brains as well as hearts, our criminal is proceeding by trial and error? It wasn't what Eleazar knew—it was the fact that he knew anything at all, that he was killed for. After all, yes, he was expert in symbols and alphabets and numbers, but maybe it as not the thousand meanings of Jehovah's name or the symbol for the second week of inundation that was stolen. Just literacy and numeracy."

I started to see where he was going with this, but Philo did not.

"But why would he need to steal those?"

"Because," Josh was racing his stepbrother now, and overtaking on a bend, "just as you would need to see that a stolen heart could beat in a chest, so you would need to see letters and numbers in a mind that hitherto knew them not."

Philo looked baffled.

Judas jumped back in. "If some wretch who knew nothing, suddenly can count or read, it proves that the magic works, even if he could not duplicate Eleazar's last lecture."

"He's buying the most useless and decrepit of slaves," Josh said, "because it's easiest to see that the stolen hearts beat, or stolen thoughts do their work, in chests that were failing and brains that were empty."

I turned to the legate, who was scribbling away frantically. "He is going to the slave markets at the end of the day. And buying what is cheapest and least useful. There will be bills of sale…"

37

The legate nodded. "You think we can find him? Just by attending the slave markets and watching who buys last? I'll round up an armed patrol or if you let me have a whole maniple we could surround the whole area and sweep through it like reapers at harvest."

"That would be heavy-handed." I have seen Romans do this sort of thing, and it usually left many people dead, none of them the ones being looked for. There are many among the mighty who would laugh aloud at me, the Huntress, lecturing on the virtue of subtlety, but among Romans… I sighed. "I know most of the slave-traders in this city, much as I have a distaste for their work. I make sure that they do not sell people for purposes of which I would disapprove and they have occasion to fear me. I shall visit them later in the morning, once they have breakfasted, and spoil their mornings with searching questions. We do not wish to alarm our wizard, though I am sure he will know by now that I am helping you."

Gaius tapped the arm of his chair grumpily. "We need everyone to see that the power of Rome is with you in this."

I am always reasonable, though that is not my reputation. I pointed to the bright young legate. "He will do, all by himself. If he has men to command, his mind will be busy commanding and I need his intelligence, untrammeled by such concerns."

Besides, his high-crested helmet and carefully draped cloak were so very decorative. I am true to my loves, but there are some young men stylish enough that it pleases me to be seen with them occasionally.

"No need to get up before the slave-owners"—I needed him to get some sleep, at least. "I will call for you at the barracks at the fifth hour."

I nodded to my young friends, and bowed my head to Gaius, and went from the palace into shadow. I had time free while mortals slept and I wished to spend them with my love, even if, as was the case, she was sleeping too. I had spent so many years waiting between her lives that watching her sleep and knowing she would wake in a few hours was a perpetual pleasure to me, and one which she tolerated gladly.

I fear that is a pleasure I have lost forever.

I sat and watched her sleep until the cocks of Alexandria crew and suddenly a line of light washed across her sleeping face and she woke with a drowsy smile of certainty that I was, for once, there. I fetched her flat bread, and oil, and the infusion of boiled mint leaves she liked to take at this time of day, and I shared a few mouthfuls of her meal. All without speaking, because after so many lives together and so many lives apart, but dreaming of each other, we could speak volumes to each other with a wink or a frown and yet did not need to.

Information, though—we needed speech for that, and when she had eaten, I told her of the night's events and discoveries and my plans for the day, and she talked of the steps in the work she planned.

She looked thoughtful. "You may need me, later, and so I shall not venture into shadow this day, but perform those tasks and rituals which the mundane world makes possible."

For this is the great secret of the Work, which I tell you for nothing and never told Newton, for it would not have served the world well to do so—the steps of the Work have, as is well-known, to be performed in order, and some steps need to happen in the mundane and some in shadow. As above, so below—you know that formula—and yet, in shadow first, then in the light, in the light, and then in shadow—that formula is lost, with Paul of Tarsus' phrase almost the only memory of it. In a glass, darkly—that is how the Work is done—and then face to face with light. And omit those steps or do them in the wrong order, or the wrong realm, and all is undone and forever undoable—and you undone too, in all likelihood.

Sof, or Maria as she was known in this life, had spent lives working through this truth, and many of her deaths had been the source of that knowledge. Hers and those of her sisters in Art, like Cleopatra who was not a queen and Cleopatra who was.

She knew all metals and many elements, and she knew every herb that grew in the parts of the world where she had spent her lives and the parts of shadow into which she had walked. And that too was the secret of the Work, as in metal, so in flesh and flower. The quest is for the perfect thing and the perfect thing is metals that grow into flower and life that does not end.

And that is all I will tell you, Crowley, for you are a man not to be trusted and perhaps you cannot trust me and I have told you lies, or not told you truths, that you would need to do the Work and live and prosper and not die in flame.

Sof who was Maria was my true love, and we had lost Lilit our sister and love and had never found her again, nor I since; we had our different work and we had each other and we made do, and wept for three young girls who had not died or changed, and what time and chance and evil men had done to us. And those were the thoughts of each morning, the bitter herbs that flavoured the sweetness of our love.

I stepped out into the brisk sea-air of early morning in Alexandria, and the foul smells of tanning, and the muddy swelter of Lake Mareotis and the sweat of bodies new risen, and stale wine and perfume from last night's debauches were all sweet in my nostrils, for I was in the crown of cities in that era.

Rome was power and Athens was intellect and the cities of the lands of Silk and Spice were civilization and good manners, but Alexandria was all of those things and people came there to learn from all of those places.

As you walked the streets, you would see tall black men from the lands below the Nile wearing heavy worked copper on their arms and ash and oil in their long straggles of hair; women of the far Celts of Britannia with the blue of paint and incised ink making patterns on their cheeks and breasts; young lithe castrates who worshipped Cybele in Anatolia and the goddesses of Hind, and Sarmatian women sworn to chaste manhood and the riding of horses.

Nor was Alexandria a place of humans alone. Centaurs still came there to study and teach, their hooves kicking up dust and their voices loud and bawdy in the wineshops; often they made love in the street and people politely ignored them, for centaurs are wise in many things but fools when it comes to rutting, the males' smallcocks erect between their fore-legs and the greatcocks with which they sire their young a perpetual hidden heavy presence. There is a reason why few speak of centaur women and why so many centaurs steal human brides—there is a heady lushness to centaur women, a perpetual carnal scent and ripeness that makes men, and women too, sweat with desire, not for them but for the act itself. For centaurs, like satyrs and fauns, have the nature of human mortals and the nature of doomed beasts as well—they have intellect and to spare, and in the pleasures of the flesh, well, not excess to be sure, but plenitude and perhaps even surplus.

There is an old friendship between those two peoples, a love far greater than the mere liking they have for humans, and they like humans well enough.

I came to the high-embankment of the harbour and walked along it, staring out at the Pharos isle and the vast long causeway that led to it and the great lighthouse that dominated everything. Great ships were there, and small boats and everything between, for it was early on a working day for every day was a working day in the city where East and West and North and South came to do business and be amused or informed.

The market was the place where most of that business was done and it gave its name, the Emporium, to such places for many years to come, just as the greater of Alexandria's libraries, the Museion, is remembered yet in the names of such places. If the rest of the city was heavy with wine and sweat and sweet and sharp and heavy perfumes, and thick oil frying batter and charcoal grills singing meat and fish, and the cries of pedlars and the seductions of dancers' little cymbals and the barked orders of men of power and the wheedling of creatures unseen but not human, then the Emporium was all of those things and more—the centre to which all of those sounds and scents and flavours flowed and from which they permeated the city.

To the east of the market was the great brick bulk of the barracks, a building that the Romans had constructed in the crudest way they knew, a building that said, we are here, we control you and if you disobey, we will kill you. Its flat roof had crosses upon it, raised above the market place so that those who bought and sold could see the slow agonizing death of those whom the Romans chose to kill, and the whipping block where men and women might die or might live, but would know agony.

All this so that Alexandria knew that it bought and sold, and learned and taught, on the sufferance of those who might have razed it as they had Carthage, but for now would let it be.

And right up against the western side of the barracks was the sprawl of booths and auction blocks that constituted the Emporium's market in slaves. Once it had been kept to the dingy warehouses of the Western Harbour, because the Greeks and the Egyptians thought it a dirty business, but the Romans had moved it here, saying that dirty businesses were best carried out in the full glare of the sun and where everyone could see what was done and who did it.

If this sounds improbably moralistic for an empire built on blood, gold and slaves, it is worth remembering that the Romans were very good at lying to themselves about such things. Also, the placing of the slave market right against the barracks wall had much to do with getting armed soldiers to the site of any unrest immediately; Spartacus failed, but his failure left the Romans pissing their beds in the night for three centuries.

The young legate was waiting for me under the awning at the barracks' front, scribbling on his tablet. Periodically soldiers would come up to him, salute smartly and whisper quietly; clearly he already had matters in hand, though I could have done with his doing so more subtly.

I joined him and was pleased to see that the two men

unobtrusively guarding him snapped salutes at me. Having no relish for being seen as part of the imperium of Rome is one thing; having it shown that at least I am taken seriously is another.

I nodded to the two guards, and then to him; politeness dictates such things. "So," because I am all business at such times, even at the cost of brusqueness, "have your men found anything out?"

He looked at his tablet, but only to give his remarks a semblance of authority, since his face was that of a man who has made his mind up and knows that he is right. "I asked, as you suggested, for men who come late in the day and buy in bulk the slaves no one else wants, and only three names came up. One of them owns a quarry; another a chain of cook-houses I shall be avoiding in future, and having inspected as soon as possible; the third sounds most like our man."

I waited a second, determining that the cook-houses should be checked even sooner, for those who develop or cultivate a taste for manflesh are often of interest to me.

He went on, with enthusiasm. "There is a man whom we have noted as a person of interest, a Persian, though one who seems not to be an agent of their Kings. He describes himself as a Magus, though he is not on my lists as one who attends their fire-rites or pays respect at their tower of silence."

Persians are rarely impious, I have found, but the exceptions are very bad men indeed.

"So where does this Magus live? And perform his magics?"

"He owns a villa on the other side of the lake, far enough from other inhabitants that no one has complained of screams. Once I had ascertained this, I sent a messenger to instruct him to attend at my convenience."

"You do realize that you sent that messenger to his death."

The legate looked a little outraged. "My messenger bore a warrant that said he was delivering a note written with the authority of the Prefect himself."

"I think it likely that the Magus did not bother to read his warrant before killing him."

He shrugged. "In any case, I sent an Egyptian servant. No matter."

I really did not think it a good idea to warn this man of our interest—it pretty much ensured that anything vile he planned to do with the slaves he currently had in his possession would by now have been done. And he might regard it as a provocation.

A hubbub grew from the Emporium, screams and cries and indignant flurries of gulls. One of the catapults that were stationed with the crucifixes on the roof above us twanged and its great spear whizzed above our heads. I looked up in the direction that the spear had gone and there, clutching it in one hand, walked a man, a tall thin man in a patchwork tunic and a black cloak, some twenty feet above the ground.

He hurled the spear back at us, but not with so much force that I needed exert myself much to reach and pluck it from the air before it could come near us.

"This would be him, then."

I hurled the spear back at him and it tore through his cloak and into his side, and on through, without his showing any great effect. I hate it when I have to deal with men who have already found some way of avoiding mortality—in this case, though, the spear had actually torn a rent in his side, through which I could see dry things flapping in the currents of the air.

He winced and then clutched his side a second and it was whole again. I had hoped that he would have been foolish enough to remove his capacity to feel pain, as many seekers after invulnerability and immortality do, making it easier to damage them beyond repair without their noticing in time.

Still, I had cost him a little strength, and he chose that moment, probably not coincidentally, to alight.

His accent, when he spoke in a great booming voice that stilled the market, sounded like no Persian I had ever met. An Assyrian, perhaps, though I thought their colleges of magic long gone and their spell tablets melted or burned.

"I am Simon the Magician. I recognize the power of no passing empire. I am above the justice of her who calls herself the Huntress. And I kill slaves, and whomever else I choose."

With that, he cast at me, and might have had some better fortune, save that I had expected some such trick and when he pulled at my heart, like men do fish in wild northern streams, my heart pulled back like that fish and near snapped his power as a great salmon might a rod and line.

He staggered a second. I myself was winded enough that I could not, as I would have planned, step forward and strike at him with more mundane weapons, for he cast again, and for a second I was blinded with blood, the blood of the young legate whose every organ had burst through his bones as fiercely as if he had been struck by one of the weapons of your last great war. His heart and his brain and his liver and his guts sprang coiled from his torn skin and broken ribs and fell flop into the dust, and the light, I swear it, went out of his eyes as he gave a great cry and fell among them.

I wiped the legate's blood from my eyes and reached for my spear to try the strength of this butcher some more, but young Judas dashed some ten feet out of the crowd that had gathered and then shrunk back and struck with his great knife at the Magus' outstretched wrist and slashed his left hand from it.

With a great cry, and no gout or even trickle of blood, Simon leaped some fifty feet into the sky and was gone from my sight into the clouds. My attention did not follow him, though, because his hand had seized the blade on its backstroke that had severed it from the wrist and run, two fingers balanced on the edge as men on a tightrope, up the sword and down his arm and needed to be pulled from the young Judaean's throat before it could tear out his gullet or stop his breath.

No hand that might do this would be a natural hand to be sure, but this, as I seized it, and hammered it to pieces with the haft of my drawn spear, was a thing of magic but also of jointed ivory pieces and little wisps of steam and a tiny furnace in its palm. A thing that might have repaid study, had any there been minded to take it slowly apart, and a thing of beauty and ingenuity, but a killing thing and a thing of dark magics which I took pleasure in destroying and taking out of the world lest it find imitators.

My care for a second was for Judas of the Knife, a brave if foolish young man who had perhaps saved many by driving the creature Simon away, and then I turned to see his foster-brother rise, covered in blood from the red ruin that had been the legate, rise with his face pale under the blood and then sway and fall.

I had seen him work healing before, but nothing like this, for the legate, who had been rags of flesh and bone and innards was whole again, though still. I have seen men struck by apoplexy that lay as still as that and drifted into death, and so I reached down and pressed hard, once and twice and thrice, and breathed the air from my lungs into his suddenly gasping chest, and I finished what young Josh, for all his miracles, had not had the strength to finish. And the legate coughed, spat blood from his mouth, coughed again one great gout of blood from his throat, and was pale and whole and alive again.

"I had no coin for the ferryman," he gasped, "and Charon struck at me with his punt pole and said be off, I have no room for you, and I heard that young lad's voice say come forth, as one who has authority, and out of Hades I came. Back into the flesh."

Then he wept for joy and surprise, and I patted him absently, as men a dog who has thrown from his throat that which might have choked him to death, and turned to where Judas knelt, with his foster brother Josh pale and weak on the ground before him.

I thought for a second that I would have to punch life back into his labouring chest too, but he was weak and fainting rather than in imminent danger of death. Thin though—thinner by far, almost to starveling—than he had been moments earlier, as if he had consumed his own flesh to give life back to what was torn or broken.

"You can't keep doing this," I said to him. "There are other ways to save people."

His laugh was hoarse and hollow. "Says the Huntress." He coughed. I worried for a second that there might be blood, but there was not. He looked intently into my eyes. "You've sacrificed yourself for thousands of years, Mara. We all do what we can."

I picked him up from where he lay. I could not cradle him in my arms, for his head and feet would have dragged in the dust; nor could I sling him across my shoulders like a lost lamb, for I carry my weapons there. I hoisted him up and supported his arm on my free shoulder and Judas took some of the weight on his other side, to the extent that he could, and we carried Josh into the shade of the great awning before the front of the barracks, where the sentries stood.

Though the legate had been shreds mere moments before, he pulled himself up, and from where he stood, shouted orders to one of the sentries, who fetched clean water from the flasks that were there that the sentries not faint, and then a cup of the nourishing weak millet beer that the Egyptians drink.

Josh sipped from the one and then from the other, but no colour returned to his cheeks, and I started to be concerned. I looked at the legate, and put up one finger and then another, and he called for two soldiers to run for me, one to my home to fetch Sof and the other to Philo's house because I would not leave the youths' guardian uninformed.

The legate knelt by Josh and took his hand. "You saved me." His voice was ardent as a lover's but there was no lust in it, though I know you think so. "I swear if ever…"

Josh waved his free hand as if what he had done were a trifle. "God sees and provides for all; do not swear to what Providence may bring in ways we shall not like."

His step-brother put a firm hand on the legate's shoulder, as if to draw him away. "Give my brother some air; don't crowd him."

This was after all Alexandria, and flying men and miraculous cures did not happen every day even in this city of wonders. Idling youths, off-duty whores and soldiers, merchants concerned about their trade—there was the makings of a crowd here that the people

47

we needed to be here would not be able to get through.

It is important that I remain patient at such times. Yet I worried about my friend and grew irked by the tiresome din of people's wonderment, of how they explained to each other the miracles they had just witnessed as if by repeating it over and over they could hold it in their mind's eye more clearly.

In my experience, the reverse is true.

I clapped my hands for silence, and was not disappointed.

It was the legate who spoke, though. He stood up, half-drew his sword and fixed one after another random member of the crowd with a glare that threatened rage. "In the name of the Princepts Tiberius, and of Gaius Valerius, disperse before I have my men whip you from this place." His voice was surprisingly loud and steady for one just returned from the shores of the Styx.

Quite unfairly, soldiers who had been part of the crowd themselves pulled back into seriousness and started to shove the people around them away. The absence of any new wonders would probably have been enough to disperse them after a few minutes, even without kicks and punches and the smack of sheathed swords against backs.

I needed no other wonder than the sudden touch of my Sof's hand against my back and the scent of her mouth as she bent to kiss my neck. I might not always recognize her face instantly, from life to life, but that touch, that smell, remained the same somehow—I treasure them even though I may never know them again...

That day, though, she was all business within moments.

"The youth, Josh," she said. "He raised a man from the dead?"

"I have rarely seen a body so torn, and he restored it in seconds, and called the legate's soul back home from the shores of Hades."

"That would take it out of most gods," she said. "And the boy is mortal, is he not?"

"As far as I know," I said. "I cannot see our old friend raising even his own son to godhood without some very pressing reason. He does not like to share."

48

Sof giggled, nervously. There had been lives in which she took a whole childhood to come to her knowledge of who she was, and in some of those lives, she had worshipped Jehovah with a child's simplicity, right up to the moment when all her lives, and her more than casual knowledge of him, came flooding back, washing that simple piety away. Most of it.

She knelt where the legate had been and took Josh's hand, not in loving kindness or gratitude but to feel the pulse of the blood within, to sniff the skin for any stench of death, to look at the nails on his fingers to see that they were secure and not brittle. She smiled at him when he looked up at her, and then sniffed the breath from his mouth and nose, and stared deep into his eyes, for she had made a study of eyes, and could tell much from them.

She reached into the wallet at her side and produced three small phials. "Turmeric for cleansing," she said, putting a phial the colour of yellow mud to his lips. "Shadow iron in wine for the blood," as she made him sip from another. "And for strength," she said as she raised the third, "a dragon's tears of grief."

A stick touched her hand before it could reach his mouth.

"I am not sure," said Philo, "that such is lawful for him to drink."

"It is neither the flesh of something unclean," she said, "nor its blood, for though men may sometimes weep tears of blood, dragons never do."

The philosopher looked down at her indulgently. "You argue well," he allowed, "for a woman, and for a foreigner you have a grasp of the issues involved. But what if I were to say, that we cannot be certain and that perhaps blood refers to all fluids that issue from the body. After all, we are to refrain, in some circumstances, even from the milk that the Lord made to nourish us."

Like so many clever men, he loved a quibble more than sense, so much so that he dignified quibbles with the name of law, and their proliferation with learning.

"The youth will fade and die if you do not let me treat him as I see fit. And then you will answer to his father."

49

"I know the man Joseph." Philo's voice was full of dismissal. "A rich artisan who will obey Law when he hears it, as did Abraham."

I thought I had better intervene.

"That is not the father she means…How came you here so fast? I sent a runner to your house, but…"

He looked embarrassed, as the wise sometimes do when they are caught in the simple everyday actions of life. "I received no message; I was here in the market with my mother, buying fish for tonight's meal. I saw a crowd and saw it disperse, and thought I would see what it had been about. I should have known you, Huntress, would be at the heart of it, and that you would have dragged my wards into your deadly affairs." He looked at Sof, who stared back at him, angrily, in a way he doubtless considered brazen. "I'll thank you not to meddle with my ward. He is under my authority, as if I stood in the place of his father."

"I do not meddle." Her voice was clear and crisp. "I am the boy's physician, and I tell you he will die if I do not help him. He has over-taxed his strength by saving that man, and he needs tonics to recover, or he will fade and all his promise be undone."

A old blind woman carrying six fish by a piece of strong yarn strung through their lips approached, led up by a young slave girl. She laid her hand on her son's arm, but turned her face to the sound of Sof's voice in wonder.

"Maria? Maria, I thought you were dead and gone."

Sof, whose name was Maria in this life, as it had been in others, looked up in delight. "Little Abigail…"

Philo put his hand on his mother's shoulder, "Come away, mother, this is some trickery."

His mother looked up at him, blind but furious. "Son, I know what I know. This woman was your great-grand aunt, whoever she is now. She was a healer, best I ever saw."

He blustered, as men will who find the universe not constructed as they had thought. "How can you know that?"

His mother spoke to him as she doubtless had when he was a

small child who needed the world explained to him. "She sounds and smells just like her."

"She smells of her work, of herbs and acids, and she sounds like an Egyptian woman of the streets, with that awful accent they have."

"I know all of that, Philo, and this is Maria returned." Her voice had both tenderness and patience in it, but also a measure of annoyance at being contradicted.

While Philo was distracted a moment, Sof took the opportunity to put the third phial to Josh's lips. He drained it and colour started to come back into his face, but nowhere near enough.

Now she reached into her wallet and took out a small jar whose contents she applied to the old woman's unseeing eyes, and then kissed them gently. She took a corner of her garment, new clean that morning, and wiped the salve away, and crystal dirt came with it, rheum hard set and tears of pain dried into paste.

The old woman blinked, and her face looked, not younger, but certainly more alive, as she focussed and blinked again, and then raised her hand to shield herself from the bright light of morning.

Philo looked at his mother tenderly, then more grudgingly at Sof. "I accept you can heal. But transmigration is a superstition, not allowed for in Scripture or philosophy."

She smiled her most maddening smile. "That's because Plato hated the idea that a young woman juggler had taught his master everything he knew, and Solomon took rejection badly. Men lie."

A soft cawing interrupted her before she could say more.

In a flutter of wings, Josh's other guardian was with us, and the bird Ghost cawed in gentle sorrow at the sight of the boy. It had brought him a crust of that manna from Jehovah's table, which is more savoury than the ambrosia of Olympus and less intoxicating than the soma of the Gods of Hind. It is tough to bite and to chew, though nourishing, but Josh took a small mouthful from it, and worked it slowly in his mouth. Then he took another, and after a while he breathed more easily but was still pale.

"And what is this supposed to be?" Philo's voice was full of irony. "One of the ravens that fed Elijah?"

"Yes," said the bird, then held more of the crust to Josh's mouth. He reached up and stroked it as if its touch were a comfort in sickness.

For all its gentleness, the white bird had the cruel beak of its parent and sibs. It slashed at its own breast and then at Josh's wrist; with the ease of one who had done this before, he held his bleeding wrist to the bird's breast for long moments, then bulled it away. Both wounds were healed as if they had never been.

"Give father my love," Josh said. He kissed the top of the bird's head and it pecked gently at his left ear, whispering something I could not catch, before fluttering away, up and up into the heavens.

There was a moment of stillness, which I did not care to break.

"Come." Sof took Abigail by the arm. "Let us take Josh back to his lodging with you. And catch up on family; did Hannah marry young Boaz in the end?"

Josh rose to his feet and leaned on his attentive brother, and the two women, the old and the young, led them away.

Philo was not happy. "I might as well be worshipping the Olympians," he grumbled. "Transmigration, magic birds. And I take it that when Josh talks of his father, he does not mean Joseph."

I shrugged. "Well, no. But really, Nameless is far less of a thug than that crowd of drunken lechers. You're better off as you are."

There was heartbreak in his voice. "It all seemed so clear—the One of philosophy and the God of my fathers."

I took pity on him, because I needed his eyes in default of better, and needed him to stop whining. "Plato said it was all shadows." I am not happy with this sort of thing, but needs must.

He breathed in sharply with a new happiness and a new interest in his eyes. " You mean..." I could see his mind racing behind his eyes. "That boy's father is God, but only in the sense that he is a shadow of the One."

"I wouldn't know about that."

Never get caught in dialogue with philosophers if you can help it; this man might not have Plato's shoulders, but that barrel chest indicated to me a capacity for going on and on.

"And the law—we obey the shadow of Law which is human and fallible, but still the shadow of the real Law. Thank you thank you."

"No trouble. It will all make even more sense later. Now, I find, when I have some hard thinking to do, it's best to have the idea and then walk away for a while, and do something else."

I really needed to move on. I required someone to come to Simon's villa with me, and though the legate deserved to see whatever had been done to the messenger he had thoughtlessly sent there, he had died in agony once this day, and I am not unreasonable. Philo was an irritating pedant, perhaps, but he was by the same token a serious person—also, he had already turned out to know some of Simon's victims.

I got the legate to draw me a map.

"I need to have a look around with only one person to protect, should Simon be foolish enough to return to his home, or have left watchdogs. Send a cohort along later to help clear up whatever vileness we find there, without disturbing the populace." Roman legionaries were very good at fighting, but they were even better at digging, and I suspected there would be a need for a number of shallow graves. "Tell them to wait for me to bring them in, and if we are not waiting for them when they get there, tell them to withdraw. Then burn the villa and all that is in it, with catapults, from the lake."

I always try to assume that I may not survive encounters, and that anyone or anything strong enough to take me down is a considerable threat to other people. It is always best to take precautions, even if in practice they are usually irrelevant.

I turned to Philo, who stood shuffling his feet as one who would really rather be elsewhere, scribbling notes on philosophy, or teaching, while his mother prepared his fish dinner, and clapped him on the back. "Cheer up, you're probably in no danger. I will make sure to have you home for supper, though I suspect you may not feel like it."

I took his left arm in my right, and pulled him with me into shadow.

The villa was not, if you crossed the muddy lake, all that far.

I've been observing your house from shadow, Crowley, and like most mages, you have no aptitude for house-keeping, or for retaining servants to do it for you. Your gutters are full of leaves, and there are tiles missing from your roof—you would do far better to pay attention to such things than to turning your old acquaintance into camels.

But at least what servants you have, generally leave at night in the same condition they arrived in in the morning. And if the place stinks, it is of tobacco, wine-dregs, opium and cats, not of anything worse.

The air around the house of Simon Magus had a sickly sweetness, the sort of smell that is usually accompanied by sheets of black flies, and other eaters of carrion. Here, though, there was a dryness in the air, even though the squelching of the lake's shore was but mere yards away.

Mareotis is a delta lake, where water-birds call and coo; gulls blown in from the harbour shriek; and you hear the dark flap of the wings of vultures, kites and other birds from the barren lands.

Round this house, though, there was silence, no cry of birds and not even the smaller noises that insects make. That cloying scent everywhere, of decay and worse, and just a hint of incense and of natron and other desiccants.

Philo coughed in the parched air, harsh deep barks almost like something tearing.

"If you want to vomit, do not blush to do so. I sometimes forget the need—it is a human thing that I mislaid so long ago that I cannot remember when." I put my hand on his shoulder in fellowship—fellowship, and I was pretty certain that he would need to vomit properly once we saw the contents of the house and I did not want to be bothered to tell him he could then, when I might be busy.

54

I beat on the outer gate of the villa's courtyard but there was no noise from within, just the dead note of my hand against the door, and the splintering of the wood as I kicked it off its hinges, and the dull thud as it landed on the plain yellow brick of the pavement inside.

The way to the heart of such places is usually to follow the buzzing of flies, but the stench that usually goes with them is as good a guide, and that was here and grew more intense as we walked across the court and into the main door, which lay open, and swinging gently, but without a sound.

Once through the door, I saw two stairways, one leading up the second storey of the house and the other leading down into the ground. The worst of the charnel stink came from below, but from above came that mixture of natron and incense and other things, and, now we were at the foot of the stairs, a whisper and a buzzing that lay just at the brink of hearing and was not insects, but something worse.

I kept an eye on Philo—many men, some of them more obviously strong, would by this point have staggered away, crouched over and vomiting, but he did not. At times, he sighed deeply or winced as if bile were rising in his throat, but he held steady.

I had chosen my witness and I had chosen well.

I hate these moments of choice, when whatever I do may be wrong, and being wrong means that people will die. This is why I act in ways that make people, some of them gods, accuse me of being a creature of impulse, because there is a thing worse than making the wrong choice and that is dithering, and still making the wrong choice.

I thought I knew what lay at the bottom of the down staircase, and that it would not be going anywhere, but I went down there first, so that there would be no surprises later. Philo followed me with his mantle pulled up and around his mouth and nose.

It was as I thought—mere charnel and spoilage, bones and meat and skin and the inner parts of what had been human and what had been animal but was now just decay and stench, though without the small crawling things that usually go with such. I spoke of this later to Sof, and she said that she had often thought there were smaller things than insects, things like the blue mould that makes some cheeses soft and salt, or the yeast that turns millet into beer.

She was, in this as in all things, the wisest of the wise, and I hope one day I shall see her again and know her.

On this day, she was from my side, and about the business of healing, and all I had at my side was Philo the scholar, who peered at the rotten things with horror and compassion in his eyes, and managed to retain his breakfast, though he went pale save for a slight flush at the top of his cheekbones. He pointed at the small glowing stones in the wall, by the light of which he was seeing.

"I have not seen those before." He gave a short bitter laugh. "Simon could make himself rich with such and yet prefers to kill and maim."

I reached out my hand and felt the stones, which were cold to the touch. "Not so much," I contradicted him, "for these are shadow sapphires from the ice caves of the furthest North, and men and other things have died to bring them here, so many that you could buy a small realm with them, and the army to guard it, and Simon uses them to light mere rottenness. Clearly he despises wealth, for wealth is a human thing and a thing of life, and he thinks to have moved beyond such. As we will see upstairs, for there is nothing to concern us here."

"What could be worse than this?" Philo said. "Men and women carved and left to rot like so much kitchen rubbish."

"I do not know"—because I did not—"but worse it will be."

The rooms of the ground floor were mostly empty. One room, set back from the rest for fear of fire, and under its own roof, had been a kitchen once. Simon no longer ate and its cupboards were bare, its oven cold; another room had a bed frame in it, but no mattress upon it, for Simon no longer slept. He received no company and he lived alone, save for the dead and the worse than dead.

He bought so many slaves, and needed no servants.

I have walked most of the halls of Hell, not only the Christian Hell but the Buddhist Hells where worms eat their way through every nerve. I have walked the halls of the Inquisition, Spanish and Roman, and the temples of the Aztecs. The long, well-lit gallery that formed the upper floor of the villa of Simon Magus was a place full of more inhumanity, and more of the demonic, than any of these.

And yet no screams, and no squalor; everything was laid out neatly, as a man might his favourite scrolls for study, or placed on pedestals, as a man might his favourite table-bronzes.

In the gallery we saw a long table on which a man's guts had been laid out and dried and then inscribed with charms; a stand on which a woman's rib cage sat stripped of all its flesh save one breast that still dripped milk, and inside dried lungs with charms written upon them so that they still fluttered, and a withered heart that beat still. In one corner was a rack with heads upon it—heads that still wept for the bodies and lives that had been taken from them and that whispered their screams, for they had no voice bar that whisper.

All this, and much more, and none of it had ever been mere jape or nightmare, for Simon was his own best creation and had built himself a step and an organ at a time. He had learned his craft, learned to take organs and dry them and charm them that the dry husks would work as well as the originals, and done this over and over with slave after slave, and then prepared the best set he could for himself and taken out and replaced his own, and prepared those too. And more besides—what little I had glimpsed of the interior of his chest had given me sight of more lungs than two.

In a corner of the cellar, I had seen brains left to mulch; in a corner here, I saw scroll after scroll of papyrus that, if you lifted it, smelled gently of the same. As I feared, Simon killed for knowledge.

I cannot hear thoughts; I read faces well, and some who speak my legends have misunderstood that fact. These scrolls, though—they pulsed gently to the touch and if I held one against my face memories whispered in me that were not my own.

I don't think even Simon would have prepared his own brain so, but doubtless, in his largely empty chest and loins, there was room for him to store those scrolls for a while, and listen to their wisdom, and select those from which he might learn more.

I would have to be sure to kill him, and destroy him utterly, for my Sof might become his prey and so might young Josh, if he knew of them.

Where the long room turned a corner into the western wing of the house, the gallery changed into what had been Simon's laboratory and preparation area, but I could only tell this from the fact that its tables were empty and its floor scrubbed even clearer than the rest of the room. One of the tables appeared to be decorated with glittering mosaic, but when Philo touched it, the glitter slipped and slid and some particles of it fell on the floor. Simon had used beetles to devour the flesh of living and dead things, and when he was done with them, he tore off their wings one at a time, and used them to make pretty patterns. I could not see the beetles' other parts, but doubtless he had tipped them down the chute at one side of this workroom, the chute that led directly to the cellar of rot and filth.

I looked in compassion at Philo, who wandered that sunlit room alternately looking in fascination and averting his gaze. "I am sorry to have put you through this, but I guessed that I would need at least one witness."

He looked at me as if it were he that should be apologizing to me. "This is what you deal with all the time?"

"Rarely bad in quite this way, but yes."

"For thousands of years?"

I nodded, and he placed his hand on my shoulder a second. "Sometimes philosophy makes me forget to be kind."

"As does my own work—or, rather, I remember but have other things I need to do more."

He nodded, and I could not quite understand why this ageing pedant's approval mattered to me, but it was nonetheless so.

And then that moment was over.

"I need you, Philo, to write to your colleagues, leading figures among the Jews in all the cities of the Inner Sea, and tell them what you have seen. Simon is no longer safe in Alexandria, but I do not trust the Romans. Their emperor ages and it is all too likely some clerk will try to buy his favour by telling him of this man, and his way of defying death."

I have overthrown empires whose rulers adopted the Rituals, or things of the same sort, and it is more effort than I prefer to take. You have heard of few such empires? That is because I take a pride in my work, and the history of the world is long and rich, but has rooms that are now left dark.

"But for now…" I walked to a side-table where there lay, held down by a child's skull, another length of gut, this one with letters that needed little work to decipher. 'Insolent Roman Fool,' it said in letters of blood, 'this is all that I left of your messenger. Imagine what I shall make of you, and of your Prefect.' "I think,"—I took the piece of gut, rolled it and tucked it under my arm—"that for the moment, at least, the Romans will be angry enough that I can rely on them."

What Simon had done already was enough to turn the gaze of power on him, a power he was unwise to set at naught. This, though, was insolence and threats, and no empire tolerates those.

I led Philo down the stairs and out of that place and down to the shore, where boats were waiting, and a platform with several large catapults, and braziers full of flame, and bowls of hot pitch.

I had not expected to see the young legate there, but he had come, carried on a litter by slaves, and was waiting at the head of his men. I handed him Simon's letter, and he glanced at it, as men do with mail from taxman or doctor, whose contents they know and dread already. "The villa?" He looked up from the letter and cast it from him into one of the braziers.

"Nothing you would wish to have haunt your dreams."

He nodded acceptance and looked at me questioningly.

"Oh yes, burn it to the ground and then pour liquid fire deep into its cellar. Let no brick of it remain." And he waved his men into action almost before I had done speaking.

So it was done, and for some few weeks, it was almost as if we needed to think no more of Simon the Magus.

I kept an eye out for his handiwork, of course. Each night the young legate and I inspected the sites of any street killings, and interviewed the mothers of young men who disappeared, and there was nothing, no evidence that he was active in Alexandria. There were rumours that he had been seen, of course. A flying man who blasted people with an ivory hand was enough the stuff of tales that people wanted to hear more about him. Years later, long after he was gone for good, parents told naughty children that he would come and get them, but I heard that for the first time within weeks of that first encounter.

I became pretty certain that he was hiding somewhere deep in shadow—not far away as mundane miles go. A centaur tribe found a family of dead fauns—not exploded, just with their throats slit where they slept and the largest of the males cut. They brought me the youngest faun, who had hidden under his mother, but he had seen little in the darkness and could not speak that for weeping. Sof gave him a candied fig and he started to smile as he ate it, and then wept again.

I enquired in the brothels if any of the regulars had developed sudden potency, but that lead was barren of results. Simon, I thought, was either practicing the magic of sex, or one of those men who cultivate solitary vice. After all, in many places, we call such men magicians.

We could not rear the faun for I was often away, Sof kept dangerous substances in her workroom and he belonged among his own, so we found an elderly couple of fauns who had left the woods of shadow and fetched scrolls for the scholars in the Museion, and they adopted him. Sof visited him often, in this life and later ones, and watched him grow to adolescence down the years, but that is part of another tale.

Over those weeks, we sometimes walked of a cool evening from our home over to the Delta district, for Sof wanted to go on treating the eyes of Philo's mother so as to preserve her restored sight, and old Abigail would insist that we were family, and that we should take supper with them, law or no law. I never especially warmed to Philo, but he came to accept that we had both known Plato, and Socrates besides, and would ask us for tales of them. I noted with amusement, though, that he never asked for tales of Jehovah, and absented himself from dinner when Josh did.

Sof had befriended the lad—"If he is going to heal people," she said, "he had best learn more about how bodies are made and perhaps not use his powers for trivial matters, but learn some actual herbcraft." Philo had been as concerned as we had at the damage Josh had done to himself by healing the legate, and agreed to the youth's coming across the city for instruction. Josh brought his brother, who was determined to watch over him, but had no interest in healing.

Sof taught Josh much about medicine and much about her work, and of the herbs from Shadow and the mundane world that she used in both—for the violets that grow in those far fields first intoxicate and then purify the blood, and the garlic you pluck there oozes a salve that is good for warts. She knew all herbs and plants and the different properties—and she knew how to filter and distil them alone or together and make the veins and arteries of the body sleep or dance.

She took the boy as far into shadow sometimes as they could go in a few hours—to the cliffs that tower above the shadow's Nile where it meets the sea in a great rush, where cormorants and harpies fight over shellfish and cast aside blue shadow pearls that, dissolved in wine, wash the liver clear of debauchery's rewards and give a finer sleep than innocence. Cleopatra the Queen knew of such pearls and fed them to her love.

Rather than have a bored youth lounging around our home, I took Judas with me a short way into shadow, where there was room for exercise that there was not amid our kitchen and workroom, and taught him how to repair the deficiencies in his knife play. He had learned much from his earlier instructor, and had been lucky, but luck will only favour the young and brave for a while, and he was brave enough to get himself killed rather than run away from those who knew knives better than he did. I had not entirely taken to the boy, but I did not want him harmed.

As we sparred, he would ask me whether I had taught Jehovah this move or that, as if he could turn knife-play into worship through emulation. Where Josh wanted to know everything about his father, his step-brother wanted to learn just this one thing—what choke-holds or wrestler's throws I had taught his god back in the days of his youth.

"Why so interested?" I asked him once, after he had almost managed to worm out of my grip, "I thought your master had decided that the Jehovah I know is just some earthly shadow."

The youth looked at me with the seriousness of the diligent pupil who is less clever than his master. "He says that service is a good in itself, is a way to knowledge. My brother has studied arms a little, but has no great gift for them. I need to be able to protect God's son. And that will help me serve the One."

I laughed, and pinned him harder to the ground, but he worked hard, and managed to make me sweat a little to twist the knife from his hand. He had a neat upward stab to the guts that I had not taught him, but which we worked on improving.

He asked me much else and I answered freely, for the lad had almost as lively a mind as his step-brother and I had promised Jehovah's Bird that I would help with their education.

One day, when I had his arms up behind his back by his thumbs and he would not yield and I would not break or dislocate an arm to make him, because I do not tire—he looked over his shoulder at me in pain from which he wanted to distract himself. Perhaps he thought he could distract me, because young men sometimes forget that I have been doing these things for a very long time, and do not shift my focus because a young man asks me an interesting question.

"What happens when we die, Mara?"

Always an interesting question, especially in those days.

"Some, like my sister, come back. Over and over. Gautama in the land of Spice promised an end to that, and perhaps he found one, at least for himself. Others just wander—not unhappily for the most part because being dead is a boon to the curious. Jehovah and the other gods take some of the dead for courtiers—it's a good way to get staff, after all."

Judas chortled and I twisted his left thumb a little to remind him to take things seriously.

"Oh, and Lucifer and Hades and some of the others have this whole weird idea that you should go on punishing the evil dead forever—which some call justice but I call a sickness of the heart." And then I let him go because he was so good at ignoring pain that I feared I might actually hurt him. He stretched and laughed and stared at me with insolent eyes that glistened like the salt of the sweat of his body.

Sof came to us with honey and curds in bowls; she kept bees and goats in another part of near shadow. The boy sat himself down and lowered his head to the bowl and I thought no more of our conversation, for he asked me for tales of Hannibal and Alexander, as ambitious young men will.

I offered to teach him sword, and lance, but he said that with the Romans ruling everywhere around the Inner Sea, showing competence with their weapons was a good way to get himself killed. That was prudent of him, but his prudence has always been one of the things I liked about him least, because it is not natural to him. It is something he learned.

I have never needed to fight with staves, but I found a tavern-keeper who was a master with staves and sticks, and he taught Judas much, and among those things was prudence. Stave-fighting teaches you that, or so they tell me—because a smart blow to the pate or ear is something you learn to avoid.

Judas learned from that tavern-keeper, and from me, and from

Philo, and above all from his brother. He is not what we made him, but what we helped him make himself, which is what his reputation states, but so much more besides.

And I will tell you that part of the story in its proper place.

Josh and Judas were young men away from home with money in their pockets, and as such young men go, they behaved remarkably well. I have known many who behaved far worse—neither of them had a taste for wine, which is fortunate, because neither of them had much a head for it, then or later. And in a city known for carnality of all the obvious kinds and some more recondite, they were both of them more or less chaste.

I remarked on this to Sof, one night as we walked back from the house of Philo. "He keeps them studying hard, and so do we, but they really are living as if they had sworn some vow."

Sof laughed. "Sometimes, my dear, for all your years, you miss the obvious. And I might have also, save for the little sheets of papyrus I sometimes find among my scrolls."

She showed me Josh's poems; it is a shame that they have been lost. But much that is lost is not gone, and perhaps they will surface one day and charm you all.

Let's just say, Crowley, that he was considerably better than either you or your friend Mr. Yeats. As he was at most things when he set his mind to it.

"Do I need to worry?" I laughed, for we had the same arrangement as we had had in her first life even if she rarely chose to exercise it, and I never, save for that once time of which I have told you.

She smiled, with a hint of regret because young Josh, though a little lanky and thin, was a very beautiful young man. "He just isn't very carnal. I pecked him on the cheek one day when I particularly liked the poem he had left for me, and he blushed and stammered. I took him by the hand as if to lead him somewhere soft, and he kissed me very gently on that hand, and equally gently pulled away."

Like most of the tales about him, this is one that oath-bound priests will never understand. Josh—I think—chose restraint in most things, not because he was sworn, but because it suited his temperament to.

"So, Josh is smitten with you and is acting like a poet. But what of his brother? He seems not to go out roistering."

Sof's laughter was like the pouring of wine into a cup made of the finest Alexandrian glass-ware. "There is only one woman for that young man. And he has his body handled by her every day, smells the thin film of sweat on her arm as it wraps itself around his throat. I am sure that he writes poems to her, but I doubt his are any good."

I had been naïve, but thought it best to say nothing. Judas was as shy and sensible as his brother.

Perhaps I should have spoken to him about it.

Some days we walked the city with them and introduced them to its less carnal pleasures. The lads had, as they told me, a particular desire to look at all the great buildings of the city and we spent hours in each of the palaces of the Ptolemies, with Judas making a little frame of his fingers and reckoning angles and proportions, and Josh scribbling notes. Yet they paid little attention to the decoration of the rooms they reduced to numbers and shapes in their damn tablets, though Josh shed a quiet tear when I showed him the room where Anthony had stabbed himself and the room where his Queen had met her end. As I have remarked, he was a young man with a taste for stories and much moved by them—and now he has become one…

We walked the slums of my quarter, where few put up new buildings, but some try to add a floor; sometimes the boys would steady a ladder while they shouted up their questions to the men who were hauling up new beams and taking down old ones. They would help shovel dirt for a ramp, or look carefully and help place a door-frame by dead reckoning, and tap in the wooden pegs that held it in place with the hammer Judas bore in his belt; I had noticed that their hands bore the marks of labour as well as of scholarship and now knew why.

We trudged every inch of the causeway out to Pharos island with the boys examining what seemed like every paving stone and cobble, with Judas tapping them periodically with his hammer, calling out numbers and Josh scribbling away. Inside the building itself, they took even more notes; Judas was fascinated by all the stage machinery which worked the tritons on the exterior, while Josh spent hours staring at the levers that pulled the mirrors around, and at the great furnace whose bright blaze served the mirrors.

One of the artisans who maintained the great pumps down in the bowels of the Pharos showed them how water was drawn up a long syphon from the canals of the city and Mareotis, all the way under the causeway, to power the tritons and other machines beside. I did not share their fascination with such matters, but I listened all the way back into town as they explained to me that there are impurities in sea-water—salt, but other things besides—which would corrupt the copper parts of the machines and stop them working in a few years.

"Ptolemy built it to last forever," they said in awe, forgetting to whom they spoke and that I know what forever means. And as human things go, the great lighthouse of the Pharos managed its millennium and went some way to its second.

I had a dispensation to use the Museion for all that I was a woman and a foreigner, and I took great pleasure in affronting those lecturers who cared about such things by bringing with me my beloved and these two young Jews.

I cared not that they sometimes spat at our shadows when they thought we could not see, because I had a permit from the Prefect of Egypt; more, my rights had been written into the Museion's charter by that fine old bully Ptolemy himself, who thought himself served by what had been my duty merely.

When he seized Egypt for himself, as the finest prize a strong man could hold who was not Alexander, who seized all, there were things awake in the land that Nectanebo had called to his side. The Magi had held those things in sleep, but let them go when the Greeks came. I solved that problem, forever, and, asked for my choice of reward, asked for access to the books Ptolemy was gathering. After all, books are my trade as much as weapons, for all I carry none about me.

On one particular day, Sof had need to consult notes she had made several lives previously, on a scroll that she had given to Solon, which had passed from him into the treasury of Athens, and thence in due course to Alexandria, whither all books came.

"I remember what I wrote," she explained, slightly embarrassed because she was proud of the way her memory worked from life to life, "but I sketched a flower in the margin that I have not seen since, and which may have passed into the further parts of shadow or gone for good." She was carrying a wax tablet and her brushes. "The centaurs we spoke to recently are going far into shadow's north and they said they would look for it."

She wandered off on her errand, and I went about mine.

I had only glanced briefly at the message sent by Simon to the legate before it was burned, but it had occurred to me that I had seen the writing before.

Simon was older than I thought, and his current activities not his first—he had been a clerk in Cambyses' army, the one in charge of burning the priests of Egypt. I had wondered about his diligence at the time, but he seemed ignorant of the Rituals, as some are who profit by them nonetheless. His ledgers of death were there, deep in the stacks, and it was as I had thought. I had considered his current use of other men's organs to fall within my areas of concern, but it was good to know that he was a man who had escaped me once, but would not do so forever. I too am diligent.

It had been unreasonable of me to expect two young men to spend more than a few minutes poring over such things, and Josh and Judas had wandered out into the sunshine, and the Museion's great colonnades, where other young men were lounging, whose right to be there was less questionable, young Greeks and the occasional Roman.

67

There are strict rules about rough-housing on the Museion's grounds, and things had gone little beyond cat-calling, when I joined them, and the youths around them fell suddenly silent.

I had said nothing, but it is surprisingly easy to intimidate when you have practice.

"As I said," Josh said, "my father's friend, and our guardian, the Huntress. Whose right to be here, and bring whomsoever she chooses with her, I trust you will not dispute."

A willowy young man whose accent placed him as coming from Ionia struck that annoying attitude that all trainee sophists seem to adopt. "Granted," he waved his hand in airy fashion, "granted that you have a right to be here in terms of the Library's rules. Still, should you be here? You Judaeans believe you are servants of one true and only God, and the knowledge we teach here has Apollo, and the Muses for their patron. Surely your god…"

"Ah," Josh laughed, "I think I know more about our god and his wishes than you do. All knowledge is useful."

Judas was more serious. "It helps us serve him."

The young sophist was not about to let things rest. "I see from your hands that you are working men…"

So many Greek scholars have an aversion to physical labour; that, and their love of a quarrel, were why they fell to the Romans, I have always thought.

"We are students of Philo," Josh said, "but we have been known to work with our hands."

"My father owns estates on three islands." The sophist was pulling rank, because he sensed that his companions were losing interest.

"His father," Josh pointed to his step-brother, "has built half of each of the Ten Cities, save Damascus alone."

"Trade?" The sophist's tone was that of a man who thinks his opponent has defeated himself.

"Trade," Josh agreed, "which is a source of much knowledge you will not find elsewhere. And moral instruction beside, of a kind not to be found in Plato, nor in Aristotle." He smiled, and where the sophist's smile was all teeth and malice, Josh's was that of a young man who expects, rightly, that all will be charmed by him.

"I remember"—and suddenly he had the attention of all the young Greeks, even the sophist. Judas smirked, for clearly he had seen his brother tell stories before, and knew them all. "Joseph my stepfather once had a overseer, who went for him to Gerasa and Pella and Raphana, to cities too far to travel easy back and forth to Nazareth in a day or overnight, yet not so far that Joseph could never visit and see how work progressed. And this overseer stayed in inns where men play at dice. They gave him strong drink and he lost the little he had, and my stepfather's money besides, and then the men beat him for he had no more. And the overseer sat in the dirt and poured dirt over his head, and was ashamed. So he went to the seller of bricks and said 'Give me a hundred score bricks, and write that I took a hundred and fifty score' and to the seller of scaffolding, 'sell me eight score cubits length of wood, and write that I took one hundred,' and to other men, he said such things as well. And each time he sent word to my stepfather that things were costing more, and thus he hid the money he had lost in the extra money my stepfather was sending him.

"But then my stepfather sent word that he would visit to see the dwelling that his overseer had built, and the overseer became afraid that Joseph would learn what he had done. He struck the great roofbeam with a hammer once twice and three times, and of a sudden the house fell down. And some of the builders escaped, but the overseer was caught in the wreckage, and his blood was upon him."

"I do not understand," the young sophist said, genuinely baffled.

"He that has ears, let him hear." Josh looked at him patiently, then put his hands out to his sides in feigned exasperation. "False in one thing is false in all. The wicked man can always find companions in wickedness. The trickster will always out-trick himself."

69

And then he laughed. "And it's very hard to get good help these days."

The young sophist recovered, and sneered, "If that is philosophy, then so are the words of mimes and vagabonds who tell such tales in the marketplace."

And one among the hearers, an older man in a torn tunic and leaning on a stick, rose in a fury and struck the young sophist about the shoulders. "Sophist," he shouted, "is Diogenes so forgotten that young men like you cannot recognize his doctrine when you hear it?"

He turned to Josh, and bowed. "Young man, I am no longer allowed to teach here, or at the Serapion, but if you would care to walk with me in the marketplace of an afternoon, I would gladly exchange with you knowledge and ignorance. And we can watch mimes and vagabonds together, and learn philosophy from them."

I would have expected that Philo would not have approved of Demetrius of Corinth, and yet I was wrong. Josh asked his tutor's permission and Philo laughed and said that Demetrius was a good man for a heathen Greek and his conversation could do no harm.

Demetrius believed that wisdom was both rare and universal, and took Josh with him to speak to all the kinds of philosopher who came to Alexandria, from the Druids of Britannia to the breathing men and scholars of the lands of Spice and Silk. And Josh learned much, and talked of it with Sof.

In later years, Philo and Demetrius travelled together to Rome, to plead for Alexandria and both its Jews and its Greeks with the tyrant Little Boots. Demetrius mocked the emperor, refusing a bribe of two hundred sesterces, by feigning humiliation.

"Am I worth so little?"

"And what does the great philosopher think his virtue is worth?" the emperor leered suggestively, and the bystanders knew that the old man was at risk not of death alone.

Demetrius pondered a moment, then shrugged. "This palace, and the city of Rome, and the lands of Italy, and all you own"—and then he paused—"would be a start," and then he shrugged again, "but not I think enough." And Caligula laughed, and Demetrius outlived him and five emperors beside.

This then was a man from whom Josh learned much, and these were the pursuits in which he spent his time in Alexandria. Time well-spent? You may judge for yourself.

All of this time, the young legate and I kept up our watch and our enquiries, and there was no sign of Simon, yet I suspected that he was not done with Alexandria, and knew that I was not done with him.

The first sign of his return was something that we might almost have missed save that one of the men and women who quarry dung-heaps and middens, both for what is supposed to be there and for the small valuable things that end up there by mistake, came to my door. As these people often did, because Sof had a use for many things in her Work and some of them were unclean.

He stood wringing a leather cap in his hands, while she went into the house to fetch copper money to pay him with for the special variety of filth he had brought her; he would not look me in the eye, but nonetheless had something to say to me.

"Men say, Huntress, that you and de Romans look for a man who is more and less than a man. Dat you burned his villa on the far side of Mareotis and dug out its cellars and burned dem too."

"Men are right to say so, and the man Simon called the Magus is an enemy to all, so if you know anything, speak of it."

Besides appealing to his virtue, I tossed a silver coin in the air and caught it over and over again as we spoke, because I was tired of waiting.

"It might be nothing, but dat's not for me to say. Would dead rats be of interest?"

"Dead, how?"

"Deir innards pulled out and laid out neat, as if dey were an augury, and deir likkle heads all burst like fruit."

I tossed him the coin. "Show me."

It was as he had said: the rats' skulls were open like spring buds and their guts spread out like geometry, and I knew with the thrill of the hunt that Simon had returned, and yet I could not imagine what he was doing with rats. After all, it is with small animals that killers start, and then move to humans.

Yet somehow, he had learned to do with a knife what he used to do with magic, for there were delicate knife-cuts at the edges of the wounds that had not been there in his other victims.

Philo had no idea, nor Sof. We had grown used to asking the lads Josh and Judas, but they could not think why rats would be of interest to the monster Simon.

A day later, early in the morning, the legate came to my door in high excitement, breathless from running. "A death, found this morning, in his bedchamber, skull hammered open and guts pulled out. Same as with the rats. But only a part of the brain missing."

That was something new.

Sof looked unwell. "Perhaps he has learned to take only the part of the brain where what he wishes to learn resides."

She retched slightly, in a way I was not used to see her do when we discussed my work, but she had a tender heart and the memory of great pain. I looked at her in question. She stared back at me, angry, but not with me.

"Think how many more he must have killed than you know, to have his art down so fine, now."

She was, of course, right—the years have hardened me and I do not always think of such things.

I turned to the legate, and at that moment Josh and Judas arrived for that morning's lesson.

"Whom did Simon kill?"

"That's the odd thing, no-one very much. A clerk who worked in the archives of the Pharos, but not one of the engineers who maintain it, or one of the administrators. Just the man who kept the scrolls in order."

I was baffled. Josh and Judas though, positively bounced with self-satisfied excitement. Sometimes I needed to remember how young they were. Josh looked at Judas, and Judas looked at Josh, who took a step back, leaving his elder brother to explain.

"It's probably the secret chamber; you do know that there's a secret chamber, right?"

The legate, and Sof, and I, had never heard of or considered such a thing; the Pharos was one of the biggest things we had ever seen, and we did not think of it as having secrets, just the miracles of its construction.

Josh stepped forward and explained. "We spotted it the first time we went there with you. We thought everyone knew and were just keeping quiet about it. It's really kind of obvious."

"Obvious how?"

They looked at me pityingly, then at Sof and the legate as well when neither of them stepped in to explain to me. Judas clearly found it hard to believe.

Sof looked at them both and then smiled at me. "I think it's something to do with the whole building thing. Boys, you'll have to explain it to us—it's not what we know about. I am sure the legate here could tell you a lot about how to set up a Roman camp or fort, but it's not really his thing either, not big permanent structures full of machines. So, it's something about how the building looks."

I thought back, to when I had been round the Pharos with them, and what they'd looked at—the levers that pulled the mirrors, but that was obvious; the place where the water from the siphon bubbled up; and the chamber where the pumps directed it, but none of those... And the big square area of blank wall between the two arms of the staircase that led up to the workrooms, the offices, the furnace and the machines.

"It's the bottom of the stairs, isn't it?"

They smiled as at the antics of a child who had just mastered walking on two feet.

"I mean," I went on, "it's not really holding all that much up. And it's just sort of there, a big cube."

73

And for a second, I saw the world as both of them had been taught to see it, all structures and supports and beams, all in proportion except for the bits that were not, and all planned in advance, not only by an architect but by the person who costed everything, and bought the best materials.

There is more to Josh than that, of course, wherever he is, but he always had that side, and I think it is the fundamental truth of Judas, and what he has become.

"I wonder what's inside it. That Simon wants." The legate asked the obvious question for all of us.

"Something Ptolemy thought important enough to hide there." I had no idea, so I might as well be the one who helped things along.

"Treasure from the land of Spice." Judas went with the commonplace.

"No, he can clearly take whatever gold and jewels he wants, and his needs seem few." Sof seemed to have a pretty good grasp of the man. "Knowledge?"

"Again," Josh cut in, "he can take whatever he wants. And Ptolemy put so much in the library; surely that would be the place to look for knowledge. It was the clerk of the Pharos he killed, not a librarian, this time. This is a man who deals in flesh, and its secret learning."

A horrible thought struck me. "I was there." I was remembering and trying to hold the picture in my mind's eye. "I was there when Octavian, whom they later called Augustus, asked that the sarcophagus be opened. And he bent down and kissed the Conqueror on the cheek. He lingered a second, and then the nose fell off and the cheek crumbled into the skull and the skull went to shards, and the leathered skin went to powder, all inside that golden armour. And…"

They all looked at me, questioning.

"I wondered why Ptolemy had hired a second-rate embalmer for his King and Master, that the corpse had only lasted a couple of centuries. Now I know."

They still weren't with me.

"That wasn't Alexander," I explained, "that was one of his doubles. Poor man, Ptolemy must have killed him so that he could serve in death as he had served in life."

They started to understand, the legate and the boys and my darling dear, and all shuddered.

I went on. "What Simon wants to steal, is the body and brain and heart of Alexander son of Philip, the Great, the Builder and the Burner of Cities. He wants his knowledge and he wants his courage and he wants to take the world."

I did not know for certain that Simon could steal the things from the long-dead that he could steal from those he had just killed, and it was possible that he did not know this for certain either. Magic is, as you know well, often a chancy business. But there are some chances one does not take, and the possibility that this would not work and whatever was left of Alexander had no virtue in it was not one I was prepared to take.

The legate had already gone outside, and sent one of his men at a run to the barracks, another to fetch him a mount. I went out into the shabby street and whistled a call I know that I had promised five centuries earlier I would only use in dire need.

I could be at the Pharos in moments through shadow, as could Sof, for she had learned much in other lives that stayed with her now, but we needed the boys with us.

She could not travel as fast as I, so she gathered a few things she might need in the satchel she wore at her side, and wrapped a scarf around her throat against the fierce winds, some cold and some hot, that sometimes blow through shadow, and started to run, and was gone from my sight.

As chance would have it, I knew the centaur who came, several centuries old and past her youth, who had worked in the brothels of the city for many years as a whore and now as a head-breaker and cup-bearer.

Then I looked at her more closely, because when she stopped at our door, she stamped hard on a paving stone, hard enough that there were sparks.

Centaurs do not, as a rule, go shod, save for she-centaurs past child-bearing, who sometimes take on missions of death and vengeance, and endure the agony of shoeing to harden their will as well as to make their hooves into deadly weapons.

She saw me glance down.

"I am sworn to avenge our friends the fauns."

She spoke as if this were a small thing, but an honour.

I took and clasped her hand.

"Then we are well met, for it is the murderer Simon that we go to seek."

She smiled with her mouth and not with her eyes; it was not a smile I would wish to see as a reaction to mention of my name.

I gestured to my two young companions.

"I know how your people hate to be seen as beasts of burden, but—"

"Huntress, my darling, our debt to you still stands, that you just called on but which I choose not to regard as called." Musk dripped from her every word. "It is a while since I have borne such tasty man flesh upon me as you are offering. Where do you want me to take them?"

Josh and Judas reddened; it was not the centaur's words alone, but the way she eyed them, as if they bore no clothes but only the sweat of their bodies after hours of play.

I smiled guardedly. "The Pharos—dark magics are afoot and there is no time for dalliance."

"Him as killed the fauns and cut their chief?"

I nodded.

"He is owed for that." Her voice was grim. "I will take the lads there by a quick route I know, through alleys and shadow and alleys again, and through a part of shadow where there is a gentle slope to the island, and not the harsh stones of the causeway on my feet. And there will be no dalliance, though I yearn before I die to one day taste a lad that is clipped as these two are."

She reached down with her strong arms and took Judas on her back, and then Josh leaped up behind him. "Hang on," she laughed. "I shall be at a gallop and you may bounce a little."

"Hang on to what?" Judas blushed as he took her meaning.

She leered. "I need to take some moments of pleasure for my pains."

I suspect this was just teasing, because I refuse to believe she would take much pleasure from his hands. Though who can say with centaurs and their games? In any case, she would take good care of the boys; she-centaurs are fierce and creatures of their word. And those who work the vengeance of the two Peoples are more focussed than they care to seem.

I made my own way through the nearer parts of shadow and caught up with Sof on the causeway, touching the back of her neck to let her know that I was there. I was glad to see the legate on his way, as we passed him. And, coming along the harbour embankment, some twenty legionaries at a fast run.

I came to the great door of the Pharos and, though it was open, beat hard upon it, to attract the attention of those who worked there.

Clerks and engineers and officials stumbled over each other down the staircases to a mezzanine that overlooked the entrance hall and gawped as I stood there, beating on their door with Sof beside me, and the legate mounted on his horse, and soon Josh and Judas set down by their centaur, who made no immediate move to leave, and the legionaries, who formed a circle around the door to protect it, swords drawn and shields ready to lock.

It was a plain, businesslike place, free of decoration save for a single torch-sconce made of gold on the wall by the bottom of the staircase, and the simple bubbling spring in a bowl of stone that seethed perpetually in the middle of the floor. It was lit by windows, five stories up, and a skylight set at a slant at almost the very top of the tower. Above us, between the winding stairs, a metal plate that glowed showed where the furnace roared like a great beast. Not so loud that we could not hear other things, but a perpetual bass note that almost made us strain.

"What is the meaning of this?" A white-haired man hobbled down the stairs toward us, taking his time because he was leaning on a stick, but also because he had an older man's sense of the dignity of his office and the respect owed to his experience.

I remembered him: Dion, Guardian of the Pharos. He had been there, man and boy, so long that he remembered kind words spoken to him by the Queen and had paid his respects to Augustus Caesar. He could seem vain and pompous, but no man who was only those things could have guarded the lighthouse so well for so long.

"Dion. Guardian of the Pharos Light and the Pharos isle, Chief of its engineers, and Lord of the Harbour of Alexandria." I think he had some other titles beside but I had never taken the trouble to learn them, and he should consider himself grateful. I am, after all, a Power who expects to be recognized, and am not known for wasting people's time.

"Dark magic is coming to this place of light." I pointed to the, now I considered it, suspiciously blank cube in front of us. "Open it."

Dion looked blank, then looked at one of the engineers, who scratched his head and said uncertainly, "I think it's just a reserve tank for the hydraulics."

For a moment, I thought that I had made a terrible mistake in listening to two young and inexperienced men. I have made mistakes of my own from time to time, and listening to other people has not always gone well for me. I stepped back into shadow, and then back again and deeper.

With enormous relief, I stepped back into the entrance hall of the Pharos which I had left moments before. "If that were the case," I tried to keep relief out of my voice, "it would hardly exist several planes deep into shadow. Few trivial things are built that impermeable."

And yet, as I spoke, there came a tapping and a clanking from inside the cube, though I could not imagine how anyone could have got inside something so bizarrely solid. I looked at the engineer. "You really have no idea how to open it."

He shrugged. "We could fetch crowbars and sledges."

That did not seem a good idea, and if the noise from inside, which grew steadily louder and more impatient, were Simon, we were up against considerations of time.

"Let me." Judas stepped forward and I was glad to see that for once he was being rash with his hammer and not with his knife.

"Where do you think?" He looked round at his brother.

Josh was looking intently at the cube. "Three cubits up from the bottom corner, and two cubits in. There's a patch there that's a slightly different colour. I think there was a sconce there at one point, but it got broken off and the area sanded down."

He really did have the most acute sight, I realized; now he pointed, I could see what he meant, but I would never have spotted it for myself.

Judas took a step back, and then, precisely, and very gently but firmly, tapped the area with his hammer. And then again, as if he had been making his mark before, he tapped it with more force.

There was a creaking, and a noise of water rushing and then gurgling away, and the entire front face of the cube rolled up and disappeared.

There have been few craftsmen who could make use of shadow in their machinery—Leonardo used it for trivial things like stage machinery, as did Inigo Jones who had the secret from his manuscripts. This unknown craftsman of Ptolemy's surpassed them all.

Inside the cube, caught in the light of day like a kitchen insect, was Simon the Mage, who seemed more unwholesome than when I had seen him before. It was as if his skin were more like parchment, and his body gaunter even than it had been.

The legate shouted to his men "Seize him!" He stepped forward to take Simon by the shoulder, and three men pinned the magus none too gently against the wall of the cube.

He let himself be taken and held, merely whispering as the legate took him. "Your messenger had succulent flesh. And I felt the quality of your liver when I pulled it from you." He giggled when the legate struck at him.

These were things that happened, but none of us were paying as much attention to them as they deserved, because the other thing that was in the cube was a thing of note.

A great glass ball, man-height and then some, and in it floating naked, Alexander, whom I had last seen on his death-bed, and then on the litter that the Followers carried shoulder high before his armies, to prove that he was dead and they had the right to whittle away at his empire for their own gain. He had died wasting and with that particular thinness that afflicts some men who drink too much, but he looked no worse now than he had then.

Not a mummy, then, for his flesh looked soft.

The fluid in which he rested from life was a rich tawny brown with streaks of yellow dust in it. "Honey and gold." I said in wonderment. "Ptolemy preserved him in honey and gold."

"That's disgusting." The centaur pulled a face as if she were about to vomit. "The things you humans do to each other." She planted a kiss first on Josh's forehead, and then on Judas' lips. "I am going somewhere cleaner. And if you have any sense, you will leave this alone. You are human and have none, but if you walk away from this, unchanged by it, come and find me. The Huntress can bring you to me; she is in charge of your education, they tell me, and I give lessons that men and women never forget."

She tossed her head and was gone.

I wondered for a second why she was leaving the vengeance of the Peoples to Rome, and then realized that she thought Rome would fail.

In the short moment in which I wondered how he had been taken so easily, Simon threw the four soldiers from him. He rose in the air just outside the cube and gestured, and the glass ball came loose from its mounting, and floated up to join him, as he floated up towards the windows, or possibly the sky-light—I do not know what he intended.

It was imperative that he not be allowed to leave with it, and I took two of the knives from my hair and threw them one after another. My aim was true, but they bounced off the dark stones that were now his eyes; he had made himself less human than I thought. A couple of the legionaries threw their spears; they thunked off his skin as if it were made of wood, and not the parchment it resembled.

It was a shame, but Judas' choice was the right one. He took his hammer and hurled it, not at Simon but at the glass ball. It rang, high and clear, and for a moment it seemed as if it had taken no hurt from the hammer, but then, with a higher note, it rang itself to shards. Shards that did not fall, but hovered and whirred for a little like a crowd of angry flies, and then attacked Simon, tearing his cloak and his skin and what lay within, darting in and out of him like needles or hungry fish or a pack of dogs that are cowards one by one and dash in and nip and run, and yet the pack is fierce.

Simon screamed, a scream that went on and on. I would have sworn that there was no blood left in any part of him, but the cloud of glass grew red about him.

The glass stayed where it was in the air, all but a few random shards, but the honey flowed free and in mid-air became a sphere again.

Alexander, though—where was that thin naked body we had all seen? For a second, as the honey reshaped itself in mid-air, that face that I had known shimmered in the flow. It opened its eyes, and shut them, as if it had made a decision and then it was gone.

And the sphere of honey fell with a splat on and around young Josh, washed over him, and then was gone.

Josh staggered a little, but managed to retain his balance. Momentarily he shook his head as if he had been soaked in water and could dry himself that way, but all that happened was that the honey smeared across his face as if it were crawling there.

High above us, Simon burst free of the glass shards that harried him and dived towards us with a cry of pain and loss. He was in rags, great rents in his cloak and his robe and his face and his body, and yet, even as he fell, I saw the rags start to repair themselves. Then, before we could throw more missiles at him, he plunged into the bowl at the centre of the room. It seemed far too small to hold him, and yet his body, his limbs, his features, collapsed in on each other as if they were a scroll that is being wound up tighter with a finger at its centre. There was a small hole, where the spring came up into the bowl, and he was gone into that hole, and gone from the Pharos light.

"Where does that go?" I shouted.

Dion's engineer said, "Down into the siphon, and out into the lake."

Even racing through shadow, I would never catch him. Nor did I see him for some years—and that is a part of this tale, but not this part.

"So that is what the rats were for." Sof looked thoughtful.

She stepped over to the bowl and moistened her scarf in its fresh water. As she dabbed honey and glass away from Josh's eyes, eyes that he had managed to close in time, she explained.

"Rats and mice can enter spaces that would seem far too small for them. I know not what part of them gives them that virtue, but Simon has found it out. We should be glad that he is badly hurt, for it may give us respite from him for a while."

Josh had been quiet, but now he suddenly coughed, great racking coughs as if he were trying to cast something out of him, then bent and vomited onto the floor, a pool of honey clear even of sugar crystals. He spluttered like one saved from drowning. "My mouth was closed. How is it in me when I had my mouth closed?"

And why? I wondered, and knew the answer at once. He was the only man in the room who, like the Conqueror, had a god for a father.

I held my peace though, because there was no point in jumping to conclusions, and he had cast honey from his body; it might be that all he had vomited was the excess, or it might be that he had rejected it altogether.

Sometimes, and this may be a fault, I leave things be and wait to find out what comes.

Outside, I saw the she-centaur and looked at her with a shrug.

"I knew." Her voice was calm. "I read the stars and threw the odds with dice. This was not his time—it might have been, but was not. Yet I will be there for our vengeance."

That night, Sof and I dined well on goat-stew from one of our quarter's better cook-shops, with flat bread, and vine-leaves stuffed with millet and dried fruit. She took to her bed, which that night I was minded to share. She glad of the company, but there came a banging at the door.

It was one of the legate's men, with a summons to attend the Prefect; the man was surly, for one we had stood in arms with earlier the same day, and I noted with disquiet that two of the soldiers who accompanied him started to put chains on the door after we had left.

I looked at Sof, and she smiled wistfully. "There is nothing in the ovens that need concern us. The Work has reached a temporary halt while I consider my next step in it carefully. I am steeping some herbs easily replaced, and I have a fragment of the Stone that I keep about me at all times. Most processes of a higher rank than that, all of a lesser, can be started with ease with that. And though I needed the Elixir to make the Stone, the Stone will always bring me back the Elixir, no matter where I am."

"I was thinking partly of what dangers our neighbours might risk, if we were prevented from coming back."

"None," Sof laughed. "I can always contrive a smoke or a noise or a blast, should I need to, but they are not tricks I find of use in the Art."

And thus we talked pleasantly until we came to the Prefect's palace through a pleasantly cool evening that was to be our last sight of Alexandria for a long time.

The others were there, under guard but not in chains: Josh and Judas, with Philo fussing around them and even Demetrius the Cynic and the female centaur whose name she had never told us, for it is not a thing that centaurs do. The legate was there, in that best armour with a new horsehair plume on the helmet that usually tokens imminent military disgrace. Dion was there, leaning on his stick wearily like a man who had already been subjected to hours of harangue.

They brought us before Gaius Valerius, the Prefect.

He had been drinking—his speech was very slightly slurred and there was an unhealthy bloom and sweat on his cheeks. He was angry and he was afraid, and he was angry, almost a maniac, because he was afraid.

"What am I going to tell the First Citizen?" he shouted. Marginally, and for a few more years, his sort of correct old Roman still pretended to think Tiberius was not a monarch, as they had pretended Augustus was right up to the moment they named him a god.

"All that belonged to the Ptolemies became the property of the Divine Augustus, including the tomb of the Conqueror, which you let Simon desecrate, and the body of the Conqueror which you destroyed. What will I tell him?"

I let the young legate speak for us.

"It was unavoidable—we needed to destroy the corpse in order to save it. Simon would have made himself a menace to Rome. We wounded him severely."

His voice ran down into silence because it was clear to all of us that Gaius Valerius was not listening, but rather drumming his fingers on the arm of his chair and waiting for silence.

This struck me as almost theatrical and I looked again, and caught him looking at the legate's reaction. I considered, and this was not something we would gain benefits from pointing out. I was, and am, immortal and invulnerable, but I had to be aware of the risk to my companions should the rage turn murderous.

He continued to bluster at us all—I caught Sof's eye and she put her finger to her lips, confirming that I had best keep silent. Gaius Valerius said harsh unjust things to which I paid little attention and which I will not repeat for your amusement.

Finally, he grew quiet as men will when they get to the meat of what they have to say and all before it has been a stormy prelude.

He made much of his mercy in letting the legate keep his rank.

"You have disappointed me, and your noble parents, I am sending you to my colleague the Procurator of Judaea to see what can be made of you there. Something less demanding, perhaps."

He went on, gradually raising his voice back into the bluster as if he were daring me to react with equal anger. I chose to disappoint him.

"In consideration of the youth of the two Judaeans, who have shown such a knack of being present where there is trouble, and the pleas of their teachers, I have merely decided that they have learned all they can in Alexandria, and should return home. The woman Sof is no longer welcome either, I have decided, both because she might so easily turn to the brewing of poisons and we have had enough of potions and magic in Alexandria of late. Plus, she is the companion of the so-called Huntress, former associate of the Witch Queen of damnable memory. Her I cannot compel to leave, but I can reduce her reasons to stay."

As he ranted, I watched Josh very carefully. He was paying no attention to the Prefect, not out of contempt but because he was concentrating on something, something small and white that hovered in the air. He seized it between two fingers and I thought no more of it for a few minutes.

Gaius Valerius was starting to annoy me—he was not even allowing Sof or the boys to pack. Her papers were destined for the Museion, again; where I might consult them for her, if I chose to come back to Alexandria, but I was to remember that I was not welcome. Further, since we had jeopardized—oh such nonsense— the stability of the lighthouse on which the city was so dependent,

85

he was not allowing us to leave by sea, but making us travel, on horse or litter, under guard, through the Sinai.

This was mere cruelty, but Sof's raised finger kept me bound to silence. I would have a reckoning with this jumped-up knight, one day, but for the moment, he had power over people for whom I cared, and over innocents like the philosophers. So I kept my peace.

As we left, under guard, to begin our long journey at once, Josh showed me silently what he had found. It was a single white feather.

Some people say that the Sinai desert is lovely in its desolation. I've known people who like to feel positive about toothache.

The thing is, both will bore you, both are excessively unpleasant and both can kill you if you let them.

As deserts go, the Sinai has a bit of variety—occasional outcrops of scrub or spiky desert flowers. High hills made of crumbly rock that threaten minor landslides. Scorpions. Snakes. The sort of track beaten into something that almost becomes a road by travellers taking the least unpleasant route and trudging wearily and heavily along it. In places, the Romans had cleared fallen rock, or shored up what had fallen away—it's one of the things they were always good for.

I could have skipped this journey, and so could Sof, with a bit of help. I really felt obliged, as did she, to share the misery with the step-brothers and with the legate whose career had, as far as I could see, been drastically damaged on the personal whim of Jehovah and some odd little conspiracy between Ghost and the Prefect.

It was particularly unfair that the she-centaur had been sent with us—and with chains hobbling her that meant she could not simply remove herself into shadow.

She amused herself by teasing the soldiers. The legions of Rome had a large repertoire of bawdy marching songs, but she knew verses that had been forgotten, verses that speculated about the sexual habits of generals as long ago as Fabius Who Delayed.

Somehow, she had either got hold of, or had composed, new verses to the old song about the Emperor's Mighty Weapon, verses

86

about Tiberius and how His Mother Kept Him Upright. The legate told his men not to listen, but I saw hardened old soldiers, men with their donations of land picked out and already farmed by slaves, blush with shame at even knowing what she meant.

Also, I was worried about the honey, and so was Sof. We really needed to keep a close eye on Josh, but without letting him or Judas know that there might be a problem.

On the third night, we struck camp in the lee of a hill that had ages ago fallen away and become a cliff overhanging the road. It had ended up, once the fallen rocks had been moved away, in a sort of crescent formation whose arms protected us from the wind. There was even a small brackish spring.

Sof walked a little way into the shadow Sinai that surrounded our road, and picked silphium and datura there where they grew beside the far larger spring that shadowed ours. If you pound them together, with a little oil, the salve can be used to outline a space into which small creatures will not go. Of course, you still have the ones that are already there, so you leave a space by which they can leave, and whisper to them. No, not really—you move any obvious hiding places carefully, and sweep the ground, like a sensible person. Scorpions would really rather not deal with human beings—we have large feet and they cannot eat us.

Hardly had the fires been doused for the night after a brief meal, than our escorts started to snore.

Sof and I had lain down together, and carefully and quietly sat up—she made the noise of a desert fox and it became clear that the two young men were still awake, and the she-centaur too.

There was a fluttering of wings and, to my not especial surprise, Ghost settled on the standard embedded in the soil next to the legate's sleeping mat. Rather more unexpectedly, a second child of the Bird arrived—the flame-coloured high-songed fast-darting creature that guarded Lucifer's throne in Hell when he was walking the world, or attending Jehovah. This was the first time I had encountered it in the mundane world since the unfortunate business in Uz.

87

"Come," Ghost cooed and the other trilled. "Our masters would speak to you."

The she-centaur rose up on her haunches. "Does that apply to me?" she yawned. "Will there be wine? If a person gets dragged through the desert on some godling's whim, she should at least get a drink."

She voiced what I had also assumed—that the whole theatre of the Prefect's displeasure was aimed at dragging us to some sort of conference about the lads' futures as much as at removing them, and us, from Alexandria.

Ghost looked abashed, tucking its head under its wing a second, and pulling some heavenly flea out, crunching it in its beak, and swallowing hard. It was as if it were waiting before saying anything, and so I made it easier for the creature.

"I know that you gave Gaius Valerius his orders. Though I am at a loss as to why a senior Roman officer has to listen to Nameless' pet."

Ghost looked more embarrassed. "He exceeded his authority. We're sorry. You can go."

The centaur bellowed her displeasure. I thought she might awaken the soldiers, but she did not—clearly their sleep was magical. "Oh no," she said, "bring me three days out of my way into the goat-fucking Sinai, pleasant as the company has been—pretty boys and fascinating women—and the least your coney-catching God can do is give a girl a fucking drink before she goes off about her business."

I struck off her chains. The birds led us back to the trail and around to the other side of the further arm of the cliff.

There were torches, there, all the brighter for the darkness of the desert around us, and tables of rich food. We came out of the silence of the night and heard the noisy chatter of angels and demons as they drank vintages out of shadow and ate manna, and clustered around two unfeasibly high thrones on which lolled, crowns on their heads and gold-cloth wrapped around them, Nameless and Star, as I still chose to think of them back then.

Though not for much longer because those days of our youth were entirely, as it happened, over.

The demon who had once been worshipped as Baal-Melkart in several sacred groves ushered us through the throng. I put my hand compassionately but firmly on his shoulder. "You used to have a proper job. You were an honest little god, and not a flunky in Hell. We stood shoulder to shoulder once in battle, and in those days Jehovah and Lucifer were no more than your equals. What has become of you?"

"Times became hard, Huntress, and we all do what we must."

Gods grow old, sometimes, or lose their worshippers, and some fade back into humanity and some try desperate remedies, and those I perhaps slay, and some find honest work. And some become hangers on of someone else's pantheon.

There are reasons apart from my moral sense why I have never chosen the role of divinity, and nor should you.

I wandered among them, the former gods of Canaan and its surrounding lands, and I nodded to this one and that. Most acknowledged me, sulkily, and Aserath, who had once almost persuaded Jehovah to take her as consort, pecked me on the cheek in a way that was not wholly sisterly. And then did the same to Sof, but with a less good grace.

Of those I had once known and fought alongside, all were here, save Dagon, the fish-headed. I reflected that I had not heard his name in an age.

"Aserath?" She looked down at me with her wine-lustrous eyes that had no pupils save the darkness of rich vintage. "Lord Dagon, what of him?"

"His worshippers were defeated, and the followers of Jehovah left them in great piles on the battlefield and sacked their towns, and threw down his temples. He had seen what becomes of gods who lose, and Lucifer made him an offer, and he refused, saying, 'I had rather be a fish in the sea, so mindless that it takes a hook and drowns in air, than serve you or Jehovah' and leaped from the harbour into the depths of the sea. I spoke to Poseidon once, whom the Romans call Neptune, and asked him how he felt about this incursion into his realm. He said that Dagon asked for parley and passage, and Neptune speeded him on his way, and perhaps Dagon dwindled to a great fish of the deep seas of shadow, or perhaps he found new worshippers off the coast of some other land, but we never heard of him more."

I remembered Dagon as the poor stupid thing he had once been, and as the mighty lord he became, and I thought of how things pass, and was sad.

Sad in the midst of rejoicing, for Jehovah stood in front of his throne and called Josh to him, who had hung back, talking to his brother and the she-centaur. Jehovah waved for silence and laughed aloud like a trumpet, and then he waved again, and trumpets and sackbuts sounded and great cymbals clashed, and his laughter was above them all.

"I am the Lord God of Hosts, and this is my son, in whom I am pleased, a fighter, and a healer, who has studied my law, and studied the philosophies of the Gentiles, and will be a great man one day, or who can say, perhaps more."

Lucifer, whose throne sat a little forward and a little lower, reached down his hand and pulled Josh up to stand on the steps between them.

Those boys do love their little games.

"I am your father's dearest enemy and worst friend, and I would know you, whom I have not been allowed to meet until this moment."

His red bird flew up and perched on Lucifer's shoulder and whispered in his ear, though it looked as if it chewed gently on his flesh at the same time.

"Come, let us play a game, if it please your father."

Josh looked at Jehovah, who looked back at him, love and yet steel in his eyes. I liked the lad and did not think he need prove himself worthy, but Jehovah has never been able to leave well enough alone and Lucifer has this perpetual need to prove himself. Thousands of years, and he still wants to be the one Jah loves the best.

"So let me put you a question, boy. Here we are in the desert, and say you had been here forty days and forty nights, and were starving. And I came to you and laid out this feast in front of you and said, 'Boy, you cannot worship your father in heaven if you die, so, why not bow down, and worship me for a day that you may eat and live.'"

Josh stared him in the eye.

"I would say, that the worshipful man feeds by the grace of God from whom all things flow, and that there is a heavenly food that excels all earthly viands and sweetmeats." Then the boy reached up into his hair, and pulled out a fragment of manna he had somehow abstracted from one of the tables, or perhaps kept from another time, and loudly crunched on it. "Also, God helps those who have forethought, and take food to the desert, with which to end their fast."

"And if I took you up to the Dome of the temple, and said, 'Cast yourself down that your father send angels to bear you up'?"

"I would say that one does not tempt God, or the workings of time and chance. And that I would not do it, because I am his son, and he fathers no fools, though he keeps one at his side for jests."

"And what if I showed you the kingdoms of the earth, and said, 'I will give you these if you will adore me'?"

The throng of angels and demons had grown silent, and as Josh spoke, the silence grew ever deeper.

"If it please my father to ask me to win kingdoms, I will do what I can, humbly and worshipfully, and without your help, Lucifer. I will tell the poor of how the rich treat them, and tell the rich of how they sin, and I will do what I can to bring justice to the world, and with it, the worship of the one true god, who is at once my father and the One of whom he is the shadow. As is my duty, to my Father Jehovah, and to the One, whom he is, and is not."

That did not go down well, I thought—and I was there once in Britain, when a king asked his daughters to show how they loved him, and one was as honest as Josh.

I also thought that it was fortunate that Philo and Demetrius were not with us, for it would have gone hard with them.

Then a shadow passed over Josh's face, and he staggered for a moment as one in the early stages of the falling sickness. When he spoke again, it was with a harsher and less gentle tone. "Or, you can let this lad foment unrest for you, and then give him, or rather me, seven detachments of these spirits who cluster round your banquet and look as if they have power enough for all that they have become lackeys and courtiers. We raise the people of Judaea in revolt, and march on my city of Alexandria, and liberate it from the Romans. Then we march a forced march to the cities of Tripolitana and New Carthage, and thence, like Hannibal to Spain, and then to Gaul. With troops like these, and your worshippers to die in the front line, I could give you Rome in three years."

Sof and I looked at each other in dismay.

He spoke with such intensity that even Jehovah caught his breath.

"And then?"

The spirit that had taken Josh laughed, and it was a full-throated but high near-hysteric laugh that I had heard in Babylon. "Persia and India—lands I conquered once before."

Then he staggered with the falling sickness on him full-blown—Sof rushed up the stairs, ignoring the two gods, and took his hand and checked his pulse.

In a few seconds, the fit was from him, and it was Josh who looked at her with concerned eyes. "Did I disgrace myself in front of Father?" The boy was anxious, and clearly had little idea of what had just happened, and I did not want to be the one to tell him.

Jehovah rose from his throne and stepped down, and knelt by his son. "Not all, boy. You were fine, good to see Star put in his place from time to time, though you had best make him your friend

92

sooner or later. He means well and he has a role in our lives. But I am intrigued by your new friend, I have to say."

I could see the calculations working behind those intense lovely eyes. He had such charm and yet is such a terrible cheat and liar when you get down to it.

"The spirit of Alexander spoke through you, Josh." There was no more tactful way to say it, so it had best be said by me, who had no reputation for tact to lose. "He seems to have entered you with the honey."

I spoke then to Jehovah and Lucifer, who had joined him at the lad's side. I thought I had best make myself perfectly clear.

"If what just spoke through Josh is even the faintest echo of the Conqueror, let alone the man fully returned for a while, do not think that you can make use of him. He will try to eat your son from the inside and you cannot allow that to happen—that is the most important thing. And the second important thing is that Alexander of Macedon is a man to whom treachery is the air he breathes."

I knew, I knew without ever having certainty, that somehow he and his appalling mother had been behind every little bush-fire of the Rituals, every little blood-soaked godling that I had killed along his trail through Asia and Egypt and back in Greece and the Isles. I never caught them at it; I was busy for a decade doing little bits of damage control and never getting to watch them properly. It is the nature of my duty, my geas if you will, that I must run around killing certain evils and sometimes miss those so discreet I can hardly be sure they exist.

I did not say this aloud. I did not want Jehovah thinking that the spirit which had possessed his son might be a certain evil and best killed with fire now. I thought that Jehovah would listen to me. I was a fool.

Jehovah stood and clapped his hands, and though the trumpets and sackbuts brayed and the cymbals clashed, his hands and then his voice were easily the loudest, like a great wind that passed through us and left us staggering.

93

"Now that my son is grown to man's estate," he shouted, "it is time that he be wed. Come, come all of you, to Cana in Galilee, where men and women, as well as angels and demons, come to witness and celebrate. Come, away."

Sof whispered earnestly to me, "Things are moving too fast, something is not right about all this."

I smiled at her. "He gets ideas into his head, and he loves to show off. There is no harm in him."

She looked at me with that pity the young reserve for their deluded seniors. She was my sister and my lover from the dawn of time, but she had lived many years and many lives since, and here she was young again, and looking at me like that. "Mara, my love, sometimes you are a sentimental fool. He and Lucifer may have been your friends once, but they are not even reliably each other's any more. They may have avoided the Rituals, but their hands are soaked in blood."

I knew this—but we had stood together against the Bird, for all that they harboured its chicks as their intimates, and sometimes seemed to think of me as men do the hangman who gets his fee, or the rat-catcher who gets his fee, or the man who empties the cesspit and gets a kick for his fee.

I was about to learn that she was right, but not for a few moments yet.

Four great seraphs had descended from the shadow sky and stood at each corner of the lush carpet on which tables and thrones and dais and partygoers stood. They raised first their hands, and then their four great pairs of wings, and they started to circle in stately measure. Slow they went and then faster and faster, and the great eyes on their wings opened and the air throbbed at their gaze, and started to rush and to whirl; the carpet was stiff as marble although there was no longer anything to stand underneath it, and the air around us was a cloud of darkness and yet angels and demons continued to take food and drink, and the she-centaur, who had much drink taken, stamped and kicked a dance in the centre of the carpet, although there was naught but miles of air beneath her hooves.

Sof stood, her hand still on Josh's brow to calm him, and I slipped my arm around her and we kissed, briefly and gently, for we did not know that we would only kiss once more in many months.

Then, as the seraphs ceased their dance, and in a brief moment of rocking and disorientation, we felt ground and solidity under our feet, I felt several heavy hands on my shoulders and at my sides, and a strong arm around my neck. I struggled and a couple of times had almost thrown all of them off me, but the sheer weight of Lucifer's companion demons was bearing me to the ground. I saw Lucifer tap young Judas on the shoulder and whisper in his ear, and they took Sof by the arm and led her away from me into the large villa in the Greek style before which we had landed. Josh looked up at his father, who raised him gently with his right hand and was suddenly, solicitously carrying the lad.

Weight after weight bore down upon me—I saw the she-centaur rush at them and be knocked sideways by an ungallant kick. I could not move, and when I tried to slip sideways into shadow, the bodies that were holding me down slid with me, still holding me down. They held me down so tightly that I could not reach even the knives in my hair, let alone any other weapons, nor did it seem likely that threats of serious violence would have deterred them.

What could I have done? I do not kill gods—or the demons these former gods had declined into—merely for affronting me; I bit and scratched a little, but there was little point, and they were offering me no violence save the utter immobility and helplessness into which they forced me. Of course I could have summoned strength enough to throw them all from me—but that would mean tapping into deep resources of power that I had taken from workers of the Rituals, and to use such for merely personal matters would be an abuse.

Lucifer came out of the courtyard gate, his red bird chirruping on his shoulder. His robe was loose, revealing his trim slim body and chains of gold about his neck. The crown was gone from his head and replaced with a garland of flowers, though no flowers that grew in these climes. He smiled down at me, and his voice dripped poison syrup. "You know, I promised myself this day a very long time ago."

"Really?" I affected boredom, and indeed I find malice tiresome in those who are supposed to be about serious business.

"When you rebuked me for striking my faithless sister-bride, and she slipped from me into the morass of the Bird, to dissolve and to be lost. I swore that one day, when you had found your sister-lover for a life, I would take her from you. To see how calm you could be."

As I say, petty spite. I was perfectly calm, save for my concern for Sof, who is, after all, mortal in each of her lives. I was determined that he not see me weep, or even show distress. "So, she is to be the bride of young Josh. She could do worse for herself."

"When Ghost reported to us that she was not only a beauty, but a healer and great in the Art, I turned to Jah and said, 'The time has come'. We had not expected the Conqueror to come to our hand, of course, but a female wonder worker to travel at our Chosen One's side—even better than taking one such from you."

"He cares for her deeply." And my thought was, that he cared too deeply to be satisfied with a forced marriage to her, a thought I would not reveal to Lucifer.

Lucifer laughed. "It will be their wedding night, soon enough, and we shall see. And you will tarry outside, with my demons for company. The night is not cold, but their bed will be warmer." He is petty in a way that Jehovah is not. "I will send them out drink, and perhaps if you ask nicely, they will share."

I had rather be unmade.

As he left, he kicked the she-centaur in the side of the head where she lay already stunned.

The hours that followed were long—drink was brought the demons and, one at a time, they loosened from me, took a swig from the cups that were brought them, and returned to their task. I had thought that they might loosen their grip enough for me to be able to break free, but no such luck. Occasionally one cuffed me about the ears, although they knew they could do me no hurt.

"Baal-Melkart," I kept pleading from my voice and managed to replace it with the pity I had shown him earlier. "Baal, is this not an ignoble task?"

"It is a task given to slaves." There was anger and self-hatred in his voice, and in the voices of his companions who echoed him, or gave him their grunting support. "Slaves is what we are, and you helped make us so."

"How so?" For I had had no part in their enslavement that I could see.

Aserath, who was among them, and occasionally revealed herself in a stroke of her hand against my cheek, or a pinch that was almost but not quite a lover's, was the one who finally spoke for them.

"You let it happen. You and Hekkat. The Olympians too and the Gods of Egypt, but our curse is on you two, who might have stopped them for old time's sake because they might have listened to you."

"Star and Nameless go their own way, and have not listened to me since Atlantis." I did not speak of Hekkat, because, for the most part, I do not.

"How many of us did they need to kill and cow? How many of our priests strike down with swords? You could have acted."

"Star and Nameless do not work the Rituals of Blood. I have no quarrel with them. Other things are between you and them."

Indeed, though I did not say so, I had had to act—Moloch and some of the other small gods of groves had not listened to me, and had had their worshippers cast babies into the flames that they might fight back. And in the name of those small charred skulls, I had fought and killed them, and aided Nameless, as I had aided the Romans against Carthage. I have work to do, and I do my work, and I do not right other wrongs. For there would be no end to it and I will not have men or gods make me a goddess. But I did not say this to them, least of all to Aserath, for I had said it to most of them before, and to her when she pleaded with me to love her, and I refused her that as well.

For the most part, I did not speak to them at all, but strained against their weight, as much as I could do without using power that was not mine to use.

After a while, Nameless wandered out and sniffed the night air. He was not wholly sober. I worried for a second that he would do as Lucifer had done and abuse the she-centaur, but he ignored her altogether.

"Look, Mara. I know what Star said. It's not just spite, you know. Though I admit you drive me mad with your stiff-necked airs. We do good work, you know that, which is why you let us alone to get on with it, and get our hands a little dirty."

I ignored him. Somewhere in the pile of demons that were holding me down, someone made a farting noise with their lips.

"I heard that. Ungrateful lot. We let you live. I mean, Mara, look at them. Whenever whoever it is out there shows their hand, you know half of them would have decided to lick it, the way they do ours."

I retained my silence, if not my dignity.

"And it's for the best. You know it is. Ghost tells me the boy has real feelings for her."

That much was true. I had read the poems.

"We all have these feelings when we're young. Look at—well anyway, they're to be grown out of. My followers all tell me so. And it will bind us all together, you'll see. One big family against the one who created the Rituals."

I laughed. "Which of you plans to wed me? You or Star? And what of the boy's mother? You fathered him, and then fobbed her off on some carpenter. Not good enough to be your consort?"

I caught a glimpse of his face through the bodies on top of me. I am not perfect and sometimes I am glad that I have inflicted pain.

"Too much of a bitch, Mara, for either of us. The boy Judas likes you well enough. Good lad that, tells me everything."

He was silent for a while.

"And another thing, what's all this Shadow of the One that the boy was coming up with? I'll see about that. Load of Greek nonsense. Personally, I blame you for this—you were told to take charge of his education, and he gets ideas." He looked sad a moment. "I don't know what goes on in his head. He never prays to me, just to this One he's found. At least young Judas prays to both me and the One, otherwise I really wouldn't know what they're up to."

I laughed at him again and then returned to my silence.

After a while he went away. Aserath whispered in my ear. "I really wanted to fuck him once, can you believe it?"

From within the house came music, and the stamping of dancers, and the cheering of revellers. The noise was wild, wilder than I would have expected from a Judaean wedding, where joy was usually more restrained as befitted what was more often a property deal than a celebration of love or lust.

After a while, in the twilight before dawn, I found the resistance of my captors less, and I realized that half of them were snoring even as they strained. By the time I had eeled my way from the pile, I realized that they were full asleep.

The villa too had gone silent.

I walked over to the she-centaur, to see whether she lived; at the touch of my hand, she flexed her hind thighs and sat up on her haunches. "No point in getting myself hurt more." She smiled through her bruises. "That last one nearly took my head off anyway. Friend of yours, was he? And the other one?"

"I thought so, once. But no, not for a long time. Colleagues perhaps, even now, but."

"That's what they always say about you, Huntress. Fair to a fucking fault, and all about the work. Piss on that, I say, but I'm only a stupid centaur with actual friends."

My mind turned to what I should do next, but hardly had I started to form the thought than two forms slipped from the villa, almost in shadow, but not quite. Josh and Sof, husband and wife.

The lad was all apologies. "I did not know; I'm so sorry. They sprung it on me."

Sof was harsher. "He wants a bloodline."

Josh looked at her, and so did I.

"He thinks that if you and I have a child, there will be a line of semi-divine beings to whom Mara here will feel some sort of obligation."

Josh's face fell. "But I wouldn't. I mean, I like you but you're with Mara, and."

I was still trying to comprehend the cold-blooded treachery involved. "He wasn't like this before that bloody bird. I know I should have wrung all their necks."

Josh frowned, side-tracked from his embarrassment. "You mean, there's more?"

I really did not feel like explaining Atlantis to him because there was a more pressing question.

"How are you out here? And why have all the demons fallen asleep?"

Josh and Sof looked at each other smugly—actually, in other circumstances, I'd have seen them as soulmates.

"It's something we were working on. For the Art." She clearly wanted to get terribly technical.

"There were these big water jugs"—Josh waved his hands around and I realized that these were very big water jugs indeed—"and we turned all of it into wine. Only the quintessence we added was a bit strong."

Sof looked even smugger. "The host said that it was the strongest, best wine he had ever tasted. Couldn't understand where it had come from. And somehow no one could stop with just one more drink…"

"Very clever." There was something bothering me that I hadn't thought of, and we really needed to get out of here before I was forcibly reminded of it.

"Where can we go?"

I started to think—somewhere far enough that a very angry Jehovah could not find them. "I don't know. Rome, or somewhere farther. Massilia maybe, or the land of Silk."

In the end, it was a moot question, because a great hand was upon me, holding me firmly. And another and a third, and a fourth—and from behind me great wings struck at me like planks of wood.

"Seraphs don't drink." I'd known there was something.

Another seraph held me, and one held Sof. I could doubtless have fought free, but only by using my full strength, and I could have fled with Sof, but what then of Josh, and Judas, and the she-centaur?

From within, a shofar blew; bleary-eyed, several of the wedding party staggered out—Jehovah and Lucifer among them, both tugged by their birds by an ear, so hard that those ears streamed blood and it was no wonder that Jehovah was in a rage, the worst that I had ever seen.

"You dare?" he shouted.

I tried to reason with him. "No-one's hurt, everyone had a good time. Sof and Josh just tried to do people a favour and work a little miracle, all of their own. You should be pleased."

He raged on. "Ungrateful brat."

I realized, with some concern, that he was very very drunk still and so was Lucifer.

"I should kill you all," Jehovah raged. His face was flushed with blood as if he were burning from inside and there was a blankness to his eyes that his dark long lashes made more terrifying. I'd never seen him like this, or perhaps had never let myself. Suddenly I could believe in all the massacres of Canaan.

Josh stepped forward. "If you must, Father, kill me. I involved the sisters in our affairs. The world needs Mara and she needs Sof."

Jehovah looked at him calculatingly. "I need you, boy, and I doubt I could harm Mara even if I wanted to. You both have to learn though."

He clapped his hands.

"Kill my son's wife."

Several of the drunken guests stepped forward, among them one I recognized: Simon called the Rock, whom I had last seen on his cousin's ship. Three angels were suddenly among them, bearing heavy stones and passing them to their human companions.

The seraph who had been holding Sof flung her to the ground, and held her there, his foot on her neck. I struggled to break free of mine, but I was tired, from wrestling with demons all night, and I could not get loose.

Jehovah was still drunk, but angrier than drunk. Lucifer was at his side, shifting his weight from foot to foot in prurient glee.

"After all, next time Sof is reborn, Mara will know not to offend us, and lose her a second time."

Jehovah was not even pretending to think ahead. "See to it." And he turned his back and walked back into the villa.

How many times had he had things done that he did not want to watch? I asked myself as I stamped hard on one seraph's instep and bit a chunk of heavenly flesh out of the other's arm. Most other angels even, and almost all humans, are so in awe of bloody seraphs that they don't think to try the obvious ways of resisting them.

As I got free of my seraphs, the she-centaur stood up, reared up and planted her back hooves firmly into the back of the seraph with their foot on Sof's neck, just between the first and second pair of wings. I head a shoulder blade crack, and the angel crumped to the floor. The she-centaur stood over Sof, her firm legs either side of her. I took up a stance beside them.

From behind, Josh seized Simon's hand, that held a stone. I heard the fisherman's thumb break as he dropped the stone. For a moment, I saw Alexander in his eyes, as he turned to the man standing next to Simon and started to wrench his neck. Then he was Josh again and pulled back his hands, looking at them in horror.

Only for a second, because he looked round at the angels who were still advancing on us with their stones. He dropped to the ground and drew three symbols in the soil, then stood, one foot poised to scuff them out again.

The angel at the centre of the group looked down and saw what he had done. I have rarely seen fear that I had not put there on the face of an angel, nor ever fear so intense. "You dare threaten us, you, your father's son."

"You menace my wife, and you expect no consequences." Even without Alexander behind his eyes, this was a Josh I had not seen, truly the son of a god. "Know all of you," he shouted, "that I will erase the name of any who come against me, or against her, and you will not have been."

There was something as pitiless as the North Wind in his voice, anger and love and despair and yearning for something not to be attained. The lad had steel in him and that steel had been tempered in his love for my sister-lover. I wanted to clap him on the shoulder and tell him that it would be all right, and yet I knew that nothing I could do, and nothing Sof could do, would ever make it so.

The lad hovered his foot over the symbols a second more, and the angels shrank back, knocking the men with them sideways in their hurry. He drew more symbols, these in the air, and they hung and burned, and he pursed his lips to blow; the seraphs made gestures of fear and submission.

And then they were not just shrinking back, but flying away from his wrath and Jehovah's as far as they could, high into the air and deep into shadow. The men with them broke and ran, all save Simon, who stood still, cradling his broken hand. "Go," Josh shouted after them. "Go, and sin no more."

And then he reached down his hand and pulled Sof up from the ground, and for a second she leaned into his shoulder with no glance at me, and he kissed her on the forehead and she looked round and took me by the hand. I held her by the wrist and kissed her on the lips, and then kissed Josh, for the first time in all the time I had known him.

I kissed him a second time, later, and a third, and those have a place in this tale.

The she-centaur whinnied in disgust. "Humans. All this kissing and no damn rutting. So very fancy and so very fucking sad."

The moment was over and I looked at Sof and she looked at me. Josh walked over, and at a touch Simon's maimed hand was unbroken.

He knelt. "What am I to do, Lord?" He looked up in supplication and I saw tears in that big man's eyes. "Something tells me that you are my master, who forgave me once before, and yet he is the Lord God."

"He is a shadow of the One." Josh spoke with a new authority. "As perhaps are we all."

He reached out his hand to Simon, who kissed it.

"No, Simon." Josh shook his head. "There are no masters, and we forgive, even ninety times."

A shadow passed across his face, as if Alexander were screaming inside him.

Sof put her hand on his shoulder. "I think he felt that," she grinned. "He talked, when he had the reins for a moment, of sowing unrest, but he is a king, and kings think of unrest as something useful to whip their enemies with. Not as an expression of the will of the people."

He grinned back at her. "No masters then. Not husbands, not priests, not Romans, not gods. Save for the One."

"Perhaps," she said with wonder in her voice, "the One is like the Stone, or the thing at the end of the Work beyond the stone. Transformation, not servitude."

They might never be husband and wife in a standard sense, but at that moment I realized that she was his partner as much as mine. I would have to put up with sharing.

There was a tap on my shoulder. It was Lucifer, sober, but still full of glee and malice, and his bird at his shoulder. "Huntress, you have been neglecting your work. There is a new god among the

104

Scythians, and a snake queen among the Ossetians, and blood sacrifice among the Yakuts, the Sofa and the Samoyeds."

Sometimes my duty calls me even when it is convenient for others that I be elsewhere.

"You saved this to tell me now, why?"

But my heart was not in rebuking him and at this moment it was not even with my love; it was on the steppes and the high places, finding out the wicked and requiting their sins.

Sof came over to me. We did not kiss, merely placed our hands upon each other's arms in a moment of farewell.

The she-centaur trotted over to us, grinning in anticipation. "If you need a companion…"

I hunt alone, but I was going among the riders and breeders and their great horses. "If you can keep up, we can travel together for a while."

She loomed over me, and smiled.

I had hardly noticed Judas in some time, not since he had helped Lucifer lead Sof into her wedding. I chose to think that he had been misled, but nonetheless was not feeling benevolent.

"Huntress." He bowed his head, and then looked up at me pleadingly. "Mara. Would you take me along?"

I felt pity for the boy, and a certain remorse. "I could say, I hunt alone, but she is coming with me and so that would not be true on this occasion. So I will tell you the truth, Judas son of Joseph. Which is, in part, that you are not ready, you could not keep up and you might not be able to survive. I go to the steppes and to the great cold of the Northern forests and I do not know what I will find there. I do not choose to have your blood on my hands." I softened my tone. "Your path lies elsewhere. Your brother has my Sof with him, for the moment at least, and she will help him fight the Prince who haunts him. She sleeps sometimes, and the Prince does not, so, I entreat you, bear the watch. And if needed, do what has to be done. As brother, and as servant of his father."

The hinges of the world, they never creak as they turn.

105

The Caucasus was wet and cold that year of famine and misery. The forests and dead cold plains of the far Northeast were grimmer yet.

There is always a price when Lucifer does you a favour, even if the price is only that you know he thinks he has scored some petty point in the endless tally book that is his relationship with you and the rest of the universe. He was right, and there was an outbreak of the Rituals that spread from the suburbs of Colchis all the way to the lands of the Yukagir. A shaman of the Yakut had had a vision of how men could attain godhood, and so not starve, and had wandered in and out of shadow, north, south, east and west, with his new power, spreading the happy word to the like-minded. He would wait a while, until the killing stopped, and then harvest his rivals— only he was outwitted and eaten, and replaced, several times over.

His tale was told, over and over, and he became Kaschei Who Avoided Death, which he did not, and kept his life in a magic egg, which was another man, elsewhere. Such is story. Interesting that when the Rus took the story and made it theirs, they added in the Bird of Fire. A suspicious person might wonder whether Lucifer's companion had been whispering in his ear, but I know that such suspicions could never be proved.

I thought for a while that the outbreaks among the Scythians and in the Caucasus were separate things, but it was the same wandering bloody shaman Kaschei, about his travels.

It was all so stupid and pointless, and got muddled up with all the petty feuds that nomads and their semi-sedentary cousins, and the herdsmen who drive great deer in the far north invent to keep themselves warm in winters that last almost forever. It meant spending months among people who smelled continually of dung-smoke and rancid fat and half-cured furs, listening to the whiny excuses of people who wanted to claim that they had not known that killing all the people they knew to become powerful was wrong, and that my killing them for it was not fair.

I am not fair. I do my work and I do the task I was given and I leave justice to others, though I often suspect that I am the closest thing to it that there is. I slit throats that have chanted spells of murderous evil and I paunch guts swollen with the flesh of babies and I sever heads full of thoughts of malign power.

I am not fair, but I like to be certain, and I only kill once I am certain of guilt. None of these petty gods ever thought they might need to hide, and wandered around with blood on their hands and guts in their teeth. Certainty was never a problem.

I am the Huntress and sometimes I become massively bored with the unimaginative iniquity of most of those who work the Rituals. Killing them is a task I cannot avoid—they are the little gods of blood that might one day aspire to be a Chernobog or the like and be a real menace—but I take no pleasure in it or in the fact that I derive small amounts of power from each one that I kill. Necessity is my life.

Still, I have had worse companions of the road than the she-centaur, who left most of the killing to me, but would occasionally help me round up gods who fled, or stun them with those great hooves, or pierce them with her arrows.

And she sang, not just the legionary songs I mentioned earlier, but centaur love-songs which go on for hours and which humans rarely get to hear, or have the patience for. I had it, and to spare, and was in the mood for the wistful bawdy eloquence with which centaurs woo each other.

Towards the end of our time together she shared with me one of her own compositions, and it was my own story, done as one of the three-day epic recitals that centaurs regard as their highest art, have done since they began.

It was flattering, and reasonably accurate. I heard it once more, centuries later, when I met a group of centaurs in deep shadow, and they greeted me with it, to show they knew my name. They range far from here—they have lost their taste for human company—and are gone from the fields I know, gone from Arcadia and Thrace and the high hills. Perhaps I will meet them again before the end.

But what, you ask, of Sof, and Josh, and young Judas?

You know, for the most part, what they were doing, for you learned it at your mother's knee and in Sunday School, and won little prizes for knowing it.

Of course, the stories I heard in the letters Sof sent to me—one copy to Alexandria, one to Colchis—differ in some details from the versions that Mark and Matthew cobbled together from them. I have not her letters to hand—they were stolen from me long ago and are safer in the Vatican than carried with me or left in the dusty rooms where I sometimes sleep. If I need to look at them—for I sometimes wish to see tokens of Sof rather than merely remember her, now that she is gone for so long and perhaps forever—if I need them, I know where they are.

No-one could stop me going there even if they wished me to. I was, by his end, the friend of the first bishop of Rome, however ill we liked each other at our first meeting, and I kept safe during the persecution of Nero the precious thing that is buried in the grave of Simon the Rock—but I digress and will tell you that story in its proper place.

The Christian church will never, of course, allow Sof's letters to be seen by anyone save me—yet they are scared to burn them as they have burned so much else. Sappho, for example—nice girl, wrote me an ode once. Marcion had a heart attack from which he nearly died when he even glanced at them; Eusebius deduced from this that what had killed a heretic might be safe for him, but changed his mind half way through the first paragraph he looked at. I think it was the chariot race; I've always thought that one of the best bits.

You've always wanted to read the Gospel according to Mary Magdalene; well, I suppose that's who Sof was, but what she wrote wasn't really a gospel. For one thing, a lot of the time what she sent me was her notes for the letters she was too busy ever to get around to writing, and she would jot down bits of her Work less to tell me how things were going than to remind herself of filtrations and distillings she was not able to do because she didn't have her equipment with her.

Together, she and Josh were better at healing than either of them was by themselves but she didn't write much about that, just kept a running tally of who they'd cured of what and where. It's not that they didn't care, but obviously people came for the healing and stayed to hear Josh talk—healing was a way of worshipping, but it also meant that they got an audience, an audience made up of people who were feeling grateful.

Josh—and sometimes Judas and sometimes Simon—talked of the One, and the worship of the One and of the Lord God Jehovah, and if a lot of the time the people who heard them did not make a distinction, well that was partly tact on the part of the preacher and partly because, let's face it, most of the inhabitants of Judaea had never heard of Plato, let alone neo-Platonism.

Sof didn't speak, though he wanted her to. No, not because it wasn't the done thing—someone as young as him preaching wasn't either. She simply didn't do public speaking, in that life.

Let's not talk about that, though.

In any case, Josh was not all that interested in talking about the nature of gods. It fascinated him, but he didn't really think it was important. What he wanted was for people to behave better, and to get angry with the rich, of course. And the high priest and the rest of the temple staff, because they were rich. And the Romans, because they supported the rich who for the most part did very nicely out of having been conquered.

He wasn't preaching rebellion, you understand, because he was always a realist and armed revolt was never going to go well. Sof was never sure how much he talked to Alexander inside his head, but after a while, the Conqueror, when he surfaced, would tell Sof, in between leering at her, that he had been optimistic, that you couldn't turn the Romans out of Judaea, let alone Egypt, with just local forces.

What you could do, was make people laugh at them.

Take the thing with the tribute money—started off as a temple police spy asking an awkward question, but they made it a thing. People always asked because they'd heard you'd get a different answer every time—which wasn't true, because they had three or four bits they alternated. Sometimes it would be the rude noises, and sometimes it would get produced from behind three or four kids' ears, and just once in a while, Sof would use the Stone.

Get people going ooh, and ahh, or laughing, and they think about things. Best of it was, the Roman soldiers who were stood around being bored and curious—they laughed too.

He got better and better at the Parables, too, or so she told me. That's what they didn't teach you in Sunday school—people laughed when he told them about the foolish virgins, or the man who built on sand, or the priest and the levite who left the man in the ditch. He'd pull the fact of the priest being snooty or throw up his hands when the man's house collapsed and they'd laugh. All those times we had watched the street performers in Alexandria—totally not a waste.

Sof taught him all the things she'd learned back in Socrates' time when she was Diotima the rope-dancer.

Oh, and of course he could do miracles, but he tried not to, because that was when Alexander came closest to the surface. Who knew what he'd do if he got the chance? Like the thing with the fig-tree, that was him. Knowing he was there, that meant Josh couldn't ever relax. Because bad things might happen.

As of course they did...And I was killing godlings in the Caucasus or the shores of the Yenisei a thousand miles away.

Look, I'm not sure I want to go on with this—I mean, you know most of what happened, sort of. It's upsetting—it's one of the worst things that ever happened. Ask me something else, anything else.

Well, that's typical. Yes, that's another very bad thing, that's why I hadn't talked about it you silly man. No, I've never ever seen Lillit—Sof in various of her lives, but never Lillit. Nor has Sof, as far

110

as I know. Maybe she doesn't come back—that's why I don't talk about it. Or maybe she just doesn't want to see us ever again.

Stop going on about it.

You're trying to make me go back to talking about Josh, aren't you? Oh very well.

It was early in the morning when the birds came for me. The red one from the East and the white one from the South—they'd taken short cuts. They got there at the same time, so the red one kept its silence and it was the white one that spoke, so upset that it forgot its normal cooing croak.

"They're going to kill him; you have to come."

I didn't have any doubt as to who it was that they were going to kill.

"They? Who"

"The Romans. Well, Herod and Antipas and the High Priest, as well. But the Romans mostly."

This was bad news in some ways, better in others—because it meant I had time. They pretty much do stonings at once, whereas the Romans take their time. They like to put up a bunch of people at a time—some clerk worked out it saved time and money. And they're both nasty ways to die, but stoning is quick beside the cross. Some people last days, hours for certain, which is what you want if you're going to get them down. I mean, Josh would be in agony, but if I got him down, he'd eventually get better, probably.

It meant going up against Rome, of course, and they'd never forgive me for it, but I brought down an empire once before when I had to. No, not one you've heard of, that's the point.

I turned to the she-centaur. "I have to travel faster than you can."

She pulled a sorrowful face. "Don't worry about me. I'll be all right." Then she addressed the birds, asking the question I hadn't quite felt able to. "Why do you need her? Boy's father has a whole army of spirits at his disposal."

The birds looked innocent, but took their time before Ghost answered.

"The Lord Jehovah says that the boy can have angels when he asks for them. He doesn't know we're here."

The she-centaur made a rude noise—centaurs can control their bowels really well, did you know that?

Of course, she had a point. I don't trust any of the Bird's children further than the length of their beaks. I knew perfectly well that my dear old friend Nameless was blackmailing me into helping him with whatever ridiculous scheme of world conquest Alexander had put into his head back in the Sinai. If I rescued Josh, I'd be starting something I would not be able to control the end of.

But Josh. Totally worth it—and he'd find a way of sorting it out. Besides, Sof loved him, and I was very fond of him. I'd save him, and I would drive Alexander out of him for good, just to be safe.

I didn't trust the birds and I didn't want to hear any more of what might be truth and might be those half-truths that are worse than lies in the way they deceive you. I was heartsick and terrified for a friend and knew I had no good choices, without knowing how terrible the choices I was going to have to make would be.

And so I ran. Through shadow and the strange winding corners of shadow that normally I avoid lest I run out of shadow and out of the world and somewhere else entirely. Faster than I had ever run before or since, because Josh was going to die a terrible death and I did not know but that my Sof would die of grief over him. Heartsick and heart-bursting I ran, as if the end of the world were coming and I could stop it with aching lungs and sweat in my eyes and an ache in my left calf that I had not felt since I was human and young.

I ran so hard and fast I almost felt mortal again. And the white bird and red matched my pace.

They led me to an upper room in a house in Jerusalem. Well away from the Temple or the houses of the Rich, in the Lower City, near the Small Market, but that was still and silent for it was the eve of the Sabbath, and the night of Passover.

Simon was there, and Sof, and some other men and women whom I did not know, sitting round a table with the last stale crusts of a loaf, and a plate of new hot flat-bread. Somewhere else in the house, I could smell the char and hear the sizzle of a roasting lamb with rosemary and basil. Sof said nothing, but she had been weeping, and I took her hand to comfort her what little I could.

"Huntress," Simon nodded with respect.

I looked around the room. "Where is Judas?"

Sof wept all the more, and Simon spat on the floor.

"Spending the money they gave him for his brother." His voice was full of anger and contempt, and I reflected that he had not shown much sign of subtle intelligence the two previous times I had met him.

Still, whatever he had done, for whatever reason, I missed having Judas at my side, for he was an intelligent lad and brave. I would make do with what I had to hand. None of the others, save Simon and a couple of men I remembered from his crew, seemed up to much; tax-clerks and housewives and a prettyboy teenager. I'd have to do this by myself, which is what I had expected.

Still, I could make it easier.

"We need diversions, plenty of them. I don't want to fight a legion by myself. I will if I have to, but it will take it out of me. Can we ensure any reinforcements have other things on their minds?"

Sof grinned. I knew that grin. "Well, at Josh's trial, they accused him of wanting to demolish the Temple."

The others looked horrified—she and I were, after all, the only Gentiles in the room.

Sof looked round apologetically. "I wouldn't do that, not really. But a little bit of a bang and a lot of smoke. I wouldn't even try to blow a door off." She looked at me conspiratorially and then added, "And I've enough of my powder left over to make some interesting noises all over the city."

She was, after all, two of the first and greatest performers of the Work that no one called alchemy for another six hundred years. Of course she discovered gunpowder, only hers was better: it used the nitre you find in great crystals in dragon's dung and charcoal from the briars that grow on the marches of Pluto's Hades and the Gehenna that was Lucifer's first attempt at a Hell.

She hadn't brought any with her from Alexandria; she must have been brewing it up in Jerusalem. I really did not want to know why, and I really hoped that she hadn't shown it off when the Conqueror was watching through Josh's eyes.

Still, if Simon and his men were running around Jerusalem doing her bidding, they were less likely to be under my feet when I went to rescue Josh.

"That's a good idea." Simon looked at once impressed and slightly put out that someone else had come up with a plan. "I still think we should track down Judas and settle accounts with him."

He really hadn't forgotten that knife in his foot, had he?

Sof stared at him long and hard. He tried and failed to meet her gaze.

"Let's get Josh rescued first. If we can. Judas can wait."

I still thought I knew the boy better than any of them—if Judas had turned traitor, there was probably a reason. Someone had probably told him that he was doing the right thing, and there were too many people he might have listened to that were older and cleverer than he was.

But that could wait. I looked sternly at Simon. "Mind you do as she says. I'm putting her in charge."

He was a good man, I found, as long as you gave him strict instructions—we'd have one good adventure together before the end.

I had no more time to spend here. "Where have they hung him up?"

The older man who looked like a tax clerk spoke up. "Outside the walls, where there's that big rock that looks like a skull."

I knew it well—I remembered when the rock had been a skull, but its magic had worn off once the creature was dead.

You really don't want to live forever, Crowley; almost everywhere

I've ever been is the site of one of my kills by now. Or more than one.

The good news was, when I had run there quickly through shadow, and observed from just outside the mundane, that Josh was still alive, and so were the other two they'd stuck up alongside him. An older woman was kneeling at the foot of his cross and weeping, with two friends standing beside her, with their hands on her shoulder.

She was in her middle-forties, by the look of her, and remarkably beautiful for any age. The sort of high-cheekboned, clear-skinned woman who ages well and whose face is so lovely because of the mind that shines through its clear eyes. Nameless has been a fool to lose her to some builder.

No wonder she wept though, because Josh was in the worst of pain. He stank of it, even from where I stood. They had beaten him and his sore striped back was pressed up against the splinters of the wood—they'd rubbed salt into the cuts and tears so that he could not bear the touch of the wood, yet needed to press up against it to relieve the arching of his back that was the only thing that was keeping him breathing.

Some joker had knotted together the supple branch of a thorn tree into a crude crown, and pressed it down on his forehead—if he let his head hang down he could not breathe, and yet if he pushed against the wood with his back, his head banged against the wood as well, pressing the thorns further in. Blood from his forehead, and the back of his head, ran down and mingled with the sweat, so that he could not see, and the flies were at his eyes.

Some Roman had really taken against him, I realized as I looked. The other two had the usual leather straps tying them to the cross-pieces and the footrest, but they'd taken a hammer to him, and bashed nails through the delicate bones of his wrist, nails that were tearing his hands apart, and a bigger nail through both his feet, that had been placed one on top of the other.

Normally, there's a bit of play in the straps, so that the victim can squirm around. It's never going to save them of course, but they can

115

fool themselves that if they get things just so it might all hurt just a little bit less. Until it all gets too much and they choke and die, or the septic rot in their wounds takes them into fever and unconsciousness. Like most of the nastiest tortures, crucifixion is a metaphor for mortal life, when you think about it.

Three Romans stood watching him, and his mother; officers by the look of them, and officers in dress uniform you'd never normally see at an execution. A couple of legionaries sat on the ground near the women, throwing dice. On a small brazier, near enough to the legionaries that they could tend it, a few skewers of nameless meat spat and sizzled.

I stepped out of shadow and one of the officers looked around at me, with a sigh, as if he had been expecting me.

"Hail, Huntress." It was the young legate I had last seen in the Sinai desert.

"Mara" Josh whispered. And then, "Where are my manners? Mother, this is my particular friend the Huntress. Sof's friend."

His mother looked me up and down, as if she did not wholly approve of what she saw. "Jah send you?"

"I don't get sent, but I came. Now, let's get the boy down from this cross." I looked at the legate. "I would advise you not to get in my way."

He and his two companions drew those short heavy swords the Romans love; slightly, but only very slightly, more slowly, one of the two legionaries leaped to his feet and did the same. The other took a moment to put the dice, and the beaker he shook them in, into a wallet at his belt, as if he had all the time in the world.

"Huntress, it has been decreed in the Emperor's name, and that of the Procurator of Judaea that Joshua Bar-Joseph, whom men call King of the Jews, or the Chosen One, should die as an enemy of Rome and a blasphemer against the Jews' god, and all other gods as well."

"And I, Mara the Huntress, slayer of gods, am here to save him. I repeat, do not get in my way."

He took a formal pose, his sword pointed at my throat. I had not yet drawn a weapon. "I have my orders. We will resist you, and you will kill us, and you will be an enemy of Rome."

I shrugged. "As empires go, it was one of the better ones. I shall try not to kill you."

His two friends pointed their swords at my throat as well. One of the legionaries leveled a spear at me and at that, I took affront, pulled my own spear, and knocked it from his hand in a quick blow. On the back-stroke, I twisted the spear and smashed it down across the sword hands of the three officers in turn, faster than they could see, so that they dropped their swords and stood defenseless before me, with the pain of bruised fingers showing in their eyes.

The other legionary backed ever so slightly away. There's always a sensible one.

On cue, there was a loud explosion from the city, and then another and another. The air filled with smoke and the ground shook. I really did hope that Sof had not done too much damage to Nameless' city. He gets petulant when he is vexed.

I repeated, "Stand aside."

The young legate bent, picked up his sword, and held it to his throat. "I will not be dishonoured again," he said.

Amid the continuing explosions from the city, there was a moment of silence that Josh broke. His voice was hoarse and whispering, because he could hardly breathe, but it seemed louder than the noise of Sof's little diversion.

"No, that won't be necessary. Mara, Huntress, put down your spear. I need to die."

Another voice spoke, though not all of us could hear it, and a shadow stepped out of Josh's tortured body and down onto the ground before him, looking up at him with as much concern as the three women, who had not spoken at all during any of this.

"You need not die," Alexander said, "to be rid of me."

His ghost was a lot taller than I remembered him as being, but then, the ghosts of the proud often are. There was something different about him, and it was not just that ghosts have to be sober.

Interestingly, it was clear that the legate could see him too, and Josh's mother.

"Get away from my son, unclean spirit."

Alexander looked almost hurt. "You misjudge me. I have been shown the error of my ways."

He looked at me again, and pointed up at Josh, whose face maintained composure, but whose body still writhed like a fieldmouse under the harrow. The labouring of his breathing grew ever louder.

"Huntress, did every person who died in my wars experience agony like that?"

"Of course, Conqueror. Did you think it otherwise?"

He shuddered. "Then I have much to atone for. I must find a way." He turned and spoke to Josh. "I will keep your secrets, as you keep mine."

He shimmered and was gone. Where, I do not know. Nor do I know what secrets of Josh's he possessed or perhaps still possesses.

I turned my attention back to Josh, and to the legate, who had not taken the sword from his throat, and held it there still, for all that one of his companions had placed a restraining hand on his wrist.

Josh spoke again. I did not know how he could be so loud with so little breath. "Longinus, put down your sword. Mara will not try to save me."

I was not sure, at that moment, whether I had ever heard the legate's name before.

"If I live, my father will try to use me, and I will not serve."

I looked up at him in frustration. Noting my distraction, the last of the legionaries finally made his move and I cuffed him to the ground.

"Jehovah has this scheme to spread his worship by conquest," Josh went on. "He has to learn. So many sons of fathers and so many daughters of mothers would die. I have seen it, in Alexander's mind when he still thought he could usurp me and start his conquests again; I know how many would die. He reckoned it up for me. And it is fitting that I die, to save the peoples."

"But I can save you."

"If I wanted. Even now. I could summon a host of angels. All I have to do is call them and they would come, and they would kill, and there would be no end of it."

He looked up at the sky, and cried, "Father, why could you not leave me be?"

Then he looked at his mother. "I am sorry. I would live. But I am not worthy. There are things…" And then he fell silent, for he had no more voice.

He seemed to sleep for a second.

The legionary who was still standing walked across to the bucket they keep for such purposes, and threw water up into his face, water mixed with salt and vinegar, to sting him awake.

Josh looked at me with eyes red with tiredness and the effort of pushing and pulling his body into positions where it could breathe. There was no appeal in it, just quiet sorrow.

His mother stood and tugged at my arm. "He does not want to be saved. For the love you bear him, do something."

Longinus put aside the sword from his throat.

"Huntress, my orders are that he suffer to the end, but if you chose otherwise, we would say that we could not stop you."

My spear was still in my hand. I looked at Josh's mother, who nodded, and, as I had so many years before with the young god, I struck home.

Josh sighed once and then was still. I felt a rush of something from him and then, for a moment, a rush of something from me. I took the spear from the wound I had made in his side, and his heart pulsed blood from his side one last time and then was still.

I looked around; the two men they had crucified along with him had been silent all this time except for the occasional hoarse groan.

119

They seemed unconscious, or already dead, but I slashed their throats with the point of my spear, just to be sure, just to be kind.

And then it was done.

Longinus, who had done his duty as a Roman officer would, fell to his knees and wept, great bitter barking sobs. He looked at me, his eyes full of shame. "I talk of honour, but an honourable man would have disobeyed his orders and killed him myself."

This was true, but I was not about to make him feel worse when there was something useful he could do.

"He would have told you to sin no more. I ask you, as one of his friends to another, to help me take him down from the cross, and give him to his mother to hold, one last time."

With his help and that of his comrades—I do not know whether they acted out of decency and shame, or out of fear of me, and I do not care—we took that obscene device of torture from its place in the ground.

I took the thorns from Josh's head and wiped what I could of the blood from his face with the piece of parchment that someone had pinned to the cross. Then I flung both thorns and parchment into the brazier to burn away to nothing.

With one of the knives from my hair, I levered the nails from his hands and feet, and flung them away.

I did what I could with the water in the bucket to clean his face and wash the worst of the blood and filth from his body, and only then did I turn to Mary, the wife of Joseph and once beloved of Jehovah.

"Mother, behold your son."

She had managed a calm almost like marble. She stood, walked over to where her son lay and collapsed over his body. Her friends fussed around her; one singed a feather in the brazier and held it under her nose until she coughed. I hauled Josh's body up—he was so thin—and she sat up cross-legged and took him into her lap as if he weighed nothing at all.

I have never borne a child nor have I regretted not doing so—

and at that moment I regretted it least of all.

Suddenly, out of shadow, stinking of flame and powder, Sof was there. She gave a single sob at the sight of Josh in his mother's arms, and stood there with her hands on his mother's shoulders and her face turned to mine with questions in her eyes.

"He would not let me save him; I did what was needful."

She sighed; for a second there was a flare of anger in her eyes and then compassion and love took their place.

"Once we had managed the little diversion you asked for, Simon and his brothers went looking for Judas. You had better stop them doing something stupid. I'd like to know why he did what he did, but I do not want him hurt."

I knew she was right—I knew the lad as well as you know anyone whom you have trained in arms and he was not one to betray his brother for coin, whatever Simon thought.

Mary the boys' mother looked at me—poets and preachers have said for centuries that a sword pierced her heart. Unlike most of what such men say, this was true, because I was there, and saw her face.

But of course, it was two swords, and not one.

"Huntress, I would not lose two sons this day."

I knelt, briefly, and kissed Josh on his dead lips, and then I was gone at speed from Golgotha, the place of the skull, back into the city of Jerusalem.

The streets were still dark with Sof's smoke and there were cracked walls wherever I looked. Few people were on the streets, although it was still only the middle of the afternoon, as if they had treated the darkness as real twilight and started the Sabbath early. Jerusalem, that great city, normally bustling even at night, was as quiet as if it mourned Josh, and for all I know, it did. After all, it had been only days ago that they cheered him into the city and rioted with him in the forecourt of the temple.

Even the Romans—I heard distant marching, but it was all away from the parts of town I was running through, down alley after alley and round corner after corner, out towards their barracks and to the palace of the Procurator. In places, the smoke was still so thick that I had to retreat into shadow to be able to breathe.

And then I heard a pair of running feet, heading towards me, and three other pairs further away.

Judas came into view, his chest heaving and tears in his eyes—he flung himself at me and knelt at my feet. "Did you rescue my brother? He did not want to be rescued, but I know you."

So Judas had known.

"He would not let me, and so I gave him the mercy stroke."

"He begged me to do it, and I thought he would relent, and Ghost told me that he would and that he would let Alexander take over, and that doing what Josh asked me to was my best way of serving Jehovah, and the One, because then he would see the wrongness and repent, and...Everyone will hate me now, won't they?"

Which is true, after a fashion. He so wanted my forgiveness and he still looked at me with that adolescent devotion in his eyes and I knew, in justice, that he had only done what people had told him to. But I had Josh's blood on my hands and I was not feeling gentle. Or just.

He saw no mercy in my eyes and he got up again, and walked slowly away.

When Simon and his brothers arrived, I put up my arms, and spear, to bar them. "Whatever you think, it was not the money. I think Josh told him to do it. I think he didn't think Josh was going to die. I think he will be harsher upon himself than any of us would be."

"Harsher?" Simon's voice was mocking. "I want to kill him. How much harsher could that be?"

Mary had been concerned that she not lose two sons in a single day, and I realized that I had made one of the worst mistakes of my life. I raced down the street, but Judas had ducked into an alley and was gone from my sight, and whatever he was doing, he was not running and I could not hear the pounding of his feet.

"Come back," I shouted. "I'm sorry." And then, "Do not leave your mother childless."

All I could hear was the silence of empty streets.

I had nowhere better to go, and so I went back to the tavern where Josh had eaten his last meal. A few gawpers had gathered there, in spite of the empty streets, for Judas was hanging from the window of the upper room.

He had tied a rope around the legs of the heavy table. He had taken a dose of the nut which makes you die as arched by cramps as Josh had been on the cross. He had leaped from the window. He had slashed his stomach open with his great knife as he choked and arched. His emptied bowels lay in the street below him, alongside them a burst purse of silver coins.

I do not know whether he had known that a triple death, with plant and steel and rope, between air and earth, is a powerful magic. He was always a clever lad, though, and he hung on every word I ever spoke in his presence. I talk too much.

Jehovah and his white bird were there, as if Judas had summoned them, and he stood there, calmly, under his defiled corpse, in quiet conversation with them.

I was too late to prevent it, and not the boy's death alone.

Jehovah embraced the spirit of the dead youth and Judas whispered in the bird's ear as it perched on his shoulder. I do not know or understand the bargain they struck that evening or how much of it Judas laid out then and there, had planned in his clever scheming head as a thing he might suggest one day. Or perhaps I had taught him well, and he had had no plan, just made it up on the spot.

He died in the most terrible of pain and rose to be the greatest of the dead, seated at the right hand of Jehovah, and serving him, and the One he believes to be the true God, as faithfully and as cleverly as he can.

I do not understand, but that boy I taught to fight was the architect of Heaven and Hell and of Jehovah and Lucifer's avaricious hoarding of the dead. People think that they worship

Josh, and they do, but his foster-brother too, who betrayed him and replaced him and did it all out of love for his brother and love for a One who, for all I know, does not exist.

As they walked and flew past me, there was no love in any of their eyes for me. As he looked back at me coldly, Judas' face changed, and became that of Josh, whose place he has taken ever since, even with people who thought they knew him.

Yet even that I cannot, in fairness, put down to jealousy, but to a desire to serve. He does what he thinks is needful and takes no pleasure, I am sure; I know this and yet I cannot forgive him for any of it.

I did what was needed. I cut the boy down, and bandaged up the great rip in his belly, and closed the agonized eyes, and made him fit for his mother to see. Sof came and found me, and told me where Mary and the legate Longinus had taken Josh's body, and I carried what had been Judas with me in my arms.

My hand slew Josh, and yet it is Judas that I fear I killed.

Joseph had built his wife a country villa near Jerusalem, with a small farm attached, and a grove where she might walk, and a hollowed out cave in the side of a hill where he planned they would spend eternity together. It was a peaceful place.

When she saw me, with another of her sons in my arms, Mary their mother threw up her arm and covered her face with her mantle a second that she not see, and then she cursed at me, and spat in my face and struck me three times, and I bowed my head and let her try to hurt me.

Sof put her hand to my shoulder, and after the third blow, Mary flung her arms around my neck and kissed me on the forehead.

"I have lost two sons, but you are my daughters now."

Yes, of course she knew how things stood between us. She was an intelligent woman, after all, the woman Jehovah nearly took as his goddess but was too jealous to share his power; the woman who made Joseph one of the richest men in Judaea; the woman who trained up two of the cleverest young men I have known. I wish I had known her for longer, but events meant that I never spent much time in her company, and then her husband died and then she died, and they went to the Heaven of her lover and their son. Where I am not a welcome guest.

We washed the bodies of both boys a second time, thoroughly and piously and not the hurried job I had done at first for decency's sake. We wrapped them in two shrouds—Mary wanted to wrap them in one alone, but it was the Sabbath and the Passover and the merchants were eating or praying. Sof brought what she could find—and it was two.

Then I rolled a stone in front of the tomb and Longinus and I stood watch before it, for that night and the next day and the night after that. Simon joined us, and his brother Andrew, and they talked much with Longinus of the One, and after a while he wept and they embraced him.

I kept the watch when they slept, the first night and then the second, but then my eyes closed for a moment, and when I awoke, the stone was from the tomb. I looked inside, and there was only one body.

At first I thought Jehovah had come and taken Judas away—I put the shroud aside expecting to see Josh, but it was Judas that lay there. I replaced the stone, and shook Longinus awake, and told him what had passed. He left Simon to sleep but took up his watch while I wandered the grove and the gardens and fields beyond it.

There was a man, standing picking wildflowers, with a broad-brimmed straw hat to protect his eyes from the glare of the sun even though it was only just past dawn.

I wandered over to him, thinking to ask whether he had seen anything and he turned and looked at me, and it was Josh, and he was no spirit. "I told you to leave me be,"—his voice was more mocking than angry—"and somehow you both killed me and brought me back into the flesh."

It was the lance of course, my spear with which I had killed so many gods and the young god first of all.

125

Josh embraced me and I kissed him on the lips one third and last time. He handed me the flowers he had picked. "Put these in my brother's tomb."

I thought I had best tell him. "Your dead brother has come to some arrangement with your father."

"Good. He was always more what the lord Jehovah wanted and I have the business of the One to be about. Things would be so much simpler were I dead. Farewell, Huntress. You will never see me more. The boys you and your sister trained are dead."

With that, he was gone from my sight into shadow, and the workings of time and chance, and I have never seen him again.

Rome was on fire. It had been burning for three days and would burn for three more.

I had been on my way there, even before.

Sof had died, as she always did, of age and too many hours stirring herbs and metals that smoked as they simmered. She made the Stone, and she made the Elixir, and she made the Alkahest, and the Adamant, and the Fifth Thing, of which we do not talk.

I will not talk of her last years, nor of her last words which were of meeting and loving again, nor her last breath, which I heard.

Sof, Mary of Egypt and the wife of Josh, whom Simon (whom men came to call Peter, forgetting that it had once been a joke) admired as the widow of his friend and Lord, but whom later generations turned into various things that she never was. Not in that life, anyway.

Simon Peter, the Bishop of Rome, needed his staff, his shepherd's crook, for more than a token of his office. He bent over it and coughed from the smoke of wood and flesh, even though he shielded his mouth and nose from the worst of it, and from the sight. His old anger burned deep somewhere under the white hair and the ash.

"They say the Emperor, that great beast, ordered it done. He was in Antium when it started, so who knows? They say much of him, and much of the worst of it is true and much is lies. I try to love him as my brother, as Josh would have done. But it is hard."

I did not care about forgiving Nero. He was a bad man, but it was just not clear to me that he was a bad man to whom I needed to pay attention. His mother had died on his orders, but that was politics and not the Rituals; his adopted father and brother had died, but it was her and not him that killed them; Britannia was aflame, but it was rape and greed and a grieving mother.

I wait and I watch, because evil men draw other evil men to them.

"Huntress, Josh once mentioned a man whom you fought in Egypt, a man self-made of parchment and bone, who was called Simon."

I felt a shiver of anticipation. "There was such a man, and I had hoped that he was gone from the world, for I have seen no sign of him for years."

Simon Peter chuckled and then coughed again, for the smoke was very thick. "I think I met him. Nine days ago."

He had my attention already.

"A man wrapped in cloaks and robes and scarves, who creaked and flapped a little as he walked, came to me with gold, and the promise of more than gold. If I would sell him power, the power to loose and bind. Men say that Josh gave me that power, but it was one of his jests. I laughed, and I sent the man on his way."

"He offered to buy the power? That is not the man I knew in the old days."

"We all grow old, Huntress, except for you."

And Josh, perhaps, I thought but did not say.

Once Simon Magus would have torn a man's organs from his body one at a time to find where magic power rested, discarding the spoil in a bucket, but Judas had taken his ivory hand and perhaps that was where his spell resided. When he had killed Longinus' messenger, and the rats, and the fauns, he had used a knife, like an ordinary killer.

127

We said nothing for a while, and watched the flames, and thought of the people who were dying down there. I might have gone down, and saved some, or many, and thousands would still die, and if Simon was in Rome, I might save thousands and yet thousands more would die.

A man like Simon sometimes takes a patron, I thought, and if Nero had not been in the city when the fires started, perhaps someone had set the fires for him.

I watched a while, and saw that, sometimes, whole districts that were lit with flames would die back into the embers and then flare up again, in sparks and flame and smoke. I stepped aside, into shadow, and I looked again.

After a while, the district known as the Caelian sputtered and died, as the wind caught its flames and took them elsewhere, and then, quite suddenly, one of the great tenement blocks that men called islands, was aflame again, and, in shadow, its flames were green and purple.

There are powders, known to those who do the Work, and if Simon had never come after Sof, perhaps there were skills and knowledge he had found elsewhere. She was, after all, the best at the work but not the only one doing it—and the others did not have me at their side.

Simon would not risk himself on the ground, because parchment, no matter how magical, is a thing that burns.

So I watched the skies, patiently, and when he saw what I was doing, so did Simon Peter, whose eyes had not failed him with age. He held out his arms in prayer, and those prayers were answered. No power to loose or bind, perhaps, but within minutes the white bird, the Paraclete, and the red bird whom Hell calls other names, were perched on his wrists like hunting falcons.

I looked at him, impressed.

"My Lord has given me much. Since he said farewell to us, and ascended, and since he sent these birds to me for the first time who taught me and the others gifts of tongues and power."

He would not have been pleased to know that his Lord was the man he despised and not the one he worshipped. I had never spoken out, for either no one would listen, or they would, and it would be a waste of all that had been done.

I say this clearly to you, for you are a mocker and a charlatan, and if you told the world what I have told you, they would shout Blasphemer! Yet be bored at the same time. It is what you do.

Simon Peter looked down at the two birds who sat heavy on his wrists.

"See where the flames die and flare up. That is where Simon the Magus is flying, dark against the night. Harry him to us, that the Huntress may take charge of him and pull him from the air."

The birds fluttered off, and they cawed into the night, and suddenly the night air, the smoke-filled air, of the burning city was as full of birds as the air of Atlantis had once been, when the Bird tried to take me. The eagles and buzzards from which Rome takes its auguries, and gulls come up from Ostia, and even the water fowl of the miasma-filled marshes around the city—cawing and screeching and making all the noises that the birds of the air make.

I had had such attention on me once, and I neither envied Simon the Magus, nor felt ready to pity him. "And how am I to pull him from the skies?"

The old bishop looked smug behind his beard—he reached the crook at the top of his staff and, as he pulled it away, I realized that he had had something hidden by the best of glamours, that which changes the look of a thing in plain sight, but not its form.

"Mara, Huntress,"—his tone was gently mocking—"how long have you known me? What would I do with a shepherd's crook? I whom My Lord called to be a Fisher of Men again, as I was once fisherman and slave-taker."

He handed me his real badge of office, which was not, and is not, the shepherd's crook Rome claims, but rather the great cruel-barbed fish-hook I had held in my hand once before and given to Ghost to take to his Master. Only now, it had a thin strong coil of rope attached to it, that had been drawn out of Simon Peter's staff as he pulled it loose. I do not know precisely what that rope was made of—angel's tears or dying baby's breath or some such recipe as Odin used to bind Loki; I am not bothered with such matters—but it was strong cordage and weighed nothing to speak of.

Amid the noise of birds, as the great flock passed to my left, then to my right, and then rose, and then dived, I heard the angry voice of Simon the Magus cursing and the gentle caw of Ghost mocking him.

He was far from my reach still, but not out of range of my casting arm, for I have fished the seas of the world and those of shadow too, nor was this the first time I have pulled down a prey that swam in air.

Once I threw, and it missed him; once again, and it tore a great rent in his side and tore important scrolls from his entrails whose writings might have been strange knowledge or merely charged with keeping him in his unclean life—and he gave a great howl of pain; and then I cast again and this time, I felt the hook strike home and when I hauled on it, it pulled that thin tattered dried up husk of a man out of the sky and down to smash against the rocks at my feet. Simon Peter made as if to throw him down into the flames, which lapped the base of the rock on which we stood, but I stayed his hand.

Out of shadow, there trotted the she-centaur, as I rather thought she might.

Simon's face, that dead mask which haunts dreams still, showed a proper emotion for the one time I ever saw him do so, and that emotion was fear.

She spat in that face once, then turned and reared up on her front legs. Once—and the thin bones of his legs were as kindling and tinder; twice, and his ribs and breastbone were shattered like a lute that someone has grown bored of hearing; and on the third kick, that face and the skull it was so tight drawn against, and all that skull contained was paste.

She looked at me, knowing I needed no explanation, but out of courtesy to my companion.

"The stars were right, this time."

Then she trotted off into shadow, singing.

I lifted the fish-hook from the wreckage of Simon the Magus and wiped it clean on a clump of grass, and then I handed it to Simon Peter, to keep as his badge of office for a little while. Until Nero crucified him upside down for a jest.

I miss them all, but they made their choices long ago, as did Jehovah and Lucifer in the dawn of time. We all take friends into our lives and friendships always end in parting. And the last of all our friendships is always sorrow.

I am Mara the Huntress, and I hunt alone.

The Easy Way

Emma realized that they were not, as she at first assumed, going straight to Hell.

The shadows around her and Josette twisted and turned as they raced through the night. London was gone and they were over fields, but then they were skimming the surface of a desert of blue sand, on which giant scorpions danced, twining their stings. For a second she wondered if this were Hell, but it felt like a place with less room for humans than that. The scorpions did not know or care that they were there, and a second later, they were not.

Then, an endless meadow of red grass and tiny purple flowers, and then—

They were under the sea and yet still breathing air, and not wet. Then they plunged through mud and then rock—layer after layer flashed past Emma's eyes though it should have been dark, a moment of fast passing light, a moment of being wrenched from one

132

kind of movement to another that made her dizzy, and Emma found herself sitting at a table on a train.

She tasted the coffee that was in front of her. It was mediocre, bitter and cloying at the same time. Still, it helped settle her— Josette had swept her up rather suddenly and she was horribly aware that she hadn't had a chance to change from the opera except to take off her jacket and—shit—put down her bag.

And not pick it up again.

Emma looked across the table at Josette, who was now wearing a business suit and slightly tinted spectacles, with her hair in a school-mistressly bun.

"Eurostar," Josette said. "Your most important enemies won't be looking for you here and by the time the train gets to the Gare du Nord, we won't be."

Then she turned her attention from Emma a second and her lips moved, as if she were talking to someone else, as presumably she was. Several someone elses, in turn, Emma realized.

Josette turned her piercing eyes onto Emma. It would be a disconcerting gaze if it were not for those eye-lashes, Emma caught herself thinking. They'd be amazing if they were false and stuck on with glue, but they really aren't, are they? Not even the posh ones someone does individually. She was just born with them. It must have been awkward, before…

"Now," Josette was all business but quite charming in the way that people who do business best always are, "I just had to check in with my other sources and tell them to take a break, go on holiday, go hide. It's been a good network, but the people are more important."

Emma felt dreadful. "Are you sure it's worth sacrificing the rest of whatever it you do? Just for me and my problems." She felt obliged to say it even though she didn't think there was much question that Josette knew precisely what she was doing, had probably planned it for years.

Josette smiled. There were a lot of teeth in that smile, as if it were a preparation for something complicated and sinister and pleasurable for all concerned. "You've always been my most special agent, Emma Jones. I almost never have to tell you or Caroline what to do—just point you in the general direction and wait for outcomes even I can't predict."

Emma had always known she was an object of utility rather than ornament, in this game, but it's never entirely pleasant to find yourself getting a job appraisal, from the employer you have worked for some twenty years, and never met before.

"So, where are we going? Presumably not Hell."

"Not yet." Josette's voice was husky with excitement and a sort of regret. "You're not ready, or armed, for Hell. If Caroline is there, that means all sorts of problems, to be dealt with when we have to. There's forty-two safe houses to check first, that I know of. Lucifer's property portfolio is extensive, though I am trying to narrow it down. Drink your coffee, nasty as it is, and I'll just do something I need to do, about—right now."

As she spoke, several of the phones being used by people elsewhere in the restaurant car started up, trumpet calls slightly out of sync with each other, as if they were all getting the same notification but not quite at the same second.

A couple of people went "ssh" as if they were in a library; several others looked at their own phones trying to understand how some people were getting reception many feet under the sea.

Emma had not thought that a phone could sound that much like a trumpet; obviously these were people with super-special magical phones not yet on release to the general public. Bit tinny in the upper register, still, though.

Still, it was the "Tuba Mirum" from the Verdi Requiem which always, Emma thought to herself, sounds a bit like that. Suddenly Josette was not opposite her, but at the far end of the carriage, and in full House of Art armour, like an art deco samurai.

The man at the table on the other side of the aisle looked at Emma across the top of his dark glasses. He had the sort of suit people wear in old French thrillers, but it was new, almost shiny

134

new, and obviously meant to look like that. He smiled, and reached into his waistband, producing a small but efficient looking gun.

All around the carriage, Emma sensed that guns, and knives, and weapons of mass destruction were being readied. Several men and women, all of them in black tailoring of a tasteful retro kind, stood up and were clearly trying to get a better view.

Josette coughed loudly.

Her cough was echoed from the other end of the carriage by a whisper of air, and the slight clunk as Tom's wheelchair landed in the aisle, and the meaty slap of two wet clawed feet as Sobekh appeared in the aisle right next to Emma. She reached out and stroked the scales of his belly with the tip of her left index finger and he looked down at her, and smiled toothily.

Josette had a spear in her hand—Emma had no idea where it had come from—and suddenly it telescoped out and from the other side of Sobekh Emma heard a sharp intake of breath and the clatter of the man's gun against china and the top of his table. Two fingertips rolled across the table top and into Emma's field of vision.

"I hope, I really hope"—Josette's voice was mellow and rich but could convey threat for all the honey in it—"that my colleagues and I won't have to make a further example of any of you."

Tom picked up where she left off. "I make a perfectly good job of our shared profession in spite of some disadvantages, but I don't see many of you managing it. It takes more talent than any of you have."

Sobekh said nothing, but opened his jaws very wide, and then shut them with a loud click.

The carriage fell silent and the people who had stood up to get a clear look at their target sat down.

"You'll all have been notified," Josette went on, "that various contracts against my friend Emma Jones have been reactivated, and in some cases increased, now that she is no longer under the protection of the Lord God Jehovah. Let it be known, and I will rely on you to notify the managers of the website known as The Hit List, that Emma Jones is under the protection of the House of Art."

"And Miss Wild and the Lord of Cliffs and Shores," Tom said. "Also under my personal protection, and if any of you don't know who I am…"

It was clear that everyone did.

Not to be left out, Sobekh rumbled, "I'm here from the United Pantheons Against Jehovah, but I also have a message from the Lady Morgan who was Morgana and was Hekkat. She just says 'Don't'."

"Are we clear?" Josette continued. "Or will I have to execute a couple of you motherfuckers to make our point? Emma Jones is still off limits."

No one protested or made any move, save to put weapons away, close their phones and return to their coffee.

Emma realized that only about half the people travelling with them were actually international assassins because some of the people she could see were still showing signs of shock.

She stood up and clapped her hands imperiously. "And cut!" She'd seen this done by actual film directors. "Thank you everyone, it's a wrap."

There was a collective sigh of relief from the civilians as she sat down again. Lucky everyone was so used to special effects that no-one asked awkward questions about Sobekh. A couple got out of their seats to look for hidden cameras, but seemed happy they had found one in an air blower.

Josette stalked back down the aisle, and as she walked the armour shifted and turned and became the business suit again, completely, by the time she took her seat again opposite Emma. Tom rolled forward and parked beside the table. Emma wondered how Sobekh was going to manage, but he wriggled and changed and shifted his mass so that he was thinner and more sinewy. He eased himself in next to her, draping his tail across her knees.

She smiled at him, and then at Josette. "I've realized that you two have been in some sort of cahoots for quite a while."

"Really?"

This wasn't any sort of test, but Emma was sufficiently irritated that she had taken so long to work this out that she felt like sharing it.

"Somehow, you were the fourth cayman." Tom looked intrigued; Josette and Sobekh looked smug. "This was a few years ago, Tom. Sobekh manifested himself in Morgan's Brazilian palace and helped me eavesdrop on Morgan and Jehovah talking about me. He was being three small caymans, but later, when he was talking to Morgan, there were four. Josette here was in the ballroom—but I'm sure she's capable of controlling small reptiles from a few hundred yards away while carrying on cocktail party conversation."

Sobekh clapped his little forelimbs together, and Josette smiled her infuriatingly knowing smile.

"Did Morgan know you were listening? Or Jehovah?"

"I stay out of his way." Josette spoke with a slight but definite vehemence that Emma took note of. "Morgan? I don't know. She's very hard to read sometimes."

"Always has been," Sobekh rumbled.

"And the pair of you know Tom precisely how?"

"Oh, around." Josette waved a vague hand. "People in our line of work tend to find ourselves meeting up sooner or later, after all. Look at all the people and beings you know."

"So." Emma glanced around the compartment again and noticed that all the people in dark suits were studiously avoiding catching her eye. "Do international assassins always travel back and forth on Eurostar, or was this special?"

Josette gave her a pitying look. "Where else would they be? Much easier to carry guns here than on a plane. "

"Anyway,"—Tom's voice was clipped—"time I was back at the office." He reached under his wheelchair and handed Josette a sheet of paper. "That's our list, probably about as reliable as yours."

Josette ran her finger down it. "The Shanghai house moved six weeks ago,"—she obviously enjoyed telling him this—"and he has builders in at the Mumbai one."

Sobekh's voice was mild in reproof. "The Cairo house burned down two nights ago, and he closed the New Orleans place down. Said he didn't fancy its chances in the next storm."

Josette reached over and took Emma's hand and Emma put down her coffee cup. "Thank you both, but we must be going." Josette nodded first to Tom and then to Sobekh, and Emma smiled her agreement.

Josette put down a stack of coins for the tip and set the top one to spinning with a flick of her fingers. It caught Emma's attention for a second, and before it toppled, they were elsewhere. In a luxury apartment that someone had already torn apart, and which had clearly been stripped of all its valuables even before that.

"Things are moving faster than I had hoped." Josette's voice was tetchy.

It took until the seventh apartment before they caught up with some angels, or rather cherubs, who were clearly getting bored to the point where stripping all the cushions off the sofas had become a pillow fight.

Emma made a note to herself, that cherubs had a childish streak. They were whizzing round on hummingbird wings pulling faces at each other and trying to pull each other's nightgowns off.

"Don't mind us." Josette was almost charming to them, almost maternal. As much as she could be, given that she was back in full armour and her helmet covered her face.

"You shouldn't be here," one of them chirped, trying to sound officious. "Don't you know whose apartment this is?"

Emma thought she had better take charge. "Of course we do. He has something of mine that we are looking for."

The officious one decided to be truculent as well. "And who are you?"

Emma stood over him—he was only a cherub after all, and most of him was wing. "If I decide to take a job offer I got earlier, I'm your boss. So don't give me a hard time."

One of them had a list in his hand. She took it off him and

showed it to Josette, who compared it with hers. The cherubs had actually done most of the safe houses already.

"All of these stripped already?"

Job appraisals were on Emma's mind, and so she thought she might as well give one to the cherubs. Right now, she knew exactly how vulnerable it made one feel. "Very good, on the whole." She walked over and wrenched the curtain down, snapping its rail and breaking off all the elegant rings it had ridden on. "Now, check inside the seams. You haven't been doing this?" She raised her voice a little. "Well, you'd better go back to the other apartments and do them properly. And check inside the washing machine detergent drawers."

The cherubs looked flustered. One of them spoke up, its voice and wings trembling. "But that will take hours. We're already late for the invasion, and with Hell on its own time, that means we won't catch up for weeks."

Emma kept her face very still, and very calm. "The sooner you've done it properly, the sooner you can go play at war." She was being very strict and Josette was doing a very good job of not giggling. "Meet us back here in an hour," she went on. Then added impatiently, "We'll go on ahead and check Dubai and Berlin. Probably nothing there, but best make sure. And we don't want to be too late for the invasion, any of us."

The cherubs started pulling down all the curtains, and carefully unpicking the seams with, what, Emma realized, were very sharp little nails. She made a note to herself: never get in a fight with them, they'd be mean little so-and-sos.

She tapped her watch. "One hour. See you back here. And mind you recheck all the other apartments properly. I'll be doing random checks." She turned to Josette. "Dubai, first, I think."

The Dubai apartment had been stripped, but not tossed. Josette, now in a t-shirt and jeans, flung herself onto one of the sofas. It was really quite impressive how often she could change her outfit given they were actually tangible and she was doing it by proper magic as opposed to whatever Caroline did, being a ghost.

I must learn that spell, Emma thought. Twenty odd years and I never knew I could compete with my sweetie. But I'd never have her gift for style. And then she remembered that Caroline was somewhere far away, and in trouble, and so she just looked out at the view—she was not sure which floor they were on, but everywhere else seemed to be down, and there was a skylight through which the sun beat down.

She looked over at her boss. "I hope you didn't mind…"

"I value your initiative."

"Only I sensed you didn't really want to have to deal with them. The whole, covering your face thing. What is it with you and Jehovah and his team?"

"Long story."

There followed a long silence that made it clear Josette had no intention of telling this long story. Which, Emma thought, was all to the good, because there was a more important conversation that they really did need to have, and this breathing space seemed to be a good time to have it.

"When Caroline was killed"—she was aware that anger was creeping into her voice—"you couldn't have stopped it, could you?"

Josette suddenly looked deeply sad, but not even slightly defensive. "No, I couldn't. I didn't even know it was going to happen until it did. I didn't know who you were, just that there was the odd bit of gossip going around. I felt her die, though, because she called on me, and I caught her soul before it could go anywhere. I couldn't save her, but I did that for her."

"And all the Chosen one, destined for Mara, crap that she came out with, that first night? Which is so not going to happen, by the way."

"I don't know where she got that from. It wasn't me."

Emma had been prepared to make a scene; she really wanted to get this sorted out. Somehow everyone she ever dealt with had secrets and many of the secrets had to do with her, and she was getting fed up to the back teeth with it. The trouble was, she looked

140

into Josette's eyes and she couldn't see any dishonesty there at all.

What she did see, reflected there, and hear *bathunkabathunka*, even before Josette threw herself and Emma sideways on to the heavily carpeted floor, was some sort of big machine lumbering through the sky at them, *bathunkabathunka*. Rotors and men with big guns that they fired and the glass of the windows held for the moment. On the side of the gunship was an insignia she'd seen in the White Corridor, and on the uniforms people had been wearing there.

"Shit!" Josette was clearly angry, presumably mostly at herself. "I thought we lost them under the Channel."

"The resources Burnedover have," Emma pointed out, "they've probably staked out half of Lucifer's apartments on the assumption we'll turn up sooner or later. And given their presence in Iraq, even after I destroyed the white corridor, they're in the neighbourhood already."

Josette shrugged and the jeans and t-shirt started to flow and harden and flow and harden. "I really need to get you some protection of your own; this is going to be a little snug." She rolled over, on top of Emma, and behind her there was a cloak of armour that came down and wrapped itself around both of them and it was hard and it was flexible and it covered both their heads, which was a good thing because with a rip of sound there was glass flying everywhere and the sofa Josette had been sitting on disappeared in a score of small explosions of splinters and torn thread and feathers.

And it was very snug in there and Josette seemed to have converted absolutely everything she was wearing to armour for them both. She pressed in tight, and it wasn't sexual but it could hardly not be.

One question settled itself rather forcibly in Emma's mind. Whoever Josette had been, whatever her past, there was nothing hidden about her naked body. Nothing unexpected except for a jagged scar under her left breast. And the other scars Emma had felt earlier.

As the bullets continued to spray into the apartment and rip everything apart except for Josette's shielding armour, Josette rolled over on her back and Emma rolled with her and got the message and they continued to roll across the floor until they came to the window on the other side from the gunship. Or rather where the window had been because it crunched under them as Josette heaved them up and over the lip where the window-frame had been.

They were falling, falling free and Emma screamed in terror because she knew that they were not going to die because she trusted Josette that much and yet there was an animal in her brain that knew she was going to die and die now and another animal that screamed in sheer exhilaration at the moment of the drop and the wind and the sense of falling that was not quite like it is in dreams.

The floor on which they landed, from a height of about an inch, was hard cold marble and Emma could not resist going "Ouch" because she was underneath and Josette's armour had suddenly become a decorous business suit.

Emma stood up and looked around—she knew this place even though she had never been here. Barrel vault ceiling, a hideous canopy with snakey columns, various statues she had grown up knowing as images. "This isn't one of Lucifer's safe houses."

"Not technically," Josette smirked, "though personally I don't regard it as much of a House of God. Den of thieves, more like, and in need of a looting."

Emma looked around—she hadn't expected to find herself in St. Peter's.

"Go and look at the Pieta," Josette ordered, "it's the best thing in the main basilica. I'll be back in a second."

Emma dutifully looked at the Pieta for five minutes—it reminded her of the other one she had seen in Morgan's palace. The one with Mara helping. So many stories and so many versions of them, she thought, and no particular way of knowing which one is true.

She felt a hand on her shoulder and turned. It was Josette. She had a smudge of dust on her cheek which Emma reached up and brushed away. As she did so, she felt a sudden transit and stumbled, as you do at the edge of a dream.

They dropped on another institutional beige carpet and Josette said, "Berlin" quite unnecessarily and pulled herself up and off Emma and was dressed in jeans and t-shirt again and the armour gone. Not, though, the memory of Josette's complicated flesh pressed up against Emma; it was the closest she had been touched since Elodie and she felt like an ache the sensation of flesh and the guilt of for a long few seconds not missing Caroline.

She looked around, as did Josette. This apartment was not like the others—some of the art was off the walls but leaning against them underneath the places where they had been, some of it hung untouched. The place had not been disturbed by searchers and even the people who had started to clear it had not finished the job. It was as if they had run out of time.

"So," Emma asked, "what was that about an invasion? I think I know, and if I am right, it's sort of my fault, but can you clarify?"

She'd meant to ask in Dubai, but events had intervened.

Josette reached up and patted her on the cheek. "Not your fault, Emma Jones, though you may have been instrumental in setting things in motion that had been poised and ready for centuries. It was bound to happen, sooner or later, and they both had preparations made for what they thought would never actually happen."

"Heaven and Hell, right? Only I thought they fought that once already and isn't this time the end, according to mythology?"

Josette looked at her patiently. "They never fought before—none of that even happened. Milton and the others made it up. It was more like what Blake called the Marriage of Heaven and Hell—a comfortable business arrangement." She stroked one hand with another, cynically. "Jehovah didn't let himself know about any side deals. Then you showed up, with evidence that Lucifer's side deals are just a bit more sinister—providing technical staff for

143

organizations with magic no-one ever saw before. That's more serious." Josette shrugged. Her smile seemed to indicate that serious issues for other people were an opportunity for her.

Emma realized that she really had triggered something. Actions have consequences, and the trouble is that we don't know what those consequences will be.

"I imagine,"—by which Josette clearly meant, she knew because she knew the people involved, but hadn't actually been there or heard anything direct—"that Jehovah asked for an explanation, and Lucifer declined to give one, and Jehovah fired him, and Lucifer said you and whose army?"

She knows them both, Emma thought, and far better than I do. It's a long story she's not telling me yet, and they're both in it. It was as if she had put up an incident board in her head, and Josette's name and face were at the centre of it, and while everything else was going on, Emma's mind was gradually drawing circles with names in, and little lines of connection. Sometime soon, she thought, I won't need to be told that long story—I'll have it.

Josette went on.

"So I imagine it's going to be messy. Evenly matched sides, usually allies against some minor pantheon or other, one or other side, or both, buying unpleasant magical weapons from sinister unknown sources. And an awful lot of dead human soldiers for both sides to draw on when it gets very messy indeed."

"This is you, imagining?" Emma decided to be impressed. "That's pretty damn specific imagining."

"What can I say." Josette could be horribly smug when she wanted, even though it sort of morphed into suave most of the time. "Thieves always fall out, cheats never prosper and it is always a good idea to think four moves ahead, and never forget that neither the All Highest nor Him Downstairs are remotely as clever as they think they are."

Emma allowed that this was true, but thought to herself that it was a bad idea to get too smug about it, because none of this quite made sense. "How can all of this have happened in less than 24 hours?" She didn't know for certain how long the trips through Shadow had taken, but surely they were quicker than clock time, rather than slower.

"Because it will have happened in Hell." Josette managed not to sound as if she were giving a lecture. " Not the least torment of Hell is that time is different there—you can be tortured for a thousand years, and that is still just your first day in Hell. That's why I was hoping that Caroline was in one of the safe houses, here on Earth. Because the alternatives are, well, not so good."

Emma could very well imagine those alternatives, but chose not to think about them right now. "Well, then, we need to see if Caroline is here, and then decide our next move."

Josette was very slightly abashed. "Yes, but everything is moving so fast." She stalked into the next room and Emma followed her.

There was a safe there and no attempt to hide it—it was a monstrous great object, a blue steel cylinder with no obvious door or dials. If Emma had been told that it was not a safe at all, but just a sculpture that tried to capture the essence of safes, she would have been forced to believe it. *Here I am*, it seemed to say, *and your stethoscopes and your drills and your explosives will be useless against me. I am the ultimate safe for the information era.*

Josette pulled a small electronic box from somewhere—obviously she had a capacious pocket of space-time, a sort of miniature universe, about her person—and stuck it on the side. It whirred and whined for a second, and then its whine became that of a whipped dog and it fell apart in a catastrophe of chips and wires and springs and circuit boards.

"Shit." Josette was clearly, like most highly competent people, not especially good with failure.

Emma did what she had been meaning to do ever since the Eurostar. She whistled.

Her bag popped into existence at her side and scratched at her leg affectionately with its little feet.

145

"Missed you too." Emma reached down and scratched it just behind the clasp and it purred. The thick strap reached up, looped itself over her shoulder and pulled itself up as she stood. The little hand tentatively came out and touched her finger.

"I need you to do something." She stroked it delicately as she walked over to the safe.

Josette had knelt and was listening intently, her ear pressed against the steel. "I don't know how it works." There was a not of deep frustration in her voice. "There's no touch pad, no iris-reader, not even a DNA scanner."

Emma held her bag against the safe and the little hand came out to play, stroking the steel even more sensuously than it did her hand in the dark of night sometimes. "Clever little thing," she said encouragingly.

It tapped the steel once, twice, three times, and a pattern—or was it writing in some unknown script?—suddenly flowed over the steel from top to bottom. The hand traced a particularly complicated series of curlicues half way up the cylinder at chest height and then tapped again.

There came out from the side of the safe what looked like the hilt and hand-guard of a sword, and the little hand tapped Emma on the back of her own hand. She reached over and grasped the hilt and pulled.

It wasn't something that looked like the hilt and hand-guard of a sword—it was, and suddenly Emma was holding a blade that looked more like a sword than anything she had ever seen. It felt warm in her hand and the dark red velvet wrapped around the hilt stroked her fingers until she wrapped them round it just so, and then the blade felt like part of her, as if she had suddenly an extra foot of steel that was like a finger with which she could point and kill.

She gasped in pleasure and fear and then she let go, and suddenly the blade telescoped in on itself and became something that might almost have been a pen except that she knew it was not, and the small hand took it from her and placed it carefully in her bag.

Again the hand reached out and stroked what Josette and Emma had assumed was a safe. More symbols appeared and it tapped them, and ten holes appeared in the cylinder's side. Without having to be prompted, Emma slid her fingers and thumbs into those holes, with a moment of terror that maybe this was the worst thing she could do, followed by the sudden tingle of something enfolding every inch of her hands and flowing up her arms to the elbows, and then the shoulders.

Her arms were living metal, and she knew that, if she chose, the metal would flow further and encase her all the way from head to feet and yet breathe with her, dance with her, fight with her. It was like a promise of the best sex she could ever have and a moment of utter brilliance and wit and charm as well. She reached up and tugged at the upper edge, just by her shoulder and first one glove and then the other peeled off delicately and became what looked like small leather gloves with a slightly silvery quality. The hand took them from her, and placed them carefully in the bag.

"I planned to make our next trip to a Sister Armourer, but someone has taken your needs in hand. I wonder who." Josette's voice was full of wonder and mild envy.

"Somehow," Emma thought aloud, "I don't think it was Lucifer or any friend of his."

"I thought I was your patron, but clearly someone else is looking after you. Morgan, perhaps?" Josette's voice was slightly teasing with just a hint of hurt.

"Not her style to do something like that and not leave a note, vain old dear. She does like to get credit for things."

"I'm used to being the secret player, but perhaps there is someone hidden even from me." Josette was beginning to sound almost sulky.

By now, the cylinder was far slighter and less impressive than it had been, and when the small hand touched it again, all the patterns and script faded away, and all that was left was a single squiggle. From inside, there now came a delicate tapping, like someone trying to get attention but frightened to presume.

Josette's helmet was back and her face invisible so quickly that Emma did not even notice for several seconds. For a moment, Emma let herself hope that they had found Caroline and their quest was accomplished, but then the hand stroked the squiggle and, with a squeal, a hatch opened in the top of the cylinder and a single clawed finger appeared, groping round as if trying to feel its way out and yet not risk too much.

"An imp." Josette sounded less than surprised, less than enthusiastic, as a two-foot-tall red personage pulled herself out. Apart from the horn, the hooves and the tail, and skin the colour of Emma's hair, she was pretty much identical in her features to the cherubs Emma had been talking to earlier.

Except that, where they were like plump dangerous babies, she had the knowing smile of someone older and more experienced than she looked at first sight. She had no wings, and her silk gown was tight-cinched at the waist.

Oh, thought Emma, someone in Hell has heard of the little black dress. Logical, really.

The imp pivoted on one of her hooves, tapped once, twice with the other, then looked at the two tall women standing over her with a cheeky, knowing leer. The curtsey that followed was fascinating, utterly deferential and at the same time both a sardonic hint that we know this is all a joke and a sultry game of offering her services to whichever of them was prepared to bid. Services that, in spite of her size, would be, she implied, unforgettable.

"Mesdemoiselles, I am Luxuriette."

She had one of those French accents which might be fake or might be merely extreme, drawled out of the side of a mouth with black lipsticked bow lips out of which a cigarette did not need to be currently hanging for you to look for it, almost reach out to it with a match.

Emma declined to believe that Luxuriette was her actual name. Possibly a working title.

Josette was all business. "And you were in the safe because?"

148

"I was taking the pictures down, to be taken off to Pandemonium, and I heard someone knocking, knocking at the door. I thought it was angels, so I hid. I am not equipped...for war."

"Your role in the household here?"

Luxuriette caught Emma's eye, as if she could divide one of her new captors from the other by making sure she was in on the joke. Emma decided to cut this short. "Look at her, Boss. Obviously she was the maid."

Josette wasn't quite getting it. Or perhaps she was, and was refusing to be drawn into the joke.

"The *French* maid."

"Well, yes, that obviously." Josette sounded a little impatient. "But in my experience of Hell and its inhabitants, little is that simple. Especially when it seems to be, or there is a joke involved. Lucifer is the father of lies, or to put it another way, disinformation."

Luxuriette looked up at her and batted long lashes. "But you can trust me. I am just a serving girl. And I can serve anyone."

Emma had taken Josette's point. "So who was it that came through the door?"

"I do not know. I was in the safe. And then suddenly there was no way of getting out of the safe because, when I opened the hatch from the inside, there was singing blue and silver metal closing it off."

Emma looked at Josette. "I think that's us done, then. Nowhere left on Earth to look for Caroline...Which means?"

Josette reached down, grabbed Luxuriette by one ankle, or possibly fetlock, and held her upside down for a second, before Luxuriette curled impossibly up and round, and stroked the back of Josette's hand. "We can play rough. If you like. Or I could tell you what she said I should tell you."

Josette put her back down on top of the safe and Luxuriette preened a little, straightening her gown. She then struck a pose. "I was inside the safe, inside its new casing, and the metal sang to me, songs of blue and silver and swords and armour, but you know that already. And a voice whispered in my ear, as if she were in the safe

149

with me. It said, 'The sword and armour are for Emma Jones, who will be here with her companions and her mistress to free you shortly. Tell her that the road to Hell will not bring her to her heart's desire, but it is nonetheless her road, and she will attain her heart's desire, in the end.'"

Sodding destiny bollocks, Emma thought, but did not say. "And who was this woman?"

"I have no idea." Luxuriette shrugged expressively, all the way down to her pointed dangerous fingertips. "She didn't say."

"It is my experience that mysterious women who hand out magical armour don't feel the need to show their good faith. It's a mistake to ask them to."

Emma was still fuming about this new destiny nonsense, but could see Josette's point. "And so I have to go to Hell to look for Caroline, knowing in advance that she probably isn't there. Because magical anonymous women that hand me armour probably have my best interests at heart."

Josette smiled. "If there's a war between Hell and Heaven, I should probably go and observe it. It takes precedence, much as I want to help you look for Caroline. There might be people to help. Not everyone in Hell ought to be there, and no one else is going to care about them. As it is, Caroline is probably there too, so there's no clash anyway."

She had the grace to sound apologetic, and Emma knew she was right. "So we go and harrow Hell, because what else are we going to do?"

"Perhaps you could drop me off?" Luxuriette asked, in an almost bored voice, as if they were going past the end of her street in a London taxi. "If there's a war, well, I don't like to think what might happen to me, small, unarmed, and helpless."

Emma seriously doubted that Luxuriette would ever be helpless, but she was undoubtedly small. And probably had no arms except her nails, teeth, hooves and horns. She looked at Josette. "What do you think?"

Josette walked over to the stack of paintings in the corner of the next room. "I think it's oddly convenient that she was here and surprising that Lucifer entrusted retrieving two rather good Monets and who knows what else to a tiny comedy servitor. I'm not convinced, but I rarely am, these days."

Josette was, Emma reflected, one of the coolest people she had ever met, but she did have the knack of making you feel like an inexperienced child. Morgan had never done that—but perhaps that had been because Emma was such a child to her that she hadn't even bothered to explain things to her. After all, Josette had been watching her all these years and she must pretty much know all Emma's weaknesses, which was worrying because she had no idea about Josette.

Old, but maybe not Morgan and Mara old. Bad wounds and a lot of disillusion. Stays well away from Jehovah and masks in front of his servants. And this imp, who is a servant of Lucifer. Really really values their privacy.

Also—well the whole business with the House of Art, where it seemed like she was a very junior member going up through the ranks—and, when you think of it, what a good way for an immortal to be part of something they may well have started without anyone particularly noticing them specifically. I bet she's done things like that a lot down the centuries, Emma thought, and no one has ever known she was there.

So not just someone who stays off everybody's radar, but someone with a colossal secret; well, apart from the obvious, which they don't seem worried about people knowing. Because cool with that bit of her past, and so very past, Emma thought, because she had seen her naked and could not have told.

Also, so very hot. Can't help noticing. Goes with the armour and the scars.

Josette looked at Emma, considering. "Since you've got the armour and the sword, you may as well use them. That way, we're two people in silver armour, wandering around a war zone. You're no warrior, but I suspect the point of that sword, and that armour, is to make up for that. And I don't think Hell is going to be comfortable for a civilian right now."

The hand reached out from Emma's bag and passed her the knife and the gloves. It stroked the back of her hand.

Emma stroked it back, and then stroked the bag. "I came out without you, and it's been lovely getting to say goodbye, but I don't think, I really don't think, that I can ask you to come to Hell with me."

If the bag could have mewed piteously, it would have. Emma looked at it hard and spoke in terms that brooked no disagreement. "Go, the pair of you. Hang out with Morgan's luggage." Probably the safest place for them.

The hand waved from the bag, which wagged its tail and suddenly plunged into a hole in the air. They were gone and Emma's eyes were moist.

She passed Josette the knife, which her employer held very gingerly, remembering that it was not hers and that magic blades can be tetchy. Emma shook out the left glove and then the right, and put on one and then the other. She raised her hands above her head as if she were about to dive, and watched with fascination as the metal flowed down her arms and then down her body and up her neck and around her face. It was like plunging slowly into a perfectly warm and scented bath, but it was also like running and feeling the burn, and like sexual arousal. As a thin film spread over her eyes and mouth and nostrils and ears, a film that felt at once like the lightness of a kiss and the security of a mother's arms and the hide of some great and terrible beast, she relaxed for a second, but when she tensed again, it was as if she could suddenly run a mile and strangle a tiger.

The metal was her and more than her, and it made her more.

She pirouetted on one foot, and then leaped up and touched the ceiling.

"This is all too easy." Emma took the knife from Josette, and it changed back into the sword, only, when she took its basket hilt in her hand, the metal on her hand flowed over it, and it was as if the sword was part of the armour and both were part of her.

Josette saluted her with her sword and Emma found her blade, too, rising in a salute. Josette thrust at her and her sword parried; thrust and counter-thrust and feet in shoes that felt improbably high and not at all the sensible pumps she had been wearing for days were dancing around Josette, who was a whirlwind of speed herself and Emma realized that somehow she knew what she was doing, knew it so well that she could decide to move to left or to right, and yet the armour knew more and when she made that choice it was always a right one. Because the armour and the sword were knowledge and power and bloody hell!

Emma would always be more in love with her intellect, and occasional moments of controlled physical energy but for the first time she could understand, really understand, how some of the beings she had fought and outwitted could be so lost in power, so lost in the dance of mind and body and sword and claw.

And suddenly, it was over, because she and Josette both had swords at each other's necks and lowered them, and smiled.

Luxuriette looked up at them knowingly. "I wouldn't want to be an encumbrance, or an intrusion—" her cynical soubrette voice was like a moment of cold water bringing Emma back to herself, "—but something was said about a journey to Hell."

When Emma lowered her sword, it shrank back, not into a knife but into another layer of metal, an embossment on the metal around her hand that swirled round her wrist and up her arm. Yet she knew it would be her blade again in a moment should she need it.

I sent the bag and the hand away to safety, she thought to herself, and these are my new friends, my friends for war.

Josette stretched out an arm, and Luxuriette swung off her perch on the safe and swarmed up the arm to sit on Josette's shoulder, where her armour had reconfigured as a perch.

"Comfortable?" Josette asked. "Now, I know some fairly quick ways to Hell, but I am sure you know a quicker one."

Luxuriette looked at the pair of them pityingly. "This is Lucifer's safe house. There is a lift in the hallway that goes directly to his throne room. Where you'll have some explaining to do, my dears, but I'm sure you will manage. After all, beautiful silver killing machines—that's the sort of thing Star likes."

Emma noticed Josette react just ever so slightly to that name. Bloody immortals and their long memory for secrets. What good is it being smart as anything when half the time people are reacting to contexts millennia old?

So, Emma thought, and realized how totally she had come back to her comfort zone; Lucifer—star of the morning—Star, or maybe, it's the other way round—it's an old name. And this little puppet-like creature nonetheless knows him well enough to use an old name, or a pet name, maybe both. Also, Josette reacts, so she knows that too. Just how old is she, and what was her context? Back in the day.

There was a cupboard in the hall, and you could pretty much tell it wasn't where you put your umbrella from the small metal plate on it that said Lasciate Ogni Speranza. Oh, honestly, Emma thought, don't tell me that I needed to brush up my Dante weeks ago. I suppose they liked it when he wrote it, copied it and it gradually became part of their brand. Spin and snappy slogans are universal it seems, alas.

Inside, though, it was just a lift, buttons and slightly art deco mirrors in which Emma caught sight of her hair, caught up in a chignon at the back of her armoured head, yet bound about with the same silver. Crumbs, she thought, this is the best I've ever looked and it's a suit of armour.

From her perch on Josette's shoulder, Luxuriette pressed the button that said -29 and the lift made a delicate buzzing noise and started to descend. It felt like hot chocolate must feel as it goes down your throat smooth and pleasurable and warm; it was like running your hand along silk, the right way.

And the best of it was, in a way, that she could enjoy it for what it was, Emma thought, without having to worry about what people thought of her reaction. Her face, her eyes, were masked and she understood now why people might want to go masked, why having a face that was not your own might seem like the best and most sensible thing, if you were used to hiding your thoughts and your desires.

And the other two—Josette had her helmet over her face and Luxuriette was clearly no-one you'd want to play cards with if you valued your soul and your guts and your tiniest finger bone, because she would have them all, and would not even need to cheat. Just bluff forever.

Then something happened; the universe shook and there were afterimages of bright red light wherever you looked and if you shut your eyes they were there and if you looked into the mirror, they were there too, receding into infinity and yet at the same time coming back from it fiercer than ever.

The lift was moving sideways, and jolting and swinging back and forth. Luxuriette fell off Josette's shoulder, slipping and sliding around the floor under the others' feet, and they were having major difficulty keeping their balance. After all, Emma was wearing about the highest heels she had ever managed, and though the armour was perfectly capable of managing them in a sword-fight, it was not nearly as good at coping with a plummeting, swinging, probably about to kill them all lift.

She might be the only one to die, Emma thought, die and be left like strawberry jam on the mirrors, while Josette walks out with every hair in perfect order and Luxuriette would do and say what she does and that would be that. This would be the worst place to die—Lucifer would collect her forever and love doing it. Or whoever takes his place. Or they'd hand her over to Jehovah, who'd be smug, tell her he told her so, and set her to work.

And she would never see Caroline again.

"This would be one of those weapons too dreadful to use, being used, I suppose." Emma decided to sound a lot calmer and more intellectually intrigued than she actually felt.

Josette nodded. Whatever had happened, it was too vast for any more words.

Luxuriette just whimpered.

Only, luckily, the lift stopped spinning and swinging; it stopped, with a jar against your feet that was like a blow, but nothing broken so pick yourself up and start again.

"We need the door open," Josette said, with the same precision with which she would order a cavalry charge into the sea to fight the land's last hope.

Emma—*I seem to be a natural subaltern, in this woman's secret army*—found herself with her sword unwound from her hand and arm, pushing it between the doors and levering. She was not labouring, there was no sweat on her brow, but the suit, though it could take it, was clearly close to the beginning of its limits.

The mirror-glass in the doors smashed as she pushed, but the doors themselves swung open and Emma looked out—they were on a pathway that seemed to lead up into crags and down into a sort of swamp. It was many yards away and yet Emma was already near choking from its stench, even though the armour covered her nostrils and she was not breathing directly any more. A hot wind howled and swirled around them; over it, Emma could hear the harsh breaths and occasional death screams of the creatures that lived in the swamp.

At the left side of the track was a drop that seemed to go on forever, lower than the level of the swamp and from below there came no sound but a titanic moaning; it's Hell, Emma thought, and perspective does not have to make sense. On the right stood a wall that seemed to go up forever—ice or glass or steel polished to mirror—Emma glanced into it and looked away. It showed her her own face flayed and bloody and yet with living eyes; it showed her Caroline eaten, over and over again, and worse, it showed it from inside the ogre's mouth. But she looked away, and if she did not look at it directly, it was a blank surface.

She bent down a second—an idea had come to her.

She noticed Josette glance at the wall, and glance away hurriedly. She wondered what Josette was seeing, and what her worst thing was. And suddenly, she guessed and knew, all in a single thought, and hugged the brilliance of her guess to herself like a hot towel on the neck.

It was one of those moments of clarity when other things flash across the mind, not as distractions but as other things you are clever enough to sort out. For one thing, she realized that there was no way she could be smelling anything—it was a spiritual stench—and the moment she remembered that, it was gone, as if she had turned a switch. For another—she whispered to her armour "I'm on to you, whoever you are." And the armour gave a little squeeze against her neck and the side of her cheek that could almost have been a kiss.

Emma did her very best to remember the diagrams in the back of her Penguin Dante and realized that nothing she could see was going to mate with that memory and give her some sort of clue. Beyond the swamp, a long way beyond the swamp, she could see the high dark walls of the city of Dis, so far away she felt like a Chekhov sister yearning for Moskva yet uncertain how to get there and clear-headed enough to know she had no easy way.

If Dis was going still to be there when she found her way through the swamps. Thunderbolts were raining down on it and many of the towers that remained were Faerie towers that stand high even when torn to lace and tatters. And there was a black cloud at the centre of the city that must be the smoke of some great burning, but seemed to hang there and not move, even when bolts flew at it.

The sky was purple like a blood bruise. And in the hot wind, there were scraps of burning paper, fulgine past charcoal black, scraps that were a million dead angels aflame in the skies of Hell. And demons too, no doubt.

She wondered if any of them were the cherubs she had bossed around earlier, or whether by delaying them, she had saved their lives for a few hours.

In the distance, she could hear artillery and fighter planes and the clash of armour and the hiss of arrows and the whump of catapults and the screams of men and other beings fighting and tearing with fists and nails. None of these sounds seemed to drown each other out and they all went on and on in the distance like a mosquito in another room or a headache you already took something for.

Josette had said that she reckoned that Heaven would have bitten off more than it could chew but would prevail in the end—so far, so accurate.

But Emma knew that they had more immediate problems. Down the track there came five men, each on a horse with the same livery—one was slightly in the lead and had a drawn horsepistol and a big hacking knife. The next three had lances —two of them seemed nervous to be there, schoolchildren who had missed the big event. The last was wearing samurai armour and hung back a little. War is a raging lion, and round the edge of its killing zone, jackals and hyenas gather for the carrion.

Josette suddenly had the sort of long lance that they use in the joust, pointing outwards and resting on one foot. Couched, Emma thought. And stood, sword extended, with her actual self actively terrified and her outer other-self exhilarated.

Josette looked at her encouragingly. "They are dead, and you are not," she pointed out, a little redundantly. "Remember that when you are tempted to hesitation or mercy."

Emma thought she had better treat this as if it were a video game.

The man on the lead horse dropped his pistol to his side and rested his knife on the head of his steed, which stared at Emma and Josette with eyes that were not a horse's. "We don't want no trouble, misses." The spark of cunning in his eyes, the slight drool on his lips, belied his words. "You could just toss us the imp and we'll part friends. She ain't no friend or kin of yours and I am sure we could find a use for her."

"She is our companion, and under our protection," Emma said, and Josette nodded.

158

"We've been on the road for months, ever since the armies exploded," he drawled. "And in all that time, not a sniff of pussy. What's the use of being back in the flesh if I can't find myself some trim quim? Now we find three of you, and one's a demon. I ain't never had demon."

"Nor shall you ever," Luxuriette hissed and showed sharp teeth like a snakes. "Put it near me and I bite it off."

"I likes 'em mean. More fun to break. Girls and horseflesh both. I hogtie and then I brand."

"Hush, William." One of his companions rode up the few paces that separated them, lowering his lance but not by very much. "I have seen women in armour before, and they suffer worse delusions of gallantry even than men. Look at them, silver virgins who will cry at wounds. Give us the imp, or suffer with her." He had haunted eyes, a moustache that drooped in the haggard lines around his mouth and a goatee that was little more than a single line of hair from lip to chin.

On the road for months, Emma thought, but the explosion was just as we got here.

When no one said anything, the second man nodded, and turned his horse in the narrow space of the track, riding back to join his companions. The one he had called William smiled apologetically—the effect was spoiled by his crooked, rotten teeth—waved his slouch hat, and rode back.

Josette spoke softly to Emma and Luxuriette. "They will come at us, by two and then by three, and try to ride one of us off the road and down the cliff—they will sacrifice possession of her, to gain the other one and you, imp."

Emma realized that she was being asked a question, or rather, she and her armour with her, for Josette must know that it was a being with a mind, it was the only thing that made sense. Again that kiss.

"We have to kill the horses of the first two," Emma said, "because then we cannot be overwhelmed by the charge of the three. If we kill the first two riders, that is a bonus." She hated the idea of killing horses, innocent creatures, if anything is innocent that is in Hell, but she was determined not to die.

She noticed that William and his companion had joined the samurai at the rear. Josette followed her gaze. "My guess would be that the other two are just random damned souls whom they expect to use as cannon fodder, now or later. Let me engage the Nipponese—I have fought such before and there is a trick to it, as with eating oyster or lobster."

Emma thought aloud, "Cesare is the threat, I think. Billy likes his guns—he'll have at least one back-up on him—but the armour will keep me safe, won't you, dear?"

It did seem almost familiar to her, but not quite. As she spoke, the sword disengaged itself from her arm and came to her hand gentle as a lover's kiss.

"Billy and Cesare? Yes, that makes sense—but how do you know?"

"I know lots of things, and after meeting Tomas, I spent an afternoon on the internet, looking at famous faces. It pays to know which of the famous dead you're dealing with." *Shit*, Emma thought, that last came out a little pointed. She whispered into Josette's ear. "You have your father's eyelashes, and, by the way, he really is a bit of a dick, isn't he?"

And she really must remember never to play cards with this woman, because she did not react to that at all.

There was a thunder of hooves from a few yards away, and that was a problem—the samurai had dismounted and slashed his horse's side lightly with his sword so that it ran screaming between the first two horsemen.

Josette held up the hand that was not holding the lance, and suddenly they had most of the time in the world. The oncoming horses and their riders were slowed down, almost to stillness—of course, Emma thought, it was her that taught Caroline that trick.

Josette's voice was sonorous—she was, after all, known for her public speaking and commanding presence. "Even now, we do not have to do this. But as you wish."

But all that Emma could see in the eyes of the oncoming riders was hatred, determination and sick lust. No doubt or hesitation at all. Little in fact that was recognizably human.

Emma had taken the wall side. As her man galloped towards her, her left hand used the fragment of mirror she had taken from the ground by the lift to flash images from the wall into his eyes, and the eyes of his terrified horse. She had two more very dangerous men to kill, or whatever you do to damned souls in Hell, and she could not afford to fight fair.

As if any woman ever can.

Distracted to madness and agony, the man and the horse smashed themselves into the wall as if they could smash what they had seen. They screamed, on and on. Emma and her armour and her sword seized the man—his face was by no means familiar and she could not afford to be curious—and slit his throat quickly. She needed to stop his screaming.

He was gone, like dust in the wind. So that's what happens to the damned—do them mortal hurt, she thought, and they go, elsewhere. Perhaps to come back and die over and over again. And that is why oblivion is the only cure for Hell's pain.

The horse had shattered a leg, rearing and falling, and it was screaming still, its mouth wide like something in Picasso. So, a quick thrust to the space a bit up from between the eyes, she remembered, the cross of imaginary lines from eyes to ears, and go in at right angles to the line of the skull.

She remembered the time she saw it done; bad as that had been, doing it herself was worse, but at least, little blood, and it just sagged against the wall and slumped down into the path of the next two charging horses as neat as she could have wished. They slammed into the body of the riderless horse, which Luxuriette had gutted from underneath with her claws and her horns.

No wonder she is that colour, Emma thought, because she is

fucking bathing in the blood. Josette was right, a lot more than the French maid.

Josette hadn't waited for her rider, who had lagged a little for fear of being knocked off the edge by the riderless horse; she ran at him with a lance in her hand and sideswiped him with it as if it were a sledgehammer. Hardly had he fallen into the abyss, but she leaped aboard his horse, brought it up short, turned it and ran at Billy. And what had been a lance, was now a slashing sword, in the Japanese style.

He fired at her once, and twice, and, when his bullets ricocheted, turned his horse and rode back up the trail, calling to the samurai, "They're all yours, but if I were you, I'd run."

"Coward." The samurai's voice was gentle. He turned to Josette. "Come, let us fight. It is a long time since I killed a woman. I have almost forgotten the sweet taste of it."

Josette spoke to him, as to an old friend. "Izo, Izo, have you learned nothing? The men of the New Corps whipped you, and they pierced your hands and feet with spears, and they beheaded you, without honour. And you still take pleasure in killing?"

But the samurai she called Izo ignored her words, and eyed her carefully, positioning his feet and raising his sword two-handed, and waiting. Josette, with a shrug that said "As you wish" all over again, lifted her sword a little, but not, like Izo, above her head.

Emma had other things to worry about.

Cesare had pulled up his horse, short of the two that lay dead at her feet, and dismounted. Very slowly, and with his eyes intent on her silver face, he put down his lance, bowed to her with a courtier's grace, and then, silently, drew his sword from the velvet scabbard at his belt. It was a Renaissance side sword, like a rapier's butcher big brother.

"Beg for mercy, and we will see what sort of mood I am in." He was clearly used to people doing that when he spoke to them.

"Everyone feared you, but I do not fear you, Duke Valentine." She was lying, and he knew she was lying, but you have to say these things.

162

He smiled, half-pleased and half-irritated, which made his moustache droopier. "You know my name then—well enough to distort it into the barbarism that is English—and you do not tremble."

He picked his way past the dead horses with a precision that was almost mincing, and with no further ado thrust straight for her heart. Her armour hardly moved at all—it was her sword, almost alone, which batted his aside.

"Is it better to be loved than feared?" She refused to take him seriously—thinking of him as a comedy villain and mocking him, was going to be her best way forward. As she spoke, she thrust at him, without expecting any great success. He parried her sword, but she forced him to take a step back, almost stumbling over the outstretched legs of the dead horses.

He reached behind his back with his free hand, and thrust at her again with the small dagger from his belt. Her armour did not so much repel it, as reach out like a fountain of steel and draw it in and absorb it, spitting out the two rubies and the topaz from its hilt so that they lay in the horses' blood at her feet.

She thrust again, only this time when he tried to parry she used more of the strength that the armour gave her and pushed him back another step. Again, he almost stumbled, and this time, he was back beyond the horses.

"It might be answered, that one should try to be both feared and loved."

"Would you stop quoting that fucking book at me?" He stepped back without being pushed, two steps and then three, and then he ran at her, slashing wildly with his sword and stumbling as he slipped in the blood.

She crouched slightly as he came, and thrust upward, under his ribs, and straight into his heart. "I maintain that it is much safer to be feared than loved," she intoned as his body turned to dust and blew away.

She was thoughtful for a second; she had been responsible for deaths before, some of them fairly directly, and yet Cesare was the first she had killed in cold blood, even though she was fairly certain he was already alive again, somewhere in Hell. She had thought, or hoped, that she would feel sick. Is there any innocence, she thought, that I will not lose sooner or later? But what is the alternative?

It was, after all, especially ironic that this particular innocence should be one she lost travelling with Josette. If her guess was right, because after all Josette had not yet confirmed it, and seemed considerably more relaxed about such matters than one would expect. Not much turning the other cheek on display, these days.

Emma's sword clearly judged her part in all this over, and put itself away.

Emma walked over to Cesare's horse and stroked it gently behind the ears. She suspected that it was no natural creature, but it is the nature of horses, and things that have become them, to welcome being gentled. It pushed at her with its muzzle, but she had nothing to give it.

Luxuriette reached up with two sugar cubes. "It is my job to spread sweetness." Her capacity for innuendo was remorseless.

Emma ignored that, and merely said, "Thank you." She offered the sugar cubes to the horse, which snuffled them from her hand and nuzzled for more.

She continued to stroke the horse between its ears, and watched Josette and the man she had called Izo stand, glaring at each other and slightly adjusting in turn the way they stood, the way they held their swords.

After what seemed forever, but might well have been seconds, Izo leaped and slashed, but Josette was not there. She had leaped higher still, up and over Izo, and as she came down, she kicked with her right foot the crown of his head, sending him reeling as he fell to earth, and then with her left foot the shoulder and collarbone of his left side, breaking bones with a crack that made Emma wince.

Izo tried to lift his sword again, right-handed, but Josette took it from him, as one takes a toy from a child that has played too long. "I leave you one sword-hand," she said. "I would not leave you utterly without resources in the wilds of Hell. You have no horse, by your own act, and no ally, save the American you just called coward. You may wish to consider your position."

From behind the metal cheek pieces of his helmet, Izo stared at her in hatred. "You insult me with mercy." His voice was full of quiet anger.

"I do the minimum needed. Your little force is broken; one ally is removed and the other fled, and the two young thugs who fought with you are gone as well. You will find no more recruits and work no more mischief. But, if you wish, I can, with a single thrust, send you back to the blood vats of Phlegethon, to be reborn, and take your chance of winning a sword. Lucifer needs cannon-fodder so badly that I doubt he is punishing deserters with more than a flogging."

If she has a fault, Emma thought, it is that she is still too fond of her little sermons.

"Be damned to you, bitch. Fuck..." Izo drew his blade across his throat and his last word ended in a gurgle before he like the others, turned to dust.

"Phlegethon it is, then." Josette turned back to the horse she had taken and swung up into its saddle. "Come on, Emma, mount up. We shall have to make our own way to Dis, and now, at least, we shall not have to walk."

Emma felt a moment's embarrassment, because she had no idea in the world or Hell how she would possibly go about getting on top of a horse, let alone riding it.

The armour, though, clearly had other views and she found herself, almost before she could form the thought of saying she needed help, in the saddle, reins in one hand and the other reaching down to pluck Luxuriette up by the scruff of the neck and up in front of her. The imp squirmed back into her with rather more ardour than was called for. Emma noticed with amusement that the armour, far from resisting this, shifted slightly against her body to accommodate it. Clearly armour with needs of its own.

The horse whinnied and shied for a second, for it could smell horse blood on Luxuriette, but she whispered in its ear, and, whatever she said, it listened and was still.

It was a long road through the swamp and Emma did not feel especially like talking.

There was a conversation she needed to have with Josette, but how do you start it? She had tried once, but...

"We all 'ave...secrets." Luxuriette was not helping.

Josette simply said, "If so, they are for another time. Emma, I need to have a word with you, but it is nothing that cannot be said in front of the imp." Her voice was not disapproving, and yet Emma felt at a disadvantage. "What do you think happened to the two men, and the horse-being, that you just killed? And the man I killed and the one I allowed to take his own life?"

"You said something about blood vats. I take it they are reborn."

"After a fashion, but often with something missing. Billy, who has fled, has lost his nerve; Cesare whom you killed so easily, his prudence. The two nameless men—most of their identity, all of their fear. And the horse was not always a horse and perhaps will not be when next you meet her. Being born over and over is part of the torment of Hell, and knowing that any time you may come back wrong is another part."

Emma had thought earlier that Hell was like a video game.

Josette read her mind, or perhaps just knew her very well. "It is not a game. It is agony and pain and rebirth that tears the soul and makes them fear Lucifer, their judge and their master—or if it is a game, he is the only one who is playing it. Remember this."

Emma found this less than fair. "You brought me here; you and the armour taught me to kill."

"You already knew how to kill, using others to kill for you. It was one of the first lessons you learned in my service. Now you have learned to kill with your own hands. What I wish you to learn now is, not to kill lightly, and where possible, not to kill at all. The Huntress, who is famous for killing, was my tutor once, and I watched her and learned from her." Josette reached out and touched the silver skin on Emma's arm. It felt like discipline and it felt like a caress between friends. "And you, armour, heed me. I know you are a player in this game; be sure that we stay on the same side."

"I have seen the 'Untress kill," Luxuriette was clearly charmed by the memory. "She has an elegance in the act that made me dream of her for weeks. Happy dreams from which I woke moaning."

Emma was aware she was being unfair, but spoke grumpily. "I only saw her once. She killed the creature that had just eaten my friend; had she arrived a minute earlier, she would have killed the creature that had not yet eaten my friend. My attitude is coloured by this."

"And you could not save John Shallock." Josette seemed determined to be fair and firm. "None of us can save everyone and not everyone should be saved."

Emma was struck by another recognition, one that this time she could speak in front of the imp, though it confirmed her other guesses. "It was you that told Tomas he should seek oblivion, for he would not find forgiveness."

"It was," Josette acknowledged. "But that was because he would not seek either to forgive himself or to humble himself enough to seek out those he had wronged and tell them of his repentance. He had other choices but he was not the man to make them, or even hear them offered."

The swamp around them was a monotony of squelch and pain— it was blood and it was shit and it was acid and it was liquid fire and it was half-rotted, half-eaten bodies that writhed and occasionally called out as if they saw old friends and loves riding past them.

Leeches and great worms battened on them, and ticks the size of eggs. Snakes crawled in and out of their bodies, biting as they went, and where they bit necrosis spread like purple char. Yet their flesh was stubborn and constantly tried to heal itself, and the scabs and the itching of the scabs, and the peeling of the scabs, and the burning of the marsh on the new skin was the worst of it all.

"Once Hell had many many ditches—" Luxuriette clearly savoured the memory, "—and in them the damned boiled or burned or dissolved into pus according to their kind and their sin. But an efficiency expert told Lucifer that this was wasted effort, and they should all mulch up together for it was cheaper that way. Lucifer heard his advice and took it, and the man is still up to his neck in the swamp, for Lucifer rewarded him with an especially fine gift of healing."

She pointed to a man with pink skin at whom his fellows tore, as if they were become the leeches and the snakes. He screamed in pain and yet every time he was bitten or clawed his skin flickered a moment and then was whole.

"And those too will be reborn in Phlegethon?" Emma asked.

"Only when every scrap of them is gone, and in the blood vats they will long for the swamp, as now they yearn for the comfort of Phlegethon. There is no surcease for them, for they are in Hell, and all of the damned end here for a while, to teach them the humility they will never learn. For they are the damned."

"When I talked to Jehovah of damned souls who were in the flesh to the extent not merely of violence, but of complaining about the food, it was a surprise to him." Emma realized how wrong Jehovah was about everything.

"He and his accomplice are perfectly content living off a Heaven full of souls singing Glory, Glory and never able to eat or sleep or make love." Josette was quietly seething. "They never chose to enquire how you could have a Hell full of souls writhing in eternal torment without bodies of some kind being involved. Lucifer bought that secret long ago, and more recently he bought refinements on it. Jehovah may not want to know how sausages are made, but some of us have more responsibility than that."

She halted her horse and dismounted and Emma did likewise, not sure why they had paused.

"This is part of your education, Emma. You need to stand here, and listen to the damned."

After watching, and listening for a while, Emma realized that what she was hearing was not just screams, but endless stories.

"I loved her, though she was my brother's wife. He beat her and I dressed her wounds, and then we kissed."

"I stole the bread to feed my children, and then they broke me on the wheel."

"I asked why God permitted such things and they cut out my tongue and branded me and then they burned me."

"I fought for our true king and they pulled out my guts and burned them before my eyes."

She found herself sobbing, and saw that Josette wept too, and even Luxuriette had moist eyes. She felt sorrow, and she felt shock, but above all she felt anger; her eyes were dry and yet it seemed that there were tears.

She wondered for a second whether she was wrong, and they were her tears, but then she realized that the armour that covered her face was weeping tears of its own.

Then they climbed back on their horses and rode away.

After what might have been hours, or days, or weeks, they felt the squelchy track on which they rode become a gravelly incline that rose above the swamp, which was fortunate, because beneath them, on both sides of the causeway, the swamp was now aflame, with a wall of dark fire that moved slower than a man would walk but consumed all in its path, leaving dry mud in its wake. Where it passed, it consumed even flames.

"Everyone that is damned to the swamp," Josette said, "will burn in that flame, and Phlegethon will be overwhelmed." There was triumph in her voice, and sorrow. "I sorrow for the pain of those who burn, but they burned already and perhaps, some day soon, they will never burn again. Hell needs to be broken, and this war will break it."

Emma said, "Hell's time is surely broken. Whatever magic was in it, has gone wild and mad."

169

Luxuriette stiffened. "Some of us call it home."

Emma held her tongue, aware that things were happening around her that she had, in part, caused all unknowing.

Ahead of them the great black wall of Dis stood no longer, all heaps of brick and marble chips, and places where fires burned—it was perhaps sparks from those fires that had started the conflagration in the swamp. Its towers were rubble, as far as the eye could see—yet above in the sky angels still burned, and the tents of Heaven, pitched among the rubble, had been bright-coloured once, but were now stained with smoke and blood.

It had not been an easy victory and the war was not over yet.

There was small arms fire beyond the rubble, in what was left of the back-alleys and side-streets of Hell, and from further away, artillery still pounded, and balls of dark flame still shot into the sky. Not all of Dis was taken yet.

From beside the tents of Heaven, great machines spat flame in great looping arcs, or fired their own dark flames.

Sometimes the missiles of Hell and those of Heaven would find each other in mid-air, and fall to ground somewhere far away in a gout of blue flame and a noise a little like thunder and a little like the scream of a dying child.

If Jehovah had hoped for a short victorious war, then he had been out of luck.

Josette broke away, riding hard towards the tents and banners of Heaven. There was no victory, but no way further into Dis that could be taken safely without their consent.

Emma dug in her heels and caught up on a little rise that overlooked the broken gates of Dis. I am being a tourist, she thought to herself, disappointed that any inscription on those gates is broken beyond repair when I ought to be thinking of the cost. There was broken glass under her horse's hooves, and the dust of walls and the shattered white skulls of men and women. It was a desert they were crossing, a desert made of broken minds and unacknowledged guilt.

A jeep drove slowly towards them, sending up great spumes and plumes of that malignant dust, with a man and an angel in the backseat. Alongside the jeep, a large black stallion trotted, with a rider who managed to convey, as he rode, his entire lack of interest in being there.

"Oh look." Emma found herself amused that she was not even slightly surprised at this point. "Heaven has human troops fighting for it. Jehovah said that there was no one alive in Heaven except for him and someone he called Ghost, and you said the same—have I missed something? Or are those illusions?"

Josette's face was hidden from her, for her visor was still down, but her voice sounded at once fascinated and appalled. "Heaven must have been losing very badly to start resurrecting the dead in such numbers. I shudder to think how many angels must have died in flames for Jehovah to do that. The dead, in the flesh—he must have been desperate."

"A couple of days ago, my time, he talked of it as inconceivable. He wanted to kill me so that I would work for him. He said that no one ever came back from the dead, which is even more interesting given…"

"There have always been things that Jehovah knows nothing about. Let's leave it there, and deal with his servants."

"What shall we say about…" Emma broke off, because, to her surprise, the insistent squirming pressure of Luxuriette's body against hers had suddenly disappeared from in front of her. How had she slipped away so handily and where had she gone so suddenly and so invisibly?

However, with the new arrivals, it would not do to discuss Luxuriette's absence with Josette or even look around for her. The imp had made her choices and had, perforce, to be considered to be on her own.

Josette had her lance again, and dipped it in deferential acknowledgement of the new arrivals.

The jeep stopped some yards short of where they had halted their horses and the man seated in the back got out, saluted his driver, and strutted slowly towards them. The angel, a tall being with many wings that flickered around him, sat impassive—Emma wondered for a second how this angel had survived when she had seen so many others burning, and then she realized that what she had seen as many wings were waves of cold flame passing over and over his body, and yet they were wings, too. It all depended how you chose to see them.

The man on horseback reached into his pockets and produced a cheroot and a match; he stuck the cheroot between his lips and bent down to strike the match against the heel of his boot. He sat back in his saddle with hooded eyes, took a draw and watched impassively. Of the two of them, he was the one Emma suspected she would rather have dealt with.

The short man in battle-dress and a beret stopped a few feet from their horses and looked up at her. "You'd be this Miss Emma Jones I've been told to expect. British gel, which is good; some kind of perverted suffwagette, which is less good. Still, it has been willed, et cetera, et cetera."

Emma nodded, somewhat surprised.

"The Lord God said you'd be coming and that we should meet you. Then we should bwief you and then send you on your way to accept Hell's suwwender. I have a document here, with the terms you are allowed to accept." Montgomery of Alamein looked slightly grumpy. "Both I and the Duke were a little disappointed. I mean, we both have expewience in taking suwwenders. But then, so have most of Heaven's captains—bit of an elite corps, don't ya know. Still, at least they're sending in someone English, even if you are a gel. That's why they sent us, appawently, so you'd feel at ease. Help you wemember your wesponsibilities."

He reached into the front pocket of his battle-dress and pulled out a neatly folded piece of paper which he passed to her, but only after he had unfolded it, slowly, deliberately and with an almost pedantic precision.

172

He flicked it once with his forefinger, and it was as if it had never been folded.

She glanced at it—pretty much what she expected and nothing that she disagreed with.

The angel flickered, and was suddenly beside him. Its face was blank and expressionless at first but then the cold flames passed over that face and upon it there suddenly shone a flat image of the face of Jehovah, though his voice, when the angel spoke, sounded distant, as far away as Hell from Heaven in fact, Emma thought.

"Ah, young Emma, good to see you."

Given how they had parted, this was the rankest of hypocrisy.

The eyes in that face flickered over Josette, but did not really see her.

"Travelling with one of the House of Art, I see. I should have seen that coming—you hired them for protection before. Smart move even if they are all wilfully disobedient to my laws. Good fighters and clearly got you here in one piece. Expected you'd turn up before now, looking for your floozy; you've messed up our schedule quite badly."

Emma shrugged. "You know how it is. Travelling through Hell. The time just flies." Then she raised her voice slightly. "We got here as fast as we could, in the circumstances. I didn't know I was expected."

Jehovah laughed. "Oh, that little row we had last time we spoke. Forgotten about it already—what use would you be to me if you didn't stand up to me? Good show. And look, I fought this little war that you made. And it's almost won. If you wouldn't mind going and talking sense into some people—they sent us back our first herald's head in a box and I thought, I bet I know who could talk sense into that bunch of scum and reprobates. Emma Jones, I said to myself, and I bet she'll be here shortly. Sometimes I surprise myself—maybe that's why Providence works, I should get a theologian to explain it to me."

Emma looked at Josette and realized that it was not just her visor

173

that made her impossible to read. And clearly she was not going to say anything with Jehovah listening.

"I need to get into Dis and talk to Lucifer, so I may as well do it as your emissary. I'm sure he'll be reasonable."

Jehovah's face disappeared, like the Cheshire Cat.

The Duke rode up, having finished his cheroot, and drawled, "His Satanic Majesty ain't the problem."

Montgomery snapped at him like a terrier. "Heard your theory about that. No evidence, can't plan a stwategy without some intelligence."

The Duke looked down that long nose. "I know what I know. We ain't going to kill His Nibs, we probably ain't going to send him somewhere far off and unpleasant—so why ain't he surrendering? Answer, because he ain't the one who is going to do any surrendering."

His voice grew louder and more emphatic and his horse twitched its ears, as if concerned that it was the object of his anger.

"Settle down, Copenhagen, boy,"—his voice grew soft and gentle—"settle down."

He reached down and stroked the black stallion just behind its left ear.

The Metatron flickered again and Jehovah was back. This time the angel whose body he was using got out of the jeep and walked over to Emma's horse, stroking the mane just between the ears.

Emma noticed just how still and silent Josette had become.

"I think the Duke is right. I've known Star a very long time and the weapons of mass annihilation were not his style. He's never liked a situation he couldn't run away from and he'd never have willingly blown up his own army to get mine. Far too protective of his collection—but these new people he's got running things, jumped up crowd of sinners…"

Emma did not like the sound of that. "Jumped up sinners?"

"Apparently he's been promoting the dead for years," Jehovah shrugged. "Was a time when he delegated to former gods—he got

174

them to serve as demons, all the Baals and so on. After we defeated them, back in the old days." He smiled nostalgically. "Never leaves things alone. He said, oh back in the Middle Ages, that he needed to move with the centuries and suddenly Baal the Lecher and Baal of the Flies were all out of the game, and the most appalling people would be turning up in Heaven as his heralds. What's the point of damning people if you have to socialize with them again later?"

"People like Tomas and Heydrich, you mean."

"Far worse, not just politicals and believers, people who do murder for fun. It started out as the new bit of his collection, only he decided to trust them with actual jobs. Trouble with the Baals, was, they knew us back in the day, whereas all these new people suck up to him, grovel and flatter. So he got rid of the old guard and locked them in a cellar somewhere. This new bunch of Praetorians are a total shower—Tomas was about the best of them. Sooner they're back being punished for their sins, the better."

God is not an Englishman, Emma thought, why does he pretend he is one? Maybe I just hear him as if he did and he doesn't really sound like that at all. Also, a bit rich for him to complain that Lucifer has an unbecoming taste for flattery.

From somewhere inside the city, there was another fusillade of automatic weapons fire and a couple of loud explosions. Nearer, with a thud and a billow of dust, another bit of the city wall cracked and fell down.

"So I'm expected to go into the city of Dis, where some sort of last ditch warfare is going on, and talk to a variety of human psychopaths who murdered your last herald, in order to persuade them to surrender and be annihilated or horribly tortured. And then negotiate peaceful surrender with the being who abducted my lover."

Jehovah chuckled as if trying to ingratiate himself. "Oh, Emma, Emma. I have every confidence in you. You've dealt with far more dangerous beings in your time." She suspected that he was thinking of himself in that category.

175

"But it doesn't sound like there's anything in it for them if they surrender. Presumably someone needs to be punished for burning up so many angels. What's to say that they won't try to put our heads in boxes?"

He pulled the face of someone who is finally reluctantly saying what he really thinks. "It's not like you and your friend can't kill every last one of them if that becomes necessary—that armour you've got from somewhere looks excessively lethal, and your friend is sworn to the most lethal group I've ever come across. If Lucifer's Praetorians threaten you, well, you have my full permission to rescue him from them."

Was she supposed to be his herald? Or his assassin? It might have been a while for him, but as far as she was concerned, he had tried to poison her about two nights previously. But how else was she going to find Caroline? There was a lot more that she wanted to say to him, but his face vanished, leaving only the impassive flickering face of the angel, which turned and walked back to the jeep. Of course, if you're the Lord God of Hosts, you have to be able to multi-task.

"What's the layout of the centre of Dis?" She might as well be practical and she had to assume that Luxuriette was not going to be around to act as her guide.

"There are maps. We have lots of maps," Montgomery said. "One of the damned who suwwendered was this chappie who wedesigned Lucifer's Citadel. Came and suwwendered to me personally, again."

"Albert Speer." Emma wasn't even guessing. "Don't tell me. Heydrich mentioned Goebbels. Just how many old Nazis did Lucifer hire?"

The Duke chuckled. "That's why Bernard here got promoted so fast. Knows how they think. Not a flexible lot, your twentieth century Germans—same old tactics assuming that they will work better the second time. Now, if Boney had been one of the damned, different story—but he never turned up in Heaven or Hell, apparently."

Emma looked sharply at Montgomery. "Why wouldn't you think a roomful of old Nazis, leavened with a serial killer, capable of every treachery imaginable?"

"Don't know about politicians. Only know about soldiers— Wommel was a soldier and I beat him all over again. Decent enough chap."

The Duke saw Emma looking perplexed. "Whole war's been like echoes. Except for the start."

She continued to look blank.

"Angels arrive, big occupying force and Genghis or one of the others lets off some kind of modern weapon that kills just about every angel, but blows up and wipes out a big chunk of Hell's army—fries most of the demons. So we get dragged out of choral duties, dumped back into the flesh, and find what we can of our old forces. Same goes on with Hell. So the other Duke, John, finds some of the walls over there were built by his old friend Vauban and gets stuck in; I put together a few squares and a bunch of gallopers and after a bit we find Ney fighting for the other side, has some man called Pickett with him, bloody useless butcher. No art to mowing them down. And a few miles down the line, some Egyptian called Baibars wipes out what's left of the Mongols—apparently that was another famous battle getting done all over again but not one I ever heard of. "

He took one last puff of his cheroot and ditched it.

"Think you can manage this? The Lord God seems to think very highly of your abilities. Didn't use to think women were capable of much in the military and diplomatic line, but then I met Miss Wild, who disabused me of that view."

"Awful woman," said Montgomery of Alamein.

"My particular friend," Which was not entirely true but a good way of embarrassing a man who was starting to annoy her. He had the grace to shuffle his feet.

"So, these plans?" Emma's watch was hidden somewhere under her silver skin, but she looked in its general direction to indicate that time was wasting and she needed to be about her business.

Montgomery reached into the jeep and produced a large scroll, which he unfurled with a flourish. The angel unfolded two pairs of arms and held it up, conveniently—clearly, when not being Jehovah's telephone, it was prepared to act as a holder for visual aids.

We all have our uses, Emma reflected, and I refuse to feel sorry for it.

She looked at the scroll and carefully memorized it. Typical grandiose nonsense—a lot of large rooms of the sort people put over-large tables in for meaninglessly large meetings, and some smaller rooms of the sort where business actually gets done. She paid special attention to the lower floors, which did not seem to make entire sense. Of course, it's possible that space is skewed in Hell as well as time…

She turned to Montgomery. "When your people interrogated Speer, did he say anything about the older palace he built this one on top of?"

She didn't really expect an answer. Oh well, she thought, you know what they say about Military Intelligence.

"Do we at least know whether Lucifer is still in his office, or the state apartments?"

The Duke of Wellington looked down his long nose at his colleague.

"Bernard here lobbed shells into the top floors in the hope of inconveniencing His Satanic Nibs—which John and I both consider damned ungentlemanly but we were out-voted by the Arabs, the Chinese and the Italians. Might as well have saved the munitions— damn place is built out of some alchemical stuff that shells just bounce off."

Oh, well, Emma thought, at least that's something. Once we are inside, friendly fire not a problem.

"Of course, shells that bounced off the Citadel pretty much destroyed everything around it." The Duke sounded regretful, which did him credit in a way. "You asked about the centre—there ain't none. Just holes in the ground and a road made of the same stuff as the Citadel. You'll not get lost."

As Montgomery reached up and took the scroll back from the angel, the angel coughed, irritatedly.

Jehovah was back, and fixed the British General with a glare before reaching up and scratching the inside of the angel's ear. He pulled out the finger a second, and then went in with a finger and a thumb, pulling out something almost undetectably small.

It grew and suddenly it was Luxuriette that the Metatron was holding, not especially gently. Jehovah held her by the scruff of the neck, at arms length, as if she were a piece of litter "Is this by any chance yours, Emma Jones?"

"We met her in Berlin. She's Lucifer's. I thought she might be useful along the way."

Jehovah shrugged, looked at the imp and then at Josette. "You have the oddest taste in companions, but I suppose it gets you results." He flung Luxuriette in Emma's general direction and the imp somersaulted in mid-air, and landed neatly in her previous spot at the front of Emma's saddle. She arched her neck back and squirmed against Emma, then turned her head and looked up.

"Miss me?"

Emma noticed that the Duke was treating this with genteel amusement, and Montgomery with a level of disgust he hardly bothered to veil and which produced small red marks on his cheekbones. Accordingly, she desultorily patted the imp on the head.

"One last thing." She thought she might as well throw this in. "A short time ago, you tried to poison me so that I would come and work for you. And now you seem to have a whole army of the resurrected. Are they going to end up queueing for sticky cocktails and going back to singing? Or have you some other plan?"

"I'm glad you asked that." Jehovah was clearly expecting a question of this kind from her. "Circumstances alter cases and everything has been moving fast. Turns out the Son had contingency plans and once the campaign is over, my new army will have the option of retiring to Heaven, or forming a colony with their former partners if they wish, in a pleasant location we've found them somewhere in shadow. The Son knows the details."

Emma noticed a very faint stiffening of Josette's spine when Jehovah mentioned the Son. Clearly the backstory on all of this was hugely more complicated than she knew.

"Do we get some sort of banner of true?"

"They'll know," the Duke said. "No one who wasn't a herald would be riding into Dis from this side of the walls. Hell's forces are broken and the blockade is total."

"What about the gunfire? Do you have marauders in the city?"

"Not any more. That's just demons and damned humans killing each other. You'll be fine—no one is going to want to risk taking you on and you have a Court imp with you. She is as good as a letter of transit, because Lucifer is still supposed to be in control."

He spoke with the certainty of a serious man who knows his business. Emma was aware that she sometimes over-rated competence as a virtue, but she was inclined to think that in this instance trusting him was not going to be a bad idea.

Emma stared hard at Jehovah, who glared at her a moment and then smiled, as she spoke.

"Here are my conditions. When I get to Hell, I will use my judgement about who surrenders and on what terms. You will honour my choices or I will not go. We cannot assume that Hell has no more weapons of universal annihilation and we need to make this work, for all our sakes."

He nodded.

"I need to hear a yes, because a nod is not a contract."

"Yes," he said, "but be sure that you can live with the settlement you make. Including the violent parts."

She nodded to Josette, who raised her lance in salute to the two generals and their Employer, and together the two faceless silver warriors rode down past the jeep and onto the broad road of hard black stone that led to and through the ruined gate of Dis, the city that men call Pandemonium.

But there were few living demons or to be seen in its streets. This was a city in ruin and it was also a city in mourning, hung with torn black banners. It had been a place with its own beauty once— obelisks carved with forgotten victories and temples to whatever gods demons privately worship and villas, but all were dust and rubble now. There had been great gardens beside the road to the Citadel where black fungus had flourished and red and purple flowers had grown, and all that was left was pulp and rot and ash with just the odd torn petal or leaf to show what had been there. She saw limbs among the rubble and some of them had hands and others claws and hooves, and some of those limbs still twitched with life, and some were still.

On one street corner she rode past a stall where a creature with many eyes sold rats and pieces of bleeding flesh; on the next, she saw a pile of not-quite dead, but horribly mangled, humans that demon guards stood over, jabbing with spears but carefully, and carefully severing limbs that one would then take and place on the stall. One of the victims would die and blow away in the winds of Hell and then the pile would shift and those remaining groan at the motion and the guards would curse that one had escaped them, back to Phlegethon for a while.

Demons could not eat the severed limbs of the human dead, she realized, but the arms and legs of those who still lived, those were another matter.

They were here to stop all this, Emma knew that, and yet they were here as a part of what had been done and what was being done doing the will of the one whose will all this had been.

After a while, she spoke to Josette. "This was always a vile place, wasn't it? Whatever people did to be sent here."

Josette was silent for a moment. "Now you know why I wanted no part of any of it. Heaven or Hell."

"I have not seen Heaven yet. Maybe that will change my mind."

"You will, and it will be another part of your education in disgust."

From the very start of their relationship, this woman had been grooming and training Emma for this. It was almost irrelevant who she had been and who she was now compared to Emma's sudden conviction that Josette was absolutely right, had been totally entitled to do this.

She said, reassuringly and with utter certainty, "We will end this war and then we will find a way to bring it all down."

Much as she still wanted to find and rescue Caroline, there were other things that mattered to her as well. Was it possible to still find Jehovah entertaining company and want first to slap his face hard and repeatedly and then to cast him down from his throne? Apparently so, yet she could not imagine the complexities of how Josette must feel.

But first, the lesser Satan, as her friend Saeed would doubtless put it.

She had never, she saw now, needed to worry about finding her way through Dis to the Citadel. The broad empty road along which she and Josette rode was only the greatest of a network of radial boulevards and circular avenues, and at the centre, where all the boulevards headed, there was visible a great black dome. She had seen it when she first arrived in Hell, but had thought it a cloud of smoke and dust that hung over the city and now she knew better. Higher than skyscrapers or most mountains it stood, and a statue of Lucifer at its top.

Bloody Speer, she thought, he palmed off Hitler's designs as if they were his own.

Yes, a hideous series of rectangular buildings arranged around a centre and that dome above them—the biggest construction she had ever seen.

"The ziggurat was so much nicer." Luxuriette had been silent ever since she returned from the Metatron's ear and what had she been doing in there? Emma shuddered to think. Dropping the fake

182

French accent for one thing, it seemed. "But it reminded him too much of old friends betrayed. And some philosopher or other told him it was a relic of antique barbarism and he should tear it down. Horrible as this is, it's better than the imitation Versailles he had for a bit. Then some man called Malevich turned up full of clever things to do with concrete and a tower that went round and round like a corkscrew, only it fell down in a Hellquake. At least this one looks evil."

"I'd expected a pyramid, or some sort of tower, not an overblown knockoff of the Pantheon."

You get moments of clarity, she thought, and then you're back with the incessant chatter of the active mind and that is probably because you can't bear to live in the clarity all the time. Or maybe other people do—Josette for example. Perhaps two thousand years of concentration and one becomes more focussed.

They rode for what seemed like hours down ruined streets. Hours during which sights of horror became repetitious but the worst horror of all was that this vast city was mostly empty and mostly rubble in which, the nearer they got to the centre, less and less moved and fewer and fewer buildings were even partly standing.

Then they came to the last circle, where theirs was the only road and everything around it for as far as Emma could see was compressed brick and granite and marble and burnt flesh, a mosaic laid by artillery and representing nothing more than pride, brutality and death.

"For the moment, bring peace," Josette said. "But only on terms that are righteous."

Emma answered, "And later, cast down power. For all power is guilty."

She was almost embarrassed, a second later; she was not this person, she did not say such things—but perhaps, in Josette's company, she did.

Luxuriette said nothing, but did not flirt, squirm or make a smart remark.

The ruin was so total that their horses did not stumble, or pick up stones in their hooves; all that happened as they crossed that devastation was that dust sifted up where they stepped and then slowly filled in the marks of their passage.

Of course, the road ended in a courtyard surrounded by steps, because sometimes the cliché is the way to go, and it is always convenient for tyrants or oligarchs to surround those who come to see them with guards on three sides and then have another rank of guards close in behind them. Emma heard feet march down behind her and take their stance. She did not look to see how they were armed or even pay much attention to the troops above and to the side on the steps—either they would fire or not and either the armour would protect her or not.

Even Josette's fate was not important except that they might stop this war and go on to prevent others.

With that in mind, Emma's focus was on the people—they were almost all men who had formed up on the top step to meet them. She scanned quickly—Lucifer was not among them, which might mean that he was waiting for them in some throne room or other, but might equally mean that Wellington had been right and he was no longer the one with power.

Their horses arrived at the steps. She and Josette dismounted and Emma reached up and helped Luxuriette down too.

Their horses sniffed the air and whinnied. Both Emma and Josette stroked their muzzles once and then patted their rumps. The horses looked into each other's eyes and then trotted away—the guards that had closed off the courtyard let them through, to take their chances with the flesh-mongers of Dis and the deserts of Hell.

Josette reached down, and Luxuriette sat once more on her shoulder. Emma's sword disengaged itself from her arm and manifested itself at her side, held there in a scabbard grown from her armour; she placed her hand firmly upon it as she climbed.

Whatever her views in the matter, she was here as the envoy of a victor to the rump of the defeated and they had best be aware of that fact from the beginning.

As befitted her companion and guard—which is what her employer was for all that anyone else, save Luxuriette, knew—Josette similarly had her hand on the sword at her side which is what her lance had changed back into.

Once she was at a level with the coterie that ruled what was left of Hell, Emma scanned their faces silently. Some she did not recognize, others she was surprised to see here, others were largely inevitable.

Wallenstein the Bohemian and Phillip of Spain, Aurengzebe and his ancestor Timur, Richard of England whom men called lion-hearted and Shaka who built the Zulu nation, Cixi of the Qing and Catherine of the Russians, a man in papal regalia whom she took to be Alexander Borgia, with whose son she had dueled, but who might have been his successor Julius. In a small group to the side, the Germans—Goering, Himmler, but not their master; the Russians—Dzerzhinsky and Beria and Yagoda, but not theirs either. Oh, and Kitchener and Mao looking like their posters. Several emperors of Rome and Sultans of the Ottoman realms and a couple of American presidents—Jackson and Nixon.

Nonetheless, monsters all in their way, and she was going to have to talk to them as if they were proper people.

She struck a pose and spoke, before any of them could say a word. "Oligarchs of Hell,"—that seemed the best title for them—"surrender yourselves and Lucifer your prince to the mercy of Heaven."

She was, after all, the emissary of Jehovah and the companion and pupil of Josette and a Power in her own right. Who were these scum that she should be abashed in their presence?

A couple of the purple-clad Romans and the Empress of China tittered genteelly behind their hands, and a small dark hatchet-faced man in a plain black suit limped forward from between two pillars and out onto the top stair almost within reach of Emma and Josette.

"It will cost your Master much to take this citadel, and he will have to destroy all of Hell and most of what remains of those who work or suffer here. And in the end, Hell will need a viceroy to run it, and maintain the blood vats and the ditch of punishment; if Lucifer has proved untrustworthy—and we are shocked to know this—then perhaps we can serve in his place." He sounded mild, pleasant, almost reasonable.

Emma laughed, and not behind her hand. Her voice was clear and loud in that space as if the armour were amplifying her. "Joseph, Joseph, you are surely Hell's jester. I am not here to dicker with those who stand condemned to a second eternity of pain. There will be no deals with any of you, but rather a process, to find which of you were complicit in the use of weapons damnable even by the laws of Hell, weapons that annihilated angels and demons alike, weapons purchased from the Enemy of All. Failure to surrender will be taken as strong evidence of guilt and punished accordingly. If you have any more such weapons, you will hand them over."

She paused, looking hard into all their faces, and they tried to out-stare her and failed.

"Your dead leaders did not trust any of you enough to leave an arsenal here, did they? For fear that you would use them in spite and despair or in petty conflicts with each other."

None of them could hold her gaze. She could not be certain beyond a doubt, but she felt sure she was right.

She scanned their faces again—no sign of Lucifer. "Where is your Master?" she asked. "It is him, and not you, that I am here to see."

"He is not our Master any longer." Joseph spoke with contempt. "He wanted to surrender the moment Heaven's army arrived. Defeatism is always punished."

There was a shuffle of agreement from the rest of the oligarchs, and Emma looked round at the thirty or so pairs of piercing mad eyes glowering at her. Were it not for her armour, she would have felt in danger from those looks alone.

186

"Nonetheless, I wish to speak to Lucifer. Who is at least competent, most of the time."

Goebbels smiled, and it was not a pleasant smile. "Our former Master is in no fit state to receive visitors. But as you wish."

He gestured, and the oligarchs opened a space for Emma and Josette to pass through into a vast empty atrium and down an endless corridor high as an aircraft hangar. Along the walls there were empty plinths and hooks with no pictures—clearly the new regime had removed all of Lucifer's celebrations of himself but not been able to agree what art to replace it with.

Apart from anything else, presumably several oligarchs had been annihilated in the earlier disaster, and others captured or defected—these were the current beneficiaries of those misfortunes. It was not a comfortable feeling, not looking round but knowing that so many nightmares were real and walking just behind her, anxious to show what they had done to someone who had crossed them.

You don't ever let them see you are afraid, and by not letting fear show, you forget that it is there. Mostly.

She was very conscious of Josette at her side; could her employer read her mind through the link she had had with Caroline? She felt, she thought she felt, approval but with the visor down, it was so hard to tell.

Emma also noticed that somehow Luxuriette had slipped away again, gone from Josette's shoulder. Not really the safe place she hoped for—they'll need a cleaner, of course, this place must be the very devil to dust at the best of the time, but I can't see this lot welcoming a cheeky demon soubrette. Even if she flirted.

After some ten minutes' brisk walking they came to the vast public space inside the dome, a space so huge that, half-lit by flaming torches as it was, you could hardly see the other side, let alone the highest parts of the dome. At the very centre of the round space was a pit with raised walls around its side, and fifty feet above the pit floated Lucifer, held there and writhing. Beside the pit there stood a tall thin man, the fingers of whose one hand moved continually in a dance of power.

Lucifer was not the suave, well-dressed figure that Emma had last seen—there was almost nothing of that arrogant sprezzatura left. Instead, his features were smeared with blood and bruising; someone had been at him with their boots and someone else with a razor, both hacking away his hair and leaving trails of cuts. Worse, large parts of his body were covered in purple carbuncles, that stank and dripped, not pus alone or blood, but small malevolent worms that whispered "Failure" and "Defeatist" as they dropped from his body into the pit.

"You can report to Jehovah," Joseph said, "that we have punished him as Herod was punished. And now you have seen that this is the case, we consign him to oblivion."

"Oblivion," the other oligarchs chorused.

"What's in that pit?" Emma heard howling come from it.

"It's where he exiled his former servants," Joseph said, "the gods and goddesses of Canaan and the Philistines. It's where he and Jehovah put the false gods of Olympus when they fell, along with the Titans out of Tartarus. So many powerful beings trapped beyond hope of rescue, and none of them love Lucifer. And what with the war, we haven't fed them lately." He nodded to the thin man, "Simon, if you will."

The fingers ceased their dance and Lucifer dropped like a stone.

"Caroline!" Emma shouted in anguish, and without a further thought ran forward and leaped into the chasm herself.

This really is not a good idea, she thought even as she did it, but at least it seemed that Josette was with her, as her companion leaped with her. It's a matter of remembering what's important—Lucifer is probably still the key to ending this war because none of that lot can be trusted for a second not to start it up again if ever they get hands on the right weapons. Whoever sold Hell weaponry in the first place has their own plans, and putting the death of everything in the hands of incompetent sociopaths would be among those plans.

And then there is Caroline, and he is the one who knows where she is, if anyone does. Or at least where she was.

The pit seemed to go down forever, but maybe that was Hell for you doing screwy things with time. Then she realized that she was falling very slowly and so was Josette—she should not have been surprised after what Josette's armour had done in Dubai, and her armour had to be appreciably cleverer. Josette's was not, as far as she knew, self-aware.

They were gliding down now, rather than falling, though she suspected getting back up might be rather more of a problem—oubliettes are not meant to be easy to leave. And some of the beings imprisoned here had been here a very long time.

At least gliding meant that, although it was absolutely dark down here, they didn't land on top of the very sick Lucifer. It was perhaps too much to hope for that magic armour would be luminous as well, but no matter—Josette produced a flashlight from wherever it was that she kept things, and shone it around.

It was a large space, full of red and angry eyes, belonging to beings that growled and, perhaps more importantly, rattled their chains. It may not have been foresight so much as sadism on Lucifer's part, but it seemed all the denizens of this lowest Hell were on very short leashes indeed.

Josette passed Emma the flashlight and then knelt over the moribund former Lord of Hell; he really did look very poorly indeed. The fall had almost killed him, on top of everything that had been done to him before.

"I didn't think he or Jehovah could be hurt like this."

"You've met Morgan—she lost an eye. And Mara has a scar on her cheek. So far the other two have been very lucky—but that thin man, he was one of the reasons why I didn't speak. He is a Magus, named Simon, and if anyone could learn how to cast a death curse on the all-highest, it would be him. He has scores to settle, not least with me."

She took off the gauntlet on her right hand and laid it on

Lucifer's forehead, ignoring the stink and the worms and the slime.

Emma noticed that Josette wasn't bothering to hide her face any more—and that she grew appreciably pale before Lucifer's flesh was clear of blight, and his broken limbs straightened.

After a while, Lucifer sat up, his face showing signs of deep confusion.

"I know your voice, Emma Jones, for all that you have found yourself a skin of living silver, but you, who have saved me, I do not know your voice or your face, though both seem familiar. But not for two thousand years."

He grew silent and thoughtful.

"I heard the legends of a blood-line, of course. And mocked them. I am the Father of Lies and know a fable when I hear one."

Josette laughed. "I was born of the flesh of the one you remember, but not in the way you are thinking."

Thought so, Emma said to herself.

Now Lucifer was not obviously about to die from his wounds and his sickness, the growling around them grew more intense.

Emma turned to him. "This is your private prison and I refuse to believe that you never came down here to gloat. Perhaps some light, and then some hint about how we get out of here."

Lucifer snapped his fingers, and winced; they were still sore for all that Josette had restored them.

"Let there be light." There was light, instantly, flaming torches some twenty feet above them. It was a joke of which he clearly never ever tired. The light revealed a long chamber, in which some hundred or so gods and demons languished in chains. Iron collars around their throats that were bolted firmly into the walls so that they could not move. Manacles at wrists and ankles with chains so short that they could just about stamp or shuffle their feet but could not have reached their mouths if there were food—which there was not—or scratch themselves if they itched. Some stank with the stink of centuries and yet, from the clear anger in their eyes, had not even had the luxury of going mad.

190

The ones nearest where Emma and Josette and Lucifer stood stank less, and their chains were looser, but not the collars around their throats.

"How could you do this?" Emma found anger almost choking her.

The one nearest her spoke, its voice mellow and almost kind. In the torch-light his great gold eyes glittered with sadness and with rage; he was a venerable man, whose beard almost hid the fangs that lay alongside his mouth.

"We were his companions for centuries, the Baals of Canaan and its neighbours, whom he and Jehovah threw down and made his servants. But then he took some of the damned into his court and they told him he should have worshippers and no fellows and they clustered around him and flattered him. And one day he turned on us and cast us in here, with the Olympians, whom we helped cast down, and the Titans they threw down themselves. And now he is here himself, as is only justice."

A light and tuneful voice, yet melancholy, sounded from further down the chamber. "It is not justice, but merely fortune's wheel. And perhaps we will rise up on that wheel as it turns."

The voice sang of Fortune and Mutability for a minute or so, to a tune that seemed to Emma both archaic and familiar. Beside her, Josette wept to hear it.

"What, Lord of Delos, are you here?"

The singer was young and so beautiful that it hurt Emma's eyes to look at him. Most of the prisoners in that hell had faces distorted by anger and suffering, had been forced into demonic ugliness, but what was terrifying about him was the sense that nothing could change him, that his intellect and his music were utterly independent of time and place. Inasmuch as his bonds would let him move, Apollo shrugged.

"I did a deal." His voice was tender in its wry cynicism. "I handed myself over to Jehovah and his gaoler because they said that if I did, they would leave the Muses alone. I could leave here at any time, but I trust them to keep their word knowing what I would do if they did not. I can think here, as well as anywhere. Now others rule Hell, and my arrangement with Jehovah and Lucifer is at an end."

He looked intently at Josette and his attention made the area around her as bright as day.

"You are familiar, but that may be only because you heal. I had a son who healed, and whom Zeus over there slew."

However interesting all this was, it was beside the point. Someone had to take charge. Emma looked to her employer, who nodded. "Lucifer, you and I have an account to settle, but that can wait a moment..."

"I don't have her. I mislaid her. She escaped."

Somehow this came as no huge surprise, and as something of a relief. After all, Caroline free and taking care of herself was considerably less worrying that Caroline in the power of malevolence.

"Which just goes to show that actions taken out of spite are usually a very bad idea, doesn't it? All this unpleasantness could have been avoided if you had simply left us alone."

"Or if you could have been trusted to keep your mouth shut about other people's business," the Father of Lies snapped, not entirely untruthfully.

"Which is as it may be. But things are as they are and I am here as Jehovah's emissary and I think we need to get out of here, with all these unfortunate prisoners, and do something drastic to the unpleasant clique that are keeping this stupid war going by not surrendering."

She looked around at the prisoners. "If I make Lucifer free you, can you refrain from anything much more than minor assaults on him? He is, whatever else happens, no longer Lord of Hell, so revenge is pretty much redundant."

This did not go down too well with the more monstrous denizens of the further corners, so she thought she had better delegate.

"Apollo, you seem reasonable enough—can you keep your old enemies under control?"

He stepped out of his bonds—he had not been lying about that—and nodded to her.

She looked at the more recent prisoners. "You're all mostly called Baal, right?"

They growled and nodded.

"Behave yourselves and I will speak up for you with Jehovah. He lost a lot of angels and there's probably jobs for you all if you want them. Not sure about the Titans." She turned to Lucifer. "Some arrangement for freeing them all by waving your hand? Or do you have to go round and unscrew their collars and gyves individually? Whichever it is, snap to it."

She really didn't know how they were going to get out of this pit, but Lucifer might have an idea and there was no point in not keeping him on edge. He had to get used to the idea that he was not in control and she was the person, for the moment, with actual, if borrowed, power.

Also, she liked the idea of impressing her employer, who was clearly choosing to remain anonymous for the moment with this lot.

"While you're doing that, tell me how you get in and out of this pit?"

It turned out that the chains and manacles were held together by magic, but Lucifer had to make a whole series of passes to remove them, and hadn't practiced, on the assumption that he would never in an eternity want to do so. He made several false starts, and Emma's hand played menacingly on the hilt of her sword.

"I can punish you for prevarication. I can hurt you really rather badly, and then have my companion here restore you to go through it all again." She really objected to torture, but Lucifer did not know that, and as far as she was concerned, he lived in a grey area where threats were lawful currency.

"I can't get in and out by myself. My bird Tsasipporash carries me. And they'll be hiding from Simon Magus, whom they helped bring to agonizing death. When he was just a courtier, all he could do was stare at them in hatred, but now he is one of the most powerful of the Grand Council of Hell and…"

Josette interrupted. "The children of the Bird are many things—cautious, perhaps, and not excessively loyal—but none of them have ever been cowards."

"But even if Tsasipporash comes, they cannot carry all of you up one at a time; they would tire and you would suspect me of treachery."

Josette smiled the smile of someone who has a plan, has had the rudiments of a plan for some time. "If she comes, she will only need to come and go once. I cannot guarantee her safety when she comes, but after that, Simon will have me to contend with."

"And if she doesn't come," Emma pointed out, "sooner or later I won't be able to protect you from all these people who are very annoyed with you, and they will have nothing to look forward to except revenge."

This was not perhaps so much a threat as a refusal to sugar the pill.

The former Lord of Hell finished his passes and, with an undue amount of creaking, squealing and raining of rust, the neck collars opened up and withdrew into the walls and the chains fell apart link by link.

"I'm waiting."

In the darker parts of the cell, there was mumbling. There were Titans there with many arms—perhaps not the hundred advertised, but more than Emma would have thought feasible—and they started to pick up the fragments of chain and braid them together, broken link by broken link.

Apollo glared at them, and they looked at him innocently, as if there were no threat implied in their pastime.

Lucifer looked where the noise of scraping metal was coming from, and shuddered. Then he looked up to the impossibly far away dot of the entry to the pit and made a loud cawing noise. He had no especial gift for imitation. Nonetheless, inside the tiny dot of light far above them, there was, of a sudden, a red speck that became a redness that blotted out that tiny light and dived and dived and was suddenly a blood-red bird, with fancifully trailing pin-feathers and tail feathers, almost effete but with a cruel beak and talons that dripped with a red as bright as its feathers.

It settled on its master's shoulders.

"It is good to tear into Simon again after all these years," it cawed. "His new flesh has more blood than there was in his old."

"I feared that he would blast you, my darling." Lucifer petted the top of its head and then stroked its beak, licking the blood that was wet there from his fingers.

Tsasipporash peered around. "This would be the Emma Jones, of whom we have heard much. And her companion? Doesn't she look like—?"

Josette fixed the bird with a glare as glittering as its own, and it fell silent.

Emma held her right index finger for the bird to nuzzle or mar as it chose. "I require your help, Tsasipporash, child of the Bird, in the name of Jehovah, whom your sib serves and whose plenipotentiary I am, charged with ending this war and sorting out the governance of Hell."

Emma still wasn't sure that she got all the stuff about the Bird and its children, but it made sense that Jehovah had one, and that it was this Ghost he kept talking about. Though she doubted it was actually Holy.

She nodded to Josette, who picked up instantly. "Fly us close to the surface, and I will take it from there." She reached within her armour and produced a vast cruel silver hook, which trailed what seemed an infinite amount of rope.

"Jehovah's fish-hook, with which he caught and pained the monster Leviathan and Simon called Peter trapped and killed Simon Magus, with the help of Tsasipporash here and Mara the Huntress. It is mine by right, for I took it from the mouth of Leviathan. I have it now from the tomb of Simon Peter in Rome, who borrowed it for a little while."

She looked round at the assembled gods, demons and Titans.

195

"Once the hook is in place, climb. One at a time. Apollo, Lucifer, take charge and come last. I trust you, Lord of Delos. And you, Lucifer, I expect to see your self-interest in making this run smoothly. Emma, come with me—we may need to establish a bridgehead and I trust you to fight at my side."

Lucifer looked concerned. "I do not know that Tsasipporash can carry both of you. I would hate for them to fail and you to fall."

"I know one of their siblings, and have seen her carry far more than that. The children of the Bird are as tough as they are old."

Emma took the red bird's left talon and Josette the right. It flapped its baroque wings once, and twice, and suddenly they were in the air and heading for the surface faster than they had glided descending.

As they rose through the air, they heard shouts and screams from above them, and the clash of weapons and the hissing of flame. A body fell past them screaming all the way down, his Hugo Boss suit torn and charred—his face was bloody but Emma knew it was Josef and was not even slightly sorry for him. Then another, and a third.

When they neared the top, Josette flung the hook. It caught the lip of the pit—it would be truer to say that it reached out and grappled it as if it had a mind of its own, which it probably did—and held even as the rope dropped and the first climbers started.

Emma saw the rope tug and the hook hold and engage ever more deeply with the edge of the pit. Then she was past and on a level with the ground and she and Josette drew their swords as they dropped and rolled and came up side by side in a fighting stance...

To find no one there to fight.

The only person in the great hall of the dome was Luxuriette, but not as they had known her.

The imp was now larger than the Titans they had left below and reclined on her side. Her red skin glowed with sweat as if she had taken exercise and her belly was distended as from a heavy meal. She smelled of blood and sex and vengeance.

"Hello girls," she said, the French accent gone altogether. "Miss me?"

196

Emma asked, "What have you done with the Grand Council of Hell?"

The being who had called herself Luxuriette licked her lips and then reached up and removed a particle from between her teeth. "About now they should all be waking up in Phlegethon—or perhaps not. There is something of a queue there these days, I believe."

"I knew that there was something off about her." Josette was slightly flustered. "Didn't I say so?"

The red cartoonish titan shimmered and shrank and became a tall, elegant brown-skinned woman in a considerably more fashionable version of evening dress, and terrifyingly high heels.

"You did indeed, and, may I say, you are not in a position to make remarks about other people's metamorphoses. Though I must say, yours suits you rather spectacularly well."

"We've met?" Josette looked puzzled.

"At the wedding. There were a lot of us there, you won't remember."

She walked over and pecked first Josette and then Emma on the cheek. "Aserath," she announced. "I'm an old friend of your father's. It's so nice to see you both again and looking so much happier." She paused and considered a second. "How rude of me, I haven't asked your name, these days."

"Josette In Arcadia Ego. Of the House of Art."

"Oh, they're yours. How clever of you. Hiding in plain sight is always the best strategy, don't you think? Though Luxuriette was quite the most annoying persona to live up to. I don't think I shall ever let anyone handle me that way again."

"You said, both of us." Emma was aware that there was something she was missing.

"Well, the wedding, obviously. You mean you didn't know?"

Emma and Josette looked at her blankly.

"You mean, neither of you know. How priceless." She laughed and it was like silk-wrapped hammers on some musical instrument. "Enough gossip. We have serious matters to discuss."

197

By now, various Baals had emerged from the Pit and were standing around looking confused.

"Help the others out, boys. Mother has sorted things out, as usual." Aserath's voice was commanding and mocking at the same time. She turned to Emma. "I fear Jehovah wasn't entirely frank with you, though I think we are on the same page on most of the decisions that have to be made. I had a chance to speak with him privately—the Metatron is his ear as well as his voice, you see. I suggested that I take over as Queen of Hell—that's what we'll call it for the moment, because the boys here are so very old-fashioned."

Josette was still looking grumpy but Emma could see there was much to be said for this. "You mean, you'd rather be, say, Co-ordinator of the Anarchist Collective of Beings Resident in the territory previously known as Hell."

Aserath laughed. "I knew we'd see things the same way."

"And no more torture."

"Such a bore and so bad for the character."

"Jehovah isn't going to like this," Josette smiled. Emma had seen that smile before.

"There are a lot of things in this world that Jehovah is not going to like, and he has been getting his own way for far too long. Or thinks he has, I should say."

Emma was not entirely sure that all of this was not too good to be true.

Aserath looked around her, disapprovingly. "This building will have to go, for a start. Something far more modest and considerably more comfortable. What was Lucifer thinking?" She turned to one of the Baals. "Baal-Meon, this is your sort of thing. Find one or two of the damned who know about this sort of thing and get them to start designing—not Speer, of course, and certainly not Malevich. What's his name, Stanford White? He should still be around somewhere."

By now, the last of the Baals were out of the pit, along with the Olympians and the Titans. Aserath helped Apollo over the lip of the pit, then reached in for Lucifer.

"I told you, Star, so many years ago, that one day you would over-reach yourself. Too clever by half, I always said so, and now look at you. Hell is mine now and there is no place for you here." She reached down and tweaked him hard between the legs. "And next time you feel like groping the help, remember..."

She turned to the bird, Tsasiporrash. "I know you children of the Bird are loyal, but -"

"I have other plans," cawed the red bird.

While this was going on, Emma felt Josette's hand on her shoulder and looked around. Josette placed a finger on Emma's lips.

"You need to go and talk to my father," she said, "and I am not ready to speak to the old bully and liar. We will see each other in due course, and I will try to get you news of Caroline."

Emma could not understand why Josette was talking as if they needed to come to a parting of the ways. Josette looked at her sorrowfully. "Remember. We will break the power." And was gone from Emma's sight, and gone from the great hall of the Citadel of Dis.

Aserath came over, all business. She put an arm on Emma's shoulder and squeezed her in a way that was almost, but not quite, intrusive. "If you've an hour or two, we need to go talk to Jehovah, and take Lucifer with us and make some arrangements. I'm sure you've got a lot of ideas and this is the time to push them through— he will be feeling vulnerable right now after losing so many angels and it's a good time to start changing things."

Aserath snapped her fingers and Lucifer joined them. He had shaken himself back into some semblance of his old smoothness, but Emma could see from the way he deferred to the new Lady of Hell that he was a broken god.

It was almost embarrassing to have him bow to her; no, not bow, cringe.

"I want you to know, Emma Jones, taking Caroline was just business, nothing personal."

Emma glared at him. "I don't care. You've tortured millions of souls for two thousand years and I am sure that was business too.

199

The sooner I never have to speak to you again, the better, because if you don't have Caroline in your possession, once I have handed you to Jehovah, I am done with you."

He made as if to say something else.

"You don't understand, Lucifer. You are not the Lord of Anything any more, and that makes you deeply boring."

Normally she didn't kick people when they were down, but every rule needs an exception.

As they walked back down the corridor to the open air, Emma noticed that the halls of the Citadel were somehow less gloomy. Once they were out on the steps, the reason became clear—the sky had changed colour and was not a sort of mauve.

And the circle of devastation around the Citadel was covered in red grass and tiny purple flowers, that she had seen before, in shadow.

She looked at Aserath, puzzled, and the goddess shrugged.

"You must have brought the seeds with you. Thank you."

"But how?"

Aserath looked smug. "I am a fertility goddess—it's what I do. Along with my destroyer aspect, of course."

She flickered, and for a second Emma was walking alongside the slithering of a great serpent that breathed fire. The serpent flickered again, into the imp, and then back into the beautiful woman.

"And the trickster aspect to keep the other two in balance, of course. Cycle of life thing gets boring otherwise. I just did some major destroying, so having the seeds to work with just made it easier to clear up all this wasteland. I'd been thinking in terms of green, but actually this works better with the sky…"

Emma thought it was no humiliation to ask for some clarification. "I thought gods and goddesses had to have some kind of massive system of worshippers, or kill a lot of people."

Aserath gave her a pitying look, "Well, of course, some very insecure beings need all that. Some of us just do the work and everything else comes along with it. You just pick what you do and

200

stick at it. Dear Thoth, for example—scribble, scribble, but it works well for him. Oh, and there are all the other things—leader of a nation, invention of a way of thinking. Night journeys, ridding the world of monsters, descents into Hell, loss of a loved one, some colossal act of self-sacrifice—those will bump civilians up to hero status easily, and quite possibly to godhood. It's all a matter of attitude."

She whistled, and after a while the two horses Emma and Josette had been riding earlier came back. Aserath swung herself into the saddle of the one Josette had been riding.

"The sooner we go and talk to Jah, the sooner he will get—what's the expression—his tanks off my lawn…"

The armour put Emma back in the saddle, fortunately since she was still unsure that she would ever get the knack of doing it for herself.

A couple of the Titans led Lucifer down the steps. They had brought the fragments of chain with them from the Pit and braided them into a quivering metallic leash, attached to a collar around his neck. They handed the leash to Aserath.

As they rode back through Dis, Emma watched the grass and flowers spread in a wave-front wherever Aserath passed. The ruins did not repair themselves, but vines and the runners of gourds started to twine round them—the red and purple and black colour scheme seemed to be universal, though the gourds as they swelled had an orange tinge as well. By the time they reached the inhabited areas of the city, the butcher's stalls and the piles of tortured bodies were gone; instead, both humans and demons stood in lines on the streets cheering, though many of the humans were still missing limbs and looking askance at their monstrous neighbours.

By the time they got close to the walls, the vines were fruiting and the populace had things to throw at Lucifer, who was soon dripping juice and pulp. Aserath looked down at him consolingly. "All for the best, sweetie. If I hadn't given them fruit to throw they'd have been throwing stones. And you need to look nice and humiliated by the time we meet Jah. It's really for your own good in the long run."

Emma really did not care. She rode in silence, thinking of what she would say to Jehovah.

The gates of Dis were gone altogether, as were the ruined walls, replaced by a thicket of roses and thorns that grew higher and higher as Emma watched them, and two rowan trees, rich with fruit, where the gate posts had been.

Aserath caught her watching the rosebushes. "Think of it as a mission statement, dear. I need to make it clear to Jah that I won't pose any kind of threat to him—I've been overthrown by him before, and it was No Fun At All. It would have been far more unpleasant, had we not come to some sort of occasional understanding."

Clearly a certain moral flexibility went with the goddess's attributes—Emma found herself missing the slight priggishness of Josette. Almost instantly, she felt guilty that she was not missing Caroline, her beloved of twenty years, as much as she was missing this mysterious employer turned new friend, with a backstory she could still not quite believe.

By now they were in sight of Heaven's camp. A couple of cherubs were blowing those silly little trumpets they have in Renaissance paintings, to announce their arrival.

Astride a white stallion, Jehovah was riding up and down inspecting troops all turned out in breast plates and hussar hats, regardless of their nationality, ethnicity, or historical period. I suppose that if you are the Lord God Almighty, Emma thought, and was aware of her own petulance, you can play gallant tin soldier with people's lives as much as you like. You'd think he would have better taste, given how many of his angels got annihilated.

Just taking long enough about it to make it clear that he was making a patronizing concession, he saluted his troops one more time, and rode out to meet Emma and the new Queen of Hell-or-something-like-it.

Aserath rode up to and alongside him and leaned across, pecking him on the cheek just above the edge of his beardline. As she did so, she tugged the leash so that Lucifer tumbled and fell.

Again, Emma felt appalled by the staggering triviality of all this theatre, and then she realized that she had said it aloud.

"Emma, darling,"Aserath cooed, "some of us older beings lack your intense moral compass. You must excuse us. You know, Jah sweetheart, she has some wonderfully radical ideas about how I ought to run this little realm of mine now you've been so kind as to give it to me."

Jehovah rumbled, "I told both of you that I was pretty much prepared to go along with whatever you decide. Under my old friend here"- his voice dripped with irony so thick that he might have well have spat it in Lucifer's face—"the place has ended up being full of death traps created by some vile enemy, and a source of personal profit for its former Lord. Frankly, I am thinking that the whole thing is more trouble than it's worth."

Emma felt that she ought to butt in. "There are some very bad people here, people you don't want running around making alliances with Beren or whatever his name is. Aserath ate them, so they are out of action for the moment, but you have to put them somewhere."

Lucifer added, "None of my business any more, of course, but there is this rather deep pit—"

"And that's quite enough from you," Jehovah snapped, clearly angrier at every word his former partner in crime uttered. "You're lucky I don't build a deeper one and throw you into it."

Aserath tutted, "I don't mind keeping a bunch of souls around that you don't want running anywhere else. Horrible people, they tasted vile in my mouth—rather not have them in the flesh again. I might be sick next time around. But yes, if we put them all in some kind of big bottle, I'll look after it."

Emma felt she had better go on while she had these people's ears. "But a lot of the people here, probably shouldn't have been here anyway. How does it make any sense at all to torture people with fire and acid, and periodically rip out pieces of their minds, just because they fought on the wrong side in some war, or stole bread rather than starve?"

"Got to make an example?" Lucifer really wasn't going to shut up any time soon.

"I don't want flaming torture swamps any more," Aserath was almost petulant in her distaste. "They're ugly and they stink, and as Emma rightly points out, they're wrong."

"How are people going to know right from wrong?" Jehovah sounded genuinely baffled.

"By setting a better example? And having a sense of proportion? I repeat again, hundreds of years being burned to death over and over again, over a loaf of bread that was probably stale to begin with." Emma was aware she was shouting and that it probably wasn't helping her case, but she had had a very vexing few days and it wasn't getting any better. Also, the nice thing about mysterious silver armour and a sword that fought for itself, was it meant that for the first time in her life perhaps she wasn't the least dangerous person in the room, and she might as well enjoy it while it lasted.

Jehovah, though, was surprisingly conciliatory. "Good point, I suppose. Son's being saying things like that for years and Ghost has too. I suppose if Aserath here doesn't want Hell to run as a place of punishment any more, and everyone's too tender-hearted about fire and brimstone…"

Lucifer butted in, still trying to suck up to the most powerful person present. "I'm surprised they're not asking for personal therapists for the worst sinners."

"Rehabilitation of serious offenders ought to be the goal of every serious penal institution." Emma found herself quoting some civics manual she'd glanced at, she couldn't begin to guess how long ago. "And punishing the innocent discredits justice."

A sly smile played over Jehovah's lips. "So what you're saying, both of you, is that we should clear most of the damned out of

Hell—except for a few dangerous people who should be locked up forever, but not actually punished, just confined."

The sarcasm was now dripping in her general direction, but Emma persisted. "I know it's supposed to happen during the Apocalypse, but couldn't we just run out the whole sheep and goats thing ahead of time? It will save time later, when you'll probably have other things to worry about and do it badly and in a rush."

Jehovah's smile got ever broader. "That's all very well, but where would I find a judge prepared to spend thousands of years of subjective time deciding who was innocent in the first place, who has suffered quite enough and who needs sticking on a box until the end of time? Where would I find this paragon, prepared to sacrifice themselves to stop injustice?" By now he was smirking.

Aserath took up his theme. "All us old beings are set in our ways. It needs someone flexible and young. Your companion, what's her name, clearly thinks very highly of your judgement. Also, you smell of immortality, so you have all the time in the world to take this on."

Emma knew she was being unsubtly blackmailed with Josette's identity, and held her peace. Lucifer finally shut up, partly because he was laughing too hard to speak.

Emma had a lost girlfriend to look for and an employer to understand, but all those poor people…

She had never thought before that a sense of duty could be like biting on a piece of accidental tin foil.

"You hate the idea of the job, which is precisely why you know you are the only person you can trust to do this." If Jehovah smiled any harder, he would break something.

For the very first time since she had met him, Emma wanted to punch him very hard on the nose and knew that she absolutely could not. He was a horrible old bully, Emma thought, but he understood her as well as she did herself.

"I'll give you a really spacious office to work out of, and we'll have girly lunches all the time." Asearath clearly thought this was going to be a consolation.

A cawing came from the sky and suddenly the red bird was perched on Emma's shoulder. "And you'll have me to give you good advice."

"What about me?" Lucifer sounded hurt. Even better, he'd stopped laughing.

"It's been swell," Tsasipporash trilled, "but you wouldn't want me cluttering your retirement suite, would you?"

"Berlin, I think." Jehovah snapped his fingers and Lucifer was gone. "Now, young Emma?"

"Oh, all right." Emma could see no way out of it. "But I'll need a staff and a big table."

And someday she would have emptied most of the damned out of Hell and be able to get on with her life.

Forgive me, Josette. Forgive me, Caroline. Some things are just more important.

As she completed that thought, she felt a tingle deep inside herself. It was like a golden flower unfolding somewhere deep in her core; it was like a strong cup of coffee and it was like exhaustion after orgasm combined with the tenderness of eyelashes on cheeks.

As she watched, incredulously, her silver armour turned to gold.

"She told you." The voice in Emma's ear sounded for a moment like the red bird, but it was coming from somewhere a deal closer and more intimate, a voice that was a little like Caroline's but different. "Night journeys, loss of loved ones, saving the world, monster-killing, descent into Hell. And self sacrifice clinched the deal. You just became a goddess, Emma Jones. Welcome to the world of grown-ups."

"Oh bugger," Emma said, and flowers wilted under her horse's hooves.

Oystershells and Ashes

The East and Alexandria 415 CE & Paris 1307 – 14 CE

"So, Hypatia?" Crowley looked at me over his glass.

"I hadn't mentioned her." I glowered at him. "I hadn't been going to."

"You've been dropping all these hints about the terrible thing that drove your sister's soul to madness and I have been paying attention. Like Gibbon. You mentioned that she talked of Cyril in her ravings and I have had a proper education. I know what he did to her, he and his young enthusiasts—it's a horrible story and I have a suspicion that what actually happened was even more horrid than the standard accounts state."

He did not exactly lick his lips, but he was showing altogether too much enthusiasm.

The trouble with talking to this man was that, companionable as he could be, he was still a potentially murderous magus with a nasty mind and unpleasant sexual tastes. On the other hand, I had needed to talk about some of these things for a very long time.

My visit to Herr Doctor Freud a couple of years earlier had not been nearly as productive. He'd wanted mostly to talk to me about the provenance of various of his curios and I'd had to tell him that the Umbrian statuette of a warrior was not a good representative of the male principle, because it was supposed to be a portrait of me. Not, as it happens, a very flattering one. He had sulked for a moment and then offered me a cigar.

Just a cigar.

It was Jung who made a pass.

I had hoped that the talking cure would be of use. There were one or two things about what had happened which were still a mystery to me—perhaps a new pair of eyes and ears would help, a new mind. It wasn't just Alexandria, it was Paris. She wasn't the only person I lost in Alexandria that year. And I had help in Paris that came out of nowhere and disappeared into nowhere.

Perhaps talking it through would help me remember something I had forgotten. And talking to this awful man was better than nothing.

So...

If I'd come any later, I would have missed her.

She'd still have died, almost certainly, and it would probably have been bad. But not as bad as it was. Her death was not, primarily, about her—it was about power, who had it, who could demonstrate that they had it and who was prepared to use it most ruthlessly and with least restraint. All that would have remained true even if I had not returned.

She would have remained the same person, pig-headed in her certainty that reason was queen and that everyone was a man of good will. Without me, she would have gone on thinking that the wild dreams that filled her nights with riot were a disorder of the humours to be dealt with by more fasting and more sitting up looking at the stars and contemplating the dance of numbers and symbols that Diophantus had left so full of enigmas and ambiguities.

Between them, Orestes and Cyril would have killed her because they could not have helped themselves.

I never understood her because I did not have time, and she never understood herself because she did not know about herself until she was old and white-haired and within a few weeks of tragedy.

Yes, she was old and white-haired, and I know the legend says otherwise, and there is a reason for that.

For most of her life save for the first three of those last weeks, I was elsewhere.

It was a busy time for me. It seemed as if every week, I came across altars and piles of the flayed, and would follow the trail of corpses until I found a warlord, his mouth wet with the grease and blood of the dead and new fangs or hair or muscles sprouting. There were new Flat Ogres in those years and other things that were harder to kill.

Those were busy years, and they were years of burning. The Goths crossed the rivers on the ice and all the others followed them and suddenly Rome, that had not been taken since the Gauls save by its own sons, was sacked by Alaric as if it were just another city.

At the other end of the world, the realm of the Han had fallen, and then the Three Kingdoms that had followed its fall had themselves fallen and crumbled into statelets. People said sixteen, but there were times when it seemed as if at any moment there might be more—or that one lord would sweep the table and take everyone's counters.

There was peace in Persia under Shapur who had beaten back Julian the Philosopher, and Shapur's son Yedzigerd, whom men would have called the Good if there was any real gratitude in men. In India, the realm of the Guptas led by example. Elsewhere, fire and blood. Behind the Goths and the rest, there rode the Huns, and behind them, pushing them both West and East were the Avars and the Rourans, empires of fire and blood.

I was kept busy in those years, because men who wish to take what is another's will seek out ways to do so with greater efficiency, and men who wish to hang on to what they have, and take back what they have lost, will do the same.

The Silk Road, which had run from one land to another for league after league, was broken, and it was gods and demons who broke it. And the monks who stole the worms and the leaves, and hid them in staves, and brought them to the West.

The legacy of the man or men who called himself or themselves Kaschei, and spread the word of how to become the Undying across the steppes and down into the Caucasus, spread and spread and I thought there would be no end of little gods grown out of the Rituals.

Sometimes I grew so sick of the filthy little games they played with victims—sometimes travellers, but as often their fellow-villagers and kin—and of killing the misshapen things that they usually became that I wandered off for days or weeks, even though there was more killing to do, into the wastes where nothing grows but straggly grass, and wild onions that only a starving man would eat and that I did not need to.

I did not expect to see any living thing save plants and the small hungry mice of the desert that feed on them, and the falcons that eat the mice, but I heard a distant calling in the sky and there, circling and calling, were two of the great vultures I would not have expected to see for leagues east or west of here.

It was late in the summer, and the desert was almost hot, as well as dry, and the vultures were doing that strange dance in the sky, coming together and locking their talons in what is almost a death-dive, the terrible mating of great carrion birds. They were a breeding pair and she was not yet gravid and there was a fierce beauty in the way they paced and plunged through the sky on dark wings.

Then they plunged again, stooping to take prey, and I heard a terrified scream from one of the gullies that break up the dunes and rocks of that part of the western desert of the land of China that is called the Gobi.

Much as I wished to be on my own, I would never leave someone helpless to have their eyes pecked and their intestines clawed out of their bellies. As a general rule, I kill cleanly even those malefactors who have tortured innocence a thousand times over—as a general rule, though I have on occasion acted foolishly out of ill temper. I am, after all, human and not a god, and ill temper is part of the necessity of that condition.

So I had followed the birds as they called to each other and did their terrible love dance, and now I watched as they hovered over the gully. Hovered, when they would have been well advised to fly far away and raise a clutch of eggs—for of a sudden great wings beat out of the gully and something that at first sight looked like their larger sibling burst from covert, soared above them and then dived, taking one lammergeier in its talons and catching the other in great hands at the ends of arms that joined its trunk just below the wings, yet no longer looked as if they belonged there.

It crammed the first, the female, into its maw and bit off her head and then took the rest of her in great bites. The male in its talons gave a cry of anguish that preceded its own similar death by seconds.

I said that the Rituals produced worse things than Flat Ogres in those years, and this was potentially one. It still had teeth inside that beak, teeth that included great canines that belong in no natural mouth or maw; its eyes still looked forward for the most part, though it seemed as if they had started to migrate to the side of its head, and among its feathers there still straggled a few long dark hairs.

I have, for my own good reasons, a distaste for magical birds and once killed a Great Vulture that preyed on the folk of the Kalahari—but that was a bird of prey grown out of the natural idea of such, as the Platonists would say, or perhaps as a god of such, because the Bird I met in Atlantis, and its children, and its other child, the Phoenix, are not perhaps the only gods of birds. This, though, was none of these. It was a man, or—as seemed likely from its harsh malign eyes that wept and the straggles of hair—a woman, who was working the Rituals to become such.

It dived back into the gully and I heard that scream again, but it was still a scream of terror and not a scream of pain, so I did not wait to find out more, but dashed to the gully's edge, drawing a sword as I ran—this was a case for quick decisive action and I was not sure that a spear thrust would serve. I have killed harpies, and their feathers are made of iron, and this was a larger and more terrifying beast; though it had, unlike harpies, once been human, I did not care to take the chance that my first thrust would go awry.

The feathers that clad her neck in a great red ruff were not, as it happened, made of iron at all. I dived into the gully and she looked up at me in a surprise that remained in those terrible, still weeping, still human, predator's eyes even when the head rolled into the dust some feet away and I wiped the sword clean on her feathers and put it back into the quiver at my back.

At its feet, tied and staked and starveling, lay five small men in monk's robes, one of whom was still screaming in terror. Two of the others chanted softly to themselves, and one was either asleep, or unconscious, and snoring gently. The last, though, hardly noticing my arrival, still murmured consolation to his friend.

"All is illusion, Peng." His voice was gentle even as it implied rebuke. "Extinguish desire and life and death are as one. To die in the beak of one daughter of evil, or be saved by the sword of another, it matters not to the noble mind. All we can wish is that we come through this particular illusion and make it to our destinations, for there is great knowledge in the land of Hind that we might learn from."

He looked up at me. "You would be Raga, would you not? Who stands for Passion? For she who captured, tortured us, bound us, and killed the birds who came to devour us was clearly Tanha, who stands for craving." He smiled ironically. "I had hoped that the next

212

temptation would be Arati, who stands for boredom, but there seems little chance of that."

I took one of the knives from my hair and cut first his bonds and then the bonds of the other four, and used its point to prick, delicately, the one who snored until he shuddered, yawned and woke.

"Thank you," said the first monk.

"I am not Raga," I announced. "I am the one men and gods call the Huntress."

There was no point in my mentioning my other name, for Gautama made sure to confuse his followers hopelessly about me. For them, Mara is a demon, a male demon, whose daughters Tanha, Arati and Raga are. Three sisters who are craving, boredom and rage—rather than wisdom, endless change and the protection of the weak against the strong. A parody, you see, of me and my sisters, and one I consider in rather poor taste.

It was very petty of him, and remarkably unforgiving. Perhaps I should not have tried to talk to him when he was meditating under that tree, but I had felt his quickening into godhood from thousands of miles away, and thought it a good idea to recruit him to the struggle against the Rituals.

We just had different priorities, and he was being obstinate about his. And has remained so, even past the point of its making any sense whatever. After all, many of his followers have been victimized in Rituals of Blood, or fallen prey to their temptations; it's not as if he doesn't know that I told him the truth all those years ago, on a bright morning, in the shade of a tree.

Perhaps I should have sat down with him in silence for a while, out of respect. I had come a long way and was impatient.

He is a philosopher as well as a god, and his ideas have not changed. He thinks perhaps that one day the one who stands behind the Rituals will declare himself and come to him, and Gautama will be able to prove to him by logic that every evil thing he has worked for for so many centuries is an irrelevance, that evil

213

can find calm from the storms that rage within by sitting still and extinguishing desire—that his reign of death is but a shadow of the tranquillity of the virtuous man.

Perhaps he is right, but I doubt it.

In any case, his servants are men and women of good will, who do less harm than the followers of some religions I can think of, which is not to say no harm at all. I took to the young monk, Xien of the Fa, and decided that rather than starve my palate, so soured by human evil, I would sweeten it with the presence of human good.

Perhaps in the process, I used to think, and still hope, I would persuade Gautama that friendship between us would be more use than enmity. He is, after all, a pragmatist.

So I wandered with them, for a while, from library to library, in the land of Hind. The two who prayed calmly were calligraphers who could do a good copy in a fair hand, and the monk who panicked was an illustrator, whose own work was charming enough, but whose true skill was in precise copying of other men's. So many scholars, as anxious to hide as to explain, put their secret thoughts in the decorations at the side of a text, and if they are one day to be deciphered, they must be copied perfectly. This was his skill.

Peng, who was terrified all the time, had a mind that, because of that fear, tried to see order and pattern in all things, and sometimes found patterns that were not there, but more often, because he was a clever lad, saw patterns that existed and that no one else would have noticed. Xien tried at all times to convince him that all things were illusion and often succeeded, and that belief kept Peng's terrors from driving him into madness. Xien, however, actually believed no such thing.

He was a man who believed in the utter realness of all he could see and touch, and in the utter irrelevance of that solid reality, an utterly virtuous and kind man who believed in the futility of virtue and kindness. Kindness and virtue were good in and of themselves, but changed nothing.

He was good company and I lingered with him and the others for far too long; I would hear of one I needed to kill, make my excuses, do what had to be done and then return. The Gods of Hind enquired politely, after some months, whether I was taking up residence in their land—Ganesh and Krishna took their time to get to the point, which was to offer me a place in their pantheon if they wanted it.

I had been useful to them all, as I so often am to established pantheons, because I weed out upstarts with nasty manners. I despise all gods, though, even the nice ones, and I resent that so many of them insist that I consider myself one of their number.

Even after Xien had left on the long sea voyage that eventually took him home, I stayed a while to guard Peng and his last companion the painter as they wandered the temples of the Gods of Hind, noting down representations that might, perhaps, have been quoted in the decorations of the manuscripts Xien had taken their copies of. I noticed that they paid especial attention to those temples which contained representations of the art of love—tantric exercises, Peng said, when I asked him, important to study those because the curves those bodies make may well be used by some scholars to denote a more spiritual love.

I was sceptical of his argument and his entire honesty, but I was enjoying their company and let it pass.

One day, as we were looking at a sculpture of a woman caressing an improbably large-penised crocodile god, the great lizard's stone eyes opened, green and alive, and my old friend Sobekh, who is enough lord of all crocodiles these days that he can speak through them anywhere. He looked down at where he was, and at the women who was teasing his flesh, and said in an embarrassed and urbane voice, "I don't know why they do that—I'm not that interested in such things…"

Not every divine being spends their whole time in rut, you know. And in his case, different species and not built that way.

Then he looked at me in alarm. "Glad I've found you. Been looking everywhere. Some angels are looking for your friend the

215

faun—he pointed his snub little nose into some papyrus or other and found something he shouldn't. Come back to Alexandria—they've been stomping round what's left of the Museion and with the Serapeum gone, it's the only bit of the city worth saving. They have flaming swords—in a library?"

So, obviously, I had to go back to Alexandria, which I had been avoiding for a couple of centuries. Nothing there for me, I thought—she's obviously being born somewhere else.

Sobekh? Well, that's a long and interesting story—I could tell you that instead. I'm sure you'd be more interested...

Well, if you insist on the short form...This was the second Sobekh, of course, the nice one. Still around, even now, though sleepy most of the time. Don't go disturbing him...

The nasty one? Well, that was the first Sobekh. Nobody liked him—showed up one day, picking something disgusting out of his teeth and hung around the judging of the dead like he belonged there. Then he did the same in Thoth's scribe school, and followed Horus round when his Birdship was hunting in the land of reeds. Bold as brass, as you English say, and just as hollow and second-rate.

Made himself popular with the younger godlings—taught them back-gammon or some such and that game Egyptians teach their children that shows them how to cheat their way through the afterlife and into the land of reeds in safety. Big half-human crocodile, made a style statement by being covered in gold jewellery and having big muscles like a human wrestler, not like a proper crocodile—tiny phallus though. Head so full of teeth it almost weighed him down.

Isis didn't take to him—said he leered at her—and sent me a message asking me to have a look at him. Now, I don't really fit in in Egypt; some of them are older than me, and a lot of them blame me over the unpleasantness that happened a bit after Crete blew. Not my fault at all. Yes, most of them are still around. Land of Reeds is off in shadow and they live there. Jehovah has some respect for gods that much older than he is, as long as they let him drive them out.

216

I hung around as she had asked. I had a few friends out there in the Land of Reeds and one or two of them owed me favours as well, favours that I did not need at that time, but was keen to remind them of.

The moment I clapped eyes on him, I could smell the Rituals on him.

Isis is squeamish about blood because finding your beloved in bits will do that to you. Out of respect for her, I waited. He slipped away from court, out through the Douat when Ra was in the sky and not using it, and I followed him.

He slipped in and out of shadow. I'm pretty certain I know how not to be seen but some people are just evasive for its own sake. We came out at a shrine by the river far, far upstream, and it had a big pool, full of crocodiles, big well-fed ones. I looked in the mud at the bottom of the pool—not a pleasant job, but I do like to know what I am dealing with, a point those who try to deceive me need to remember. I found skulls, mostly, the odd pelvic bone, and fragments of femur. Most of the rest of them had been digested.

He had started off as an overseer at the quarries, up beyond the cataracts, and he wasn't very good at that. So they put him on disposing of dead slaves, and then dying slaves, and then slaves they wanted dead because his colleagues could pocket the money sent to buy food. And he started with one crocodile and taught it to come and be fed, and then more came, and he noticed how well he felt when he threw slaves who were not quite gone yet into the river, and he had slaves build the shrine, and the pool and the crocodiles were well fed that day.

Some people who play with being a beast lose themselves, but he never did. He saw the crocodile shape as one he could put on and off, and gradually, ever so gradually, he became not just a shape-changer but a god, of sorts.

He killed the other overseers, and their clerks, and the man who came to enquire why shipments of stone had slowed, and his escort. Perhaps Hatsheput would have sent an army in the end—she was

217

prudent, that one, unlike Rameses, say—and perhaps that would have been the end of him, but, as it happens, I was.

I chopped his crocodile head off and, when it changed back to human, threw that with his body into the pool. I am careless sometimes and fail to think things through, but then, nothing happened for a long time. The crocodile that ate his head, and then the rest of him, digested him slowly and it was a while before it changed. He changed...

I heard from Isis again, because, like me, she has a sense of justice. Here was a creature, born from the Rituals but intelligent and moral enough to want no further part of them. He had been born with all the memories of the dead man, and with a moral sense, whether deduced from first principles or just natural to crocodiles, I know not. He turned up in the halls of the dead and asked for judgement—and Anubis refused it him, said it was my concern.

The thing is, the second Sobekh was born not just with morals, but with charm. He grins at you with all those teeth and it is only threatening when he wants it to be, and it is all a fraud because he does not eat people. I suggested strongly to him that it would be a bad idea, that it might lead him into bad habits, and he agreed without demur. After all, there are plenty of things that crocodiles can eat.

I worried that the god part of him might starve and I had one of my bright ideas. I do have them occasionally. Apollo had moaned to me that the minor cult of him was in charge of granaries, and diseases, and therefore of mice and rats, had resulted in mice worshipping him, which he regarded as beneath his dignity.

So I arranged with him that he gift the worshipfulness of mice to this nice young crocodile god, and it's an arrangement that has lasted to this day. Not much prayer in a mouse, of course, but there are a lot of them.

What do you mean, you thought a being had to be intelligent to pray? You know better than that. Even in a sarcastic sense.

I went back to Alexandria, because he was not a creature to

summon me lightly or to use his power to look for me through the eyes of the creatures that are his. I said farewell to the monks, and paid my respects to the nearest God of Hind I could find, which as it happened was Shiva, who merely glowered and nodded as if I were some minor deity of no account.

A little to my surprise, young scared Peng tried to persuade me to let him come with me, but I sat him down, and told him tales of my travels with Star and Nameless, and of the city of the Bird that men call Atlantis. He answered that he shared his name with the great bird of his people's legends, of how she rises from the water where she is a fish, and how this is a metaphor philosophers use for awe and freedom.

I had not known because though I understand all men's speech it is at the expense sometimes of hearing their words. On this occasion, though, I understood the words behind his words, that he accepted my counsel, but was ashamed to acknowledge the great fear I had put him in.

He was a nice lad, more a poet than a sage; I hope nothing ill befell him as he travelled home. Alexandria would have been no place for him. It was not the city it once had been.

I stepped out of shadow, and a young bearded man in a black tunic struck at me with a staff, though as one wishing to punish rather than to maim. "Cover yourself, sister," he cooed. "The days of pagan immorality are done and good Christian women do not parade half-naked."

I flung glamour into his eyes, much as it grieves me to waste power in this way, and he saw me otherwise, and brusquely apologised. Then a shout went up from down the great avenue— "Orestes is killing the holy man!" they shouted. "Come witness martyrdom. Ammonius joins the saints this night." And the like. Crowds were rushing up and down the street shouting and striking at each other—monks from the desert with their straggly beards and ragged robes, and more disciplined younger men like the one who had accosted me, and mercenaries from all nations, who seemed

219

more interested in preserving their skins than in bringing order. Also a lot of ordinary citizens, trying not to get in the way of the people inflicting violence on each other, but heading in the same direction as most of them.

I followed the crowd. Always the best thing to do when in doubt if you are invulnerable. Also when you are looking for marauding angels, prone to intervening in religiously-motivated civil unrest. As I walked briskly in the wake of the largest group, the ordinary citizens, I listened to the gossip.

"Tried to stone the Prefect, they did."

"That's not going to go well."

"Cyril is a man of God, and Orestes is some sort of heretic or pagan."

"Hypatia will calm them all down."

"She's a pagan."

"Yeah, but she's the right kind of pagan, the sort that doesn't make trouble."

"She's a philosopher."

"How does that work, when you're a woman? I thought philosophers had to have beards."

"She's way old."

"Still beautiful."

"Not for the likes of us."

"What are they going to do to this Ammonius?"

"Stone him, probably."

"That's not much fun to watch."

"It is if they use small stones."

I was sure that, when I found Sobekh, he would brief me with the same basic facts and take several times as long.

As we moved down the avenues, I noticed how the city had changed in the last century or so, and not for the better. The slums were that little bit more filthy; the big houses had not been painted for a long time; the temples were either in ruins or converted into Christian churches by slapping a cross on the front or tearing down the old good statues and replacing them with newer cruder ones.

The Pharos was still there, towering over the harbour, but there was no sign of its great mirrors, reflecting the sun in lights that danced across the water to direct the ships, and the great tritons that also helped direct the traffic were dumb and their faces marred where someone had tried to take a hammer to them. Even from the wharves, I could see potholes in the road along the great causeweay, as if someone had stolen cobblestones and they had not been replaced.

One day, quite soon, it would be dangerous to take a cart across it, and on that day the fire would fail that had burned in the Pharos for five hundred years and more for there would be nothing to burn in it. And on that day, Alexandria would cease to be the great port and become a backwater and start to fall into the sea, and the marsh.

It still shipped grain—no longer to Rome so much since the city's sack by Alaric the Goth, for the rich men who controlled the trade no longer regarded the City as a good risk—but to Byzantium—and the great grain ships still docked there, and fishermen brought there catch to market, but gone were all the medium size ships that traded jewels and books and silk and other precious things. The glass that used to ship to Rome now shipped from the Red Sea ports to the lands of Hind.

I looked down one of the avenues as I crossed it and saw where the Serapeum had burned and fallen, with the scholars of its library martyrs in its ruins. Some of its walls had been shored up and a roof, with a cross, placed across them. It looked like a rotting wooden peg where once there had been a healthy tooth.

The marketplace stood where it always had, but was a shadow of itself. All save the slave market, which prospered as ever. And the barracks; they had painted the red bricks white, and had stuck above its door a crude image of Josh in torment, but the barracks stood in the bright sun as brutal as ever. Before it, a great crowd watched in silence, as an army executioner gave the monk Ammonius an almost gentle stroke with a three string flail. The

221

white back of the assassin was criss-crossed already with marks of the flail and yet he had hardly started to bleed—it was as if the executioner were just stroking him to death, was taking his time.

On a curule chair, close enough to watch every agony on the monk's face but not so near as to be splashed by blood when it came, sat a handsome man in his thirties, his face marred by a great bruise and his laurel wreath placed over a bandage around his forehead.

I hoped that the silence of the crowd was compassion and grief, but from the looks on their faces it seemed more likely that it was enjoyment, and worse, appreciation of artistry.

Ahead of me, elbowing their way to the front of the crowd even though they could have flown, were the two angels that Sobekh had spoken of, their flaming swords held above their heads and yet somehow unseen by the crowd, even the people prompted by their invisible presence to get out of the way.

Angels do have a taste for watching people die. Jehovah likes to think they are just obediently waiting to take souls to their proper destinations but that's just one of the areas in which he is a foolish optimist.

I sidled up behind them and placed a firm hand on the left shoulder of one and the right of the other, shoving them gently together as a hint that I could have knocked heads together had I chosen to.

"You've been bothering a friend of mine?" Though I was pretty certain these were the angels I was looking for, it was just conceivable that two other angels were in Alexandria and up to no good. I've told you before what I think of angels.

"Oh shit, it's the huntress," one of them chanted in that annoying way that angels have, even when caught unawares.

The other tried to bluster. "We are on a mission/ working the will of God./Do not come between us/and our missi…"

I cut him short before the other could come in and harmonize the final cadence. "Don't lie to me." I kept my voice to a monotone because angelic singing can be infectious if you do not watch yourself. "I know ill-disciplined, corrupt, free-lancing angels when I see them. It's something about the eyes—you get a violet tinge."

They looked at me truculently, as if they fancied their chances.

I laughed. They were, after all, at best jewel spirits and at worst random afrits and dust devils that had been lucky when Jehovah was hiring a lot of help and lowering his standards.

"Better beings than you have tried it, and ended up whimpering. I could make this official—I could pop to Heaven and check with my old friend Nameless and be back in three minutes with a squad of Seraphim. Or you could just leave town, now."

One of them cast a wistful expert eye on the execution.

"Now." I had no patience.

And they did that thing angels do, where they recede not only into shadow but into what seems like a long corridor of perspectives. I could do that, but I refuse to waste power I have harvested from the murderers of innocence to do flashy little tricks.

From the west of the market, a chariot drove up, pulled by two absolutely white horses and shod with gold. A woman held the reins, but was not tugging at them even when the chariot drew almost to a halt, so that the crowd could let her through. I noticed that she carried no whip, either, either for horses or pedestrians. She was tall, thin and elegant, and dressed in white, a white mantle cast around her head and largely hiding her face from sight.

The crowd parted for her, and not out of fear that she would trample them.

"Said she'd come," one of the people standing near me spoke in hushed and reverent tones, even as he bragged about having guessed right.

She drew up the chariot—the horses halted completely without any obvious word of command—some paces short of the whipping post and the executioner, placed the reins delicately on the handrail of the chariot and stepped down, so carefully that not a single crease of her gown or mantle altered its perfect line of fall.

Though he was clearly in pain, and found standing difficult, the man in the chair rose to greet her and made a hand wave of respect.

"Hail, learned Hypatia." His voice was full of genuine admiration.

"Hail, your grace, Prefect Orestes." Her voice was soft and mellow and I knew it well, though I had never met her before in this one of her lives. "I have come to plead for mercy."

"It does your tender heart credit." There was a firmness in his voice in spite of the grimace of pain it was costing him to stand even for so little a time. "This man has not only tried to kill me, Prefect of Alexandria and Lower Egypt, but he has raised tumult and disturbed the Emperor's peace."

I could see her smile through her veil—age and good humour had drawn soft lines around her mouth and moderation in diet had left her cheekbones prominent, but not jutting. This life, and the sixty years of it she had clearly lived, suited her well.

"I would not ask you to set aside justice, merely that you exercise restraint." Her voice was quiet and clear and precise, as if it were she that sat on the magistrate's chair. "He tried to kill you with a single blow, and you should do likewise rather than torture him to death. Whatever you do, Bishop Cyril will declare him a martyr, but the people will know what you did and what you did not do. Kill him cleanly with one simple blow, not with an elaborate performance of painful death; he is, after all, however ill he serves him, a man dedicated to the God you share with him."

But not, I noted, with her. This Hypatia was still a pagan of sorts, a dangerous thing to be in this city, now.

"I would comply with your request, but I am indisposed, as you see." Orestes returned to his seat, and indeed he looked genuinely ill. "And Leo here takes a genuine pride in his work—he would hate to leave the task I have set him half done. Of course, if you were to give the mercy stroke…"

She nodded, and turned to the monk. I could not know whether Orestes knew her only too well, or not all that well at all; in any case, she had come prepared, and was not here for half-measures.

"Ammonius, we met once, years ago, when you were still a philosopher."

He spoke with effort. "When I was still damned for the sin of pride in intelligence, you mean. As you will be, unless you repent."

"Has abandoning philosophy for fervour and violence made you a happier man?" she asked, and when he did not answer, said gently, "Go whether to your God, or to the One who made us all."

She took a small thin blade from the girdle around her waist and placed it expertly into his heart. He gasped once, but his eyes were blank and dead in moments.

She nodded to Orestes, once, and then to the executioner Leo, to whom she handed three gold pieces. "I would not take a working man's employment away without compensation."

He touched his forehead and bowed to her. "If someday you could teach me that stroke, I would be grateful and so would the wretches condemned to die."

His voice was at once impressed and wheedling, but she treated him with utmost seriousness, as if, for a moment, they were colleagues. "Find me at the Museion. I will take you to the lectures in anatomy there, and you will learn much, and perhaps teach more. Not enough is known about the ways in which the body experiences pain, and like other honest working men, you know as much as scholars."

Clearly, the life of the mind in Alexandria had changed, and in some ways for the better—Aristotle's distaste for the practical had bedeviled the Museion for centuries, so that even a man like Hero had had to pretend his little steam whirligig was just a toy, because the practical was beneath the true sage.

She rested her hand on Leo's shoulder in friendship, and then she turned back to the man she had killed, closed his staring eyes and kissed his forehead.

She turned back to the Prefect Orestes. "I have willow-bark tea for you, if you would like me to bring it to you. Do not take the poppy; it sorts ill with injuries to the head." She curtsied to him, with just a hint of flirtation. "Do not rise. I know my way."

She stepped back into her chariot and her horses whinnied once and wheeled and turned.

"Sof," I called out from the crowd. She looked back at me in panic—the veil fallen from her face—then turned and pulled the reins once, twice and was gone at speed, back in the direction of the Museion.

Where my path led in any case.

If the lady Hypatia, whom I must learn to call by her name even if I still thought of her as Sof, had hoped by her bold action to bring peace, she had been naïve. Hardly had she left, but a detachment of the young enthusiasts in black tunics gathered together and started after her with cries of "Kill the murderer of Ammonius," only to be attacked by a group of their co-religionists, the filthy monks of the desert, shouting, "Blessed be her who saved Ammonius from torture". Many of the ordinary citizens stood a little way off, and showered both groups with rotten vegetables from the market stalls; I even saw some of the more prosperous element buy particularly vile vegetables in order to throw them.

I found myself remembering why I had loved this city for so many years.

Then Orestes rose from his chair, aided by his executioner, and shouted "Clear the streets" to his soldiers—those immediately in view and a detachment who appeared from within the barracks, and another which he had concealed behind the slave market. Which the troops did, none too gently, but using the flats of their blades rather than the edges.

If this seems harsh, remember, he had served his apprenticeship in governing on the streets of Byzantium, where a minister can fall if the wrong team wins the chariot race, where the mobs have been known to burn a quarter of the city, and where the putting down of a riot can leave twenty thousand dead. I did not stay to see how the riot and its suppression developed; it was not my concern, whereas I had a faun who might still need protection, and a long-lost love to perhaps rekindle.

You look askance at the idea of my pursuing a woman who, in appearance at least, was so much older than myself, and that just demonstrates how utterly superficial you are. An eternal love does not reckon such things—or so I thought, to everyone's cost.

"Love is not love which alters when it alteration finds?" Well, precisely. Oh, the Stratford man. Wise as often as not, that one, no wonder you people made him a god.

I had seen two angels off, and it seemed unlikely that they would come back, but they had an employer, clearly, and there was the question of what my foul-mouthed young friend might have done to interest someone with enough power and wealth to bring angels into the game.

Even ordinary angels cost a lot—not as much as the seraph Newton hired, of course, but then he had the mint of a mighty nation in his power. I cannot think how much it would cost to hire a Power or a Dominion, or the consequences if you approached the wrong one, and I have never known for certain that there are any Powers or Dominions that a person could corrupt, if she needed to.

Like the rest of Alexandria, the Museion was in disrepair. Hero had built great fountains in its gardens, but there was no one left who knew their secrets, and for the most part they were dry and filled with dust, or played in sudden spurts that were more likely to wet passers-by than have the delicate aesthetic effect for which he had striven. Another generation had had a taste for peacocks, and those had flourished, almost suspiciously so; I can concentrate no matter what is going on around me, but I cannot imagine what it was like for scholars late at night with so many of those useless birds screaming outside.

The question was, how would I find the faun? He was presumably hiding from angels, and was likely to be good enough at it that the rest of us would have some difficulty in finding him. He had been working in the library almost since his orphaned childhood some four centuries earlier and was still irritatingly adolescent. Fauns take a long time to come to maturity, if they ever do, and there is no point in being irritated with them. They are naturally delinquent.

Nonetheless, he knew the library better than almost anyone—both how to find forgotten scrolls and how to hide books no one should ever read. I relied on him to keep records of the Ritual from coming to light more than occasionally; he had ethics that precluded his destroying anything, but putting scrolls in holders that seemed to be just a fourth copy of a treatise on rhetoric, or the sermons of some Christian divine, that—though even such tricks pained him—was something he might do if he thought it needful.

All of this meant I was liable either to spend hours wandering aimlessly in the stacks, or to have to hope Sobekh would turn up, and have set up some sort of system for meeting him periodically in a safe place. For the moment, I just wandered randomly, noting how shelves that had once been filled to bursting, and yet carefully ordered, were sometimes almost empty and at others spilling onto the floor.

The quality of what was on the shelves had gone down. I was not so old-fashioned that I regretted the increasing replacement of papyri and other scrolls by parchments bound into codices. What worried me was that little of what was actually in the codices was worthwhile—good poets were being forgotten, while the uninteresting decisions of Christian councils were being endlessly and tediously commented on, and every word preserved as if it were by Plato or Plotinus.

Once you would never have seen a moth anywhere in the acres of rooms that the Museion consisted of—now, in the darker rooms, they swooped and twisted in the beams of light that pierced the heavy shutters, which had not been, from what I could see, replaced in decades. In the walls, there was scurrying and squealing—once the Museion had magics upon it that kept rats away, and now they had to borrow cats from the grain warehouses and leave them to breed and hope that they would keep the rat population at least under control.

Scurrying? I listened carefully and above me I could hear tentative hoof-beats, several stands along and up to my right. I backed carefully to the end of the row I was standing near, as silently as I could manage without using magic, so as not to alarm him.

Rather too quietly, as it happened, because as I backed round a corner into the next aisle, I met someone, also backing up and coming the other way. We tumbled over each other in a flurry of white linen.

It was the Lady Hypatia. This close, this intertwined, it was even more obvious to me that she was Sof, but from the look of horror on her face, it seemed that she was not entirely aware of the fact.

There was an embarrassed silence during which she stared at me long and hard, as if I were the first thing she could see on awakening from deep sleep.

"Are you the Huntress? Mara? Of whom the old pagans speak and the newer romances?"

"I am."

"But that cannot be." She spoke as one trying to convince herself. "Such things do not exist. There is the world we see, and there is the transcendent realm of the One, and of the forms he created. And all is susceptible to reason."

I wanted to kiss her, but not as much as I wanted to smack that smug pedant Plato around the face a time or two more. If you ask me, he has caused more mischief in the world, and more self-delusion, than Gautama and Lao-Tse put together.

There was no point in not confronting her head on. "The world is not as you think. I am Mara the Huntress, who protects the weak against the strong, and you are Sof, who sought to understand the workings of time and fate. You are wisdom, who dies and is reborn, over and over. And I have loved you, in one life and another, for five thousand years, and mourned with you our sister and lover Lilit. Who has been lost to us both, for five thousand years, and one day, perhaps, will return."

She reddened; it suited her. "Is it fleshly love of which you speak? Unnatural, and doubly so because incestuous and thus beastly?"

I was clearly going to have to explain a lot of things to her. "I thought that you were not a Christian."

She drew her lips together tightly and pulled away from me.

"It is a foul lie, far too often found in the mouths of Christians who should tell the truth, that true philosophy by itself leads to sexual immorality. That is not what reason tells us."

I looked deep into her eyes. "Forget what reason tells you, my love. What does your memory tell you, of all the lives we have spent together?"

She was still trying to deny the truth to herself. "My father Theon listened to my stories, when I was a child, and told me that they were no more than dreams, which seem real for a moment when you come awake, but then vanish. He told me many children have an imaginary friend, who seems as real to them as any other, just as the Christians have their guardian angels and their protecting saints. But true philosophy..."

"Everything your memories tell you, is true."

"But that cannot be, because that would mean I was both Miriam the Jewess and Maria the Egyptian, who devised alchemy, which we know not to be true. It would mean that I was that Maria who married Josh, whom the Christians say was the son of God, and—"

"All true." I was aware that a slight asperity was creeping into my voice.

"Bugger me with the phallus of Osiris," came a voice I knew from somewhere above us. "I thought you two were supposed to be protecting me from murderous angels, and here you are, arguing about your love life. Kiss her, Huntress, and get it over with before we all die of thirst and hunger and winged hooligans rip my balls off and feed them to the peacocks."

It wasn't bad advice, but I also saw that she was frightened, and feeling every one of the years that lay on her shoulders, so I kissed her, once, very gently on the cheek. "Your father, who loved you, no doubt, was wrong, but meant well. I did not know you were protecting the faun from angels too."

230

"And you think I'd have no other reason for wandering round the library?" She was slightly indignant, and defensive. "As my father's daughter, and as the editor of Diophantus, whom no other scholar here seems able to make a fist of understanding, I have rights here that no other woman has."

I coughed gently and pointed to myself. "I have always had rights here. Ptolemy put them in a clause of the charter and Callimachus renewed them. As you would see if you studied the charter."

"I read the charter, but thought those clauses…"

The faun sat on the top of the bookcase we were now standing against, tapping his hooves against the upper shelves. "I always wondered what women did together, and stick a radish up me but it's more tedious to watch than I expected."

"We're not—"

"She's not—"

The faun laughed at us. "You so obviously are. It's obvious now. I don't know why I never noticed it before, but I was very young when Maria was still around. Lady Hypatia, you do know that you used to,"—he made a noise with his lips that was clearly supposed to imitate sexual congress of some sort—"in another life, of course, which you may feel does not count."

I thought I had better explain the situation to him, since the longer we spent on it, the longer it would be before we could consider his situation. And he was obviously tiresomely fascinated. "She doesn't precisely remember."

Hypatia got slightly flustered. "I do too. It's just I didn't believe— because transmigration, goetia, marrying the Christ, the Great Work of the stone and the elixir, monsters and sorcerers, oh my."

"You're used to having me trotting round stacking shelves." The faun pointed at his naked chest, furry thighs and personable horns and hooves. "What did you think I was?"

She looked embarrassed. "Father Theon always said you were an unfortunate freak of nature, but I must not think that meant there were whole tribes of you or that centaurs were real."

231

"Freak of nature? Oh that's so fucking charming. I am one of a proud people, just the only one who stuck around once it became clear that Christians thought we were some sort of demon, and started pointing two fingers at us in the streets. We and the centaurs exist, we just sodded off into shadow because we know when we're not wanted. And I was an orphan who'd mostly been reared by humans, so I stayed."

I thought we had better get back to the main issue, and that was his safety and not her beliefs or our sexual past. I am good at priorities. "So, angels? I had a word with them and they've gone away for now. But that probably means they will be reporting to their employer, whoever that is, and if he or she or it doesn't tear off their heads and eat their wings, they'll probably end up coming back. Obviously, if I am here, I will drag them back to Heaven and throw them to an archangel...But that still leaves their employer. What on earth have you done?"

An unbecoming whine crept into the faun's voice.

"I was just shelving some scrolls and I sometimes look at them, in case there are smutty pictures in the margins. And there was this one, it was very old and it fell apart when I looked at it, but it said something about how the sleepers would awake and the Ring of Flesh would burst and all would be undone. Do you think it's important or something?"

I had not heard a single being utter those words, save the young god on the day he made me what I am and gave me my mission. Except for myself, obviously, when I tell the story of that day. I was taken aback, in the way you are when something you thought was a secret proves to be less of one than you thought. I still had no idea what it meant.

Hypatia looked blank. She opened her mouth a couple of times as if still thinking and not quite as ready to speak as she had just thought, and eventually ventured, "It's clearly some sort of apocalyptic prediction, but not one talked of in any religion I can remember reading about."

"I heard it once. I've known many gods but none of them have ever mentioned it to me. Come to think of it, even the Bird can't have known. Jehovah knows about it, because I told him and Lucifer back when we were all much younger, but that man lives in denial about everything that doesn't suit him, so he's probably forgotten. It may be that only I knew it, up to now. Neither of you should probably ever mention it again, though."

The faun looked piqued, as if this were something that made him special, and which he was not going to give up on anytime soon.

"Maybe it's a message. Maybe I'm supposed to tell someone."

"And maybe when you do, you will get yourself and them killed." He might have a point, but I was not going to concede it. "Maybe somewhere a long way away and a long time in the future."

When dealing with truculent adolescents, I find the best thing you can do is put off the evil day. When it's a faun, this may mean you get to put off the evil day for several centuries, which is a plus.

"In the meantime," Hypatia had an I'm the practical one, who knew face on, "we'd better find somewhere really safe for him to hide. I mean, really safe. So that when people come looking for him, we see who and what they are without putting him at risk."

She was obviously very clever. I saw nothing wrong with her plan, except that I had no idea of what a fool-proof, angel-proof, secret evil overlord proof hiding place might be. I said so, and she looked crest-fallen.

The faun was excited. "I've got a coffin. It's got a picture of me on it and everything. You could put me into a magical sleep like in a romance, and only wake me when it's over."

Hypatia and I looked at each other wryly, and I smiled. "That's a very silly plan. So many things could go wrong."

He looked disappointed. Hypatia reached up and patted one of his hooves. "We'll keep it in mind as a last resort."

The faun smiled down at her, then jumped down and smiled up at her—he clearly had some sort of crush. Then he turned to me. "So, the Lady Hypatia turns out to be your Sof, come again. Aren't you going to kiss her or anything?"

Hypatia looked sadder than I had expected from an ascetic virginal academic. "Why would a young woman like her want anything to do with an old woman like me?"

I laughed at her.

"First, I am thousands of years old. Second, this is not the first time you've been sixty. We haven't always been that lucky, and quite often, in earlier times, you died much younger than this. You always age well, when you get to."

She blushed a little, then continued without answering me. "For the moment, let's go to my rooms and drink some millet beer."

Personally, I never liked the stuff, but Egyptians always drank it, and then the Greeks got the habit. And I am polite in these matters. These days, I almost miss it.

I have known millionaires and princesses with apartments less well-appointed than Hypatia's. Sof always had good taste and in this life, she had location, a selection of art from the Museion's vaults and a remarkable view. She had ascetic habits—probably slept on a mat and always dressed in simple white—but that just meant that the rooms were not cluttered. Everything was placed where she could reach it easily or look at it without having to walk around things. In one corner of the room there was a small table with a portrait of a woman, painted in the Alexandrian style on wax, upon it, surrounded by dolls, toy animals, and other relics of childhood. Otherwise, it was a scholar's room—star charts, several pairs of dividers, a scribe's inkstone.

Having lived with her when she was doing the great work, and there were retorts, and dried flowers, and things turned into gold, everywhere, and we lived in the slums because of the smells, I found this an improvement.

I sat on a couch she clearly kept for visitors and never used herself; the faun joined me, lay back and put his hooves up. Hypatia winched slightly, but he patted where his hooves were with a careless hand. "It's all right, I haven't been anywhere to get dirty. Just the stacks where there's nothing but good honest book dust."

He was right, there was no mark on the plain red fabric.

She busied herself with beakers and a jug which sat unobtrusively on a table at the other side of the room, then brought it to us on a small tray. The faun drained his in five sips. I sniffed—and I didn't like millet beer any more than I had eighty years earlier when I was last in this city. I noticed that Hypatia was sipping hers very slowly and had poured herself a far smaller beaker. The faun reached across and took my beaker from me.

"I remember, Huntress, that you don't like this stuff. Well, all the more for me." He drained this second beaker and then shut his eyes and yawned. "Don't mind me. You have things to talk about. Wake me if you decide to do anything that might amuse me. Put out my eyes with Thoth's stylus, but that's strong stuff."

He started snoring. The faun didn't even wake up when a very old, very angry man threw the door to Hypatia's apartment open, walked in and slammed it shut.

"Father?" She cringed in a way that no daughter should to a parent who loves her.

He walked up to her, closer that anyone who is shouting ought to be to the person they are shouting at. He was a surprisingly short man. "Have you gone quite mad?"

He paused for breath and I took a second look at him—he had the broken blood vessels in his cheeks that indicate either habits of intemperance in drink, which I doubted, or a perpetual passionate rage that would one day soon burst his heart or his brain.

From the way that this lovely intelligent brave old woman cowered before him, it could not come too soon for me.

"Bishop Cyril is standing outside in the gardens with forty of his young black-tunicked acolytes, demanding to speak to you. I do not know what you have done, because he would not tell me, but he is very angry. And I find you here, having some sort of orgy with a deformed book messenger and some street scum you've picked up

235

from god knows where when you should be working on Diophantus and his equations. Lazy, ungrateful girl."

Suddenly she was not cowering any more, but in a passion as great as his. He could criticize her person and her behaviour, but not her work. "I finished my edition of Diophantus weeks ago—it is with the scribes and copies are being sent all over the world as they finish. You would know this if you ever paid real attention to a single thing I do. As to the faun, he has had a shock and I am looking after him because he has been essential to the smooth running of the Museion for three hundred years. But you knew that, and chose to lie to me, and say he was a deformed slave who should be treated with pity and contempt."

She paused for breath and for a second I thought she was going to cry, or start to remember to be scared of her father again.

"And this is the Huntress, Mara -"

"You think some street slut is the imaginary friend you amused yourself with in childhood. You are mad..."

He made as if to slap her, and I twisted his arm behind his neck, reasonably gently in token of the fact that he was an old man. Then I marched him, against his will, but gently still, and put him down on the couch next to where the faun was sleeping.

"I will treat you with respect because you are father to the Lady Hypatia, and a philosopher in the fine tradition of this place." As I spoke, I fixed him with a withering glare that belied my words. "I knew Socrates, and Plato, and Aristotle, and Philo, and you are not the equal of any of those men. None of them would have worried about the opinion of Bishop Cyril, even if he threatened their lives, as he almost certainly would if they were here."

Theon quailed for a moment, then rallied and turned his attention to his daughter again.

"And you expect me to believe with the Pythagoreans or the folk of Hind that metempsychosis is true and you have lived many lives."

She went to the table with her childhood toys, picked up three balls and began to juggle them. "I never learned to do anything like this, simple childish games of skill, father, because you wished me to be the best mathematician, the best astronomer, to excel all save you. And look, I can do this"—she made a complicated pass and catch above her head and then behind her back and then spun the balls as she caught them on an upturned finger of one hand, steady on top of each other.

He gawked at her. "When in Hades' name did you learn to do that?"

"When I was the mystic that Socrates called Diotima, father." She giggled, as if she were a young girl, and for a moment, she was that young girl again, rope-dancer and expert in many erotic skills whom Socrates loved and considered at once his greatest teacher and his greatest pupil. And who had died of a flux, in her twenty-second year, mourned by us both.

Thinking of her, and the other lives in which I had known and loved and lost Sof and found her once again, I walked over to the table of toys and looked at the portrait again. I could see the resemblance, and, seeing it, could see how closely Hypatia mirrored both parents, mingled, and for that I found myself losing my anger to the father who bullied her but had also reared her.

He saw me looking at the picture of his dead wife and I told him that I was sorry for his loss.

I put my hand on his shoulder, in compassion, but perhaps a little too firmly. He did not flinch which might have the beginning of some sort of trust between us had things been otherwise.

It was a moment though, and he moved to business. "That's all very well, but what are we going to do about Cyril, and his young thugs?"

The door opened—not this time as an expression of rage, but as the slow exercise of control and threat, and in walked a man in the prime of life, with a spade beard, a robe of black brocade and a mitre perched firmly on his head.

His voice was rich with irony and hatred.

"Yes, what are you going to do about me? Murder me in public as you did the sainted martyr Ammonius?"

Hypatia's voice was firm and haughty and without a single edge of doubt to it, because, after all, the bishop was not her father. "I did not murder Ammonius. I saved him from excruciating pain. But he deserved to die, for he had tried to kill Orestes, the lawful governor of this city and this province. I am sure you do not mean to imply that he had your support in that act."

From her face, and Cyril's, it was clear that she thought and he knew that his role in Ammonius' act had been as instigator.

"What are a few hours of agony compared with the eternal delight that awaits the Blessed Ammonius in Heaven?" His voice was that of an actor, not a divine, though for all I know he believed what he spoke and clearly expected to join Ammonius, in Heaven, in the fulness of time. "As you would know, were you not an arrogant pagan, and doomed to the flames of Hell. All of you."

Then he saw the faun, whom he had not noticed before, and jumped back in alarm, crossing himself. No, I do not remember whether he did so in the manner now considered Orthodox or the manner now considered Catholic.

"Hell, whose devils are here!" he shouted. "I should burn this place and all it contains, as my uncle Theophilus did the temple of idolatry called the Serapeum, and all the pagan knowledge it contained.

"Your Grace!" The faun was probably not helping matters by intervening on his own behalf, but who could blame him? "I am no demon out of the Hell of Lucifer, but a poor orphan faun, whose family were killed by the evil magician Simon Magus. And avenged by Simon Peter, the first Pope and Patriarch of Rome. He blessed me once, with blessed water. It did not boil or burn when it touched my skin."

Cyril's face grew red and his eyes bulged slightly. I would have believed in his utter passionate sincerity if I had not seen actors do as much, in farce as well as in tragedy.

238

"Lies and more lies. It is what a demon would say. I shall burn this place, see if I don't."

I realized that, if other alternatives failed me, I would probably break my usual rules and kill this man, for he offended me in the core of my being. Perhaps my heart knew that I should kill him before he could do more damage and my heart would have been right.

He met my justice eventually, though, and that is a part of this tale.

In the meantime, I reached down and picked through the carved wooden beasts that lay among Hypatia's dolls and other childish things. What I looked for, was not there.

The faun smiled at me. "He'll be here. Don't worry. He said to whistle."

From outside, there came the noise of hammers hitting things and the crackling of flames. Theon cried out in anguish. "See what you've caused, you stupid girl?"

He dashed from the room. She followed him, at no great speed, pausing only to take each of the three balls poised on the finger of her left hand into her right, and throw them expertly, so that they narrowly missed Cyril's head.

I whispered to him as I walked past him. "Do not underestimate that woman. I have known her in many lives, and she is fiercer than I have ever known her."

Then I reached down and seized his left hand in a come-along; there was no need for me to break his little finger, because, for a power-hungry fanatic, Cyril was a self-protective man. He had flinched when the balls whizzed past his ear and over his head, and now did not resist for even a token second.

"I may need you to control your followers. I promised Ptolemy I would protect his Museion as far as I could, and though it is a sad shell of what it once was, I keep my word."

"What are you?" It was as if Cyril had not even noticed me before, so intent was he on the faun and on Hypatia.

239

"One you would be wise to fear."

The faun jumped up from the couch and pattered along beside us. "She's the Huntress. She kills gods."

"Only ones who deserve it, little one, and none of them any concern of this man who follows Jehovah and his Son and his Ghost, though knows them less well than I do, and thinks better of them."

"I will hear no blasphemy, woman."

He wanted me to believe him caught up in holy rage, but I caught his eyes watching me and calculating. A wicked clever man, of a type that gravitates towards priesthood no matter what the god, and worships in that choice of god his own pride and his own anger. Blasphemy, to him, meant any statement about divinity that offended his own sense of self-worth.

His men were trying to smash up the fountains with hammers, and had tried to set flame to the laurel trees that lined the courtyard. They were having little success with the trees, which had been sent from the island Delos and blessed by Apollo himself.

They withered and passed from the earth in the end, of course, when Apollo departed, but that was not yet.

Theon had dashed out into the courtyard and tried pleading with the young black-tunicked acolytes, one of whom felled him with a blow. Other library staff had come from the nearest buildings. Some of the younger scholars had swords that some of them knew how to use, and some of the older ones staffs that they were not leaning upon.

I put my free hand on the faun's shoulder. "I think it's time you whistled."

Normally, these days, Sobekh is a portly little god who waddles along comfortably. He prefers not to waste effort on being terrifying unless he has to.

The manifestation that appeared in the centre courtyard of the Museion that day was the largest and most fearful that I have ever seen; of course, he was bluffing, because of the geas I had put on

240

him years before, but none of the people watching knew that. He stood on his hind legs, as he normally does out of sensitivity that people not think him a mere beast, but his small vicious front paws were on a level with the roofs of buildings, and he snarled.

It was a bellow that most dragons and other great beasts would have been proud of. Three scholars and two of Cyril's acolytes fainted on the spot.

Cyril broke free and I let him go without a broken finger. From somewhere, he produced a glass retort. I thought it holy water, but it sizzled and charred when it bounced off Sobekh's armoured hide and smashed on the pavement besides his feet. I was not, in those days, used to holy men who tried to inflict the judgement of God in the shame of aqua fortis and aqua regia. Usually they relied on faith alone. A safer prospect.

I feared I was going to have to intervene directly, because though Sobekh can put on a good show, he is in no position to follow through with people determined to be unreasonable, as it seemed Cyril was. Fortunately, however, at that moment, we all heard the tramping of feet, and a command: "Clear the courtyard."

The scholars scuttled back to safety, but the acolytes were left in the open. Those that had cudgels and torches and hammers, dropped them and tried to look as if they had always had empty hands. The soldiers advanced with drawn blades, held as if they planned to beat with the flat rather than hack with the edge or slay with the point. The acolytes broke and ran—the soldiers let them pass.

Two burly soldiers, one of them the blond executioner Leo, caught up with the troops, bearing a litter in which Orestes lay. He nodded to a couple of soldiers who accompanied them and they seized Cyril, considerably less gently than I had.

Another soldier picked Theon up from where he had fallen, and where Hypatia was ministering to his wounds.

Sobekh, in the interim, had disappeared, surprisingly quickly for so large a creature. He had not, in the end, been needed; perhaps he saved a few decorations, a few shrubs, and if we had known Orestes was going to arrive as promptly as he did…

I am not foolish enough to feel guilt over the actions of the wicked, but I have my regrets and this is one of them. Sobekh is a card we played too soon.

Orestes beckoned to me, where I stood on the steps and I walked down to him. "Hail, Prefect."

"Hail, Huntress," he acknowledged. "One of my agents saw you in the crowd and realized who you were. Various of my predecessors have left standing orders that I read when taking up my post. I noticed that most of those orders were centuries old."

"Might I ask what they contain?"

"Firm admonitions that you be taken seriously."

I smiled; it is always pleasant to be shown respect. Still, respect too lightly given…

"How, pray, do you know that I am the authentic Huntress and not some impostor?"

"It is said,"—I really could not tell how much this man was speaking ironically—"it is said that the real Huntress can be told by the utter terror she strikes into the hearts of the sensible man. I never believed this, but now I do."

He paused.

"There is, of course, an infallible test of the bona fides of anyone claiming to be you, which is to have someone like Leo here swing a sword in the direction of your neck. I don't think any of my predecessors have had the nerve ever to try it. And there was only ever one fraudulent Huntress."

I was surprised to find myself amused at the idea. "How much did she take the Treasury for?"

"Luckily, she contented herself with freeing all the slaves in the slave market, leading them into the palace of the Prefect of that time, stripping his kitchens of all food and drink, and causing them to disappear. She then reappeared, a week later, at an audience between him and the leading citizens, read them a lecture on the iniquity of the trade in slaves, criticized the fiscal policies of the Emperor Caracalla, who was at that time on the throne, and announced that she was not you. Then changed her face into someone else entirely before disappearing again."

I confessed to myself that I approved of this imposter, whoever she really was.

He then turned his attention to Bishop Cyril. "You have endless jurisdiction over the souls of your flock, but not over the public buildings of this city. My predecessor was ill-advised enough to let your uncle destroy the Serapeum, which was a place of pagan worship, but served many other useful purposes. I do not propose to let you have free reign to damage the Museion."

Cyril glowered at him. "It is a place full of pagan things like her, and like that." He pointed at the faun.

Orestes looked at him as if sad for his errors. "That's a perfectly ordinary faun. A family of them used to live on my family's summer estate. Nothing pagan about them at all—they dined with us every Easter. As to the Huntress, it's clear from her file that she has a better relationship with all of the persons of the Holy Trinity than either of us."

I found myself wondering precisely what the file said. I never pursued the matter and a mere two centuries later, the city fell and its administration passed to other hands who were not bothered by such matters. I was not spoken of in their holy book and so did not exist, for administrative purposes. On the whole, it is better that way—I can keep my dealings with the authorities simpler when they are based on occasional sharp lessons.

In any case, Orestes and Cyril snarled at each other for several minutes more, the Prefect more urbanely and the Bishop with greater fervour. Cyril threatened to deny the Prefect the sacraments and Orestes threatened to have him arrested for heresy on some abstruse point or other to do with whether Josh had a foreskin or not.

I paid no attention, because Hypatia was weeping for her father.

He lay on the ground, breathing hard from his mouth, and blood was flowing freely, not just from the wound to his scalp but from his left nostril and right ear. His eyes were open, but seemed not to see anything.

She broke a phial under his nose and he seemed to revive. I could be of little assistance, and I loved to watch her use her skills, in this life as in any other.

I did not know that I had only three weeks left in which I would ever be able to do this again. Always remember time and chance, Crowley, and be mindful of your pleasures while they last.

I stood there watching her, and after a while the men were silent, and watched me with that sort of impatient observation which usually means that they wish to speak to you again.

"We are not done with each other." Cyril seemed to think he could threaten me. "Nor am I done with you, Prefect."

"Any time you wish to commit the capital crime of raising a riot in my city, Leo here will be only too happy to oblige you." Orestes drew a finger across his throat. "As he would have done your catspaw Ammonius had the Lady Hypatia not handed out her own brand of justice and mercy. I will not permit her to do that a second time." He nodded to me. "If you wish to talk to me, my door is always open. My predecessors are quite adamant that, unless you ask, I shall be better off not knowing why you are here, and what it is that you are going to kill."

I smiled at him, showing my teeth. "I am here to protect this faun, whose family I helped Simon Peter avenge. Apart from that, I am here on private, personal business, which should not be the concern of anyone here, unless they choose to make it so. Which is never advisable."

"Just so, Huntress." He nodded, tapped the executioner Leo on his shoulder and was, with surprising despatch, gone, and Bishop Cyril with him.

I hoped I could avoid being caught up any further in their struggle for power. Neither of them had any compassion on those whose pain was the cost of their games—like Theon, who had roused a little under his daughter's ministrations, but was death pale nonetheless, his speech slurred and his mouth drooling a little. He tried to raise his hand a little and could not.

I had seen him as one of those men whose anger and ill-humour was one day going to catch up with him, but that was before some young deacon chose to beat him about the head. He was already a man of some eighty years in any case, an old man who was now a dying man.

Over the next ten days, he declined slowly. He had regained consciousness but drifted into longer and longer sleeps. His breathing became at once effortful, more and more shallow, and his voice was a slurred whisper.

Yet it served him for what little he had to say. He asked what had passed between Hypatia and Ammonius, and when she told him, thought hard and then agreed. "There was no other way—and I sorrow that you had to make such a choice, because he was my pupil once, as Synesius was yours, and you taught yours better."

Another afternoon, he called the faun to him and they jested until his voice failed, exchanging foul witticisms. For his daughter's sake, he made the faun his friend.

Before the end, early one morning when he and Hypatia were newly awakened, and I had been watching over them both all night, Theon gestured that I should sit with him and then pulled his daughter to him and placed my hand over hers.

He looked up at her, and tears came into his eyes.

"When you talked of her as a child, I knew. Give me credit for that much—I knew of the Huntress and I knew of Maria of Egypt and that there was more to her knowledge than Zosimus understands."

"But if you knew, why did you tell me it was all dreams and lies?"

I stroked his forehead and then looked her in the eyes. "Because he was afraid that if I came when you were young, that you would leave him, and not become the scholar you are. Leave him to go adventuring with me, and perhaps die young, as has been your fate in many of our lives together."

She bent and kissed her father and then reached up and touched my cheek with a single finger. Just here, where I now bear a scar.

"I gave you the other things you asked for—a sextant, the poems of Servilia, your first little chariot and the pony to pull it." His voice was almost pleading still.

She smiled at him nostalgically.

"And the bigger chariot, and its horses, that you..." His voice failed.

"True, though my chariot is Zenobia of Palmyra's that was given to the Museion as a gift. And the horses were a gift, from a desert chief whose son I healed of a canker. Still, you set me to medicine and astronomy and mathematics. You haven't said, Father, but you gave me the world." She kissed him a second time.

He never spoke again, except with his eyes, and then those dimmed and closed and within the hour he was done.

I saw his spirit pass, young and bright-eyed. He looked at his daughter in tenderness and then at me in respect, and I saluted him as he left. I hope that he found his Empyrean, that he is not too sad that his daughter will not have joined him there. Philosophers know sadness, for all that they like to think that they will not.

Later, in the evening of that day, his colleagues bore him out of the city, along the wharves of the West harbour and then up onto a small rise that looks down on them, on which there has never been building. We burned him there—had Hypatia been his daughter alone, she might not have been allowed to be the one who placed the torch, but she was his fellow-scholar too, and no one questioned her right.

So, of that last three weeks that we were able to spend together, until the time we crossed France some fourteen centuries later, half was spent nursing the dying and the other half mourning the dead. And yet I treasure the memory of those weeks, those days, those hours.

And will not profane them by speaking of them in any detail.

246

Mostly we talked, of the past, because it was too soon to talk of the future. We walked in the streets of Alexandria together, and I reminded her of buildings that four centuries had taken away, and she showed me new beauties that I might otherwise have missed. We went to the market and bought radishes, and olives, and grapes, and goat cheese, and made frugal meals of them. Usually, the faun was with us, our chaperone whether he wished to be or not.

I thought that we had time. She feared that any time we had together would be short.

We did not lie together, or not as you mean. I lay awake next to her on her sleeping mat, but I did not do so much as take her hand. It was out of respect for her mourning but she feared, without saying anything, that it was because she was old.

There was no sign of the angels, nor of any other threat to the faun.

The city was quiet. Cyril announced that Ammonius was a martyr of the church, and many venerated him as such, but the woman who had taken responsibility for his death was not placed under any threat as a result. Too many people had seen what she did for it, or her motives, to be misrepresented.

Orestes' men patrolled the outer walls of the Museion for a few days, but after that, a single sentry, with a large rattle. A rattle which was never needed, for it was a quiet time.

And then one afternoon, as I sat watching her plot the axes of a triangle with her dividers, for some purpose that passed from my head within seconds of her telling me, a voice I knew sounded out of a bronze mirror that hung on her wall.

It was my friend Xien, who had, after many troubles by land and sea, returned to his homeland, that troubled and divided sea of small states and temporary kingdoms, through which he wandered, spreading the doctrines of Gautama the Buddha, and his own brand of good-will and righteous kindness.

As I told you, though, he was not a foolish idealist, and there were occasions when he was prepared to accept help.

247

"I am concerned, Huntress," he said, his voice only a little altered by the bronze mirrors—Hypatia's and the one he spoke into. No, there was nothing special about them; what was special was his need and his sense of need.

You're the one who talks about technologies of will, but you have never experienced will or need at that level of seriousness, have you?

"I would not trouble you, but you have often told me that, at times, just as it is better to treat a disease before it becomes mortal, so too the time to prevent those diseases of humanity called gods and monsters is at the first, before wicked mind and wicked heart have combined into wicked deed."

I turned to Hypatia. "I do not want to leave you. Things are quiet, with Cyril, and the angels, and yet…"

She smiled at me. "You are the Huntress, and you hunt alone and you protect the weak against the strong. Sobekh will help, and it is in Orestes' interests to protect me. But stay an hour, for I would not send you away unfed."

She disappeared for an hour, and when she came back, she had produced from somewhere those small cakes of ground sesame and egg and honey and flour that were known as enchitoi. She placed one, still warm from the oven, between her lips and I ate it in a kiss, our last kiss.

And then she put the others in a twisted palm leaf, for my journey.

And thus it was that I was called away by duty, as I had been so often before to my cost, and was busy preventing a great evil when the worst thing of all the bad things happened to me and the woman I love.

I went to the Western Kingdom of Wei. It was needful because what I found there was a man of many virtues, whom Xien judged harshly, on the brink of becoming bad under the most intense of provocations. It is said—and I say this with due respect to your claim to be the Wickedest Man in the World—that the worst thing is the corruption of the best.

248

In any case, as I said, Alexandria had gone quiet, and the angels seemed to have gone away for good, and Hypatia said that of course I had responsibilities that I should not neglect for her, and the faun said he would always be there, and Sobekh promised to come again, if he whistled.

Hypatia remembered a life in which she too had known how to whistle loudly, and Sobekh promised he would come if either of them whistled, and that all seemed sensible enough.

It was not enough. The worst of things happened while I was turning aside evil in the northern hills of Wei.

Tufa Rutan was not, precisely, a good man. He was a talented general and the weakest king of his short-lived dynasty; he was merciful and self-willed and one who gambled with lives and kingdoms out of a misplaced optimism. Xien judged him harshly— he was Wu Hu, one of the jabbering peoples who had come when the Han lost the mandate of Heaven.

Tufa Rutan deserved to lose his army, and lose his kingdom, but he did not deserve to die in agony, with his skin peeling from his flesh and his flesh melting from his bones. He did not deserve to be murdered in the foulest of ways by a man he had pardoned over and over, and with whom he had made the best deal he could when that man won.

Like many of the northern peoples who had come into the sixteen states that had been the empire of the Han, he was at once the Chinese noble dressed in silk that he wished to be and the Xianbei warlord dressed in furs and armour that he hated himself for being as well.

At the end, in pain, he called for shamans as well as for monks. It happened that one of the shamans loyal to him, knew of the Rituals.

If I had not gone to Wei, Tufa Rutan would have avenged himself on Qifu Chipan. He would have become a monster to do so, and would have been far better at being a monster than many villains. Between us, Xien and I persuaded him, by preaching and by threats, to die in agony rather than become what the Rituals would have made him.

I have to believe that saving him from himself was a thing of importance. I did not just bully him into a virtuous death—I spoke for him to Guan Yu, that red-faced general of the last days of Han who is worshipped as the God of War. He appeared to the dying man, and they talked of battles lost and won, and Guan Yu promised him a place in his Ministry, and, when he had died, honoured that pledge. It all worked out for the best.

But only in China.

I was gone a little more than a week.

As I stepped out of shadow on the quayside of Alexandria, I noticed three things. Up on the western hill where we had burned Theon, the smoke of another pyre was rising, thick and black. A dromon was being loaded in the harbour, hard by the barracks, loaded not with weapons of war but with the travelling chests of a noble. The corpses of a score of Cyril's young thugs lay unburied on the space where a crowd had watched the death of Ammonius.

Each of them had, in their right hand, a shard of oyster-shell, covered in blood and other fluids. And each of them was covered in blood and other fluids. The blood had dried and flaked away, so that tunics that had been black, and then been red, were now almost black again. Their hands though, and their feet, and their faces, were covered in blood and it was not theirs, because each of them had died of a clean sword-thrust.

I had no business with the dead, and so I walked towards the ship, already dreading what I might be told there. If Alexandria had erupted in violence again, while I was away, then I had misjudged, and put my love and my friends at risk.

Orestes was supervising the porters; I did not recognize him at first because there was a great white streak in his dark hair and he looked a full decade earlier than he had a mere month earlier. He already looked as sad as a man dying of some long slow disease, and when he saw me approach, his face fell further.

"Whose pyre burns on the headland in the West?" I asked, and knew before he got the words out.

He stammered, "Th-they k-killed her. I asked her to dinner, to show the dignitaries of the city that she would come if I asked, and she set out in her chariot and they took her, and they killed her. To prove that I do not rule."

Which was all I needed to know. "The faun?"

"Dead, I believe? There was a funeral."

"The crocodile?"

Orestes pointed to where Sobekh sat, leaning his scales against the wall of the Emporium, and weeping, weeping human tears before you make the joke.

I needed to talk to my friend, and learn the worst, but before I walked over to him, I looked Orestes hard in his eyes, which were red with tears of humiliation, of knowing that you are not the person you thought you were. He tried, stumblingly, to explain. "I don't want it enough. I thought I did, but now I know I never really wanted power, or control, because I watched him and he wanted it all and he has taken it all."

"Cyril." There was no question in my voice because I knew.

"Cyril," he echoed, and then, "Even if you kill him, I won't stay. He showed me that, not wanting it *enough* is not wanting it."

I did not hate him—I do not hate weak men—but I had nothing more to say to him; he had failed himself and failed Alexandria. So I turned my back on him, and I do not know when he left, or what became of him, whether he was allowed to return to his estates and live quietly, or whether they blinded him with hot irons and put him in a monastery to pray for his sins. And his omissions.

Sobekh looked up as I approached. His small eyes were dry with desolation and he wrung his small hands endlessly as if he could cleanse himself of what he had seen.

"They slung ropes over me, and I could not tear myself free. Somehow they knew I could not, and would not, kill them, and they tied me down and they mocked me and they made me watch. What they did to her. Huntress, you do not want to know what they did to her. It will make you mad."

And indeed, if I could run mad, I would have done.

"Oyster-shells."

"Yes, and they made me watch. They pulled her from the chariot and they tore away her gown and the veil from her, and it was as if she were young again, and they were blinded by shock and lust and terror and then one shouted 'witch' and dashed forward and slashed her across the forehead and down her cheek so that skin hung loose and she was not beautiful any more and that gave them permission. She was blind, so they would let her escape a few paces and then they would move in and slash, until they took the tendons from her legs so that she could not stand and broke the bones in her legs so that she lay there screaming. They would take a finger, and then a toe and then a sliver out of an ear. They pulled things half out of her and sliced them holding them against the tattered white skin of her belly so that they could see clearly through the flood of red. She did not die well, Huntress; she died in terror and pain. And they went on cutting and she went on screaming. I think that she screamed long after they had cut so deep that there was nothing left for her to scream with."

"And then?"

I could not speak more, for fear that my voice would break into a scream, and then I would run mad and tear down what was left of this mighty city. I held control until my head ached with it.

"The monks came, the monks of the desert, and they had swords and the men in black tunics greeted them as if they were brothers, shouting, 'We have carved the feast and you come to help us dine'. And the monks fell on them and stabbed each to the heart with a single stroke like that with which she killed Ammonius, and they fell and were done."

"And then?"

I looked down a second, and the paving stone on which I had been standing was now ground to dust under my feet.

"Two of the monks had brought great buckets with them, the buckets that men carry water in, on a yoke across the shoulders of

252

two men. They picked up the scraps that were all that was left of Hypatia, your love, and they filled the buckets with them, as butchers do with discarded fat and tendon at the end of the slaughter and the butchering, and then they scraped up what was left on the ground, and then they left, heading to the West, where yet her pyre burns. After a while, with none to stop me, I got loose, and I had nothing to do save wait, knowing that you would come, but come too late."

He held me in his stubby little paws, against his scaled chest, and for a moment it was as if I were a child again, and he were my father, because he knew that I needed to weep. I had wept for Sof and Lillit, great raging sobs, and I had wept for Sof each time she died of age or sickness, the tears of sadness and joy that someone has died and will come again.

This time though—I had thought what was done to her and Lillit at the start of things was a masterstroke of evil, and it was, but this surpassed it. They had held hands at the last, but Hypatia had died alone; they had spat, I think, in their killers' eyes, and that handclasp was token of it, and she died screaming.

Then I thought—and it was as if she were young again...

I wondered ,because after all, Hypatia was Sof, who had been Maria and Diotima and so many more. But I did not have time to consider further at that time. I could only bear it if I found friends to care for, or someone to kill.

"The faun?" I had good reasons to forget, but he was under my protection and perhaps I had failed him as well.

Sobekh hugged me tighter, so that I knew the news was bad even before he spoke. "There were rumours, just rumours, but it was enough to make him panic again. Someone said that they had seen the angels, consorting with Cyril's men in black. I do not know if that was true, but he thought it was, and he grew ever more certain that they were going to come for him, and burn the books he cared for. So he went to her and begged and begged, and she had no better plan than his, in the end."

I pulled away and spoke harshly to him. "Could you not have stopped them?"

Sobekh looked at me ironically. "You have known her in how many lives, and known him for how many centuries? I suggested that they wait and you did not come back and the faun grew more scared and she was frightened he would find something more stupid to do."

It was hard to think what could have been more stupid, but I let him continue.

"She found her old work-room, in the slums. There was still a guard on it, four centuries later, and nothing had changed, under the dust. Dried flowers had become dust, but she remembered her way into shadow to pick more, and she lit the old oven, and she washed the glassware and then set it to bubble. And she made him a sleeping draft, one that counterfeits death and holds you still in death and time's arms. He sleeps, and sleeps forever, or until she comes again. Only her presence can wake him—she made it so."

I could see why she had done this, but it was a disaster. Time and chance…

"She warned him that, if he chose this, he was putting himself in the hands of fate. What is done by the Great Work can only be undone by the Great Work, she said."

Sobekh told me that, and I heard him say it, and I did not understand the full tragic import of it for many many years. I did not think, because I was mourning my love, and mourning our friend who was lost in time and a sleep like death, until she come to wake him.

Sobekh hugged me one last time. "What will you do now, little Huntress?"

"I will go see this man who claims to be a man of god, and who has killed my love, and I will hear what he has to say, and so will his god. For I will pull Cyril to Heaven by his beard, and, when he is condemned, kick him every step of the road to the Hell of Lucifer."

He looked even more sorrowful. "That is no place for me, and I would not be a good witness in your cause. Jehovah has no fondness for the pantheon of which I was once part, and I still live in this land of Egypt, which is his and not ours."

This was true.

He went on. "Beware of Cyril, for he is a man of subtle intellect, who plans ahead. He will plead his cause before his God and he will have prepared his excuses like a lawyer. You know best what you wish to do...As for me, I need a period away from men and women and their stink and their wickedness. You forbade me to eat their flesh, or take their lives, and I thank you for that, because, at this time, I want nothing of either."

"What will you do, Sobekh? Where will you go?"

"Somewhere beyond the cataract. To lie in the sun and watch the mud dry and listen to the prayers of mice. Until she comes again."

And I have not seen him since.

Cyril was expecting me.

He stood, not in his brocade and mitre, but in the plain linen of a simple man, though someone had cleaned it of all stains and starched it near stiffness and pressed it with hot stones that it hang straight and clear. I doubt that that someone was Cyril, because he was a lordly man even in his pieties.

"Why?"

He looked at me, down his long and commanding nose, and did not deign to answer. I was some pagan thing out of the past and he owed me no answer, whatever his god thought.

I have my own fast ways to Heaven as you know by now, and generally I disdain to greet my old friend where he sits in state, with the impostor at his right hand, and his white bird on his shoulder or perched above his head. I detest what he and they have done with the souls of the virtuous dead and I still do not understand why they do this—endless flattery, endless chanting, endless incense. At least Zeus and Odin threw good parties.

Nonetheless, there are things that have to be done and said in public, before all of the Host and in front even of the Impostor and the Child of the Bird.

I took Cyril, shoving him ungently rather than, in fact, pulling him by his beard or kicking him, and flung him to his knees before Nameless who was now Jehovah, and made my plea.

"I charge this man with the foul murder of Hypatia, who was Sof, who was once the widow of Josh your son. He did not even act from hatred—or not of her at any rate. He killed her to prove to his rival that he would go further, that he would will darker things, that he would always win in the end because he would do anything to win. He had his men kill her in the vilest of ways, and then had them killed by his other men, to prove that point even more fiercely. He is a murderer, and a traitor to those who followed him, and a blasphemer, in that he claimed to do these things in your name. I ask you for Justice."

Cyril made his plea like a lawyer.

"You are my Lord, whom I serve, and they are pagan women, driven by unnatural lust. I know not this Mara, who is some creature out of old pagan times, who presumes to talk of you as if you owe her anything, who are Lord of all and created all."

The trouble with Nameless is that he laps all this nonsense up even though he knows it to be utter lies. I am surprised he has never tried to destroy me, because I am one of the few left who know him for the fraud he is in these matters—perhaps the only reason is fear, or that without me, and Hekkat, and a few others who have stayed their own mistresses and masters, there are so few who know the truth. He and Lucifer are held together by many things, and one of them is the fear that the other might suddenly mock them for their pretensions.

Most of those they have made their servants know and are silent—Aserath, say, though I suspect that one of harbouring sharp thoughts about those she once loved.

Cyril went on, "As to these charges, I respect her grief but she is misled as to fact. True, I sent my acolytes to bind the dragon, and

256

prevent the Lady Hypatia from attending dinner with Prefect Orestes, a man too prepared to court the good will of pagans like her. I knew her to be a pious woman, in her pagan way, and hoped that if I had her placed in a cell and starved a little and taken away from bad and corrupting company,"—he looked at me harshly—"I could win her to your worship, have her see that this One she talked of was none other than you."

I realized that I should just have killed him, and taken the consequences. Like that John whose voice was gold, Cyril's was dark honey, laced with poppy and lies.

"Why would I kill her? I wanted her at my side, a holy virgin rededicated to chastity, to advise me with her wisdom. But alas, it was not to be. When the acolytes saw her, they realized that she had somehow been restored to youth, whether by dark sorcery or some other means, and being simple men, unlearned in such things, they took the law into their own hands—'Thou shalt not suffer a witch to live'. Had I been there, I would have stopped them for even a witch deserves fair trial under law before she is stoned or burned. They acted rashly, and excessively and, yes, in cruelty, for her beauty provoked their lust and they were men sworn to chastity."

I seized an opening. "How unfortunate that none of them are here to confirm your story. Or should that be your lies?"

He ignored me as if I had not spoken or were not worth the listening to. "Tragically, the wild monks of the desert, who owe me allegiance, but whom I do not control, had taken a fancy to Hypatia, for saving one of their number from Orestes' torturer. True, no Christian woman would do murder in such a way, but they too are simple men and thought well of her, for that. Outraged by what was done to her, they could not save her, but avenged her. They are a lawless bunch, who raised near fatal riot against the Prefect only the other week, and I have sent them back to their pillars and caves and out of my city of Alexandria, which is now yours."

He was so convincing, even though he lied. I made one last effort. "How came these simple hermits to have military swords under their robes, which they knew how to use so well that they killed the acolytes with a single thrust each?"

He shrugged, "I know not. Some plot or other. I rule Alexandria, but I do not yet contain every thought or sin of its people." He struck a pose that, if it was an actor's, was that of a good actor playing an innocent man. "I swear before you, that I am guiltless in her death."

Nameless looked at me, heartless, from under those lashes. "Huntress, for the long friendship we have known, even if we have been estranged of late, I have heard your case. I am not convinced—for my servant Cyril has an answer to every item. What has happened is sad, and awful, but, after all, it is not as if Sof will not return in a year or a decade. She may already be reborn and you should be looking for her, not troubling me. What's done is done, but I find no fault in this man."

He looked at me sternly. "I will have angels take him to his home. We must not put temptation in your way. Perhaps you would prefer to stay away from Alexandria for a while, lest it remind you of your guilt and anger. You have your tasks in the world; I am sure that Cyril can ensure no gods of blood arise in his city. Go, search for criminals and monsters to kill, and perhaps you will find your love again. Soon."

I should have known better than to trust him—he is, after all, a fraud, and a god of laws not of justice.

I went from his Heaven to the far North, where I hosted with the Gods of the Balts, and then the spirits who rule the Samoyeds. I learned the ways of peoples forgotten by history and saved them from gods and demons, and never let them worship me. I travelled with the great hordes that rode across the steppes and with the simple herdsmen who watched them go by; I watched plague and famine take their toll and war, wars of people, wars of religion and wars of kings.

I had seen it before, the slow fall and then the fast fall and then regrowth; I have seen it several scores of times, and will doubtless see it again, before the end.

258

The old order fell into decay, a crumbling brick at a time, a scribbled-on parchment at a time, but it was not all loss. Clever peasants learned to use the land better; smiths cast ploughs that ran deeper furrows, and suddenly horses had collars that did not choke them as they pulled them across the fields. Running from barbarians, people who had been citizens of Rome built cities on the marshes and islands of the lagoon, cities that became Venice and, for a while, Torcello, cities that learned pride and empire.

I could tell why Torcello rose and fell, from a great city to an empty cathedral, a few walls, and sheep pastures, and it is a story of killings by night, and creatures that swam in the lagoon that had once been men, but it is a long story and for some other time.

In the north, people pulled land from the sea, a clod at a time, and started to turn the great forest into charcoal to smelt the iron that was hammered into ploughs. People learned to cast bells in great moulds, bells that sounded as loud and high and clear as a legion trumpeter bursting his heart in battle.

I could tell of Ys, which was claimed and which the seas took back, and whose bells sometimes toll in the deep. I have told you of another city that drowned, and all such stories are ultimately the same. There was transgression, and then there was nightmare, and then there was punishment. I will not speak of it.

Cyril and those like him asked for centuries Jerome's question: what has Athens to do with Jerusalem? And scholars in the West forgot all poetry save the psalms, and all their rhetoric save sermons, and most of their mathematics save the counting of gold, and astronomy save what they could see in the sky at night. The Arabs kept much and invented much, but much was lost, even by them.

Still there were new musics in the land, catches of the north that went round in an endless dance, and slow ululations from the south that caught at the heart, and these blended into something new. Later, cymbals and drums joined them, but not in the time I wish to talk of; it was a time of stately dancing and songs of hopeless love.

There were wars of gods, in which I chose to take no part for they were no business of mine and I had friends on each side. Jehovah took the gods of Olympus prisoner one at a time and he and Lucifer cast them into Hell; the Gods of Egypt crept away and the Aesir retreated further and further into shadow.

One set of Jehovah's worshippers fought other sets of his worshippers, over and over, but he profited each time, somehow, whether it was Cyril driving the Jews of Alexandria out into the desert, or the followers of Mohammed coming out of their desert and sweeping halfway around the world imposing and persuading their kind of worship as they went, or the descendants of the Franks and the Goths and all of the others heading back into the East and taking back Jerusalem for their sect of his worshippers. So much of the time they talked of Josh and they meant both him and the imposter, and understood neither.

I travelled back and forth in the wake of those armies, because so often both victors and defeated fell into ways that interested me. The wars and the persecution were no concern of mine, but starving children will sometimes do things I cannot ignore and so will greedy brigands. I slay both, when I have to, and some of them I mourn as I do so.

I cannot save them all, the weak or the strong, from what they do to themselves and to each other.

People talk of the war for Jerusalem as if it were several single wars, and indeed it can be seen thus. For many of those who fought on both sides, though, it was a war to take land and then a war to keep it. I have mentioned Queen Melisande, whose true history is so much more than books tell, and Hassan, but I could talk also of Saladin, that most perfect of knights for all that he never read a romance of chivalry, or Bohemond, that great bear of a man so unabashed in his greed for gold, land and food.

None of these were of interest to me, in the end, though I have told you of Hassan and his fate, and I watched Bohemond from shadow many times. He was your sort of man, Crowley, and once tortured, killed and ate a man before the walls of Ephesus; I thought, aha!, but it was for effect merely. He did it in reality, but as theatre, and got the surrender he hoped for.

I have talked of the Assassins, before, and now I need to talk of their great enemy, the Poor Fellow-Soldiers of Christ and of the Temple of Solomon, whom men more often call the Knights Templar. They were as brilliant on the battle-field as any force, and as competent in the back-alleys of every city of the East as the Assassins themselves, though less famous for knives in the back and poison in the drink. That was because they chose not to be feared for that; they were advised well, and their adviser said that the way to wealth and to military success was renown.

For almost two centuries they rose, from a few poor knights sworn to chastity that guided pilgrims through the newly conquered lands, to a career for younger sons. There were battles that would not have been won without them, and others that were lost in spite of their sacrifices. They reminded me, though, of Cyril's acolytes in their unforgiving passion for blood.

Many talk of the chivalry with which those wars were fought, and it is not entirely a lie; kings and lords spared each other, like as not, and their womenfolk were rarely abused, when, as often happened, they were captured. The Templars though regarded the followers of Mohammed as so many vermin, to be killed unless there was more profit in temporary mercy. Saladin was, as I said, a man of chivalry— yet when he defeated the Templars and their royal allies at Hattin, he killed the Templars in their hundreds, because he knew that had they caught him, he would have suffered far worse than a single sword-blow. His sufis and scribes and poets begged from him the favour of executing a Templar each—because there was hardly a family in Syria that had not lost some relative at their hands.

They were deadly men, all the more deadly for being chaste, and people who were afraid of them told lies about them. I listened to those lies, because there is sometimes a grain of the truths I need to hear in such: they had betrayed Jerusalem; they had given Baldwin the Leper his disease; they were sodomites who lay with each other;

they worshipped strange gods. I thought nothing of any of this, for it was all either clearly untrue or no business of mine.

I am, though, sometimes curious.

There was a tale men told, of a young man who seduced and killed a maid, and kept her head in a box, where it whispered secrets to him, secrets that led him to power and a rich marriage. It always ended badly, of course, because his wife found the box, and the dead maid told her all. Sometimes she killed herself thereafter, and sometimes she killed her man; and the box was always thrown into the sea. Until the next version of the tale.

At first, I thought it just the tale of Medusa, whose flayed face was pinned to the shield of Athena, or the tale of the harp strung with the dead love's hair and made from her bones, that tells all on a feast day. Tales flow, and tales rush into each other like rivers. Yet this one stayed the same—I heard it all around the Inner Sea and the Black and up in High Germany and at a feast at Connaught. It was always somewhere else, and yet, in places where no one could have drawn you the North coast of Africa, men said Tripoli, or Trebizond. And in each of those places, yes, some young adventurer had made a rich marriage and then fallen...

After a bit, there were no new stories of this kind, though the old ones were told and for all I know are told still. The Templars gathered many precious things to themselves and with them the jealousy of men, men who told stories of their sodomies, their betrayals, their worship of a god that was a head or a face, and lived in a box, and whispered advice to the Grand Master.

I grew curious.

Some said it was a vernicle, or the real shroud of Josh; I had not seen him in thirteen hundred years, and I longed, longed almost like a lover, to see my friend again, even an image stained by his lifeblood. Also, I wondered, had some ill befallen him and, if so, should I take his relic to his father and punish his slayers, or their accomplices, or heirs?

I will say no more than that I had a feeling, a feeling of unease.

262

You might say that it was the grinding of the wheels of time and chance, whispering in my ear.

The Templars had been driven out of the Holy Land; they planned to renew the wars, but for the moment the time was not right. There were Muslims to fight in Spain and pagans to fight in the North—and as you know, I had made that latter war more costly than had been hoped. Templars had gone through the ice on that day, along with their brothers of the Teutonic Orders, and it was by my stratagem, and they knew it and cursed my name.

So it was with discretion, in the depth of night, and out of shadow that I slipped into their places of power. Not that I feared them, but that I do not borrow more trouble than I need to.

I went to the Castle Almourol that overlooks the Tagus, and the keep of Kolossi in Cyprus that their old allies the Lusignans ruled. I went to their holdings in London, and, not last, but not first either, their great estate, the New Town, that had been carved from a marsh hard by the wall of Paris, and it was there, in one of the seven turrets of the great Tower of the Temple, that I found the truth I sought, a truth that broke my heart.

I watched from shadow as Jacques de Molay, an old vain weak man who was the Head of the Order, went about his daily affairs; he was not a clever man that I could see, and yet his decisions always seemed to be astute ones. I followed him to a room where the Chancellor of France De Nogaret asked searching questions of him, about the wealth of the Temple and the needs of France, and de Molay would look blank a moment and then answer, but not as one who had known, but as one who had been told and learned by rote.

It was on the second night that I watched him that he went from long hours of prayer to self-torment with a knotted rope that had nothing of it of pleasure and all of asceticism—I will say many bad things of de Molay, but he was not a hypocrite. He twisted the rope apart when he was done, and there at its core was a key.

His chamber was stark and empty with nothing to sleep on but a straw pallet, no furniture save the small image of the virgin before

263

whom he knelt on bare stone, and a single candle before the image which served to light the whole room. He lit a taper from the candle and left, through the small chapel, hung with rich tapestries, that adjoined it, where he said his Office, and mass once a day, and where his confessor called on him, and along a short corridor up to what looked like a blank wall. He took the key and suddenly it became clear to me that there was a keyhole in the wall and that what looked like brickwork was actually just the sides of bricks glued to a door.

Behind the door was a small chamber, just enough room for a table and a chair. And nightmares.

On the table there stood a candlestick, a veil, a brass cylinder, a small incense burner, a row of small metal instruments—awls, pincers and the like, a bowl with some small black pellets in it,— and a box that stood on four small cat's feet and had a cat's face grinning savagely on its lid. It was a plain box carved from some black wood, and the cat was elaborately carved in a full relief that made it look almost real.

De Molay lit the candle with his taper, which he blew out, and then sat down in the chair, his bones creaking, and reached for the box. From under it, he pulled a small tray or drawer that sat between the cat's feet, a tray of what looked like slices of veal and inner parts like kidneys, and then he reached for the lid.

It was not locked and its hinges were not stiff. When de Molay opened it, the lid opened so that the box's contents were hidden from his gaze, but he placed the veil over the inner lid and the open box nonetheless.

He whispered—I could not quite hear him from shadow—and then placed the bronze cylinder to his ear. When he did not like what he heard, he raised his voice a little and I heard the word Nogaret and the word King; he took up the pincers and heated an awl in the flame of the candle and then picked up one of the slices of kidney and touched it with the hot awl. Then he listened to the cylinder again.

264

This time, he smiled—he pulled open the jaw of the carved cat on the lid of the box and I saw that there was a small hole behind it that pierced the lid. He placed one of the pellets in the incense burner, placed the burner on the lower part of the open jaw, lit the taper and held it against the pellet which issued a gentle aromatic smoke which was partly hashish and partly poppy, and he blew the smoke through the lid in regular breaths for a while, taking none of it himself. He had clearly done this many times before, perhaps nightly.

Then he listened to the cylinder one last time, crushed the burning pellet between finger and thumb, wincing slightly, took out the incense burner, closed the jaw, and pushed the tray of flesh back between the feet until it clicked shut, and then closed the lid. He relit the taper once last time and blew out the candle, leaving the room in darkness that became absolute when he left, and closed the door behind him.

I have no need of light—I can, if I need, glow, but more importantly I see clearly with the light that is in shadow. I waited until I could no longer hear his weary footsteps in the passage, and walked around the table so that I could see inside the box when I opened it.

In all the legends, the wife who opens the box is blighted or blasted by the sight of what is within.

I had not understood why de Molay cast a veil over the contents so that there was no chance of his catching sight of what was inside.

I looked down and saw, blinking at me with eyes that saw me clearly, the face of Hypatia, younger than I had ever known her in that life, with a great gash from forehead to cheek crudely stitched by one who had no great care for results. Her face, flayed from her skull and yet with ears that heard and eyes that both saw and wept continually.

They had taken the scalp as well, so that the face lay like fine leather or silk in a nest of hair that was still white.

I realized, then, what the slices of meat and offal were, and why de Molay pierced them, and why, once he was satisfied, he gave her a moment of surcease from pain. For almost nine centuries, she had lain in that box or one like it, and wicked men had asked her questions and advice and punished and rewarded her.

It is no wonder that, afterwards, she was mad; the wonder is that, when I saw her first, she was still sane.

Her eyes moved to her left a little, the most she could do by way of volition, and I saw that she was trying to point me to the cylinder. I lifted it, and held it to my ear as I had heard de Molay do, and from within, I heard the sifting of fine sand, like that in a glass that tells the time, and yet it was also her voice.

"They burned most of me to ashes, ashes and charred bones, and then they took every scrap, and picked out the wood of my pyre a splinter at a time and ground it, slowly and slowly, in a jeweller's small hand mill until all that was left of me save my face, and some small fragments of my flesh that they kept so that they could encourage me to counsel them, was fine white dust."

"Cyril." I think I whispered but it may have been a howl of grief and execration.

"Cyril, yes," the ashes whispered, "but so many many others too."

I had already guessed what she had done, and the folly and wonder of it.

"You made and took the elixir? To be young again?"

"I found the elixir that I made when I was Miriam, who also made the stone, and stared at both for years in my workroom, and that Mary found where Miriam had hidden them. The elixir—I wanted to have so many years, and to have them with you. I found the phial and I was weak, and thought it for the best. It was such a little thing that I be punished for it."

Her eyes wept continually, but the whispering ashes could not sob.

"Tell me -" there was no point in rebuke or in sympathy, because they would not help and I could not bear not to be about saving her from this, "- how do I end this life-in-death for you? How do I free you?"

"I do not know. What is done by the Work can only be undone by the Work. Cleopatra, not the Queen, followed Miriam and made That Which Dissolves, and that which contains—but they and the stone were gone from the workroom when I found it, and only the elixir left. Someone had been there and taken them, and left it, which was a cruelty and not a kindness."

I wondered, then and later, who had done this, and why.

"I will learn the Work, for you, though it take me many years." I would abandon my duties rather than leave her in this state.

"At least take me from this place, all of me that is left."

I swept through the closed door without bothering to open it, and pulled one of the tapestries from the chapel wall, and bundled into it the box and the cylinder, and the bowl of small pellets. The Templars would pay for this, but for now, I wanted to be gone from this place.

In that age, as in others, I kept a small room, as stark and bare as de Molay's, in Paris and in other cities of particular interest—Damascus, Byzantium, Delhi, Timbuktu, and Shanghai in that age. I keep such rooms still.

It was to that room that we went, so that I could, in security, speak to the flayed face of my love and listen to her whispering ashes—I say these things over and over that you may appreciate the horror of our predicament—about how best to destroy her so utterly that she would be free to move from this immortal unlife into something new and cleaner.

I threw the lid open again, that I might see her clearly and she see me, and I held the cylinder to my ear that I might hear her. We spent that night and the next day, and much of the night after that, talking, of the past a little, but more of how I would need to build a laboratory of ovens and glassware, how I would need a small forge at some point, and where I would need to go into shadow, either to gather those herbs and minerals whose shadow form is all that would do, or to do phases of the work.

Periodically, I would burn the small pellets, to give her relief.

She told me of that work which is now called alchemy, and deeply misunderstood, because its practitioners knew nothing of shadow. They might achieve the elixir, which in shadow is the First Azoth, but nothing else of note, neither in the self-forming that is a part of the process nor its rewards, which are also its stages. This is the elixir which sometimes prolongs life and sometimes blasts it, because it is fickle as the mercury which it changes into that other metal which is known as the adamant, unbreachable by any force, yet as ductile and shapeable as clay—it is the perfect metal save the Gold of the Work (which is not Gold at all but the Child of the stone). Without the adamant to contain and control it, you cannot transform Aqua Regia and Aqua Fortis into That Which Dissolves, the Alkahest as the Arabs call it—and without the Alkahest and the Azoth, you cannot transform the Adamant into the Stone. And without the Stone, that changes the nature of all things, you cannot begin to achieve the Quintessence, the Gold of the Work, the Child of the Stone, and perfect wisdom, perfect knowledge of time and chance.

And yet, she told me. There was still some factor she had not considered, some step she had missed in all of those lives when she had done the Work. She had come close enough to that Fifth Azoth, that Perfection of Essence, to smell it in her dreams, especially in her opium dreams, and be relieved by that dream and not just by the opium that gave her the dream.

Yet there was something missing for her and for all others. Some last chancy step beyond silence, beyond knowledge, beyond desire—and also beyond daring.

Or so she said, though now I know otherwise. For nine hundred years, her only relief from despair and madness had been thought, with no way to test her thoughts about mathematics, or astronomy, or the Work.

The only thinking she had been able to test was her thoughts about the practical problems of evil and ambitious men, who would punish her with pain if her advice failed them. She told me much of the ways of power, that I listened to for her sake, even though I decided long ago that the game of thrones was one I would not play, except, occasionally, for the sake of my duties, or, perhaps, occasionally, for revenge.

I once talked to an exiled Florentine, who knew much of what she told me, and an Englishman, and a German scholar who lived in London. We should never be proud of wisdom, because in the end it is all one.

As she whispered this knowledge to me, I groaned, at her pain and at the long months of precision and work that lay ahead of me. At the birth in me of that hunger and that knowledge which would change me utterly and leave the world defenseless, without me to protect the weak against the strong.

Sometimes, in my reveries, I take those steps, and do that Work, and things are otherwise than they were and are. Because I did not take those steps and do that Work because, as I sat and thought, there came a knock at the door of my chamber.

I flung it open only to see the fluttering of a cloak, as someone— perhaps man or woman, or god or demon—disappeared down the alley opposite, and also into shadow. On the ground, at my feet, lay a flask made of some metal and a large basin that looked as if it were made of the same. Above them, lighting the darkness, there floated a crystal with many sides that shone into the night as if it were the dawn.

I took the flask and the basin and spoke politely to the crystal. "Enter. If you would be so kind."

The secret of managing the Stone, Hypatia had told me in that long lecture, is courtesy, which is a symbol of Benevolent Will, which is one aspect of what the Stone itself is.

I showed the Stone, for you know it when you see it, to Hypatia and asked, in an ecstasy of hope, whether the flask and basin might be what she had told me I would have to labour many months to achieve.

"Not only might be," her ashes whispered, "but are the very flask and basin which were stolen from my workroom between my life as Maria and my life as Hypatia. See, the flask bears my mark."

Indeed, its stopper was moulded into the shape of those blue flowers of shadow which she loved.

"But who? How?" I do not trust good fortune.

"We had a sister once, who died in pain spitting at our enemies and clasping my hand. She wished, did she not, to live in delight, and mock time and chance, and turn their workings aside."

"I have never seen her in all the years of my life."

"Nor I, in all my lives. Until now, or such is my guess. When we needed her most."

I have thought of this, often, since, and realized how strange Lilit's wish had been. It is a matter too deep for me, but perhaps one day some wise man, or she herself, will explain it. This, though, was not a time for thought.

Briefly, she gave me instructions, both about how to use what we had been given, and what to do next, when she was gone. She advised me of the state of the nations, as if I were one of the wicked men from whom she had learned, to whom she had taught, statecraft.

"Place me, all of me, in the basin," she whispered. "And do not hesitate. Be resolute whatever happens. You are the Huntress, who ends the delight of gods and evil men, and what you are about to do is a mercy, even were it to annihilate me forever. I have held on to my sanity in hope these many years, in hope of this final death, and I feel my mind fraying with the wear of those years now that death is upon me. Mara, my love, farewell until we meet again."

Of all her deaths, this was the most terrible, because I had to do it. I opened the tray, and reverently placed the pieces of her into the basin, and then I opened the cylinder and poured out the speaking white dust that lay within. Lastly and with the greatest gentleness of which I was capable, I reached into the box and under her white hair and lifted face and scalp and ears in one delicate piece, and placed them too into the basin, where her eyes watched me until the last in an ecstasy of hope and fear and, yes, near madness as I opened the stopper of the flask and smelled the sweet flower scent of what lay within.

The crystal hovered, as if it too watched me.

As I poured That Which Dissolves onto the flesh, and ash, and hair, and face of my beloved, she went away from me, silently and in terror and I fear in great pain, as when ice on a pool melts in spring sunlight, and grows thinner and yet keeps its shape to the last. I watched to the last and it was the face that went last, and her mouth that I have kissed, and her eyes that gazed into mine, last of all.

Eyes that I next saw in another face, in this same city, stark staring mad as she had feared. She had hung on to herself for so long, and then the pain of dissolution broke the last strength with which she held back madness.

Then, as she had instructed me, I pulled at the sides of the flask and crimped its stopper into the body of its neck and bent and pulled and twisted it until it was a flat shape as large as the basin which I laid over the basin and crimped until it was sealed. At the last, I pressed a little too hard and a single drop of That Which Dissolves flew out, and struck me on the cheek, burning worse than the fires of Hell.

I would have been undone, for it would have eaten at me until there was nothing left, but the Stone kissed my cheek in an instant, and felt like my lover's finger there, the most sensual of caresses. See, where it left a scar.

Then something happened which I do not fully understand, because it seems to me that the crystal, the Stone, placed itself at the centre of the lid with which I had closed the basin, and became a part of it, and as it did so, the metal changed, flowing and changing to the next version of itself, like mercury and like the Adamant, and some new thing.

Was this the Quintessence of which Hypatia had told me? For it brought about no ending, but instead grew and spilled out and changed, and became a beautiful woman, of living metal, who

271

sometimes looked like Sof, and sometimes like Hypatia and sometimes like other women whom I knew not.

She flowed and she danced and her touch was hard as diamond or Damascus steel, and she touched my cheek one last time, and spun and was gone from my sight, leaving me bereft of all save my duty to serve justice—even if it looked a little like vengeance.

The rest is swiftly told, though it took seven years to bring to its climax.

I took the box in the shape of a cat, to the chancellor of France, de Nogaret, and told him, truthfully, that it was the source of the wisdom with which de Molay had thus far held off the greedy desire for wealth of him and the king that he served. Without that wisdom, de Molay was an ordinary man, with none of the gift for statecraft he had shown up to that point.

"Be bold," I told him and his good-looking power-intoxicated king, "strike hard and strike fast."

Then I wandered the streets of Paris, telling all who would listen that the Knights Templar worshipped an idol of a cat. It is not my fault that people started to shout the old stories of sodomy and treason, any more than that some street singer announced that the name of the cat was Baphomet, mostly because it fitted nicely into a ballad he was writing.

Over the next two nights, beacons flared and couriers rode their mounts to sweating death. Nogaret and Phillip had laid plans. The box meant that he could act on them, because it could be shown to the great council of France and to the Pope in Avignon—Clement needed an excuse and I gave it to him. On the third day, every Templar in France was arrested; before the month was out, almost every Templar in Europe.

I have no real regrets—they had all benefitted by my love's centuries of torment. So had many others, of course, but they were dead, and as a general rule I leave the dead alone. As a general rule. None joined the Templars save to profit by the profession of violence in the name of Nameless and Josh—who doubtless hates the idea—and if they were punished for things they had not done, most of them will have done something.

Was I unjust? Perhaps, but at the time I did not care. And this is why I limit my involvement in human affairs save for my duties.

In any case, it took seven years, during which I often had occasion to regret that there is no way of being in more than one place at the same time. I needed, and needed desperately, to be in Paris and not miss the end of the remorseless process that would lead to the death of de Molay. I do not normally bother with the dead, but I would need him one last time after my revenge on him was done, because there was another dead man to whom I owed requital. I would not be denied this.

I was, in the course of those seven years, a victim of my own success. The sheer size of the purge of the Templars made people discuss their guilt endlessly, and in some minds that had the inevitable consequence that they decided that, if the Templars had done magic of a dark kind, and been so successful for so long, perhaps it would be possible to emulate their methods and their success, but not their eventual fall.

I had continually to travel through those lands that knew or cared about the Knights Templar, which included all of Christendom, and a large part of the Umma, explaining to people who made that decision that they were wrong. Finding them before they did too much damage to others, or indeed to themselves, was rather difficult when I needed to keep track of trial, appeal, papal enquiry and all the rest of the solemn mummery. I rather let the lands of Asia slip in those years, and Africa below the desert, but the consequences were not too severe. I am, I think, allowed to make a few bad decisions in seven thousand years.

In any case, things drew to a close and de Molay and three of his colleagues were placed in penitential garb on a scaffold outside the great church of Our Lady, to receive some sort of mercy and a sentence of life imprisonment.

273

This would not have been especially convenient for me. As it happened, though, the four old men looked at each other and started to call out that they had lied, that the charges to which they had pleaded guilty were false, that they had been tortured into confession and the like. I had raised the crowd against them somewhat seven years earlier, but anything I might have said would have fallen on deaf ears. The mob started to cry out for the Templars and against the King—de Nogaret had died—and against the Pope for his weakness. I think the old men were just tired of indignity and prepared to be burned rather than live out a few miserable months more.

If so, Phillip gave them their wish. De Molay and his friends were shuffled off the stage—even the provosts that shoved and pushed them seemed to do so with a degree of respect and reluctance. Phillip was not a man to delay action if there was a risk to his authority; that very night, with no stay for further proceedings, de Molay and his companion de Charnay were burned on a great pyre that lit up the night, on the island called the Island of the Jews where now stands one of the piers of the great bridge that is still called New after three centuries.

De Molay died well, calling King and Pope to be judged with him before the throne of God, but, with respect to his courage, this was not at all my plan.

As he and de Charnay stepped, dead, from the flames, I stepped forth and seized him by the hand as if I were Jehovah's tipstaff or bailiff. "Jacques De Molay, testify against King and Pope at your leisure, but this night I require your evidence in another matter." I made to sweep him away, for I was anxious to be done with this matter.

"What of me?" De Charnay looked old as a shade, not the fierce warrior that was de Molay's image of himself.

"I do not know," I answered him. "Did you know the secret of the box shaped like a cat?"

He fell to crying, "They placed my privities in the hot jaws and

274

my foot in a vise, and asked me over and over, but I knew nothing, even when my pain would have ceased if I could tell them…"

"In that case, I have no use for you. Go to Heaven or Hell, or wherever you are called, for you are no business of mine." I turned to his Master. "You, on the other hand…"

And as with Cyril, so many years before, but a few steps and we stood before Jehovah. We were in his study, but a number of the dead were seated around his table, as well as a selection of angels and the Imposter and the bird Ghost.

"Huntress," Nameless thundered at me. "How dare you? After Chud?"

"I go where I please. In the name of justice."

I looked to where Cyril sat at the table, not merely a saint but one of Jehovah's counsellors, ranked with Simon Peter whom I counted my one friend in this room, and Moses, yes, and that other Prophet too. He had succeeded in insinuating himself into the highest of places. His fall would be all the better and more pleasing. Cyril glowered at me, and I smiled back. He started to look concerned.

The Imposter smiled as if we were still friends. His voice was smoother than I remembered it. "Mara. Justice?"

"This is Jacque De Molay, former Grand Master of the Poor Fellow-Soldiers of Christ and of the Temple of Solomon. Who burned this night, by order of the King of France, for many offenses, some of which may even have been true. Jacques"—I turned to him and smiled—"tell them about your box and what it held."

He looked a little baffled; he was hardly scared at all because I don't think he fully believed where he was. Jehovah and the angels and Simon Peter he might have expected to see—but Moses, and the Prophet? The man was of his time, and a bigot, and therefore ignorant.

"What was in the box?" I was a little more urgent because I needed witnesses for this hearing and they were not, for the most part, especially interested.

"A woman's face. It advised me. I was given it by the previous

Grand Master—he said it was the secret source of the Order's success."

"And what did the woman look like?"

"Young, but with white hair. Beautiful, if a man cared for such things, but with a great gash from her forehead to her cheek."

"What came with the box?"

"A tray of fragments of flesh, that one pierced or burned but which did not change, but writhed. A cylinder of dust, that whispered. I was told they were some pagan thing that I could use"—he turned to face his god—"to your glory. Did I sin?"

No one told him. A minor angel led him away. I do not care where.

Cyril started to back away from the table. I don't know why villains so often do this, give up and let the game go when one last throw might save them—I think they grow tired, by the end. I was at once at his side and slightly behind him, so that he could not move. "Cyril, you said once that you would not have killed Hypatia, who was Sof, who was Maria, of Egypt and Magdala, because you wished to have her advice. And yet, someone found a way to have her advice, forever, and pass it on. In a box, in torment." I did not want, at that moment, to touch him myself. It would feel like dabbling my fingers in filth. "You killed and tortured my love, and I owe you for that. But you also lied, in the face of your god."

Simon Peter seized him by the arm, the Imposter by the other. I backed away a little—the Imposter and I had not stood so close since his death, or since the sword lessons I gave him once.

I went on, so that everyone could realize how serious this was. "Who told you what to do if she took the elixir? Who advised you?"

Cyril looked shifty. "One of the monks of the desert. I never knew his name. I looked for him to thank him when it all worked out for the best...He just said that, one day, he might need a favour. When the sleepers awake, and the ring of flesh bursts, and all is undone."

This was part of the truth perhaps, but I suspected it was by no means all.

I looked around the room, to see whether anyone reacted to those words. Only Jehovah knew that saying, which was as I hoped and expected, but was interesting.

"We will not speak of that." Then he turned to Cyril. He thunders normally at such times, but when he is quietly angry, his lips go white. "I don't ask much of my loyal servants, but you do not lie to me."

Jehovah struck Cyril across the face.

Not all of the dead have a sense of self so profound that they can bleed, that you can hear their bones break, and then reform.

"I trust you. I bring you to my highest council."

Cyril tried to speak, but then his eyes blazed with pain and there was fire in his mouth. Afterwards, there was a dullness in his eyes, and his mouth lolled open, with nothing within save char. Whoever his Master had been, his power could reach even here.

Jehovah shrugged with resignation. It was clear to me that something of the sort had happened before. He turned to one of his angels—I paid no attention to which because vengeance achieved is always a sick feeling in my stomach, which is why I take it so rarely.

"The usual," said the Lord God of Hosts.

I did not trouble to think what this might mean, but many years later, when I took Charles of France to Heaven for justice, I found out.

I stood before the throne of Jehovah, glittering with jewels, diamonds and emeralds and rubies and rare crystals out of shadow that have no name. And there, in the heart of a stone, I saw Cyril's face screaming in pain, though with that lively wicked mind gone to dullness.

Nameless does not like those who betray him. He keeps them close.

Judging

Hell 2003

The Recording Angel had a sniff. Every five minutes, for a hundred years, he sniffed. It was one of those slow ruminative sniffs that you think is actually going to go somewhere, that will end in a definitive gurgle of whatever angels have instead of sinuses, and something clearing for good. Every five minutes, for a hundred years.

He'd been there when Emma opened a bubble of space and time, something she was surprised to discover she could do, now she was a goddess, at least in Hell, where the rules of space and time were weird anyway. Jehovah and Lucifer had created the whole damned place with a shared effort of will, and it turned out she could remodel.

And there he had been, sitting at the table in one of the two rooms she had created, looking disapproving.

"The Lord God thought you might need some help." He had a

voice like a whole Russian church choir, that made your toes tingle. "I'm the Recording Angel, well, one of them. I know everything, the secrets of men's hearts and women's."

"Really?" Emma said sceptically.

"I know everybody's sins." He was obviously proud of this, as opposed to being embarrassed. "I know how you hid your pink candlewick bedspread in the bottom drawer of your college room."

Which was impressive.

"And how precisely was that a sin?"

"It was a present from your mother and thus hiding it from shame was a breach of the Fifth Commandment. Especially since the shame derived from coveting the superior aesthetic sense of your room-mate, whom you were looking at with unnatural lust."

"No, I wasn't. I didn't even know I was in love with her until after she was dead."

"I know the secrets of everyone's hearts."

Alternatively, she thought, you're a prurient legalist git and no wonder Jehovah has palmed you off on me.

"So what else have I done that's bad, apart from being your new boss, that is?"

He looked thoughtful. "There was a birthday party you didn't get asked to when you were ten. More coveting."

She had a sense that he was scraping the barrel. "And?"

"I can't see anything at all after the moment you saw her killed. I always assumed you died too, until you started showing up in other people's sins of lust and anger."

Emma thought of asking him precisely who all her secret admirers were, because she knew she'd always been clueless about this, but she thought that the sort of abuse of her employer's powers she would be better off not indulging herself in. She'd never had an employee before, and she wasn't used to having to think about these things. Better keep it professional.

"OK, then. Hit me with a list of sinners."

He winced. "That would take a long time."

"We have all the time there is. This corner of Hell runs on my clock." It felt very good to say that. "They'll be queueing up outside shortly. I sent Tsasipporash out to tell everyone in Hell that wanted to appeal to come here. Look, I made an anteroom."

Actually, she hadn't thought to, until now, but there it was. Already full. She was going to need a bigger…And look, it kept expanding. I'll get the hang of godhood eventually, she thought. She felt pleased with herself at having thought of something that the flame-coloured bird could do that got it away from her for the moment. It had defected from its former master a lot too readily; she had to assume it was a spy but if so, for whom?

And talking of spies…The Angel sniffed again.

At first Emma thought the sniff was some sort of professional criticism of her. After all, she was having to make the job up as she went. Actually giving all these damned souls some sort of justice and a lot of mercy—it seemed as if none of them had got much in the way of care or consideration before. Heaven and Hell had been slapdash where they were not straightforwardly cruel; there were souls here who had been damned at the age of five for saying rude things in their last fever.

Those were the easy ones from one point of view, but then there was the question of what to do with them once you'd reprieved them. You couldn't just let them go wandering round the universe on their own, and she didn't, in the circumstances, trust Heaven with them. These were, for the most part, kids that had starved and been hit and never got a chance to play safely, and she didn't see shipping them off to Heaven to spend the rest of Eternity singing.

Luckily, Aserath liked children.

She grew a vast purple jungle for them in one of the sections of Dis nearest the bower that she had created for herself, once her vines and creepers had pulled down the citadel. There were humming birds and small mauve furtive creatures that she had shipped in from somewhere in shadow.

There were a lot of mothers in Hell too—young women killed

before their children were born for the sin of fornication which often meant being raped, and women killed for stealing bread, or for whoring to buy bread. Emma couldn't unite them with their children, because even the Recording Angel couldn't keep track, but she could send them where children were, and let them sort it out between them. She might be a goddess now, but she wasn't going to be a control freak about it.

And every five minutes the Recording Angel sniffed.

He—he felt sort of male—was big and chilly and grey. He wore big spectacles that she was convinced were an affectation. For several months she wondered whether he'd stop sniffing if he took them off.

"Hey, Parvuil," she eventually asked, "why do you keep sniffing? Am I doing something wrong?"

"I'm Vretil," he said, "Parvuil is my sister. She's still in Heaven." Then he sniffed again. After a few years, he said, "I'm an angel. In a small room in Hell. And Hell is now full of flowers. I have allergies."

Emma visualized a box of tissues, and they appeared. She added an asthma inhaler and a bottle of Olbas oil, and shoved them across the desk. Vretil thanked her, and used them, and still sniffed.

Every five minutes.

"I could block him out for you," her golden armour whispered.

"Once I use you for every little thing, I'll end up taking advantage of your good nature," Emma sub-vocalized back.

Having something wrapped round every inch of you that flowed and shifted was weird enough; knowing it was a person made it almost creepy. It was like having a maid as well as a bodyguard catering to your every need.

Right now, it was mostly just gloves, but it had left part of itself attached to her ear like one of those headsets gangsters wear at East End funerals.

Nothing comes free, Emma thought, and I really would like to know to whom I am beholden. She was not going to compromise that just because of a sniff.

"Tell me who you are, and what you're doing here, and I'll consider it."

"I can't do that, Dave," the armour whispered and giggled.

The thing about being a goddess, Emma found, was that she did not exactly ever get bored. She sat for what seemed days reading sheaves of paper that Vretil endlessly scribbled and passed to her, and she memorized the details of hundreds of lives, and then she would spend day after day calling soul after soul into an office, where she would talk to each one of them and decide what she was going to do with them.

Tsasipporash sat on a little perch she had provided it with, and preened a lot. Every so often, it would say something sensible and she let it sit in because for a lot of the damned, it was still Lucifer's bird and a symbol of continuity across regime change.

Most of them didn't want to leave Hell, especially now it was a nice place, with flowers and fields and gardens. It made sense, she supposed; most people are peasants and so long as they're not being tortured, and can grow things, and sit down to a square meal of an evening, why would they want to go somewhere else?

She always felt obliged to tell them that they could now go off into shadow and have adventures, or that they could now go to Heaven and sing Jehovah's praises, but mostly they just wanted to stay, and find people who reminded them of their relatives, and engage in light manual labour.

Every so often, there would be people who didn't fancy that. Mostly, they wanted to do filing, which saved her having to do it— imagine being so traumatised by torture that you saw filing as an acceptable improvement in your destiny.

Gradually, the simple room with a table in it, at which she and Vretil sat and worked, and the room next to it, where she talked to the damned before telling them that they weren't damned any more, grew into an endless set of cubicles.

For a while, it seemed that she was living in a space as grey and

282

dull as Vretil, but then flowers started turning up. Vases of flowers on every desk in every cubicle; potted plants on the sills of windows that she was sure hadn't been there before, that looked out on to the endless mauve and green and purple and red vistas of the vast garden that Hell had become.

Every few years, Aserath would show up for what she had called a girly lunch but was more like a picnic that lasted a week, with hampers of food that seemed never to empty, and conversations that were a sweet flow of mild innuendo.

Emma supposed that she would sleep with Aserath sooner or later, because it would be rude not to.

The new Queen of Hell sat opposite her now, being languid and elegant, and every time she licked black and yellow spice off a well-grilled chicken leg, Emma felt herself shifting in her seat uneasily but pleasantly.

Aserath eventually crunched an ortolan, picked fragments of its bones from between her teeth, and smiled. She had brought champagne, very scarily good champagne. Emma sipped gently and then, when Aserath wasn't looking, poured most of it into Tsasipporash's drinking bowl. The bird didn't mind and guzzled cheerfully.

Best stay sober, Emma thought.

Aserath reached across the table to pour another glass and also to make sure that Emma got a serious view of her cleavage.

"You're a goddess now, Emma Jones, and you could be enjoying it more."

"Every minute I'm not working, is a minute some poor soul has to wait for redemption. I owe it to them not to have too many breaks."

"Go on like this and you'll end up as mad as the poor bloody Huntress. She never ever gets laid and hardly ever has snacks. All work, no play."

"I've only met her once." Emma remembered it vividly. "She didn't strike me as especially dull. She was mysterious and kissed me."

Aserath looked smug. "Well, of course she did. But then, Emma Jones, you always were special." She was clearly hugging herself over some secret too awesome to share.

Emma decided that perhaps she wouldn't sleep with her annoying colleague after all. Let her little secret keep her warm at night. After all, if she was going to cheat on Caroline, there was someone even more interesting. But then, secrets there too, even if she had guessed some of them.

Then Emma thought of Caroline and wondered whether she was OK and where she was hiding. With a sudden flush of guilt and shame, she wondered whether she was contemplating sleeping with other people out of pique that Caroline hadn't waited around in Hell for Emma to rescue her.

"Mind you," Aserath continued, her voice velvet with mischief, "the Huntress did have that little fling with Hekkat back in the day. Did you and your ghost ever try that one out?"

"Hekkat?" All these Old Ones and their former names, Emma thought; I promise myself I'll never decide to have a special goddess name. I know who I am.

"Morgan." Aserath let the name hang in the air and drip honey.

"I suppose I shouldn't be surprised." Emma decided to play along. With women like Aserath, knowledge is power. "We never fooled around with her, but she did show us the art gallery, and her toy boy composer said as much, come to that."

"It's true about the art gallery?" Aserath was impressed. "She never showed me that, even when we…"

She looked genuinely wistful and Emma decided to head any self-pity off at the pass. A compliment now would save hours of listening to her cry, and Emma really needed to get back to the office. It was a nice lunch, but souls were waiting…

"Obviously she cared about you enough not to complicate it all by starting you comparing…She wanted to keep it light. No dramas."

Aserath perked up again. "I can do light. I should ask her down here, show her what we're doing with the place. Next lunch—put it in the diary."

A couple of air kisses that somehow lingered like incense and she was gone to another part of her realm.

Then she was back.

"Meant to say, sweetie. So far, you've got ten shrines to my eight. I'm the Queen of Hell, but you're the Merciful Judge."

"People're worshipping me?"

"Don't knock it, darling. Neither of us exactly needs it, but it's a sweet bonus. You've got all the souls you've freed and all the ones who are waiting. You've even got the ones you've locked down, because you offered them the chance to repent and appeal. Hope— it's a better deal than the boys ever gave."

And then she really was gone.

With a quick flick of her own mind, Emma was back in her office, looking at her schedule. Oh goodie, one of the former Dukes of Hell. Lucifer's back-stabbing protegé here to try and persuade her that he was not like all the rest, and had some glimmer of goodness that a kind word might fan into redeeming flame. As if.

She'd done a tour of the cells near Phlegethon where most of them were being kept, a deal less cocky than the last time she had met them. Being digested by her lunch date had been a salutary lesson for at least some of them, she hoped. She just wasn't going to be persuaded of this easily.

Still, this one…Not a mass murderer or even an associate of mass murderers. Bit of a shabby con artist if you asked her—still, there are gods who probably started off as dingy little chancers, naming no names, she thought…And he'd managed to scam his way into Lucifer's court and survive all the plots and purges.

He was thinner than any of the photos and a deal more wholesome looking—new body and no time either to bulk it out with muscle or wreck it with other things. Presumably someone like him could find a dealer even in the new liberal reformed Hell that she and Aserath were building between them.

285

Vretil sniffed—he didn't always show up for these but this one obviously interested him.

Tsasipporash fluttered in and sat preening on a filing cabinet.

Emma didn't see it herself, but obviously some beings were interested in this one.

"So." Emma wasn't wearing glasses but looked over them anyway. "Wickedest Man in the World, eh? That's a big claim."

Aleister Crowley tried to be an overpowering presence in the room—some skills anyway, but this body not bulky enough for all that charisma to work with. Also, without the jowls, weak chin.

"Yes, very nice, dear. And I'm sure it used to impress people, but I'm a goddess, he's a senior angel and they're a mystic bird companion from the dawn of time, or something."

"I saw Atlantis sink," the bird hissed.

"Well, there you are," Emma went on. "We're not easily impressed. What have you got?"

"I made love to women and men; I climbed mountains; I drank wine and took strong drugs; I ..."

"You got a lot of porters killed on Kanchenjunga; you got addicted to heroin as a cure for asthma, and how pathetic is that...Silly man, this is the Recording Angel and I've read your file."

"I performed blood sacrifice to the demon Chorazmon."

"A couple of chickens and a goat you paid twice the going rate for."

"I reformed magick..."

"You created a lot of misinformation for which those of us who've had to police the magical world are appropriately grateful."

He was starting to sweat. His reputation for evil was clearly important to him. What had Lucifer been thinking? Come to that, how had this little fraud got sent to Hell in the first place?

"The ring of flesh shall burst..."

Emma's voice was full of tolerance. "...The sleepers will awake and all will be undone. Yes, everyone knows that one these days. Who told you? The Huntress?"

Crowley looked impressed.

"Someone took a photo," Emma explained. "I saw it in a private collection." She looked at Vretil and the bird, then put on her benevolent understanding face. "You know, I'm inclined to let you go. You seem to have talked Lucifer into taking you seriously, but then you always were a good liar."

And then she realized that he wasn't scared of not being taken seriously; he was scared of being let go. She looked enquiringly at him.

"I'm probably safe in Hell," he whispered. "I'd be safest in the under-dungeon if that were still in use."

"So, who's after you?" Emma was starting to be intrigued.

"I can't say." The poor man was terrified. "I betrayed the Huntress but I don't expect she'd hold a grudge. It only inconvenienced her for a bit...But if I said who I betrayed her to..."

"He's right."

An elegant young man with soulful eyes, brown skin and a robe that looked as if it were somehow tailored entered the room, and Vretil instantly bowed. Low.

Tsasipporash chittered randomly, clearly put out by this new arrival.

The young man went on. "I saw St. Cyril blasted into dumbness and idiocy in Jehovah's own private study. Our Enemy has ways of getting to people."

Clearly, he was taking precautions against this, because he was accompanied by five, or was it six, angels who managed to flank him at all times while somehow managing to blend into the furniture and walls as if they were only partly there. Interestingly, he crackled with power and confidence, while at the same time clearly being dead.

He turned to Emma.

"I think we'd all like to know how exactly Mr. Crowley here managed to betray the Huntress. The only other people who've managed to lay a finger on her that I'm aware of are, well, the Lord God and Lucifer in collusion, the Jacobin Robespierre and the

287

previously mentioned Cyril. And the Bird, I suppose, that counted. And all of those had cause to regret it, in the end, one way or another. Yet here Crowley is...Vretil?"

The Recording Angel sniffed. Oh good, Emma thought, it isn't just me.

"I can't see her, as a general rule. So whatever happened between them is not something I can tell you about."

The young man smiled.

"I see. Emma—may I call you Emma? I know the Lord God does. Would you mind terribly if we boxed Mr. Crowley up and asked him about this in a secure location? We'll return him afterwards for you to make your decisions about him."

Crowley looked at once frightened, surly and sulky. "I don't want to go to Heaven. It's not safe and people would think I'd narked."

"I'm certainly not taking you to Heaven, you grubby little man. I mean to a secure location."

Emma did not like the sound of that. "I really don't think I like my proceedings being interrupted like this. Least of the mighty and all that, but common politeness."

The dead young man looked faintly apologetic. "I'm so sorry, where are my manners? It's just I've always wanted to know about that conversation ever since Morgan showed me the photograph."

"You call her Morgan." Emma was intrigued. "I thought all of you old souls called her Hekkat. Except for..."

And then she shut up, just in time.

"Fair point. I believe in politeness. After all, if we can't change our names from time to time, where would I be?"

Emma thought fast; this should be possible to work out. After all, everyone deferred to this young man as if...

"Ah." She had it. "You're the one Jehovah calls the Son, only you're not, are you? You're..."

"Judas." He said this quite calmly, as if everyone knew this. Everyone clearly included Crowley, she noticed, because she didn't think his poker face was that good.

Emma was silent for a second, digesting the information.

Judas had clearly explained all this, if not often, at least repeatedly. "When my half-brother tricked me into organizing his death, someone had to step up and take his place. Since somehow he managed to disappear altogether. His father and Lucifer were hopelessly wedded to old notions of godhood; the Lord God may be the person the One has chosen as his shadow in the world, but I refused to think that I couldn't serve the One best by running his affairs for him."

The awful thing was, he wasn't even arrogant. He had a puppy's eagerness.

"Jehovah still thought in terms of living worshippers, as if he were an Olympian."

Oh, she had it now. "So you talked him into putting a lot of the dead into Heaven to worship him because they're an endlessly renewable power resource. Heaven's a battery."

He looked at her with enthusiasm. "You modern people understand it. You have the language. I didn't, back then. I had to talk to him in terms we understood, like the way water pressure ran the machinery in the Pharos, or the mirrors in it reflected the fires of the furnace and made them light. He could grasp that..."

Crumbs, she thought, I always used to be glib about magic being a technology, but this guy really got it and made it work. Respect, even though...

"This place, though...How do you justify that?"

Judas had the grace to look ashamed of himself.

"I used to tell myself, well, law is a shadow of the true Law, which is the One's, and obedience is a virtue. I was stupid and wrong. I always thought Lucifer was just doing a hard job that had to be done and then I got that he enjoyed it a lot too much."

Emma wasn't happy. "So because you think Jehovah might be the shadow of some meta-God, you've fucked up most of humanity? We're in the place where good intentions lead."

"Well, there is the Enemy to think of."

She sensed that he was rehearsing arguments he'd been having with himself. She wanted to quote Josette at him, but that wasn't her secret to tell. Also, she suspected Josette would not wholly approve of Emma's own choices.

"Maybe we should deal with the Enemy when and as he shows his hand, like I've had to."

"You sound like Mara."

Oh, and there was history there. Emma could tell from the tone of voice. Poor bastard, he means well. She realized that she really liked him, in spite of everything. She wished she could tell him because it might take some of the weight of responsibility of his shoulders. As it was, she made as if to hug him, awkwardly, and remembered in time that he wasn't solid.

"Why aren't you in the flesh?" There was no tactful way of asking.

"The Lord God—well, you know—likes being the only one in Heaven in the body, well apart from Ghost, who's his Bird. And you have Lucifer's? Also, even now all the soldiers have flesh, it would be pretty hypocritical of me to take special privileges, don't you think?

Emma had never thought of being pure spirit as something someone might use as a way of punishing themselves.

"Also," Judas went on, "it's bad enough that so many people think I'm him, risen from death, and that what I did, I did to betray him. Taking flesh again, that would be the real lie."

That was impressive enough that Emma felt able to ask the really hard question. "Look,"—there really was no polite way of saying this—"I am a long way from being convinced that, even if there is some very abstract One floating around somewhere outside the universe not getting their hands dirty, that Jehovah is their chosen. Seems more likely that he's a chancer a bit more charming and lucky than Crowley here, who has been lucky in the people prepared to work for him."

Judas looked at her in horror. "If I thought that…Well, I've allowed terrible things to be done to people in his name. I'd deserve to be as deep in this place as any poet has ever placed me."

Poor bastard, Emma thought, better not make him feel worse about himself.

"Bloody Hell." Aleister Crowley was still in the room while they were having all this existential angst. "You two may like to think I'm a fraud and a crook, but at least I never tied myself in that many knots."

There were screams from the anteroom where the damned were waiting to be seen and then the noise of something huge banging against the door. The door cracked and a spike jabbed through it, a long tapering thing with corkscrew sharpness spiralling round it.

One of the angel bodyguards, who had just moved to the door to investigate, was skewered through his chest and started screaming. Then the door was off its hinges and a massive head followed the spike through. It tossed the angel, still shrieking and bleeding gold ichor, across the room, to lie broken against the filing cabinets.

Its whinny was like a turbine screaming, like a mob tearing a victim, like the wild wind in the world's last storm. It forced its way through the door altogether, shouldering the ceiling until the room stretched out of shape. Emma felt its will against hers, making its own space and she let it because otherwise it would just crush everyone under its sharp bloody hooves.

The innocent white hair of its flanks, and the bone-white plates of armour that lay among the hair of its side and face, were splashed red with the blood of its casual victims. Its eyes were mad with fury, magenta mingled with ruby and vermilion; there was not so much intelligence behind them as a blind vicious will that wanted to tear things apart and splash in the bloody pulp until there was no sign left except for ruin.

It fixed those eyes on Crowley and reared up a second before falling down at him, horn aimed at his throat, like a wave of malice.

Judas stepped forward and caught the horn in the palm of his left hand, so that it pierced it through, destroying the hand almost altogether with its brutal size and strength. With the fingers of his right hand, he dabbled in the ruin a second and flicked the blood into the unicorn's eyes, which in a second became as grey and opaque as pebbles.

If its whinny had been unbearable before, it was now like the torture of infants, like the creaking of the press in which they would be smashed to the wine drunk by executioners. It reared again and then collapsed on its side, kicking out and finishing the destruction of Emma's furniture.

The gold flowed over Emma's hand and arm and the sword came free, configuring itself as a vast butcher's knife. She walked across, wrapped her free hand in the coarse bristly hair of the horrid, beautiful, wild mad thing and hauled the head up, so that she could plunge her blade deep into the side of the neck and carve it across, silencing it and splashing fountain gouts blood over what was left of her room.

She wiped the blade clean on its mane, and the blade coiled back into her armour like a snake to its hole.

Once the screaming and terror were done with, she reminded herself that the room was in part a thing her mind made and maintained, and put it back as it should be. At a gesture from Judas, his bodyguard angels took up the dead spoiled meat that had been so beautiful, one at each leg and one the awful head, only a little diminished by death.

Their broken colleague watched them, lying whimpering where he had fallen, as they took the monstrous beautiful carcasse from the room.

"Aserath has dungheaps," Emma called after them. "Let the creature be consumed into flowers."

The part of the armour that was by her ear whispered a thing to Emma that she might do, and she walked among the crushed and terrified damned in her anteroom, healing with a touch of her gold glove where she could and, where she could not, whispering a verdict of redemption into their dying ears, and with a scalpel stroke sending them back to Phlegethon to be reborn free citizens of Hell.

Lastly, because she knew he would wish it thus, she healed the ghostly torn hand of Judas.

"How could it touch you?" she wondered aloud. "How could you blind it with your blood?"

Judas looked at her with the patience one shows to small children and the surprisingly under-instructed. "Virginity," he said, "is a thing of the spirit and not of the flesh alone."

"I hate the fucking Unicorn," Emma's armour whispered in her ear. "It always comes back, time after time. It and the fucking Lion. You were lucky they only sent one of them after you."

Emma looked to where Crowley was sitting, his head between his knees and breathing like a broken boiler. "It wasn't for me, not even as a trial of strength. Someone wanted to destroy Crowley here in as messy a way as possible, just to show us that they could. He'd be back from that, not annihilated, but it would tear his spirit apart, and he would spread the fear of their justice forever among other informers and potential informers."

Judas looked concerned. "What are we going to do with him?"

"Not Hell or Heaven, that's for sure."

Emma thought a little harder and then Tsasipporash chimed in.

"She ripped my nestmate apart, and we hate her for that. But we could send him to Morgan. You know how good her security is, and I'm sure she'd love to grill him."

"Makes sense." Emma nodded to Judas. "Can I trust one of your angels to deliver him? Crowley, we'll bundle you off like a parcel. Morgan will take care of you."

Crowley did not look especially convinced, but he was clearly a bit less terrified.

Emma had a bright idea. "Actually, you'll be able to make yourself useful. When I was there, Morgan's books were arranged in different rooms; I don't think she has an overall catalogue."

Crowley perked up. "I always did admire Casanova. He was one of the people on whom I modelled my career."

"And you get to end your career as he did. As a librarian."

A couple of angels had filed back into the room, wiping their bloody hands on their robes, and now they whisked the dead magus away expeditiously. Emma sighed and looked at the angel and the dead demi-god.

"I wish I could solve my own problems as neatly as that. How do you cope? I've already got all these life-stories and decisions rattling around my mind—and either they're ones I don't want or they're all the same. I know far too much about Mr. Crowley buggering people he didn't fancy for the sake of the"—she did air quotes—"magick; and I know far more than I have ever wanted to about ploughing and weeding. I worry it will all get mixed up by the time I've processed another million souls."

The Recording Angel looked at her patronizingly. "You just have to keep it organized. Build a memory palace and fill it room by room."

She'd read Frances Yates a long time ago but had never thought of it as relevant.

Judas was bouncy at her. "That's what I do, and I don't have nearly as much to keep track of. You imagine this huge building in your head—easier for me of course because I grew up in the building trade—and you divide everything up floor by floor and room by room and shelf by shelf. The ones you're not using any more, you put a door on, with a lock, and a sign telling you what's in there. With luck, once you've processed every single Hungarian peasant, you never have to remember anything about the conditions of their land tenure ever again." He made a turning a key in a lock gesture. "But it's still there if you need it. Because you know where you put it."

Emma had her doubts. "But doesn't that make the whole thing a bit too clinical? Doesn't it mean that all those lives just become statistics and regulations? Because presumably you lock all the emotional content away as well."

Judas shrugged. "What's the alternative? Burn yourself out on every injustice in the history of humanity? Have every damn thing

294

vivid in your head? Even Mara avoids getting involved in most of the things that aren't her business. If you don't look after yourself, and make decisions about what to care about, immortality and godhood can become an awfully long sentence."

She didn't have much to say to that, and he and the Angel left her alone to think about it. Judas made perfunctory goodbyes and the Recording Angel removed his sniff into an adjacent room.

Normally the chair at Emma's desk was hard and stiff—she'd always liked Rennie Mackintosh and now she could sit in one of his chairs every day, but that wasn't what she needed right now. And suddenly there was a sofa in the room, bigger than the one in her London flat, but with the same patches holding the stuffing in and the same huge plush tyrannosaur as a sort of cushion to snuggle up against, only she'd never actually bought it, just thought about it. The upholstery was a thicker velvet than she'd ever owned, and a darker purple, and the patches were a red that complemented it rather than clashing. It made her feel relaxed just to look at it.

She lay down and went inside her head and started to build an image. It was a bit like an Oxford college, with quadrangles and patches of lush grass and staircases with doors off them that you had to duck to get through, and rooms that were bigger than you'd expect; and a bit like an art gallery with everything in cases that had covers thrown over them at night to protect them from dust and early morning glare; and a bit like a library with alcoves and cabinets and locked shelves.

It was a bit like imagining something and a lot like dreaming it.

Emma took a whole pile of the memories of the people she'd listened to and freed, and then the few she had left in prison for the time being until they stopped being smug self-satisfied evil jerks who'd do it again next chance they got, and put them away securely in a wing of her brain. As she locked the green baize door firmly behind her, most of the first years of her judging dropped off her shoulders, and she remembered that those hundred years had been only a couple of days in the rest of Hell, less elsewhere.

295

She'd get through all of this as quickly as she could and still only be a few days late when she found Caroline, and Josette.

Except, when she opened her eyes, Josette was leaning against a filing cabinet, feeding peanuts to Tsasipporash. Emma felt abashed, knowing that she probably had some explaining to do.

Josette sounded more amused than Emma had expected.

"I thought we were going to break Hell, and tear it out of existence, not negotiate its abolition piecemeal."

Emma had been anticipating at least annoyance.

"Well, yes, maximal demands and all that, but what was I going to do when I raised the issue and Jehovah just rolled over and showed his tummy like a big friendly dog? I was assuming he'd just tell me to fuck off and do what I was told, but he was reasonable."

"He never does anything without a reason. Or without its being at someone else's expense."

Oh dear, Emma thought rebelliously, were they talking politics and ethics, or was this a television movie where she'd to deal with Josette's daddy issues? And then realized from Josette's face that she'd said it aloud.

Josette giggled. "Fair comment. I suppose. But he was a complete shit to me even without knowing, so I think I'm entitled."

Emma considered what she knew from the standard sources. "So, basically deadbeat dad until he decided you could be useful."

Josette clearly had a lot to be angry about, but she was also clearly a woman who enjoyed a grievance. "He used being the Lord God to sweep my mother into bed and then just abandoned her, as if he were Zeus or something. If it weren't for her cousin Joseph's wife dying in childbirth around then, I'm not sure he could have protected her from the village busybodies once she started to show. As it was, that worked out pretty well and I sort of think of Joseph as my real father." She looked wistful.

"Judas and I had a pretty awesome childhood—Joseph and Mary loved us, both of us, as if we were both of theirs, and Ghost used to show up a lot. And sometimes bring Tsassie here with them; they

296

wanted us to believe that they'd been sent, but actually they just came. Says something about my Father, that demon bird things cared more about me...But then there started being miracles, you see, and that finally got him interested."

"Miracles?"

"Small children's stuff, mostly. Mischief."

Emma remembered the pictures of naughty children turned into birds; her face showed it, clearly because Josette went on. "Nothing like the stories. Mostly building things and cheating on housework. Judas thought of most of it—he was always the inventive one. We'd get the pans to scour and I'd make a little whirlwind of sand, only Ghost saw us doing it once, and he told Jehovah. And suddenly I was his son, only..."

She paused. At some point—Emma had been listening too intently to quite notice when—Josette had stood up straight and taken centre stage in a room that suddenly felt like a stage set in which she was the star.

As was only right, Emma thought.

"Whenever he talked to me, or usually got Ghost to talk to me for him, all his big plans didn't sound like me. They sounded like some boy in his head, someone more like Judas, but not as nice...I really didn't know what I was thinking, because he was God and yet I resented him and didn't want to be like him and wasn't like him, not at all, or Joseph, whom I actually loved. There were thoughts I couldn't have because they were the abominations children snickered about and said the Greeks did and that was why Greeks and Romans were filthy."

Suddenly Josette was really, scarily angry. "That's why I can't forgive him. All the children for thousands of years who were unhappy in their childhoods and didn't know why. Because he wanted to keep his pet tribes from getting too close to the Egyptians and the Babylonians and made up all these rules about who you were allowed to be, and who you were allowed to love. And when just being made to feel bad didn't work, he let them start killing

297

people to make the rules stick. He'd have let them kill Mary; he nearly had them kill Sof."

Emma stuck up her hand. "Sof?"

"Mara's sister-lover, killed in the dawn of time and reborn over and over. My teacher and, not through any will of ours, my wife. My friend."

Josette wept, and Emma reached out a hand to comfort her, but let it drop again when she realized Josette was too caught up in sad memories to notice.

"When did you know?" That's so inadequate, Emma , herthought, I am being a stupid cis girl, like when boys ask me how I knew I was queer.

"Always, never...I knew something but I never knew what I knew. Only in Alexandria I saw these tall elegant slim women and Philo saw me watching them and hissed 'Abomination' at them and 'Sodom,' and then one day I was with Demetrius the Cynic and I asked him and he did not answer at the time. But then he took me to hear Valerius the Mime who was dressed like one of them, only with blood on his hands and blood at his groin. And chanted it, and I was never the same."

She was plunging deep into memory, Emma could see that. Her face changed as if she were remembering not the mime's words alone, but everything about him.

"*Attis hurries. Runs barefoot,*
takes a fast boat to Asia,
runs again.
Mad with Her love so that he feels no pain.
He loves.
Comes to Her woods and groves.
Then starts to cut,
cut with the flint that cut
feet.
Cuts deep and fast.

The blood begins to flow.
She plucks the last
Bits of her former flesh
Out by the chords
No.
Takes off their weight
loses that weight.
So
And slash
No words for what she feels
new made at her own hand
blood gushes on the trampled earth
at this new birth
of who she is,
of what he was,
of who she will be,
what he cannot be.
Her hand
Suddenly delicate white hand
Seizes the tambourine
The little tintinabulinking
tambourine
the drums, the drums as white, the calfskin drums, drums of Her sacrifice
cut from the bull-calf.
Stretched
stretched
drum beaten by the white hand
the light hand
fierce.
She sings soprano, sopranino, mezzo mezzo to the band
of her new friends, her sisters of the cut
who beat the drums
and wave the tambourines
and dance upon the ground the bloody ground

the sound, the echo sound, the piercing sound
of Goddess rite."

Josette's eyes were shut, as if she were asleep or in a trance, and as she recited, her feet shuffled in the steps of the dance she was describing. She was lost in memory and her face grew terrifyingly innocent and relaxed.

Emma hated to wake her.

"I know that. It's the Attis poem by Catullus," she said in the end, to break the spell.

"So then I knew, sort of," Josette said, "but it was horrid, pagan blasphemy of which even the Greeks and the Romans were scared. Even Demetrius was, for all his Cynic airs. She was an old goddess even then. Morgan who was Hekkat, and was also the Great Mother, though she has borne no children."

She shivered, as if she felt wind off the sea or from a mountain.

"But then things happened, and I had Alexander sharing my head and sneering at me that he knew how to be the son my father wanted and why did I not just go to sleep and dream of dolls, and I might have, because it would have been so easy. But I saw all that that man of blood would do to fill the emptiness inside his soul. Also, I feared what he might do to Sof, and to Judas, out of spite and love of mastery. So I stayed and I fought him through my mind and we talked, and I learned so much from him."

"You were possessed by the Ghost of Alexander the Great?" Emma really did not know where to begin.

"He was a tyrant and a monster, before I talked to him, but he was taught by Aristotle, and that had to count for something. He understood the governance of great states, even if he could not govern himself. And inside my head, he could not drink wine."

Josette looked serious.

"I learned a lot from Sof and Mara, and from Philo and Demetrius, and from Joseph my father. I learned most from Alexander and not just by negative example. I learned how a sword felt going into a soft belly and a prick into unwilling flesh. I learned all the things I never wanted to be—he taunted me with how he would do them with my body if I let him. But I also learned the road through Persia to India and all he had seen there; I learned sitting in justice and founding cities that will stand after two and a half thousand years and making men who had hated each other stand together as brothers. If I had wanted to learn to be a king, or a queen, I had the best of teachers."

Emma could not imagine the violation it would be, and to be able to be so calm. Josette saw the look of horror on her face, and smiled a quiet vengeful smile.

"Oh, he learned things from me he never wanted. He was locked in my head even if he thought he was the rapist, the invader, when he came there. I won't say he learned compassion, but in the end he learned that there were limits to his own courage. He stayed with me for the scourging, and the long walk under the hot sun, and he was there for the nails, but he left before the choking and the spear through the heart. I've always wondered where he is; we never met again. If there is a One, and they are just, I pray mercy for him; he was my other brother. And though I love them both, who can say which of them has done most harm."

"I've just met Judas. He's worryingly charming."

Josette laughed. "He has big brown eyes and a broken heart. Always seductive, I've found."

"A broken heart? Mara?"

"He never stood a chance, poor lamb. No one does. Her sisters have her heart, and for all she says otherwise, Hekkat a little. No man, not even Voltaire, not that he was all that bothered. Too caught up with Miss Wild."

The last long while, even now she had locked so much of it away, had left Emma feeling older than she had ever expected to be, but she realized that she was still a child. Maybe almost as old as Polly, but...

"I didn't treat my brother well, back then. I did what I had to do and I never thought it would lead to his death. I am sorry for that, but not the sort of sorry you can ever apologize for. It's not as if he hasn't profited from what I did and persuaded him to do."

This was obviously the conversation in which Emma got to ask everything, and it probably wouldn't come round again. "So you died to rid yourself of Alexander?"

"No, though I dared him to stay and die again with me. I died so that I could not be used; Jehovah wanted a general and a god-king, and I would not be that and I would not let Alexander be that a second time. If I lived, Jehovah had hostages, and I deserved to die, because I was an abomination. Remember, I still believed that the Law was a thing of the One. How could I live? Only, I came back."

Emma waited for an explanation, and it followed almost immediately.

"It was Mara, unable to mind her own business as usual. Ghost sent her to save me when Jehovah was waiting for me to lose my nerve and beg to live on his terms, but she listened to reason when I told her to let me die. Only she had to meddle and she killed me to save me further pain."

The pause that followed was only partly Josette playing the story for maximum drama.

"It was her spear. I think it was her spear. She has killed so many gods with that spear, gods of evil, but also the one who set her on her path in vengeance for his death all those years ago. The spear stored something. I died, and then I came back. The One, if there is a One, wanted me back and wanted me to find my own path, I believe. A path that had nothing to do with Jehovah, or even with Mara, whom I found it hard to forgive for a century or two."

She opened her arms in an all-encompassing gesture that Emma understood to include her body, her incarnation in her flesh, her past and her future.

"I awoke free of my guilt, of my sense that I was an abomination who ought to die. And so part of my path was clear. I needed to be where Jehovah could never find me because he would not look for me there. And I needed finally to be well, to be free of the sting in my flesh that had tortured me all my life."

She paused again.

"I am a healer, and so I healed myself. Once and for all."

Emma got up from the sofa and flung her arms about her employer and friend. Clearly, Josette needed a lot more hugs than life had ever given her. The hug went on for rather longer than Emma had originally intended and involved a lot more tongue.

At some point, they weren't standing, but lying in each other's arms on the sofa.

When they came up for air, they looked at each other with new and slightly scared eyes.

"Caroline?" Josette eventually said, pushing herself up on one arm.

Emma snuggled up against her and looked up at her.

"Isn't here, and wouldn't mind. Except for the not being here part that is."

The piece of armour in Emma's ear giggled at her. It was a very familiar giggle, Emma suddenly noticed.

"Caroline?" she said, nervously.

"Good guess," the armour whispered seductively, "but no."

"Are you anywhere nearer knowing where the armour came from?" Josette stroked the ear-piece.

"Tell her to do that again…"

"All I know for certain is that it is in some sense a person. Other than that, it's being annoyingly coy. And stroking it like that only encourages it."

The ear-piece tweaked the skin it lay against—almost painfully. Clearly it did not take kindly to being teased. Emma thought of when she was going to be entirely enfolded in armour, flush against every bit of her skin. It was a very sexual thought, perhaps because it was also a very frightening one.

"I have trust issues," she whispered.

"Trust me," the armour whispered back.

Josette looked at the same time amused and intrigued. "I can control what I am wearing, as you know, but it's never become my imaginary friend. Between that and the sword and the bag and the creature who lives inside it, you've quite a collection of magical servants."

"They're not my servants. They're my friends." Emma was aware that she sounded aggrieved.

"That, I am told, is how one acquires magical servants. I wouldn't know. I travel light."

Poor lamb, Emma thought, two thousand years of keeping out of sight, then realized that Josette was still feeding peanuts to the bird she had been told to think of as hers. And the light dawned. "Oh, Tsasipporash is one of your agents. She was spying on Lucifer for you. Does she know where Caroline…?"

Emma had previously assumed that the bird would have told her if it had known, but she hadn't exactly gone out of her way to be ingratiating.

"He left me behind," the bird squawked moodily from its new perch on the back of the sofa. "I'd have told him not to bother— which is why he didn't tell me before he came to see you and indulge his spite. Look at the consequences; he was always wilful and that's why I've never felt a huge obligation to be loyal to him."

"Tsassie spotted me when I was undercover in the retinue of the Divine Antinous. Luckily, they felt no especial need to tell anyone, and we've been feeding each other information ever since. They're a discreet bird."

Tsasipporash fanned their tail feathers. OK, Emma got it, non-binary pronoun. "Who was I going to tell? Ghost would just tell her master and the Morrigan would have used it to stir up some sort of religious war. And I've never got on with the other two."

"Apparently they were supposed to be Mara's, but so far she has always refused to take them on," Josette explained. "They're still waiting for her to see sense."

Emma was clearly supposed to have a view about this. "These would be Thought and Memory, Odin's birds?" As no one replied, she took it she had it right, and moved on. "So essentially you've been under the radar for two thousand years, doing what? Stirring up subversive sex anarchy shenanigans?"

Josette clearly would not have put it quite like that, but, equally clearly, had no other way to describe it.

"Bad as things have been, they could have been worse." She was clearly trying to be modest and failing. "I did things that needed doing. In ways that you, being young and quite priggish, Emma my dear, may find shocking."

"You mean, like the way that you persuaded Tomas that his best option was oblivion. By posing as your mother."

Emma had no particular investment in any of the mythology, but she had thought that a little raw.

"As I said before, I set out his options, and somehow he just would not consider seriously the idea of seeking out everyone he had wronged and making it right with them. And I didn't impersonate my mother for his benefit; I just allowed him to persist in a convenient misconception. And I don't see what's funny about that," she went on as Emma chortled.

"And there I was, thinking that casuistry was an invention of the Renaissance."

"I used to think that whatever was done in the service of the One and for the benefit of humanity was an act of love. I was young then, and had seen less; these days, I'd prefer to talk about love and hope because no one that I have ever met has fully understood the workings of time and chance. One I knew, who wished to, but she is gone from us, her desire unachieved."

Judas, Emma thought, was not the only sibling with unresolved and unrequited passion, but she held her tongue.

"So anyway," she started after an uncomfortably long silence, "is there anything else we need to discuss right now? Because I have thousands of damned souls to judge and in most cases liberate. You can help, if you'd like."

She sat up, disentangling herself from her erstwhile employer.

Josette shuddered. "Given that most of them were damned in a misuse of my former name, I'd have an issue with that. And there's a problem we may need to deal with. I checked the holding cells at Phlegethon."

Emma suspected that she should have done that herself, thoroughly, but she could only take so many of the human Dukes of Hell at a time. She'd rather thought of it as Aserath's job, anyway—which was probably a mistake, now she came to think of it, because the new Queen of Hell tended to be too busy remodelling and growing things to do much actual ruling.

"Who's missing? I thought she ate everyone."

"The man Goebbels, who fell past us, screaming—and he is not in Underhell either. I checked. He'd be worrying by himself, but there's another one gone—or rather never there. He flies, so presumably Aserath never caught him."

Emma was aware that she was over-fond of the significant pause herself and not entitled to complain about other people doing them.

"Simon the Magus," Josette went on, "whom Mara, Judas and I defeated in Alexandria, and whom Mara caught up with finally many years later, with another band of allies. He is not an easy man to defeat, let alone to destroy. I have no idea what his powers are, here in Hell."

That was depressing. "I suppose one of us should tell Aserath."

The red bird started searching for fleas among their feathers in a complicated set of postures that Emma took as a hint that Tsasipporash was not volunteering.

She looked at Josette and Josette looked back.

"She'd want a lot of explanations from me I don't feel like giving her. And wouldn't be able to resist making a pass. She slept with my father..."

Emma could see that would be a problem; all she'd have to do when Aserath finally pounced would be say no. Or decide not to. She really didn't want to deal with this right now, but then, she didn't have to. "Give me a minute—" and she disappeared into her

306

interviews for several months before emerging with a bunch of sad memories and the gratification of having sent a thousand souls to wherever they needed to be.

Except that, in the two minutes of objective time that she had been gone, Judas had walked back into the room without his angels but with a small mustachioed minion. He and Josette were just standing there looking at each other, their mouths open—for a second Emma thought she had forgotten to get back into time, but she could hear Tsasipporash crunching whatever they had managed to catch.

This was pretty much the definition of a private conversation she did not want to be an intruder at; after all, they'd not spoken for almost two thousand years and they probably wanted to scream at each other. Privately.

"Tsasipporash. I think you need to come and see Aserath with me. Now." Her voice was more commanding than she had known it could be. She patted her shoulder and the bird flutter-hopped up there. She gestured to the minion, whoever he was, and he followed her out.

In the adjacent room, Vretil was standing with his ear pressed to the wall. Emma glared at him and he pulled away quickly, and snuffled rather than sniffed.

"I don't know what you've heard," she said sternly. "But I suggest, I suggest really strongly, that you put it in the deepest vault of your memory palace, turn off all the lights and lock the door. It's above your pay grade."

"I'm an angel. We don't get paid."

"Whatever." She turned to the minion. "And who are you and why are you here?"

The minion looked slightly miffed. "He said you needed help with the filing, overseeing all those clerks. It's just an excuse. He always thought I shouldn't be in Heaven and now he has an excuse."

Vretil put his hand on the minion's shoulder. "The Son never especially liked the last-minute repentance rule and with Josef

307

Vissarionovich here, you can see why. But he really is very good at organizing files—that was his trouble."

Emma looked at the minion again; the moustache was familiar, now she thought about it. Imagine the embarrassment of all concerned—ruler of the largest atheist empire in history.

"It was that bloody woman," Stalin explained. "The pianist. I liked her Mozart and she said that proved I was not beyond redemption, and she would pray for me. I was listening to her on the gramophone and everything went black."

"Oh well, I'm sure there'll be lots for you to do here. I won't guarantee you won't find people you killed among the filing clerks, but then, that was probably an issue for you in heaven. At least I don't expect you to sing."

Once she got away from the long string of rooms that her simple office had gradually become—it seemed like hours of walking past people bowing to her and stacks of files that really did need someone efficient in charge—it was a pleasant purple and pink day in Hell.

Tsasipporash flew off a little way to where people were tying vines on to wooden frames, and a few yards away, picking great clumps of grapes from those vines' neighbours. They came back with a cluster dangling from their talons.

"Gods shouldn't forget to eat," they said. "You lose the taste for it, and then you might need to learn it again one day, when worship fails. We have seen this."

Emma dutifully plucked a handful and chewed them one at a time as she walked. They had almost tough skin with just not quite enough tannin to be too much, and the pulp inside was soft and delicious, soothing, almost soporific. She tossed one in the air and Tsasiporash caught it in their beak and swallowed it. She did it again, but then her arm was tired.

"Poor love, you're so exhausted. You need to sleep," whispered the armour in her ear as it flowed over her body. "Don't worry. I'll take you to your meeting."

Emma really did need to file that last set of hearings; it would be sensible to let the armour do her walking for her.

She was weighed down with imaginary folders, a double armful, and she was not in the part of her memory palace she meant to put them in. In fact, she was somewhere in the palace she had no memory of building, in an ill-lit corridor lined with padlocked doors. Except that, when she got near to the first door, her glove, because she was wearing the armour in her trance, extruded a key, that fitted, and opened, first the padlock, and then the door itself.

She knew that some doors are not meant to be opened, but just a crack would not hurt, would it? Just enough to let some sounds escape and get a hint of what was there...

Raucous jazz music and voices shouting and a sense of bones cracking that would never heal and her own voice saying calmly "Sie auch sterben so," and the pavane theme from the opera she had heard in Brazil and Le Sacre played by four hands on an out of tune piano and—

She slammed the door back to, and closed the lock and then the padlock, and the noise of that final click woke her.

She would have to find that corridor again, if only so that she could retrieve all the case notes she had left on the floor.

The air was thick with scent and pollen and the humming of mauve and silver bees and the thrumming of cicadas and the chirping of starlings, the quiet cawing of jays. Of course, Emma thought, Asareth can't do sparrows because those are Aphrodite's. Only from the heart of the Queen of Hell's grove came voices, raised not in anger but certainly in the grumpy barking of men, or was that beings, with a grievance? Emma found it hard to believe that she was standing where the citadel of Dis had been; Aserath's vines and trees and flowers had not just pulled it down but had pulverised the rubble and used it as soil.

Emma was back in control of her legs and her arms, which felt as if she had been running hard and pumping the air as she ran. She pushed a curtain of vines aside and came out beside her co-ruler, who was wearing her fertility aspect but on a scale Emma had only seen from the dragon or the trickster imp. Aserath's current size, Emma might have expected a few more clothes, but then, fertility goddess...

Yet, this was her friend and her partner, and Emma felt considerably dwarfed but not in the least intimidated as she made herself comfortable, reclining in the hollow of Asareth's shapely ankle. Tsasipporath fluttered down and perched beside her.

"She'll hear us," one of the ape-demons clustering nearest to their Queen growled. "She's the Judge."

"You sure?" stage-whispered one of his associates. "My mate Shabburakh went after her in the City of the Angels, and she had bloody Sobekh gobble him down like a tasty snack. And she had the Inquisitor exorcise us in the belly of the worm."

"Well, fair dos," the first replied. "Self-defence, harsh but fair, I'd say. Like you'd expect from the Judge."

It wasn't clear to Emma whether or not he was being sarcastic.

She was getting more cheers than groans from the crowd of demons that were gathered in the grove. Senior demons, by the look of them, with time-blunted horns, and wattles and jowls, and pronounced beer bellies most of them. Do demons drink beer? she wondered.

"Millet beer mostly," whispered the armour. "They got a taste for it in Egypt."

Emma looked up enquiringly at Asareth. "There's a problem I really need to discuss with you, but it had better wait. What's all this about?"

The Queen of Hell looked sulky. "You got me thinking so much about the Damned that I forgot about my other subjects. They're not happy, apparently."

The entire crowd started yowling and shouting. Some of them had the sort of tusks that get in the way of articulate speech and some of them were just in an amazingly bad mood. Unlike Asareth, presumably, Emma had been on the occasional demonstration, in

310

her student days and later, and she reckoned that this was about a minute away from turning from an angry confrontation into a full-blown riot. Which was probably not a good idea when the main person they were yelling at was both arrogant and a part-time dragon.

Emma gave Asareth a 'maybe I should have a go at handling this' look and jumped down from her ankle. She walked over to the demon who had spoken first and took his paw in her right hand, clasping his upper arm in her left; she'd seen Presidents do this and it seemed to work most of the time.

"I can't listen to all of you at once, so I'll let…" She paused, and Tsasipporash whispered to her, "Ah, Kretakle, I'll let Kretakle here explain." Still holding his arm, she stepped sideways into her time bubble, and created a simple stool for herself. "A seat?" she asked the demon.

Kretakle had his pride, clearly, and said nothing.

"So why are you all so unhappy with my colleague Aserath? I thought she was one of you, first among equals sort of thing."

He looked disgusted at the very thought. "Well, that's it, innit? We're just scum to her, the hired help that Lucifer brought in later."

Emma hadn't studied the demography of Hell.

"She may have fannied around for a bit pretending to be a house imp and acting like she was down with the common people of Hell, but you can't trust her kind."

"What kind is that?" Emma asked, aware that she was possibly showing too much interest. She really did rather like her colleague.

"Well, she used to be a goddess in bloody Canaan, didn't she? And all those Canaanite and Philistine and Tyrian gods, well, they're all the fucking same, innit. Think they're better than us ordinary demons; they opposed the will of Jehovah and Lucifer, but they got forgiven and started poncing around calling themselves Dukes of Hell." There were thousands of years of stored up bile in his voice. "Not that any of them ever did a day's work, you understand. None of them would know how to turn a rack, oh no.

311

Think ovens stoke themselves, they do. Only now there ain't any ovens any more, are there? That's all gone."

He chortled.

"Of course, the Lord Lucifer got fed up with them in the end and calls in a bunch of us and arrests them all and slings them into Underhell—except somehow she fixes her way out of that, doesn't she? And we think, that's our chance lads, only what does he do? Take a whole bunch of sinners, what we're supposed to be torturing like they deserves, and dresses them in robes and calls them Dukes of Hell. And ordinary decent demons get screwed all over again."

This all had a certain logic, Emma supposed. She waved him to continue.

"So then he and they get Hell into a bloody stupid war over what, your girlfriend or something, and all the gold he's been stealing and stashing away. They can't win, and they kill a lot of angels and then Heaven comes down on them like a ton of bricks. And who gets shredded? Who gets starved? Us again."

"We did manage to stop that."

"Well thanks, for nothing. So then it's peace and somehow you two are in charge. That's a bit better, all respect, but only a bit. Because you change everything, and we get screwed again."

"So, what do you want? Democratic elections? That's a fair point." She had been feeling a bit guilty about that herself. "Let me just sort out the damned—free the ones who need to be free, imprison the ones who need to be in prison—and then we'll talk about that."

Kretakle looked disgusted. "That's bloody typical of the way us demons get messed around. The sinners get to vote? That's even worse. You and she would always win, then, wouldn't you? Because they worship you and they like what you've done to Hell."

Emma was beginning to see where the problem lay. "You don't like what she's done with the place?"

He spat and the ground sizzled. "Bloody flowers everywhere, innit. And vines—I hate vines. She's put away the lava, drained the stinking marshes. She's probably going to fill in the Abyss. We're not allowed to spool anyone's guts any more, or flay them with knives— I spent years as an apprentice learning to flay. Off in one piece, an inch at a time. We're just supposed to sit around, like they do, or grow fucking flowers or sodding vines. Bloody sinners—you're just letting them off."

"So, let's get this right. You want elections in which only demons can vote, because sinners are here to be punished, and that's your job, which has been taken away from you, and you don't like flowers so you don't want Aserath growing them everywhere, or the former damned voting for them."

She realised she was raising her voice a little, and tried to rein herself back in. Not his fault, victim of a set of cultural assumptions and all that. She hated being a benevolent despot, but it was like arguing with a Daily Mail reader. "OK, you've got a teensy bit of a point. Asareth has turned the whole place into a garden of Earthly Delights which might not be to your taste. But torturing is over. Before you ask, I'm not even prepared to let you torture each other."

Kretakle looked appalled at the idea. "That's a fucking disgusting idea. Typical bloody human sinner, mind like a sewer..."

Emma wasn't sure how much magic she had, which was possibly a good thing, because right now she would be really tempted to turn this demon into a toad. After all, ape demon? Giant toad would be a step up and everyone wins.

"If you girls won't see reason," he went on, "we demons have a better offer. There's some as respect us. And they have friends of their own..."

Which, Emma guessed, was where she came in. She turned time on again for a second, shoved Kretakle back among his mates and, placing a hand on Asareth's leg, pulled her into the bubble with her.

Asareth immediately shrank herself down from titaness size to only an inch or so taller than Emma, so rapidly that she over-balanced and stumbled against Emma, who nearly collapsed with Asareth on top of her, except that the armour wouldn't let her fall.

Was there a supernatural female being in her life who didn't seem to be macking on her, Emma wondered.

Asareth's breathing was loud in her ear—clearly for this particular goddess, the idea of personal space was a new-fangled notion with which she had no truck.

"This is serious." Emma stepped back slightly. "Apparently Goebbels and Simon Magus aren't in the cells at Phlegethon. And this lot are boasting about their friends, who will see them right over their demonic right to sulphurous air and several victims to disembowel every day."

Asareth snorted, and a wisp of smoke came out of her left nostril, slightly tarnishing the silver stud there and the chain which ran to her left ear.

Emma didn't want to get her closer to losing her temper altogether, which might be messy, but felt she had to go on. "I don't want to worry you, but with both of us here, this delegation might be what it seems or might be about to try to turn itself into an opportunistic assassination attempt."

Another wisp of smoke. "Let them try. I haven't eaten today."

She shouldn't encourage this sort of thing, but—"Sobekh says ape-demons are quite delicious. Funny, he said they're vanishingly rare, but they seem to be all over Hell, and the one I talked to was full of ancient rights and long-term grievances."

"No." Asareth frowned thoughtfully. "They were never around before Lucifer used them to throw my brothers the Baals into Underhell, And then I never saw them again until quite recently; I just assumed they lived in a part of Hell I didn't visit."

Emma made a decision and squeezed Aserath's hand to emphasize her point. "I think we need to leave. Right now."

Aserath looked truculent. "I'm the Queen of Hell. I can't just run away."

This made Emma even more certain that they needed to leave. "As far as I am concerned, rule one of being Queen is 'Don't get killed'. People depend on us, and if I were a Nazi war criminal whom you'd thrown down a hole I wouldn't be too fussy about how to get rid of you. Or me."

Sometimes you watch a friend's face change as you explain good sense to them and they congratulate you on your wisdom and you pat yourself on the back and everyone takes ages actually to act on your advice.

This was not one of those times. Emma had not finished speaking before she found herself in mid-air, with great wings beating above her head and the hand that had been squeezing Aserath's suddenly hanging on for grim death to the talons of the dragon that Aserath could suddenly become between thoughts.

Emma remembered what Saeed had told her about safe distances and waited until the ramshackle string of one-story buildings that were her own court came into view before she turned time back on again. There was a flare of light behind them, a sudden buffeting wind and a noise ahead of them of every one of Emma's windows breaking.

Aserath banked and wheeled. "My grove," she roared.

It wasn't there and nor were the angry demons they had left behind them. Where it and they had been was a barren circle again, one Emma expected would not be growing another crop of flowers anytime soon. There was nothing there but yards and yards of the powdery white dust that had been all that was left of John and Tomas.

"Kretakle talked of his friends, and said that those friends had friends of their own." Emma raised her voice because she was not sure whether Aserath's dragon ears could easily pick her out among the noise of rushing wind. "I think we have a serious problem."

"I wish you didn't still have that tiresome human habit of understatement," Aserath bellowed. "This isn't a problem. This is war."

Rites

The old man clung to the rail at the eastern end of the viewing platform, his stained leather apron flapping in the wind and driving rain. He kicked his feet in an attempt to get a grip on the ironwork, and one of his galoshes came loose and fell.

"For the love of God, Huntress!"

"Which god would that be?" I pulled one of the more delicate of my knives from my hair. I pricked his right index finger with it, so that it would bleed a little. I pulled it up, but not enough to loosen his grip, then patted a square of paper against it, to get a perfect print in red. I had a friend in London who wished such a souvenir for her private collection.

"Which god would that be?" I asked him again, in as gentle a tone as I could manage. "The god you hoped to dethrone, or the god Catherine and Mary called to in vain as you gutted them?"

"That was long ago."

His voice was arrogant still, but his eyes could not meet mine. His old arrogance had worn away with the years.

"And yet you wear your apron still," I said. "And I find you in this place of power, with a dead woman at each of its feet."

"They found me." Old Jack was shivering. "They made me do it again."

"And who would that be?" I held the knife to the hollow of his throat to emphasize my words. "Some demon? Some voice in your head?"

"I don't know," he said. "They came to me in the night and held me down while one stropped a razor before my eyes, and shaved my privates raw, and held the razor to my terrified prick. And asked a favour of me as friend to friend, but not as allowing any refusal."

"Men?" I asked him, urgently, for I wished to be done with this. "Women?"

"I know not," he said. "They had black silk around their faces, and were clothed in the night."

"You have lived too long, Jack," I told him. "There was a time when you would not have been caught sleeping. You managed to escape even me, which is something few gods and no other murderers can say."

He had been one of my failures. I had managed to break the power of the Ritual he worked, and put down the thing he raised, and prevent the thing he would have become by killing it. And yet I had lost him in the fog of the streets. I cannot say I respected him, for I detest all such; but there is a stillness at the end of hunts and stories. My sorrow was for the women I had been too late to save, here and all those years before.

And yet…

"I don't know who they were," he said. "All I know is that I failed them. One of the women below us spoke a prayer as I gutted her and smiled the smile of the saved as I tore the tongue from her throat. I had not only to kill them, but bring them to damnation and despair."

317

He sighed. "And I faltered. Because my hands and knives are old. Do you never tire, Huntress, with all of your years upon you?"

"No."

"I wish I were as remorseless as you. But you are less vengeful than they will be, I fear. Good luck with stopping whatever it is that they plan." He smiled. "And I choose neither to be their catspaw or your nark. I am Jack. And my dying curse on you and them."

Before I could decide whether I wished to stop him, he released his grip and fell from my sight. I might have beaten him to the ground and saved him, but I saw little point. And did not wish to. As for his curse, I cared not. Gods and demons aplenty have cursed me down the long years, and yet I still walk unhindered and unharmed. All I knew was that I had enemies in this city, who had planned a working to which tonight's deaths were just prelude. I doubted whether Jack's slaughter here, or even his death, was intended to be much more than a taunt. I have never met a man, god or demon who was not as obsessed with displays of cleverness as with commission of evil. The small model of the tower I had found among the carved-off hooves and tails among dying cattle in the slaughterhouse of Les Halles, with the slaughterers dead among them, had been just such a boast, intended to send me here just too late.

What they seemed not to realize is that the centuries have taught me a few things, including a measure of humility. Cities fall and people die, and I cannot save them all. Just be glad of what little I can do, to protect the weak against the strong. I had not been in time to save the four women, but one thing I could do for them.

Running through shadow with burdens heavier than their weight, I took each of them to the room full of tables washed by cool water that they call the Paris Morgue, where they would be cleansed and cared for, and those who loved them found. The men and women who attend there know me, as did the monks who did their task a thousand years before, and would not ask questions.

Jack, though...I would leave him to rot where he lay, in the dawn shadow of Monsieur Eiffel's tower.

I had turned to walk away, after coming back for one last look—I admit, one last gloat over a death that was long overdue—when my sandaled foot kicked something that splashed and shone among the rain puddles.

It was a hotel room key, which had perhaps fallen from Jack's pockets or had perhaps been placed there for me to find. Thoughtfully, it had a ticket attached, with the name of the Hotel Aurore, and the room number, 23, printed clearly in indelible ink.

Sometimes, my desire for information exceeds any fear I might have of the few traps that could seriously hold, hinder or injure me. As I looked at the key, the Japanese long sword I call Needful, which was slung at my back with my bronze spear and other weapons, thrummed in disappointment and admonition.

It was right, of course. Dead is a good friend when dealing with such men; but dismembered is a better. I drew Needful, and with my other hand pulled up the head of the smashed corpse. A single stroke freed it. When I threw it in the river a few minutes later, it hardly made any splash at all. One less possible weapon in the hands of my antagonists.

The room was anonymous. It held little to confirm the identity of its absent occupant save for a leather apron, neatly folded. It had never occurred to me that he would travel with a spare. Otherwise, there was nothing save the humdrum clothes of whatever his civilian identity had been, and one thing which might, had there been no clue as clear as the apron, have made me doubt altogether that this was his room. Pinned to the wall was a poster, of an androgyne swathed in light scarves and wreathes of flowers, with a head dress of the same. Looking closely, I saw the pocking of a thrown knife at its throat, and heart, and guts, and groin; clearly Jack's room, then.

The poster read, "Theatre of Monte Carlo: Evening of 19 Avril 1911: Ballet Russe".

It seemed unlikely that Jack, or his unseen controllers, were followers of the dance, so it appeared that the dancers were most probably their target and their prey. The room yielded no further clue.

I left, not by the door, and came out of shadow some yards down the street in the heart of Montmartre. I soon found a discarded newspaper on a cafe chair and checked the notices: the Ballet Russe had no performances scheduled for three days, after which they would be giving a new ballet. Its title awakened my professional interest. The Rite of Spring? I had known many such, and few of them ended in blossoms and lambs.

The Theatre of the Elysian Fields was a new building, washed by the rain of the night until it shone. It stood a few streets away from the Opera, a building which held precious few good memories for me.

From the noises within—odd snatches of music, the stamping of feet, the hammering of nails and the discord of men shouting at each other in several languages—I gathered that a rehearsal was in progress. Everything was going to be ready, if at all, at the last minute. This seemed to me likely to apply to any planned monstrosity, as well.

I took my seat at a cafe some yards away, ordered a coffee and waited for the rehearsal to break up. I sat peacefully, and from time to time a waiter brought me another coffee or a glass of water, and, when I asked for it, a piece of dry bread and some crumbled white cheese. When he asked me for money, I stared at him and he flustered away. I have no especial objection to paying for food and drink, but nor do I feel any huge obligation. I have saved most cities at least once down the centuries, and the labourer is worthy of her hire.

As twilight fell, an elegant young person in white tie and tails, with slicked back blonde hair and a monocle, and an untidy sheaf of sheet music tucked under her arm, strutted down the street and entered the café's further room. Soon after, I heard the sound of the music I had heard in New Orleans a few months earlier, and relaxed into what had been, for the most part, happy memories. I wondered who this confident young woman might be, and then brought my mind back to matters in hand.

Now, it had been my habit, these last few decades, to cast a low level glamour when in public, in cities, so that people saw me in whatever they regarded as appropriate dress. I hate squandering on magic the power that I took back from murderous gods, but the necessities of my work had gradually overcome my distaste. Small cantrips are the start of corruption, of course, but I had grown tired of being pointed at in the street by the year of the Great Revolts. A culture of sensibility and manners, backed up by disapproval, had forced me to change that the power of Romanitas and the tyranny of churches had not. I was used to these small spells working, and so felt some mild surprise when one of the three men who came arm in arm across the road from the theatre looked at me and started to gibber aloud.

"Look!" He pointed, throwing his whole force behind that finger; for a moment, it seemed as if it were feet long. "A witch. Or a demon."

"Vaslav, Vaslav." The largest of the three, an older man with something florid about his features, shook his head. "You must excuse him, mademoiselle. He is a genius and overworked."

"Can you not see her?" Of a sudden, I recognized him as the androgyne from the poster that had brought me here. "Dressed in black and carrying swords and spears and knives, as if she were at perpetual war?"

The problem with slight glamours is that they can be seen through by the skilled or by those with the sight, or, and I suspected this was most relevant here, those of doubtful sanity, though a fair degree of accurate perception.

"I've said it before, Sergei." The third man was a dapper young dandy with a receding hairline and pince-nez wobbling on a nose that was up-turned with more than arrogance. "Clearly Vaslav is under some terrible strain. His choreography for The Rite is not the brilliant innovation you and the others think, but a symptom. A symptom of madness. We open in three days and we are staring disaster in the face."

"That for your opinion, Igor." Vaslav spat at his feet. "You can talk about dancing when you can dance your Petrushka as well as I can. You have become so arrogant since Nicholas told you that you had dreamed the soul of ancient Russia, hasn't he, Sergei?"

"The whole enterprise is doomed," said Igor. "There is a curse on the whole thing. The theatre manager's secretary falls under an omnibus and the woman who replaces him cannot spell. The whole production is chaos."

"Shhh, my little ones," the older fatter man said. Another man had come up behind them and was hovering. "Trust each other, as I trust you, and it will all do very well. Isn't that right, Nicholas?"

"Yes indeed, Sergei." He seemed distracted. He stared directly at me, and I felt a pressure in his gaze that indicated some degree of power.

"Roerich sees her too," Vaslav muttered, turning to the man Nicholas. "Don't you?"

"I see an elegant young woman with whom I shall talk once you cease to disturb her," Nicholas said. "Now run along and flirt with the pianist, all of you."

"Such a pretty young man." Sergei was staring at me.

"She's a girl," Igor muttered, and Vaslav nodded.

"As if it would matter to either of you one way or the other," Sergei snorted. "Pay attention to the music he plays, Igor. In a year or two, I shall want you to compose a ragtime ballet, because what Americans listen to. That is the real music of the future. Just wait and see."

Igor fixed him with a stare that was meant to be angry and supercilious, but through his pince-nez seemed merely petulant. Sergei laughed at him. "Come, my little ones. Let us listen to someone else make music. We are on holiday." He clapped his arms around their shoulders, hugged them close to him and swept them off into the bar.

"My apologies, Huntress." The man Nicholas took a chair from an adjacent empty table, and sat down at mine. "They are all men of genius, in their way, but they can be tedious in their relaxations. And Vaslav is being driven to distraction by the importunities of Sergei and the jealousy of his mistresses, poor thing. They need to be careful lest they break him."

I enjoyed the way this man talked. As one above the game, who observed and mocked. Of course, I have known many, especially sorcerers, who delude themselves into such an attitude, and they were most of them men who thought themselves immune to conscience, consequences or death. And sometimes I have been involved in setting them straight on the matter.

"Igor?" I asked him.

"A brilliant musician," he shrugged, "with the soul of an accounts clerk and a relentless desire to be more interesting than he is. Sadly, it is only when he is at his desk or his piano, scribbling away at music paper that he is of any interest at all."

"And what is the point of the fat man?" I asked him.

"He brings things together," Nicholas told me. "Things happen round him. Art happens round him. He goads men into genius. I am sure you have known many such."

I had, and mourned them.

"Now," he said. "To business. You have heard of our little Rite, have you not?"

"Indeed."

"It really is only a ballet," he said. "Bits of Igor's dream were a little worrying, perhaps. He is a little more interesting, when he is asleep. But I got him to take those bits out, by telling him that they made no sense. And it is quite harmless now."

"It is a death sacrifice, like all spring rites, then."

"The image of one," he nodded.

I leaned forwards across the table to him, as one confiding in a new intimate. "Powers are taking an interest."

"Good god!"

"No." I shook my head. "He has never taken to the ballet; he even goes to sleep when the dancers come on at the Opera. Darker powers. Whose names and faces are unknown to me, even if they have them."

"That's not very helpful, Huntress."

"It means that you can probably rule out the usual suspects. Just go with evil forces you feel must exist, but don't consciously know about. On the other hand, they had working for them at least one of the more famous evil-doers of the last half century."

"Had," he said, in a knowing and conniving tone of voice. I refused to be drawn. "He met misfortune. But he was more frightened of his masters than he was of me."

"His masters are braver than I, then," said the man Nicholas.

That fear is your friend." I put my hand on his wrist for emphasis, and felt an expected whisper of power there. "It will wisely encourage you to tell me the truth at all times."

"I grew up knowing that fear." He showed the suddenly unfocussed eyes of someone remembering lessons hard learnt, long ago. "Ancestors of mine worshipped the Black God and I heard tales of what you did to him, at my grandmother's feet."

"A job well done, then," I smiled. "So, no problem with your little dance that you know of, then?"

"None—good god!"

There was a noise of breaking glass, and the large man came hurtling through the window of the cafe into the street, with the sleeve of his heavy coat protecting his head, and the dancer Vaslav clutched to him. "Apaches!" he gasped.

I was puzzled for a second. "Apaches? What…"

"They're a street gang," Nicholas told me. "Striped jerseys, pepperpot revolvers, and knuckle dusters. Sewer rats, pimps and their whores."

"Oh, them," I shrugged. "I've seen them around Paris over the last three decades, but I never needed to know what they were called. I can't keep track of everything."

I drew Needful, and pushed my way into the cafe against the panicked flow of people trying to leave it. I had dropped my glamour altogether, and they saw me as I am, and were gratifyingly impressed. In these latter days, fewer have heard stories of me; nevertheless, the sight of a young girl armed to the teeth and dressed in a black leather shift makes an impression, I find.

Several of the waiters lay on the floor groaning. By a back exit, two of the gang stood guarding a retreat. I rushed forward and struck at their hands with the flat of my blade, breaking fingers that I could have struck off, and smashing their weapons to the floor.

I put Needful to both their throats. "Where have you taken them?" I had already noticed the absence of both the piano player and the man Igor.

"To play for us," one of them said.

"At one of our little parish dances," the other giggled. "Our patrons have offered good money for a little spectacle, and made us demand their presence."

More dupes, then. "And if I were to wish to attend?"

One of them made kissy noises with his lips. "We can always find room for a pretty face."

"Between our thighs," the other added.

Such men think all women so threatened by their feeble masculinity that we go all of a vapour or into madness at any sexual reference. It is a sad delusion. And these two clearly wished to defer any questioning by provoking their own deaths. They were to be disappointed. I heard the belated sound of police whistles, and slid Needful back in its sheath, banged their heads together and left them for the *gendarmes*.

I turned to Roerich. "Is this city as obsessed as it ever was with what lies beneath its streets?"

"I cannot speak for the long past," he told me, "but that would be my impression, as a foreigner."

I seized him by the hand and dashed downwards into shadow. "Well, then," I said, "let us begin our search."

325

"I have read of this," he remarked, as we passed through lead pipes and ancient brickwork and occasional cellarage. "But what little power and knowledge I have gained in my studies has not taught me of the reality of it."

I stared into his eyes as one recognizing an equal, but one that needed, in this matter, some instruction. "Believe," I told him.

He ducked as our heads passed through the low arch of a sewer junction. "Flattered as I am to travel with you, I am not clear why you need me."

"I do not imagine," I said, "that there will be many pianos being played underground this night. But if there are, I do not wish to waste my time. And you know the man Igor and his music." I paused. "You are probably acquainted with the woman they have taken, as well."

"The beautiful Berthe? Young, talented, a sapphist. Paris has many such, but she may be special. Igor thinks so; she showed him a flute trio that she wrote a year ago, when she was thirteen or so, and he was in an ill temper for days." He laughed. "The female Mozart, if some lover or rival does not strangle her first."

I doubted, though, that those who had taken her cared or even noticed that she was such a paragon. Perhaps they only wanted her to play the piano, but to the tiresomely literal minds of those who perform such acts, she probably counted as a virgin, useful fuel for their ritual. It was with such worries in the forefront of my mind that we dashed through Paris under Paris, parts of which had hardly changed in a century or more. I recognized rubble, and human remains, that were of my own making and had been left to lie.

Suddenly Roerich pricked up his ears—there was a noise of men shouting, and glass being broken, and among it all the surprisingly gentle noise of a piano: a simple tune that felt like a summoning, but which stopped and started again, then a noise of pattering like rain that became the stamping of angry feet, and the summoning of something darker and its arrival.

"There we are," Roerich said. "So fortunate that they chose the piano four-hands version Sergei had Igor write for rehearsals. The fair Berthe will have been needed and so is safe, for the time being, I would think."

He looked at me and smiled. "I have known the odd hero in my time. And you so like to have damsels to rescue. All of you, even one as cold-hearted as my friend Koba."

I know now things I did not know then about Roerich and his heroic friend Koba, whom men would later call by another name: that of Stalin. He listened a moment longer. "And she plays her half of it better than Claude did, the one time I heard it all the way through. Surprising, given that she must be sight-reading. Perhaps they knew what they were doing when they took her."

We walked quietly, still in shadow, to the door of the underground room from which the music and racket were coming. As we approached, I smelled a scent I had thought lost for centuries. I had done my best to ensure its loss, because of the smoke of which it formed a part—a smoke which the trainers of the arena used to drive their swordfighters mad. And somehow, without the giant wild garlic of North Africa that stung to tears eyes yards away, the concoction of bulls-blood and bhang and the seeds of a blue flower some called Daybreak's Joy had ceased to have a reliable effect and passed out of knowledge.

"What is that smell?" Roerich wrinkled his nose, and made a strangled noise. I tugged the handkerchief from his breast pocket and stuffed it against his mouth and nose.

"Madness and death," I said. "Breathing through silk should protect you. My informant told me that the enemy go veiled and now I know why."

We passed through the wall and into a large room, some sort of cellar, arched and built of untiled red and black bricks. Igor and Berthe were seated side by side at an upright piano. They wore scarves of black silk wrapped around the lower half of their faces as gags, but also to protect them from the smoke that spiraled from burners in a corner of the room. Two of the figures Jack had described to me stood at their sides, facing the room, with pistols clapped to the sides of the pianists' heads as they played, and pistols in their other hands pointing out into the room.

In the middle of the dance floor, two couples, male and female, were dancing jerkily to the music. At first the dance reminded me a little of how the whores of Buenos Aires danced the tango in the early days. One man threw his woman almost into the back of the other, sidestepping the other man's partner as she blew him a kiss. It was a dance that was all sex and threatened violence, even to begin with.

As the music gathered momentum, one of the women reached up and drew her nails down her lover's cheek with a force that laid bare the flesh down to the bone. The other man reached over with a razor and cut two of her fingers off so fiercely that his stroke criss-crossed the other man's cheek. As if unaware of the pain, the first man threw his partner to the floor so that her head crashed and rebounded with a crack, and she moved no more.

Her partner reached over, planting a lush kiss on the other man's lips before bringing up a knee into his groin with maiming force. This in spite of the second woman, who had let go of her partner's hand and leaped into the air to wrap her legs around the first man's neck with strangling tightness.

The frenzy spread out from them like a contagion. Within seconds, all the ruffians and their partners were gouging and scratching and biting and hissing like cats in a bag. It was too late to do more than reduce harm and put a limit to the number of the dead. I drew my long sword and passed into shadow and through the throng, to stand in a blink of an eye close up against the two shrouded figures.

"Drop all four pistols," I said, "and you may hope to live through the next two seconds."

"We know you, Huntress," one said in a snarling baritone—this one was male, then. "And your sickly compassion for the innocent, and…"

And said no more, collapsing into the gush of blood that came from his wrists as I severed both hands, pistols and all. I turned to his companion, who whimpered a little. "If you use those redundant strips of cloth," I said, "you may hope to save his life. My compassion is for the innocent, and them alone."

The other shrouded figure dropped his or her pistols and set to, to tourniquet the wrists. Elsewhere in the room, with the rampaging murderous crowd constantly spoiling their shot, a couple of their companions struggled to take aim at Roerich as he bobbed and weaved through the crowd. He kicked over the burners, stamping at the hot coals with no care for the leather of his boots. He carefully kept his handkerchief against his face.

The two pianists, realizing that things had changed when they ceased to feel pistols against their temples, stopped playing and turned their faces to look at the room behind them. The man Igor at once covered his eyes from the carnage; Berthe, I noticed, stared with interest and a measure of concern.

With the smoke fading into the air, and the music's last clangorous echoes falling from the bricks, the surviving Apaches fell to the floor among the dead and maimed as if unstringed or unsinewed. The two adepts dropped their pistols, and dashed to an alcove at the far side of the room. There was a shelf there, with a small silver box open on it. One of them reached for it.

I had only seconds to pull a knife from my hair and hurl it at him, and my aim was not perfect. I managed only to wound the back of his hand and jar the box a little, so that it spilled silver dust onto the shelf.

The adept cursed and snapped the box shut. Then he and his companion disappeared into the alcove wall. Yet there was no door there. Clearly they, if not their subordinates, had some ability to walk in shadow. And no foolish loyalty to bind them.

Once the person in black had bound their companion's wounds in torn-off scarves, I reached down with the pommel of my sword and clubbed them both insensible, before wiping the blade clean on a scrap of silk I tore from their garments. The sword sang in gratification as I sheathed it.

Roerich moved to examine the powder spilled on the shelf. "Let it lie!" I called to him, and picked my way to it myself. I picked up a few grains in my fingers, and even the touch of it told me what it was. It was the peaceful grazing of cattle and their sudden panic as they were carved alive by men with great curved knives; it was the tiredness of a slaughterman suddenly bleeding on the floor he had so often filled with blood; it was the despair of three whores and the joyful resignation of another. It was the frenzy I had just seen, the passion of the dancers and their innermost knowledge that their wills had been taken from them and that they were being forced to destroy those they loved the best. It was the best of life, and the pain of its ending.

And it was so much more. It was the rush of power into me that I knew so well from each time I had slain a god. Every time that I think I have finally weighed and accounted for all of wickedness, I am painfully surprised by how little I know. I turned to Igor and Berthe.

"At least you two are safe."

I had been too late once more, but not by quite as much. Dead thugs who had willingly served men they knew to be evil magicians, and found that they were prey rather than minions—I would have saved more of them if I could, but I would not shed tears. Igor and the woman Berthe were innocents in all of this, and probably, as such, intended sacrifices. All the more valuable, because innocent musicians of genius forced to accompany what had become a dance of death would have ended in their deaths.

There were flavours missing from that damnable dust that evil men and women had hoped to place there: a small victory, but I have learned to value such.

I wished I had noticed that box sooner—or better yet, that I had arrived at Les Halles or the tower soon enough to stop it or its equivalent being used and then taken away. It is bad enough that those with bad intentions and worse deeds take the power of murder into themselves, worse that these seemed to have found a way to gather it and store it and perhaps send it in the mail, or sell it in the marketplace. There was nothing to be done about this for the moment, though.

I gestured to Roerich to place a hand on my shoulder. Taking the two musicians by the hand, I led them from that place of blood and death by the quickest route I could. I noted with some amusement that Igor made sure to grab both copies of the music from the piano before we left.

Sergei and Vaslav had kept vigil at my table. Both of them slapped Igor on the back, and promptly ignored him and Nicholas to concentrate their attention on young Berthe.

"Some brandy for you, lad?" Sergei rested his hand on the girl's left shoulder in a way that skirted lechery, but not by much.

"No, no," Vaslav said. "She is far too delicate for strong spirits. A healthy tisane for the mademoiselle."

He summoned a hovering waiter with a flick of his hand; amid all the bustle and death of that night, I will remember the graceful fluidity of that movement as I do the singing of my sisters dead these many epochs, or the dying sigh of the last aurochs.

Berthe, though, waved all this aside with a toss of her head. She looked at me; she looked through me, almost. I have seen the windows of cathedrals and the lapis jewellery that the Great Inca wore about his neck, and none so richly blue as those eyes.

"Huntress." She spoke as one who knew every particle of my tale. At such moments I am always torn between being pleased that my legend lives, to warn criminals of their impending fate, and surprise that it still makes its way across the ages. "My father is a student of Mesopotamian antiquities," she said. "I was reared on stories of you."

"I could tell you more such stories," I told her.

"Indeed, you could, but first I need to speak to Herr Stravinsky." She turned to him. "How on earth have you orchestrated that opening? Those minor thirds?"

"Bassoon," he said.

"Oh you clever man," she cried in glee and kissed him, firmly and deliberately, on the nose and then on the forehead, as if a child thanking an elderly parent for a present. Soon their talk was all of intervals and modality, and the moment when I might have talked more intimately with her was past.

At my side, Roerich chuckled. "With artists," he remarked, "the ruling passion to know how a competitor did it will trump gratitude, or even lust. If you want to talk—" he made a sarcastic little sign with his fingers over that word "—to Berthe, you will have to take your turn after the semiquavers and horn calls."

I shrugged. "Now," he said with an insufferable air of knowledge, "about these ninjas."

I raised one eyebrow. "Ninjas?"

"The shadow assassins of old Japan," he said. "I knew them at once by their outfits."

"That's not what ninjas wear," I told him.

"But the black, and the trailing streamers, and the scarves and the hidden faces?"

"Assassins," I said, "do not succeed because they wear strange costumes. They succeed because they know perfectly well that the best way to get close to your target is to look exactly like everyone else. Preferably a someone else that is trusted for her level of access and despised for age or frailty."

Ninjas walked the roads of Japan in the tatters of a poor peasant or the robes of a monk. They did not advertise their presence with elegant outfits in the most expensive of black silk. For one thing, assassination does not pay enough for that much silk. And for another, silk wears well, but not perhaps when your stock in trade is leaping across alleys and desperate fights on lone far paths.

"Still," I said, and watched him brighten, "you may have a point. How do you know about ninjas?"

"Read of them, in books of travels."

"Which tells me," I said, "that our enemies read too much and think too little. I am always happy to meet opponents who consider themselves to be clever."

Nicholas looked at me quizzically. "Because," I told him, "they rarely live long enough to consider themselves wise."

I am, for all my years, not especially wise—people have commented on my rashness—and yet I have learned a few things. One of which is always, if I have the luxury, to learn the place on or in which I will kill and save.

I waited while Nicholas and the others slept. Then I had him walk me through the theatre from the cellars where they store as yet unpainted canvases, coils of rope and the torn remnants of dancers' slippers—for there is power in those last which strengthens the ropes, gives intensity to any images painted on the canvases—from the cellars to the high ceilings above the walkways and pulleys and up onto the roof above the great skylight at the centre of the theater's dome, and the gallery beneath it where they wind the great sunscreen across.

"I love these," I remarked. "I always have. Once Vespasian let me wind the windlass which drew the shade across his great arena."

I paid particular attention to the skylight. It was one of the places through which, if that was their plan, our enemies would introduce their drug into the theatre. I also had Nicholas show me the ventilation system and the hot air vents—this was a new and very modern theatre, with new pipes and ducts all tightly welded and secure. Then he took me to the theatre manager's office, which Sergei had taken over for a meeting, We passed through an outer room where a secretary sat hammering away at a typewriter with her left hand, a room full of mysterious tubes. As I watched, she pulled the paper from the machine, placed it in a cylinder, and put the cylinder into an opening in one of the tubes. She pulled a lever, the opening closed and there was a fascinating *whoosh*. Human ingenuity knows no end, and is rarely harmless.

In the inner office, the impresario had assembled the theater's ushers and doormen and Chief of Staff, a bunch of tough, old men with the scars of battle on their faces and in their eyes.

"Gentlemen," said Sergei, and I noticed with approval the entire

333

sincerity with which he addressed them and the grunt of respect they gave him for it. It would make my task easier that they did not despise him for being a foreign aesthete of uncertain morals, but instead listened to what he had to say. Gentlemen, we have a problem. The other night, foreign nihilists kidnapped Monsieur Stravinsky and might have killed him were it not for Miss Mara here, and Nicholas, who managed to rescue him. We believe that they plan to make a nuisance of themselves at the first night. Miss Mara has a certain expertise in such matters."

There is never any easy way with such men, particularly when you walk into a situation and have to rally them round you. I could not be everywhere at once, no matter how fast I patrolled the theatre through shadow, and I needed these men to stand guard at crucial points. Some of them would have to fight under my orders and, in all probability, some of them would die.

Any reluctance they might feel to listen to me was in part understandable, though some of it—probably the most part—would be the tiresome prejudices of such men against short dark women. I dropped the glamour which had presented me to them as a woman dressed *a la mode*, then snapped it back.

"Nice trick, miss," said the Chief of Staff. "What do you do for an encore, saw yourself in half?"

"No," I smiled. One such man always selects himself as my volunteer from the audience. "I make fat old men disappear."

I picked him up by the throat, carried him across the office, put him outside the door, and closed it. Then I opened the door, shook him by the hand and ushered him back to a place of honour among his men, smiling at him as if we had rehearsed the whole thing.

"Gentlemen," I said. "Criminals intend to attack the theatre tomorrow night, probably by introducing noxious substances into the auditorium."

"Poison?" one asked, making a note in a small book, and in a tone so bland that one might have thought such things a regular occurrence.

"Of a sort. The sort of poison which leads men and women to run homicidally mad. You've all heard Monsieur Stravinsky's new score?…"

"Bloody travesty," one muttered. From around the room came a chorus of opinions: *bloody travesty, horrible noise, I quite liked his Firebird.*

"… So you will see that it is the sort of music that arouses violent emotions," I continued. "We just don't want the audience to get out of hand. Last night we saw some victims of the combination, and I assure you that it was not a pleasant sight."

"So what's the plan?" asked the Chief of Staff.

"Essentially, to prevent their gaining access to the skylight, the ventilation or the heating ducts. We will place armed guards—you will be issued revolvers and sabres—and rattles and whistles so that you can summon help. It is possible that they will be dressed in black silk pajamas and veils, more likely that they will be posing as innocent devotees of the ballet. But none of the relevant areas is open to the public—so you will know them by their attempt to gain access."

"And where will you be?" The Chief of Staff's tone indicated genuine enquiry, rather than insolence.

"Everywhere."

They looked at me skeptically, and I summoned just a scintilla of my power. "Everywhere" I repeated and the room became still as a schoolroom when the mistress enters.

With my preparations made, I wandered over to the cafe to take coffee and relax. To my delight, I saw the elegant Berthe eating a pastry outside.

"May I join you?"

"It would be my pleasure, Huntress." She watched me intently, with some amusement in her face. Though she was an adolescent, this was nonetheless a woman of character, who knew her own worth.

"Will you be attending tonight's performances?" I asked.

"I had planned to in any case," she said, "but Herr Stravinsky has been so kind as to give me a seat in one of the company boxes. So much better than where I would otherwise have sat, and a chance to mingle with my betters. Monsieur Saint-Saens, for example, my former composition teacher, who will be so unpleasantly surprised to see me there." There was an attractive malice to her grin. "He really did not like my trio," she explained, "and he tried to have me removed from the Conservatoire as a woman of loose morals."

I did my best to look appalled.

"Silly old hypocrite." she laughed, "when it is well-known to my Russian friends that he shocked Tchaikovsky rigid by taking him on a tour of boy brothels, where he was clearly a regular."

She laughed again, and then looked serious. "Bad things are liable to happen, later, aren't they?" She saw the answer in my face. "I shall be sure to have a scarf handy to protect my breathing, then, and a hat pin and a derringer for self-defense. But I expect you will deal with any problems that arise and I will not have to use any of these things."

"I would hope not," I told her.

"In which case," she smiled, "we will doubtless get to talk further at the after-party."

I was not sure that I would want to attend any such thing. Even to talk to fascinating young women.

Before the performance, I made sure that men were standing guard in the boiler room to prevent access to the heating vents and the ventilation system, which ran off an engine in the same cellar. There was another system of pipes in the room, connected to an engine but with no obvious access. I looked at these questioningly.

"Messaging system," said the Chief of Staff.

"I see," I said, but did not.

My guess had always been that our enemies would come to the roof—they seemed obsessed with theatricals, and something ingenious and showy seemed like a fair bet. Nicholas and I, and a few of the ushers, stationed ourselves around the edge of the vast skylight. The house lights went down and we were stood in near darkness, listening to the strains of music coming up from below. The moon was up and bright, and as silver as the music. It was a sentimental confection for strings and flutes, but I recognized it nonetheless.

"Chopin?"

"Yes," said Nicholas and then fell silent.

"I heard him play, once. In his villa on Majorca." And then I was silent, listening. In the distance, the music was being broken into by the chugging of an engine. It grew closer for a while and then cut out, as if something were hovering. Oblivious, beneath us, a waltz was playing.

The darkness was suddenly covered by a greater darkness—above us was an airship that until that moment had been hidden from us save for the noise of its engine. Magic is surprisingly poor at covering such things. Since most dragons passed from the world, I have become unused to thinking of danger as coming suddenly from what I think of as the empty sky.

With a snake-like hiss, silk ropes spun down from the gondola and men in black silk were clambering down at us. Moonlight glinted from the blades some held between their teeth.

I leaped for one of the ropes, feeling it slick beneath my hand. Climbing it hand over hand, I reached up and seized the legs of those I met so that I could pull them away from the rope. I did not bother to hold on to them more than a second, but hurled them I cared not where. I protect the innocent, when I can, but these were not they.

One pivoted on one hand. Seizing the rope above him with his feet and dangling upside down, he struck at me with the blade he had worn sheathed across his shoulders. I ducked under his blade and swarmed up under his reach, twisting his neck with my free hand until I felt it crack. He fell away limp, from my sight and my concern.

At the top of the rope, I hauled myself aboard the gondola,

grabbing the handhold offered by trailing black silk, before hurling that cultist to his doom as well. Most had descended already, but Nicholas and the ushers seemed to be keeping the upper hand. I had no time to watch, but was impressed nonetheless by the skill with which he employed his sabre and needle-gun.

I reached up with Needful and slashed at the gas bag—this time, I would allow none of them to escape to be a further nuisance to me and to the world. The sword sang to me of its pride in killing so vast a beast.

"Not quite yet," I whispered to it. "There is more killing than that of something not quite alive." I clashed Needful against my spear, and struck a spark, and leapt back down to the roof. The great ship caught with a sudden *whoosh*. It burned rapidly, but with a flame that only some of us could see to fight by—the glamour that had hidden its approach hid its death as well. Helpless, it drifted away, and I was too busy fighting for some minutes to observe its fate.

It was a silent battle, with music playing beneath us, and then a burst of applause, as the last few cultists, clearly outnumbered, nodded to each other and dived off the roof to their doom. It was just as well; I doubt I would have given them quarter, even had they asked for it.

I turned to Nicholas. "I have committed a grave error. None of them seemed to have about their person enough of the drug to affect an entire theatre, and none of them seemed to be nursing an injured hand." I thought a moment. "Is it likely—because I don't know about such machines—that a woman would be employed as a typewriter who could only type one-handed?" I have lived many ages, and each new thing is, alas, a source of possible error.

"No," he said, and I did not pause to thank him, but jumped down through shadow into the auditorium, now largely empty for the interval.

I left shadow for a second and sniffed—I could detect nothing, which meant that I was perhaps in time. I rushed into shadow again, and to the ante-room of the manager's office, where I left shadow for a second and sniffed—again, nothing, which meant that I was perhaps in time. I rushed into shadow again, and to the anteroom of the manager's office, where the woman secretary, slowed down by her right hand, was placing a glass cylinder into the message system She pressed the lever just before I could put Needful to her throat.

A case lay open on her desk with cylinders in cavities—she had only had time to deploy one. I stepped away from her, and closed the case. As I did so, she lunged, not for any weapon but for a sheet of paper which had lain next to the case. She stuffed it into her mouth as if to chew and I took her head off with a fast swing of Needful. Pulling her jaw open, I pulled out the paper.

It was a list of names—Princip, Ulyanov, Djugashvili. None of which meant anything to me. Suddenly the dead eyes looked at me and the jaw and tongue spoke without breath.

"We sent out the powder," it said. "You will never find them all."

I knew this was true, but I had a job to do here, today. I went to the boiler room, where the Chief of Staff and his men were standing around looking bored.

"They got one cylinder of the drug into the messaging system," I said. "Can you turn up the fans?"

"The performance starts again in five minutes," he said. "We are not allowed to run the fans during a performance. Too noisy."

"So turn them on for five minutes. That will either be enough, or not."

"The audience won't like it."

"They won't like madness and homicidal frenzy any better," I snapped. "If anyone asks, tell them it was meant to put them in mind of the chill air of the Russian steppes in antiquity, and they will think you all terribly clever."

As I ran through shadow, I heard the fans start up. In the circle bar, there was a faint smell of the drug, but not the scene of violence I had feared. Voices were a little more heated, perhaps, gestures a little more emphatic. Berthe was there, elegant in a dress that I would have said far too old for her, had it not suited her perfectly. Her eyes were very slightly glazed.

"Hallo, Huntress." She gestured drunkenly to the old and dignified man standing next to her. "Mara the Huntress, Monsieur Saint-Saens."

"The drug?" I said urgently.

"I heard the message tube ring," she said, "and I thought to myself, I thought, that's not terribly likely at the height of the interval. So I turned to my friend Alphonse, who is the chief barman and a lovely man, and I said, let me get that for you. And it was a glass cylinder, and it had cracked in transit and I could smell it, the same as the other night. So I covered my face, and I reached in with tongs, and I dumped it in an ice bucket and I covered it up, and then I went and flushed it all in the lavatory. I think everything is all right, though I feel a little strange."

"Perhaps you should go lie down," I said. I move among gods and demons and other beings of power. They wonder often how little respect I pay them, and how little vanity I take in my work. And this is why—so much of my work is done for me by weak mortal women and men, helping me because it is the right thing to do. If I worship anything in this world, it is the kind courage of the allies fate throws to my aid.

"I'm perfectly fine," Berthe said. "Right as rain, as the English say, I don't know why. Do you. Camille?"

"I hardly think," said the old man, and turned to me. "Mademoiselle von Renssler is clearly under the weather. I don't normally allow my former pupils such familiarity, even the talented ones."

"She is excited," I said, "about Igor Stravinsky's new ballet."

"You'll love it, Camille. There's a bit for bassoon at the start which is obviously a parody of you."

He went very red in the face. He was about to say something, when the bell rang and the bar emptied. He followed them out, muttering to himself. The bell rang again, and the fans cut out. I hoped it had been enough.

"Whoops," she said, and laughed. "Trouble-making again."

"It's allowed. You did a heroic thing tonight, and managed better than I did."

"The thing about heroes," she said, "is that we inspire each other. Just like musicians."

"Don't you want to go to your box?" I asked her. "And hear the music?"

"It's in my head," she told me, "and right now I feel too sick to move."

She sat down heavily on one of the now vacant chairs and I sat beside, her to see whether she was dangerously poisoned, or would get better. And that is where we were when the music started—those chords I had heard in the sewers, only played by an orchestra and more evocative even than I had heard them before. Almost at once, there was shouting, and the banging of fists on seats and balustrades and the cheers of some and the boos of others. Among the din, I heard Saint-Saens screaming something about the bassoon, but I could not hear him distinctly enough to be clear what.

After a while, Sergei came into the bar, and ordered a bottle of champagne and one glass. He wandered over to us.

"A scandal, my little ones," he said. "Always better than a success."

"I killed people tonight," I said.

"But only bad people," he smiled, "because, dear Huntress, you are a being of legend, and that is what legends do."

And as the three of us sat in silence, the orchestra and the crowd and the riot and our silence became their music.

For a second I was lost in the memory of that music and for a second I found my eyes closing, as they never do without my decision that it is my time to sleep.

And I heard the slow deep laughter of Crowley across the table.

"They told me some years ago that you would come calling for

341

me. And that I should feign difficulty in recognizing you and act as if I were more of a charlatan than I am."

I did not waste energy on regret. A habit of mercy, of treating even the worst criminals as people—these are not bad things even if they sometimes cause me inconvenience.

I let him think me closer to sleep and to paralysis than I was, because perhaps he would say something revealing before I had to make my move.

"I met Hassan in '05. We have corresponded ever since; he sends his regards as he sent you the liqueur. It took even more of it than he expected, but luckily..."

I laughed bitterly at him. "Have you understood nothing of what I told you? You have sold yourself to masters who care nothing for you."

He looked at me confidingly. "No, I have not. One task for them, and they leave me alone, in this world and the next. I know when I am overmatched."

He was going to be unlucky in that, because he was going to have to let them down. At least partially.

I yawned. Perhaps he knew more, but I had no more time. Sleep was overcoming me.

And so I let myself sink, through shadow, deep into the earth.

Sicily is an island born of fire, and there are bubbles in the rock. I could sleep without breathing—I had once before, in great need—but I found my way still partly wakeful, swimming through the rock, to a small chamber a mile underground. The rock under my back was hard, I knew that, but it did not feel hard. It felt like featherdown.

I did not dream except for once, towards the end, when I came half awake again and it seemed to me that the rock shook. I remembered a day in June 1916 and thought I was dreaming that memory of France, when I searched the high command of three nations to see if one was working the Rituals, or whether they were all dolts and butchers without any reason.

And then I was awake. Or, at least, no longer asleep.

I saw no point in leaving the rock where I had entered it and so I cast my mind, as I rarely do, and followed the scent, the very weak scent of my betrayer, through shadow and rock and into the open air and across land and sea.

I was almost certain what I would find, from the faintness of the scent and from another thing. Some who sleep, like the faun, will do so until the one who put them to sleep returns; but that is a thing of the Work. More often, we sleep until the one who put us to sleep goes to a last sleep themselves—a problem when your enemy is an immortal, but otherwise an inconvenience merely.

I did not need to enter the tasteless Gothic chapel from the chimney of which the last smell of Crowley was drifting into the December air. I could hear a few men chanting to Pan and watched as, afterwards, they huddled in the crematorium porch, in thread-bare winter coats, sharing roll-up cigarettes that smelled of cheap tobacco and low-grade hemp.

I would not have punished him even had I found him alive, though he would not have enjoyed my questions. As it was...

I am the Huntress, and I hunt alone, and I sometimes trust foolishly. But death pays all debts, and I do not meddle with the dead.

Fighting

"All things considered, it was rather fortunate we were both still here."

Judas the Knife, son of Joseph of Nazareth, adopted Son of the god Jehovah, was looking quite remarkably smug as he and his sister Josette hovered together, summoning emeralds from somewhere and shearing them into tiles with a wave of their hands.

After a while, they had enough tiles, and Judas pulled back, to leave her patting them delicately into place on the spire of the tallest tower in the new fortress.

She would probably have been looking smug too, but she was concentrating on making pretty mathematical patterns with them, and hardly noticing Emma and Asareth at all. She was cute when she concentrated and it seemed as if the only person she was paying any attention to was her brother, as they wove around each other in flight.

It was very reassuring the way they looked at each other. As if the last two thousand years, and whatever had actually happened then, were set aside and they were just being family again.

Building things together was clearly their way of bonding. They kept looking intently at each other, just to make sure the other was real, and was there, and was not shouting.

When Emma had left them staring open-mouthed at each other, she had assumed they were in for many hours of soap-opera shouting, but whatever had happened in her absence was entirely over. She supposed Vretil could tell her, if she wanted to know, and Asareth was clearly desperate to find out, but sometimes demigods need their privacy.

That was a resolution she had made when she found herself in the middle of their confrontation, and she saw no reason to stay. She hadn't expected the results to be so—well—constructive. Emma had never thought much about fortresses, let alone thought that one could be at the same time tasteful and impregnable.

Josette patted the last three tiles into place and Judas produced from nowhere

"It's her design," Judas went on. "She was always better at the big picture. I'm better at making sure the drains work and the doors don't stick."

"Too modest," Josette corrected him, smiling. "You've done a perfectly good job on Heaven, especially that throne room. I'd never thought of those endlessly recursive tiers of choir-stalls; you're so much better at geometry than I am."

"That's just numbers. I'm not an artist like you."

The suspicious thing was, they'd clearly roughed the whole thing out in considerable detail even before they knew it was going to be needed. Within minutes of Emma and Asareth arriving and announcing the assassination attempt and the demonic insurrection and the use of annihilation weapons, the siblings had been waving their hands around and excavations were gouging themselves everywhere. Another gesture and there were foundations with wells and cellars in place and a rather tasteful water feature hovering over what was presumably going to be the main courtyard when it filled in around it.

Of course, it was possible they'd spent their childhood and adolescence designing things for contingencies and this was a design from then—but no, that couldn't be true because in that case they'd have invented a sort of gothic Baroque blend millennia too early.

Emma was at the same time worried for the ramshackle collection of rooms she had unthinkingly put together, and a little abashed about its tastelessness. Vretil suddenly grew to titanic size, picked it up in his hands and tucked it into a gap in the rising walls. It fitted as neatly as if it were a drawer being pushed back into a kitchen unit and Emma knew without asking that, when she next went into it, the doors would abut neatly into landings on staircases. She'd never bothered to think about what its walls were made of, but once it was in place, its outer walls became the same solid basaltish stone as the rest of the fortress's inner keep.

Asareth was back to her normal-sized female form and had produced a comfortable chaise longue from somewhere on which she was reclining, watching other people do the work. Nearby, Tsassiporah was alternately preening and searching their tail-feathers, presumably for demon lice.

"Shouldn't we be doing something?" Emma hated feeling useless.

"When the fighting starts," Asareth yawned, "I shall be busy as anything, so I propose to take it easy while those two do what they're good at and we stay out of their way. If you feel some remorseless need to be busy, go off and judge somebody; I'm sure you've got a massive backlog building up."

"Oh dear." Emma had hoped that becoming a god would remove at least some of her capacity for feeling guilt about deadlines not met. "They're all going to be stuck here. In the middle of a siege."

"Don't be silly, sweetie. I'm sure that if you promise a free instant pardon to everyone to sweeten the deal, all the damned souls you've got queueing up for your little therapy sessions will be only too glad to get a chance to kick demon butt. They've been tortured for hundreds of years and we'll offer them a chance to get their own back."

Emma hadn't thought of it quite like that—she'd spent too many subjective years recently being earnest social worker Emma rather than fierce butt-kicking Emma and yes, she needed to snap out of it. Shit, she thought, we need to start thinking about this as a war.

"Vretil, Tsassie," she said aloud, "there's an army of demons somewhere out there looking to restore the old order and start torturing people again. You'd better fly out and talk to all the settlers and make sure they know this, and abandon their farms, and head here or up into whatever hills are nearest."

Vretil snapped a salute—she kept thinking of him as just a bureaucrat, but like all angels, he was a soldier. He spread his wings and was gone—amazingly quickly given that he hadn't actually shrunk back to his normal size.

Tsassipporah looked sulky. "Don't send me away, mistress. The formerly damned probably won't listen to me anyway—they think of me as Lucifer's bird, not yours."

Fair enough, Emma thought, always nice to have company while she sorted out her backlog. Or, as she supposed she had better start thinking of it, her army. She didn't have the foggiest idea what to do with an army, though—perhaps one of the others would know, though she got the impression they were all going to be as useless at generalship as she was.

She stroked the top of the bird's beak and they chirruped enthusiastically. Emma reflected that she had better not ever trust them. She still needed to get straight the story of where these birds came from.

She sighed. "I'd better get on with processing people—honestly, sometimes I think of all the damned stretching in a queue that will take me hundreds or thousands of subjective years, and my heart sinks. This war is just going to make it all worse."

347

"I'm sure you'll manage." Asareth reached over and patted the top of Emma's hand. "You seem to be good at most things you set your mind to."

Patronizing bitch, Emma thought to herself before she remembered that she really did rather like the other Queen of Hell. I'm always good at things, when have I not been?

Protecting my lover, one part of her conscience reminded her before the other cut in and said, struggle of love and duty. And you were told, weren't you? Workings of time and chance stitched you up properly...

Caroline seemed so long ago now, even though in the world outside Emma's head it was mere days. I used to think I was old, she thought, and I had no idea, even if I don't remember a lot of it. Imagine how it would be to be one of the real old ones—how do they stand all the days? They can't all lock it all up behind locked doors. Or maybe that's exactly what they do.

"Denarius for them?" Asareth looked concerned and Emma realized that she must have been looking a little gloomy. "After all, any problems we've got, are as nothing to those two. It's all gone far smoother than I would have expected—the Son seems to have mellowed an awful lot over the last hour or so."

Emma shrugged, "I wouldn't know. I only just met him. Actually, I'm more surprised at Josette—she's got a lot of quiet anger stored up towards her father, and her brother has been totally part of that whole shitty system. Constructed it, mostly. Still, family..."

Then she realized that, actually, Judas, being a spirit, could creep up on you quite suddenly, whether he meant to or not, and be one of those listeners who hear everything good or bad that you might not say to their face.

"She's not letting me off a thing." His voice was not exactly sad or apprehensive but it could hardly be described as happy. "A damned thing, I should say. Can I borrow your courtroom for a few aeons? There's a thing she's demanded I do—she's obviously been storing it up for years and gloating—can't say I blame her."

Emma remembered the alternative to oblivion that Josette had offered to Tomas. She started doing sums in her head. "I was just going to have a quick session in which I offer pardons to everyone who'll fight with us, even the bad souls, because if they're with us they won't be with their former allies. But we could make it all longer if that would suit you better—my time is my own, I mean, really my own…"

Judas looked a bit embarrassed. "Also, could I trouble one of you to put me back into flesh? I need there to be at least the possibility that some of the damned will want to punch me on the nose. She gave me a big lecture about how it's all very well preaching the virtue of humility but it doesn't mean very much when you're a spirit and can't blush. Or get a pie in the face—she was big on the importance of pie, for some reason."

"I'm sure she was speaking metaphorically."

"Now, about the flesh…" Judas could press all he wanted, but Emma did not have an idea what to do—she could see that it wasn't something a chap could ask his sister to help him with, but she'd never built anyone a body before. She looked helplessly at Asareth, who propped herself up on an elbow and started to make slightly operatic hand-gestures.

"Watch and learn, young Emma, watch and learn."

Judas' face went blank and then faded out, along with the rest of him. Emma looked down and noticed that his feet were starting to come back, an inch at a time, only solid.

"You can do it from the inside out, which is showy, and rather disgusting," Asareth went on, "but personally I prefer to do it bottom up, that way the head is the last thing. The secret is, anyway, that they mostly do it for themselves, but it's a magic feather thing—they have to believe someone is weaving a body for them because otherwise it's too disturbing. Also, they have someone else to blame for hangnails and embarrassing fungal diseases they forgot to treat before they died."

By now his legs were back and Emma noticed that, for someone

349

who had been a spirit for two thousand years, his calves were attractively taut.

"Personally," Asareth was being far too blasé about this—but then, Emma thought, that's just how she is about everything. "Personally, I draw the line at doing their clothes. I'm doing them a favour as it is. Clothes are up to them. Also, this way, I don't get those embarrassing moments when it turns out I've accidentally stitched a seam to their skin."

Emma averted her gaze—Judas really was coming back entirely naked and it was probably too much information.

"As I say, they do it for themselves, really." Asareth was actually pointing at the Son's genitals. Emma found herself blushing. "I didn't arrange for him to be cut—it's just an important part of his body image that he has no foreskin."

Emma realized with a shock of recognition that this really was an important lesson. She was starting to understand that becoming a god had its perquisites, such as that, when and if she found Caroline again, she'd be able to restore her.

And Josette can teach her how to do quick fashion changes while in the actual flesh, she thought nostalgically; she really won't want to lose that aspect of being dead. If we get her back.

The armour whispered to her, "We will. We need her." Which was at once reassuring and disconcerting.

She glanced back at Judas. Asareth had been right; perhaps one of the reasons to do the head last was that without it to confuse the issue by thinking the body just remembered faster. Up he grew, rib by rib; she hadn't thought of people in first century Palestine as being buff in quite that way, but then, builder.

Emma looked away; the thought of watching a face grow inch by inch upwards really was too disturbing. Almost instantly, she looked back because she was not going to be able to be squeamish if she ever had to do this for Caroline.

"It gets easier." Asareth reached over and patted her thigh without getting up. "You're doing very well. The first time I saw someone put back in the flesh, I was sick for days, though I blamed it on the stewed fish we'd eaten earlier."

For a second, the face—it was the same face that Judas had had as a spirit but somehow not quite, more earthy now it was solid, and different without the beard—looked blank and then that lively intelligence shone through the eyes and he was totally back. He looked giddy though, as if he had been spinning and was about to fall over.

Tsassiporah cawed, "Catch him before he falls," then fluttered off into the interior of the fortress whose outer walls now surrounded them.

That was not, Emma realized, quite what she had in mind because there were a couple of things she needed to get clear right now. She slapped Judas hard on the cheek and then did the same on the other side. He winced from pain, but at least he didn't look dizzy any more. Two birds with one stone, she thought to herself.

"What was that for?"

"I imagine you're going to have to get used to it," Emma shrugged. "I wanted to get it over with so that we can move on. I hate most of what you've been doing for the last two thousand years, just so you know, but hey! Not my place to do anything more than register that. But really! I know he's charming, and he was your sibling's dad, but how, how did you ever think that that appalling old con man could possibly be the representative on earth of some inherent deity or whatever?"

And yet, she knew she was being disingenuous. Up to a few days earlier, she too had let the old fraud into her heart and basked in the fact he seemed to like her.

Judas looked abashed. "It all made sense when Philo explained it to me, and then Josh—Josette, sorry—thought so too back then. It all fitted—the only other gods we ever met were her friends,"—he pointed at Asareth—"and a couple of the Olympians. He was rough round the edges, but he seemed like the most plausible option, once you assumed that after all, with some mysterious evil around, the One had to have left someone in charge."

"And while you were getting ready to fight evil, you might as well make yourselves comfortable? And let Lucifer run his private little torture chamber?"

"But the Law?"

"You were there. Did Josette not say stuff about the letter killing and the spirit giving life?"

Judas looked at once abashed and petulant. "Not you too? I just thought, well, there's got to be order and discipline if we're going to fight evil. And I suppose it all just got out of hand."

"You think?" Asareth had joined them, and Judas winced pre-emptively. "The Baals all took to it quite readily, but I was so much happier down here when it was all a matter of spirits wandering around looking sad. Much less work for us, apart from anything else. One of the reasons for the housemaid gig was that, that way, I could stay away from the pincers and the flaying. So depressing as well as being bad for the character."

"Anyway," Emma's grin grew broader, "it's not us you're going to have to explain yourself to."

Tsassipporah fluttered down. "I've put a selection of the damned into the Great Hall. Will a couple of thousand do, to start off with?"

Emma had suspected all along that the red bird's reluctance to go out on reconnaissance had less to do with any problem the damned might have with them than with basic idleness and a disinclination to go where there might be risk if they came upon the demon horde.

She gave the bird a withering glare and they cringed—the signs of a guilty conscience apparently cross species and that bird was sensitive enough to know why Emma was vexed with them.

Asareth was suddenly all enthusiasm. "Can I come? I've never seen you judging, and him apologizing as well? Got to be comedy gold."

"No." Emma could see she was going to have to be firm about this. "We have to respect the privacy of the formerly damned. And Judas here apologizing is a serious business, not your personal cabaret. Show some respect."

She herself felt in two minds about going; poor chap was going to have to go through the most excruciating of embarrassments. And no more than he deserves, she remembered.

"Two thousand for starters," she reassured him, knowing that this was going to be anything but reassuring, really. "We'll work up gradually to a proper crowd, one that could lynch you so thoroughly there wouldn't be a toenail left and we'd have to weave you a body all over again."

He looked appropriately scared. Good.

Emma turned that tooth smile on her co-ruler. "You, my dear, had better go and talk to Josette—I'm sure you've got catching up to do. And keep an eye open. Presumably a demon army is going to surround us at some point and castles don't defend themselves. See you in ten minutes."

They kept it short, in the end. A lot more than two thousand of the damned had crammed themselves into the hall, whatever Tsassipporah thought they had arranged—people in a line to be liberated formally from eternal torment were not all that likely to do what they were told, and after years boiling in lava, standing on your neighbour's toes was not going to be a deterrent to anyone.

Emma had done the quick throat-clearing thing that usually got the damned to stop yelling and be anxiously silent. She felt bad about it, because she was trading on patterns of deference and obedience left over from an old oppressive system, but things were all going to go so much quicker if she could just get everyone to shut up.

"OK," she started. "I'm Emma Jones and I'm your Judge for appeals. Only we may cut things a bit shorter than usual because there is a demon revolt going on, and they want to get rid of me and fling you all back into the flames. So free pardons all round—if any of you want to talk about specific offenses, you're welcome, but can we do it later? After and if we win the war. Now, there's someone here who wants to speak to you all, and will be taking questions

353

afterwards. You all know him as the Son of God, but I have news for you—that's his job, not who he is. Please, a big round of applause for the one, the only Judas the Knife."

There was a stunned silence—quieter than she had got with the cough. It's like tearing off a plaster, she thought, you have to do it and it hurts but best get it over with because honestly…

Judas looked embarrassed, but followed her lead. It was a really smart suit he was wearing; she hoped it didn't get torn or stained.

He was clearly having trouble getting it all out; he kept starting and stopping and starting again. "Look, all of you, it was like this. Um. I thought Father, well, Jehovah who isn't my actual father, not really, but anyway, he was the Lord God and the only god I knew and thought I trusted. And well, neo-Platonism, right, there had to be a real true God somewhere out there, but maybe not taking a hand directly. I thought, makes sense Jehovah would be his chosen shadow, and by adoring and serving, and helping organize things— well, it seemed like a good idea. And Lucifer was his friend and said we need to punish people because, well, it worked for Olympus and we had better morals. Only my sister, who used not to be, or maybe always was, but I didn't know—anyway, she's persuaded me that I was wrong all along. And most of you have been horribly tortured and I thought that was all right because well, I did something bad, only I thought it was what I was supposed to do. And I killed myself pretty thoroughly and painfully and that only lasted a few minutes but I thought it meant I understood and I deserved it and so you did. Look, I'm sorry. Now if any of you want to hit me, I'll be over here and I quite understand. I'll turn the other cheek. Oh crap. I'm going to have to explain it all to Father now I don't think he is the Shadow of the One after all, and while I am here being a punchbag, at least I'm not there explaining. Oh, and if you want to fight demons, you'd better form an orderly line by the exit and go and sign up."

He shut his eyes and flinched. Apart from a couple of kicks in the shins from people who needed to get past him to get to the exit, no one seemed terribly bothered with him at all, except for a small group of mostly elderly men who huddled a few paces away and argued fiercely but quietly with each other, and then formed a semi-circle around him.

Emma wasn't very worried; they were people whose sense of themselves as old and wise was clearly so important to them that they went back into the flesh that way. For the most part, they looked as if, even if they mobbed him, he could knock all of them down with a sweep of his arms. It struck her that the worst stain on the suit would probably be spittle or possibly just drool.

"Why are you tormenting us so?" one of them eventually sighed as if rebuking an errant servant. "None of us is fooled by this pretense." He had a slight Scots accent and a rather magnificent beard.

"What do you mean, tormenting you?" Judas was baffled and Emma only had the vaguest idea of what was going on. "You've just been told you're free to go."

"It's a tawdry illusion." This one looked vaguely North African. "And your explanation makes no sense whatever. You look like Him, but he would never say such things or display such doubt."

The fattest of them had jowls that jutted over his neck like a toad's. "The Son of God is God; God is perfect reason without hesitation; ergo someone who hesitates and makes no sense cannot be God or his son. It would not be logical."

Several of the others just stood there weeping, as if they had lost their faith.

Emma looked at Judas with amusement. "This clearly isn't any sort of coincidence. All the major theologians? All in Hell being tortured? How did that happen?"

"Jehovah doesn't like people presuming to be clever about him; he decided it was the sin of pride and Lucifer said it would be funny if they all discovered that they weren't the elect, even the ones who got canonized. They'd been drinking—they used to sometimes—and they tossed a coin for who got them all."

He turned back to his questioners. "You all read the Book of Job. Couldn't you take the hint?" Then he raised his voice a little. "Everyone blames me for sending people here. You lot are just as bad without a war with ultimate evil to worry about."

Emma tugged the fat man and the Scotsman by the arms and the rest of them followed her to a corner ,where she left them. The Scotsman muttered something like "The Seventy-fifth blast of the trumpet against..." but the others shushed him.

She glared at them sternly. "I need Judas here to help fight demons. I don't imagine any of you will be useful for that. So why don't you stay in this corner and construct some shared rationalization as to how none of this is happening and you've never been in Hell, because you are saints or the elect, and you are in your studies having nightmares?"

There was one old man who hadn't been part of the semi-circle. He didn't look like a scholar—he had a craftsman's hands and a neck slightly twisted from hard work in cramped conditions. He tapped Judas on the shoulder.

"Just one thing, sir. I always meant to ask if I ever got the chance and here we are. Why the blood thing? You were properly brought up, after all. And he made the rules in the first place. Then you go and create all this horrid stuff for the gentiles where they talk about drinking blood, and know it's disgusting, so make up all these stories about putting it in the matzoh. Why do that?"

Judas had the grace to look embarrassed. "I was trying to make sense of what got said at that last meal. And I never thought they'd take it that way. He and the Bird thought it made sense: things to argue about meant everyone worshipped harder, both sides. Thing about the Trinity is, I often lost the vote. Besides, Lucifer was usually in on things and Jehovah always listened to him. I just thought it was for the greater good. I'm sorry, I'm so sorry."

He wept, and the old man reached an arm around him and comforted him.

"I understand, boy. You tried to be Messiah and you weren't. Now, make yourself useful—fight some demons. I'll help."

But Judas continued to weep.

Easing past him, Emma ran from the room and up onto the battlements, and as she ran, the armour flowed over her body. To her surprise, the crowd of enthusiastic former damned who a few minutes ago had been so keen to get so involved with fighting demons were nowhere to be seen.

Josette and Asareth were leaning over the parapet, peering into the middle distance. Nothing much seemed to be happening for the moment except that there was now an orchard surrounding the fortress which had not been there before. People had flooded into the orchard and watching as bright red buds burst with a noise like firecrackers, and suddenly the trees were lush with purple leaves and pink flowers.

It was spring in that part of Hell for a moment and then the blossoms were done and floated to the ground like a pink blizzard and on the trees there swelled and ripened plums and peaches and apples and lemons.

Emma looked more closely, and some of the fruit were kumquats and cherries grown to the same luscious size. Vines raced up the trees and along the branches, and then, in moments, there were blackberries and thick clusters of red and green grapes.

"I thought we should feed them," Aserath explained, "so I borrowed your bird for a moment and got them to send the former damned out to eat. It's perfectly safe for the moment, no sign of demons. And they've never had any great gift for stealth."

Clearly any qualms the former damned had about the red bird had been overcome. Especially by the mention of food.

Josette looked thoughtful. "I'm afraid that the fact the demon army hasn't got here yet probably means that they're trying to find formerly damned settlers to torture, eat or kill. It's a good thing that you sent Vretil off to warn them, but it worries me a little that he

357

hasn't come back yet." She peered off into the middle distance as if looking and pulling a worried face could actually make something happen.

"He hasn't been gone very long." Emma shared her worry. "How long should we give him before we start being seriously concerned? He is flying, after all, and as far as I know most demons can't."

"Normally that wouldn't worry me, but Goebbels got out of that hole somehow. That probably means that someone on that side is airborne, probably Simon the Magus. Thinking of which," she turned to Asareth and produced the silver hook, "could I trouble you for some dragon flame? This has been tempered in the blood of Leviathan, but a little more magic never hurt a weapon. It's brought Simon down twice and third time pays for all, but he will be expecting it."

It hadn't occurred to Emma that Aserath did not have to be the dragon, or even the imp, to produce a small but impressive jet of flame from her mouth, or that Josette could simply roll up her sleeve and bleed impressively from the wound in her right wrist. The silver hook showed no particular sign of heating in the dragon goddess' fire, until the blood quenched it and it hissed impressively.

"Can't hurt, might help," Josette shrugged.

Emma found herself losing control of her right hand momentarily as the armour reached out and stroked the length of the hook. It felt like warm velvet under her fingers and where they had passed, the silver shone with a new gleam.

"Thanks." Josette was not speaking to Emma and it was not Emma that nodded acknowledgement.

Aserath was no longer paying attention to them. She pointed into the sky as a dot appeared high above them, a dot that became the line of great wings plunging towards them. As it grew nearer, it shrank from distant titan to manageable proportions.

Vretil alighted—his robes were now chain mail, with the finest of links, but chain mail that had been stressed and battered and scuffed and scarred. Armour and angel were whole, but he had clearly known war. His normal impassivity was gone altogether and on his features shone a mixture of triumph, exhilaration and pain overcome. The sniff was gone altogether as he spoke.

"I warned as many people as I could. Some of them are coming here, with the demons hot on their heels, but most fled up into the mountains. They said that the Wild Damned would protect them."

"The Wild Damned?" Emma knew that there were things she didn't know and wasn't ashamed to be the one who asked.

Aserath was dismissive. "It's one of those stories humans tell each other in bad situations to make things seem better and which end up leading to sadness and despair. Hope is always a bad thing. The story goes that somewhere in the mountains of Hell, too high and barren for even demons to bother with, there is a valley to which the damned can flee, and where they are building an army which will one day overthrow Lucifer and all his works."

"But Lucifer's gone." Emma was also not ashamed to point out the obvious. "If the Wild Damned exist, perhaps we need to let them know this. We could do with them as allies right now, and we don't want them thinking of us as enemies sometime down the track."

"If any of the fleeing settlers find them, they'll know," Vretil reassured her, "they're desperate enough to keep running until they find someone. The demons are not waiting until they've won to reinstate the old order whenever they catch anyone—flaying and limb-lopping aren't the half of it. That's why I went down and reminded them that such things are never a good idea." He smiled a paladin's smile. "I know you think I am a dull old pen-pusher, which is fair enough most of the time. Just sometimes, I like to remember the good old days when we put down Canaan." He turned to Aserath. "No offence, your majesty."

"None taken. Those were good days, and good fights. Before Nameless got above himself."

They seemed to be having a moment, but Josette, who clearly thought this was not the time and place, broke it with a loud and not especially polite cough. "So where are the demons? Where are the refugees coming this way?"

Someone has to be in charge, Emma thought, and she was glad it didn't seem to have to be her. Aserath was an incredibly powerful ditz, but a ditz, and Judas seemed still to be having a melt-down. She trusted Josette—which was partly the habit of taking commands from her, but partly a sense that if she took control herself, it wouldn't be her, after a bit, it would be the armour being competent on her behalf whenever she did not know what to do. She did not know the limits of what it could do and she still did not know what it wanted.

"Do the settlers have any way of protecting themselves? If the demons catch up with them?"

Vretil was not as downbeat as Emma had expected. "All over this part of Hell, angels dropped their swords and shields when they burned, and the weapons did not burn with them. So many weapons lying around for the taking—good swords, better than the demons have."

A thought belatedly struck Aserath. "You mean like the ones I buried all over this area—I thought we wouldn't ever need them, which was foolishly optimistic. Oh well, since our army is out in the orchard…"

She said "our army" in a way that indicated a worrying lack of seriousness about the idea—Aserath likes having people to rule, Emma thought, but perhaps she doesn't have much idea what to do with them except give them things and be worshipped.

Aserath gestured, and below them suddenly the people picnicking on plums, peaches, apples and other less identifiable fruits found themselves tossed about as if in a storm at sea as the roots of the trees grew and twisted almost like arms and handed out weapons and shields from the ground, weapons that the picnickers gratefully took and brandished, before starting to make their way back inside the castle.

"That was handy." Emma found herself with the beginnings of

ideas. "I hadn't realized you had quite that level of fine control over vegetation. Is everything you've grown an extension of your will like that?"

Aserath said smugly, "Only about as far as the horizon. If it's not in my direct line of sight, it's harder, but yes. Why?"

Emma realized that what she brought to this particular party was not so much magic armour, or godlike gifts, as an intimate acquaintance with a lot of films that her companions had probably been too busy being goddesses, angels and international women of mystery to have actually sat down and thought about.

"It's nice to have an enthusiastic army. It's going to be important if the demons actually manage to get here, which some of them probably will, assuming they have more annihilation weapons and that sort of thing. But this means you control the entire terrain and as far as you can set eyes on is a killing field. Did you not think of that? Stabbing thorns and strangling vines and tripping roots and crushing branches. Also, routes through which the fleeing people can be brought to safety and which can be closed off, lethally, the moment that they are through."

Then she shut up, because Josette had caught her eye with a pleased, encouraging look which probably meant she had in fact thought of all this herself and had been waiting for Emma to contribute. Still, Aserath and Vretil seemed to be impressed, which was a score.

"Good point about the avenues of access." Perhaps Josette hadn't thought of everything Emma'd said. "We should go out and funnel the refugees towards them. That will also make it easier to get early sight of the demons and know which directions they're coming from."

"And most of us are capable, individually, of giving a demon army quite a fight if they turn up faster than we expect."

Judas had entered silently, and had clearly moved out of the self-pity part of his repentance into the belligerent amends-making phase. Sweet boy, Emma thought, such a boy.

"I'll go that way," Tsasipporah offered, pointing one wing in a direction directly away from the site of the former Dis and Aserath's destroyed bower.

"Are you sure?" Aserath asked mockingly. "It might not be the safest direction to go in. Demons may loop round and come from where we won't expect them."

The bird's voice was equally mocking. "We both know low-grade demons—not very bright or subtle."

Josette spread her hands in an attempt to make the peace. ""Yes, but human commanders. Some of us have dealt with Simon before and he is so very much not a nice man. He has scores to settle with me and Judas, though he may not know we are here." She looked round. "Vretil, you can fly, too, but you've already made one foray. So go high and look down at where the explosion happened and see if they're coming back that way. Come back, don't engage this time—it is the most likely direction and we need information more than we need you to give them another bloody nose. Aserath, you stay here; we need you to fiddle with the vegetation and this is the central point for that.

She reached out and gave her brother a hug.

"Judas, we'll take the two sideways routes. Most likely find refugees there and we're probably the most reassuring figures they could meet."

Emma, feeling left out, stuck up a tentative hand. She really hoped she wasn't going to be asked to do anything stupidly dangerous, armour or not.

"Yes, Emma. I do have a job for you. We need someone to circle inside the orchard just in case anyone doesn't take the conveniently empty pathways. You may meet demonic infiltrators, or the more paranoid sort of refugee. It helps that you're flexible. On the other hand, you may not meet anyone at all, so only do one circuit, don't stay out there too long."

Emma thought she had better raise another subject. "I get that the priority is the refugees, but hadn't we better start thinking about how we actually turn the people we've got, and the refugees when we get them, into an actual army? I have no idea how you do that...Aserath, Vretil—you've actually fought in a war. Any ideas?"

Aserath didn't quite giggle at the very thought. Vretil just shrugged. "The Lord God always took charge of that sort of thing— him and Michael. I was just a ranker."

At least Judas talked tough, but how much experience had he actually got? And Josette could handle herself, but more in a ninja sort of way than a cavalry charge.

For a bunch of gods, Emma thought, we really are useless sometimes.

Tsasipporah chirruped helpfully. "There are always a lot of military men among the damned and they can't all have been killed. Perhaps..."

Aserath looked vexed. "So while you're all swanning off looking for fleeing hordes, I have to interview lots of the former damned and interview a lot of generals. I don't know about you, but in my experience, most of them are narcissists with small penises."

Suddenly remembering something, Emma piped up, "Actually, what we really need is the equivalent of Regimental Sergeant Majors. The Duke of Wellington said to me that that was the key thing." In this company, she did not have to feel bad about name-dropping.

Aserath sighed the sort of sigh which means that someone is agreeing to do what you've asked them to do and isn't going to go on moaning about it. "Well, OK—and get back soon, because it's going to take ages and you can help me."

Someone had to do the boring jobs, Emma totally accepted that. Frankly she'd rather be here than helping Aserath chat up NCOs, and the armour meant that she could easily pick her way over roots and the occasional sword that no-one had picked up yet. But she was still already fed up.

It was the first time in years—years of subjective time at least—

she had been on her own, and she wasn't used to it. Even before that, there had only been a few days without Caroline.

"You've got me," the armour whispered.

"Yes," Emma said, "but either you're a person who isn't telling me anything about who you are and what you want or you've a voice in my head with nothing behind it. Excuse me if that doesn't solve the problem—talk to me, or don't talk to me, but I refuse to regard you as company until I get an explanation."

The armour said nothing.

She had gone a long way into the orchard, far enough away that the castle was only a looming presence in the middle distance, and then cut across. She came to the first of the avenues. It was full of people running, but there was nothing much coming behind them except for Josette in the distance, and so she waved and plunged back in among the trees.

After a while she could no longer hear the running feet, but there was still no noise of an invading army. She kept going. The next one will be the tricky one, she thought, it's the one closest to the site of the explosion, so... And then she heard the noise of someone stumbling as fast as they could through the trees and saw a white shape off in the distance. She flexed her hand and her sword sprang out of the armour on her arm, but almost immediately she released her grip on its hilt and it coiled itself back.

Whoever it was, was naked and gushing blood from a throat that was not exactly cut, and limping badly—though not just because of bruised and unshod feet but because they always had. She knew that gaunt face though she had seen it, on film and in the flesh, full of arrogance and sneers—a face now as tortured and agonized as when she had seen it in photographs burned to charcoal after his suicide.

That harsh vicious voice was gone forever—his lower jaw hung open and there was no tongue behind what was left of his teeth, and she realized that what was missing from his throat was, well, most of its interior. It was only because he was dead, and in the ersatz body of the damned, that he was even walking.

Right now, whatever else he was and knowing at least most of the terrible things he had done, he was an object of pity. He could not even scream, though she shuddered to think of the pain. He was also, clearly, a source of major information.

"Come along, Josef," she said to the former Minister of Propaganda, the Gauleiter of Berlin. "We need to talk to you."

Even in agony, he looked at her with mocking irony. A moment later, he collapsed from blood loss and exhaustion. His back was raw with whip marks and torn by claws—none of it enough to kill his current body, but enough to give him a modicum of the pain he deserved.

Nonetheless...

She reached down, and with the help of the armour, slung him across her shoulder. This was going to take less time if he didn't die and they didn't have to put him back into the flesh; she assumed Josette was still a healer, though she had never bothered to ask.

Weighed down, and running fast, she picked her way carefully. She could not have done it, or even dreamed of doing it without the armour.

"You underestimate yourself, Emma," the armour whispered in her ear.

As she ran, she heard the orchard trees creaking and twisting and dropping all their remaining fruit. The wood behind her grew darker and higher; by the time she was back at the fortress, it looked almost impenetrable.

Aserath was outraged. "Really? I have to help you harbour scum like that? Have we no standards? Can't I just eat him? I should have in the first place, but I was in a hurry. Then he can queue for a body like anyone else."

Josette shook her head silently as she placed her hand on Goebbels' throat, with a finger carefully inserted into that ruined mouth. As Emma watched, her friend grew ever so slightly paler and the maimed Nazi started to whimper, where before all that could be heard was the rattle of breath in his ruined gullet.

If you're a healer, Emma realized, you do it because it is who you are and not because you like the people you are healing.

"This is Simon's work," Judas said with certainty. "He will have stolen that tongue, that voicebox, because he wants to use them himself. This is what he does—what he always did back in our time—and if he has done it now, rather than at any time in all the years he was at Lucifer's court it is because he wants to persuade someone to do something for him."

When thieves, or in this case the utterly bastardly, fall out, Emma thought…Josef was lying there, clearly conscious and no longer in pain, but with his eyes flickering within that taut snake skull and his weak chin nervously drawn down so that he could fake the smile he did not feel.

"No one here is your friend," she told him, "and your best course would be to make yourself useful to us. Your former ally has turned on you and mutilated you, and whoever your secret masters are have let him; the demon army watched you fall and helped drive you out. They clawed at you and whipped you, who were once a courtier lord in Germany and in Hell. Feel that betrayal; we promise you nothing but revenge."

"Nothing else?" He laughed a bitter laugh that showed his white teeth even more. "I come to this, an informer bartering for my life."

Judas looked down at him scornfully. "We will not lie to you. We will not kill you either. If it were not for the self-deceit that has led you to this moment, you would know that is the best deal you have ever had, from any of your masters or colleagues."

Josette still had her hand at the German's throat. She kept it there as she spoke, as if she had rather be snapping his neck than healing his wounds.

"I was at the garden of the Chancellery when the Russians brought them out—your dead children in their white night-clothes. They might have lived, you know; you could have bought their lives, but you preferred to kill them and your wife and yourself in pride, rather than risk humiliation and death at the hands of your

366

enemies. I doubt you will ever see them again—but you did love them. A little and only to the extent that a man like you is capable."

"Your point, woman."

"There are children here, who have been tortured. And whom your former allies wish to torture again. Part of the reason you killed yours was fear that they would suffer before they died. In their name, help us protect thousands of others."

"Also," Aserath snorted some admonitory flame, "if you spill, I won't eat you."

Goebbels maintained an icy silence.

"We're not playing cards." Emma made a shuffling gesture. "We do not have time for your nonsense. Tell us what we need, or we will put you out of the door to fend for yourself. And when we win, we will exile you from even Hell to wander alone forever in the darkest parts of shadow."

He shrugged. "You Jews know how to drive a hard bargain. Very well. Clearly, I had no idea of what Simon now intends because part of it involved ripping my tongue out by the roots. I know that emissaries of some being he has dealt with before offered us weapons of annihilation like the ones that killed the army. I voted to refuse them, because they did little good before; secret weapons never perform as promised, I find." His laugh was like bones rattling. "Still, as you know, they seem to have given him at least one for free, behind my back, and the demon leaders who had made us their chiefs because they could not agree to serve each other.

"They planned an ambush against you, Lady Aserath, which I thought foolish of them. I do not think that the weapon that exploded had anything to do with any plan of theirs. I think Simon planned to destroy likely rivals far more than he hoped for your head. With them gone, he could move against me."

"That's bad news." Josette looked concerned. "Killing your own allies by treachery—we know that Simon eventually found his way to the Rituals because that was why he helped Nero with the Fire."

"Rituals?" The German looked intrigued.

367

"Nothing for your ears," Aserath snapped, and enhanced the point by slapping them hard.

"So," Emma calculated. "A power upgrade of some kind and stealing eloquence and a big dumb army of demons with no leader but him. I'm not getting a sense of someone who plays well with others."

Josette and Judas laughed bitterly. "You've no idea." Judas explained. "He's remembered for trying to steal the power that was given to the Apostles, but that was minor. He stole brains for their knowledge; he gutted mice and rats to steal their power to crawl through pipes; he had a blasting hand made of bits of ivory or bone."

Emma was aware of a very bad feeling. "You'd think we'd have seen some sign of his army by now. Maybe he isn't planning to use it as an army."

Even though he more than anyone here knew what Simon was capable of, Goebbels was the last to catch on to what she meant.

"Spare parts," she clarified, and, given his record, was almost amused by the irony that he looked appalled and disgusted.

"But what did he want with my tongue and throat?"

Josette looked pityingly at him—such a great villain and, like all villains, incapable of thinking things through. "Presumably, he needed to persuade them to hold still while he cut."

There was a moment of silence as everyone tried to imagine, broken by Goebbels tearing his new throat with retching and retching from his empty stomach.

Eventually, he looked round at them. "But to thus treat beings that have given you their loyalty, as those demons did, that is dishonourable." He said it again in German for emphasis. "*Ohne Ehre.*"

There was no talking, Emma decided, to someone that capable of utter self-delusion. Aserath tried to break the mood by butting in perkily. "Anyway, about the army. I found a few good men and they understood the situation, and they're on it. So much easier than I expected. A man called Bourne stepped forward almost at once, and he came up with some others, Carney, Bakht Khan, Yakov Panov. Two noblewomen friends of his two, who know all about sieges—Black Agnes of Dunbar and the Sforza woman—who thanked you, Emma, for the drubbing you gave her old friend Cesare. Who knows why they were all in Hell? Or how they came to be hanging out together here?"

Actually, Emma remembered, she did. She popped inside her head and found the relevant door and checked. It was private, though, and confidential.

"Good men, those," she nodded. "Good choices. I know them, I realize. I'll go and talk to them; several of them did well in sieges, which I guess is what we face, or something like it. It's going to depend on what this Simon has turned himself into. I'm sure we'll know before too long."

Actually, it was several of the periods of normal time Emma was still prone to think of as days. It was time spent in preparation, and in talking to their new comrades, and watching, and, yes, learning a lot, as the Siege Club—as Bourne and Panov and the two women called themselves, and the friends they had recruited and trained over the years as a hobby in those moments when the torments of pain surceased—recruited, and trained, and drilled. And found more people to recruit, and train, and drill. After a while, the first bunch of recruits went out among the formerly damned, and recruited more re-embodied souls to train and drill.

Sometimes the gods felt like guests in their own fortress, there on sufferance while others did the real work, but then, Emma thought to herself, that must be what real commanders do so much of the time.

She went off and talked to those of the damned who had not yet been properly pardoned. She listened to the heartbreak of people whose loved ones were in Heaven or some other place and lost to them, and did her best without leaving the safety of the fortress to check that they were not elsewhere in Hell.

369

That was the trouble—none of them could leave, especially those who had skills or talents or powers or attributes that Simon might wish to steal, to use against their friends. The fortress had been a response to the thought of a demon revolt, a refuge for those the demons wished to go back to torturing, and it remained one even now that it was seeming more and more likely that the demon army had fallen foul of its own ally.

On the afternoon of the seventeenth day, or perhaps only the seventh, Tsassiporah flew into Emma's office. Emma was listening patiently to two former Lords of Hell—the French king Louis that men called the spider, and that Reynard from whom some say foxes are named, the treacherous butcher whom Saladin slew with his own hand—cry into the paper handkerchiefs that she gave them that they were much maligned, and innocent of many of the worst charges levelled against them. And had fallen into bad company in death as in life, and would truly never do it again, any of it, whatever it was.

She pretended to listen and she pretended to forgive because she needed brave clever men who deserved to be in Hell, quite as much as she needed good ones who had come there by mistake or other's malice. One day they might resent her; one day their tears might turn genuine. For the moment she had to make the pragmatic choice, to accept lip service and lies.

And Tsassiporah flew into her office cawing as if it were the end of everything when it was only the end of this period of quiet preparation.

Emma joined the other gods on the high battlements. She gave them, and the men and women of the Siege Club, equally respectful nods, and followed their gaze to the air above the edge of the forest where a cloud was forming—or was it perhaps not vapour but something like insects, a cloud that had a tail that spiralled and twined down and out of sight.

The cloud grew and boiled where it was, and then it started to approach, slowly, above the trees, taking its time as if it were trying to create the maximum sense of dread and do a thorough job of searching the trees for stragglers.

Searching, yes, that was what it was doing, or rather what they were doing, because the cloud was made up of a myriad spheres and its tail was made of almost transparent, translucent filaments, only visible at all because they were so densely braided and tangled.

As they got within yards of the fortress, the spheres turned upwards.

Emma and the others found themselves staring into the eyes of Simon the Magus, the hundred thousand eyes, with pupils that were slits, or triangles or mandalas and were the eyes of—just how many demons had he cut the eyes out of? Into eyes that were bloodshot and bloodstained and dripping blood: it was blood that made the long braided train of nerve fibres even visible.

His eyes stared into the hearts and minds of Emma and her companions as if there were nought of worth about them, not anything a man might wish to steal, but then those scornful eyes revealed their deceit all of a second's breath. The fibres untwined and the eyes started to dart into the fortress and roll about its floors and float in the air of its corridors.

Looking where pikes and crossbows and machine guns were stored, at corners where an ambush might be prepared, or slits in the wall from which fire might shoot.

Tsassiporah flew up into the air and sliced down behind the air, pecking and clawing at the fibres. The eyes turned to look at the red bird and the filaments tried to engulf and strangle it but they won free, left the things that had tried to bind her floating free in the air like gossamer.

Aserath spat small flames at the eyes as they rolled around under her feet. She spat a larger gout at the untwining filaments, but it splashed off them.

Catherine reached into the wallet at her side and produced a pair of dress-maker's shears, with which she started to snip each eyeball free of its filament to fall and rot like wet summer fruit in the grass, wherever they ended up lying.

Emma's armour shimmered a little, and suddenly a sharp blade extruded from the palm of her hand. *It's like being inside a Swiss Army Knife*, she thought, *so useful.* She sliced away at any filament that came near, and if an eye came too close to her, she jabbed at it, hoping to cause their master pain. She looked around at her companions—they were all doing what they could, partly to make it as hard as possible for Simon to spy on them and partly sheer revulsion at being watched like this, with eyes that had been gouged out and taken from their original owners.

From the shouts of disgust and anger from other floors, it was clear that the eyes were finding their way in through arrow nocks and the few windows that Judas and Josette had put into their creation. At least this meant that, after a long wait, the garrison of the fortress were getting to do something, to fight an enemy.

Emma thought back to the first time she had fought this sort of creature, the artist Aurora—old tricks are the best—and she shouted out in a voice that the armour amplified for her, "Salt and Pepper!" She found that her will, and that of her companions, produced a steady shower of the stuff, that gritted under foot, mopping up the fluid from burst eyeballs.

In a flurry of motion, the remaining eyes pulled back, like a fast receding tide.

Pain had been a factor, clearly, but...

"I assume that the damage we did was only a factor." Her voice was more pessimistic than she had expected it to be. "He's probably seen everything he needs to."

"That was disgusting," Aserath's voice was rich with heavily emphasized loathing, "and I speak as one who has spent the last two and a half thousand years in Lucifer's Hell. I wonder what he will do for an encore."

"It's never a good idea to ask that sort of question, I've found." Josette's world-weariness never sounded remotely affected, unlike almost everything Aserath said, Emma thought. Poor love, she really does sound as if she is letting this get to her.

"Simon really doesn't like us," Judas explained. "Of course, he may not realize who Josette is, but that will only mean that he thinks I'm the person she used to be, which won't improve matters."

Josette laughed. "I don't know—all I ever did was heal someone he had just killed and get in the way of some falling honey. You cut off his blasting hand. It really would be a good idea for you to hang on to my old face, I think. Yours might make him spiteful…"

Judas looked even more thoughtful and regretful than he usually did. "Whatever happened to your unwelcome guest?"

Josette smiled and shrugged. "He did eventually leave, just before I died. Announced his repentance and indicated that he was going to find something useful to do as atonement. That was very nice of him, and maybe he kept his word, but I certainly haven't heard of him since. I'm something of an expert in staying out of sight, but he is even better than I am, it seems."

"He never showed up at the Court of Lucifer, which would have been an obvious place," Aserath reasoned. "And from what Judas is saying, not Heaven either."

Emma, bored with guessing, raised her hand and asked, "Who are you talking about?"

"Alexander," they chorused.

Emma felt genuinely impressed, but not so much so as to switch of her brain. "So, not anywhere where anyone's come across him, and apparently not impersonating anyone else because you'd know."

A look of mingled disgust and affection crossed Josette's. "I really would. He lived inside my skull for a long time. I really would know him anywhere."

"He's obviously doing something he thinks is very useful somewhere where no one has ever thought to look for him. It's the sort of interesting riddle that usually only gets solved when it needs to be, in this or some other desperate emergency. Either he's just dead or he'll turn up sometime, somewhere, being the cavalry. Maybe today, if we're lucky. Because we need some luck. Look there."

Out at the edge of the forest, picking its way rapidly across the tops of trees with the diminished cloud of eyes floating above its head, the filaments trailing into its empty eye sockets, was something that was presumably Simon the Magus.

"You have got to be fucking kidding," said Judas, son of God.

Simon has wasted quite a lot of the demons he had misled and betrayed, Emma thought, but maybe there will be nasty surprises later. Still, Aurora was a true artist, if a deranged one, and genuinely creative in what she did to herself, whereas Simon—well, in fairness, he's been in Hell for two millennia so he may well not have read Hans Moravec.

Then she realized that she had been being a smart-arse aloud and blushed inside her armour.

"Moravec?" Aserath turned from contemplating the approaching thing to ask.

Josette and Judas stumbled over each other to explain—of course they'd know, Emma thought, the whole builders-engineers thing.

"Most people thought robots"—Aserath looked blank and so he corrected himself -"automata would be made to look like humans, but actually that didn't work. Humans don't like what looks like them but isn't, whereas…"

"Something like that, that doesn't look human, because it has too many arms and legs and they branch off from each other, and—he really hasn't left much of his face alone has he?"

"That really is disgusting." Emma had thought the eyes an obvious gambit, but Simon had outdone himself with the rest of the body he had built himself. A true monster, for anyone that hates spiders a reasonable amount but regards Daddy longlegs as the real enemy. He really did not need an army, not with hundreds of arms. Each of them had a weapon in it; some of them were swords and spears, but he also had several of what looked like hand grenades but were probably something far nastier. Emma looked round at her fellow gods.

"Could this get any worse?"

"Actually it's worse than you know." Josette had spoken, but Judas nodded along with her. "Even when we knew him, he had made himself largely invulnerable by keeping stolen organs as backups dried in between his ribs. With that long thin body, he's probably got them all over the place, likely including backups of his brain. He dries things out and rolls them, so he may well have a kidney between two elbows or part of his brain in a joint. Mara and her friend the centaur smashed him apart and then gave him to his own flames—it was the only way to be sure."

Aserath laughed. "Well, that's easily dealt with, then. Because, hello, dragon here?"

She flickered into that shape, and flew up to perch on the very top of the tower—Emma had not noticed that Josette's design even included a place for her to do that comfortably.

"We may well try that at some point, but I would imagine he's thought of it." Emma hated to be a wet blanket, but it seemed likely that the only way to destroy the creature was going to be a limb at a time, with a butcher's bill being paid for every single one.

Still, what Aserath did next was clearly well thought through. There was no real point in keeping the forest that the orchard had turned into, since it was going to be no sort of barricade at all. Flames leaped between intertwined branches and raced up them high into the air; the air filled with the noise of the breaking hearts of dying trees and the crackling of the thorns that grew on them. By setting fire to the trees rather than burning Simon directly, she achieved greater heat, especially when she used her wings to fan the flames.

A line of fire raced out to meet Simon, who reared up on his back fifty or so limbs and sprayed red sticky liquid over the flames, sending up fumes in black noisome clouds and eventually quenching them.

Behind him, the fires joined up again and swept out in a fan of flame that seemed likely to consume the whole wood. Then Azareth raised a talon and suddenly that entire sector of wood, ash and stumps and embers was gone, leaving the expanse of grassland that had been there before she had grown the trees. Where the fire had not reached, the forest stood high and complexly twisted and intertwined as it had before.

"Well," said Vretil, a fan of the obvious. "Now we know what he did with the blood of those demons as well as their limbs and eyes."

Emma remembered how effectively Aurora had repurposed her own guts for strangling, and spraying sleep gas and digestive acid, and hoped Simon hadn't gone there. Josette noticed the look of disgust on her face and said, "The guts? Oh, no, he needs them—to dry as parchment and macerate with spare brains and the knowledge they contain. We're probably safe from his using them for anything else." This was reassuring, for a particularly disturbing value of reassuring.

There were a reasonable number of archers among the garrison, who had pulled themselves together as a group, as a sudden tightly focused rain of arrows descended upon the beast. Simon reached up into the sky with a selection of legs and arms, which appeared to be unpleasantly double-jointed, and plucked almost all of them from the sky before they even came close to hitting him.

"I suppose it's a good thing to know he can do that." Emma was more concerned to see what Simon could do that was not merely defensive. Her eyes wandered up to Aserath, who was still on top of the tower but no longer a dragon, just big—which presumably meant that she dissolved and remade those dresses each time she changed, because otherwise they'd be part of her.

Trailing behind Simon was a sort of bag of skin which possibly wasn't actually attached to him—some of his arms reached inside it and flashed something; but Emma was looking away and had time to go off inside her head.

She found herself outside the smaller of the doors she had seen before and this time opened it fully. Out of it came a shorter, blonde slightly butch version of herself in a tuxedo.

"Berthe." Emma spoke as if she had always known that the

composer was an earlier incarnation of herself. "I need you to take over my body for just a second, and get paralyzed with guilt and shame and dread."

Berthe looked at her with sardonic reproach and went over to what, in the palace of Emma's memory, were two large bay windows that looked out through her eyes.

"*Scheisse*," she whimpered, and was still, staring in fixed horror at something that Emma did not see. She had blindfolded herself, or rather, her self, before elbowing Berthe aside and taking over the body again. She was just in time to see Simon putting back into his bag the fragment of the mirrored cliff of self-knowledge and despair, with which he had succeeded in incapacitating Emma's companions.

She could see why Judas had a bad conscience and just about got that Josette might; it had never occurred to her that Aserath had any sort of conscience at all or that Vretil would need one. The Siege Club were just as badly off; thousand-yard stares on all of them—but then, anyone who survives a battle or a siege is going to have issues, she thought.

Goebbels had already been whimpering naked in a corner and he didn't seem any worse than before. That probably meant he hadn't seen it, and, truthfully, she wouldn't wish what he would have seen even on him.

She whistled to Tsassiporah, who had been swooping after severed eyeballs around the battlements and had missed the whole thing. The red bird fluttered up and dived at Simon's parchment pale face, cruel beak extended. Emma had never noticed before that they had claws along the tops of their wings, but now they were all out.

Simon snatched at the bird with twenty hands—snip, snap—but Tsassiporah was faster, and got away unscathed except for one of their more uselessly showy red feathers. Emma seized the moment of distraction to dash across to Josette, who was sobbing gently, and grab from her the silver fish-hook, which she had tucked into her sword belt. She reached around and placed it across her shoulders. The armour flowed over it, holding it in place.

Since she was there, and because it is always important to do these things while you can, she kissed Josette hard so that her lips stung, bruised by one of those perfect cheekbones.

Emma did all this so fluidly that by the time Simon's remaining eyes turned on her, she was standing nonchalantly among her moaning and paralyzed companions and whistling La Vie en Rose rather tunelessly. She was expecting the long-fingered pincer-hands that snaked around on ten-jointed arms and picked her up by the scruff of her armoured neck.

"So you're the little mortal who fancies herself Judge of the Damned, Co-Queen of Hell?"

Seen close up, that face looked more like faded scraps of wallpaper in the wreckage of a bombed house than anything human.

Distract him until the others pull themselves together, she thought, and if possible seize the opportunity to hurt him physically or emotionally. Only use the fish-hook when you're absolutely sure.

"I dealt with one of your kind before." She spoke with an insincere tone of compassion and concern. "It didn't go well for her, but then, at least she knew what she wanted, and got it after a fashion."

"There is no one like me," and he shook her like a dog with a rat for emphasis.

"Self-remodelling, self-hating, never satisfied? Trust me, I know the type. Obviously you're the famous one…"

"What about you?" His voice was sly and insinuating. Of course, it wasn't his voice, not really, it belonged to poor old Goebbels. "You weren't always immortal and young and a goddess and you didn't always have hair of that particularly vile vermilion shade."

Emma laughed at him. "I chose none of those things. They are the wages of unself-conscious virtue, most of them, including the hair. What can I say? I am the pampered bitch of time and chance sometimes. It's better that than chopping people up for the bits for two thousand years. All it got you was sent to Hell, and all it has got you there is sadder and sadder."

She cast her glance along the length of his belly to where a prodigious piece of equipment hung. "I mean, sweetie. I don't know who you stole the immense schlong from, but trust me, it's not going to get you laid. Except possibly by a desperate giraffe." She shook her head. "Sad."

Simon laughed, showing far too many teeth in a jaw that was clearly not his. Oh, she thought, that's why the skin of his face looks so stretched, because it is. Silly man.

Then she thought, that she didn't think he could cram her in there, and remembered the ogre who had eaten Caroline.

"I'll tell you what's sad," he smirked. "A so-called Queen of Hell who dangles from my arms while I kill all of her friends with a single shot. Not just kills, annihilates; they won't be coming back. Not even the angel."

One of the arms that was almost, but not quite within reach of her sword arm, raised something that looked like a gun. She looked desperately behind her; the others were still semi-stunned and not quite back in control of their emotions. Asareth was still in human form, but had slipped from her perch and fallen partway. It was only guttering that was keeping her from falling down to the battlements. Her left hand flopped into the air on the brink.

"Duck!" Emma shouted, and it seemed as if some of them started to hear her.

Simon twined several of his eye-stalks round each other so as to get the clearest possible focus for his shot and Emma tried desperately to escape from his grip or at least reach out and dislodge the gun. Oddly, her sword seemed reluctant to come to her hand.

"Wait," whispered the armour.

Simon's finger tightened on the trigger, and from out of Emma's head there burst the intangible, but very visible and very angry shade of Berthe von Renssler.

She flew at his eye-stalks like a Fury, so that he flinched and shot wide. But not wide enough. The gun howled like a tormented rabid wolf and something shot out of it that was like the rich rotten smell of sewage, a fingernail prying into the socket where a tooth decayed.

Asareth's left hand and part of her wrist sheared away to nothingness and then she was falling—but Vretil caught her and gently laid her on the flagstones.

Her scream awoke the others and suddenly the air around Emma was full of thrown projectiles. Simon reared up, catching some and hurling them back, and letting go of Emma altogether, so that she fell.

As his grip on her released, she twisted, using the momentum to swing towards the long thin tube that his torso had become.

"*Now*" whispered the armour, and rippled. The giant hook that had been flush against her back came to her hand, and she swung it out ahead of her. It pierced Simon just below the throat.

He screamed, and the scream as she tore apart the voicebox he had stolen from Goebbels was the most eloquent thing she ever heard from him.

She heard the shouting of the garrison and the noise of trumpets and hoofbeats. She paid no attention because she was leaning into the hook and putting her weight into it, feeling Simon's grossly elongated and distorted breastbone yielding under her pressure. She heard his windpipe gurgling where the hook had caught it, and suddenly the bone cracked and sheared and she was riding the hook down as it caught on a rib and snapped, it and then another, like the breaking of sticks for kindling. Oh dear, she thought, this was going to be a very messy ride, all the way down to that ridiculous dick, with innards spilling all over her.

When it came to it, though, there really wasn't much left inside Simon beyond dried parchments and nameless solid lumps. As she rode the hook down, she reached in with her free hand and snatched, and threw, doing as much damage as she could. Some of what she grabbed was wet and slick, but most of his organs were like thin paper or the wings of dead moths.

Below her she could hear the cracking of bones and the squealing of joints as they torn apart; above her, from the battlements, people were hurling rocks and shields and weapons. Some of them glanced off her, but the armour protected her even from the jar of strikes.

Simon screamed on, like a siren running out of air that would go on for a while yet, diminishing a little at a time.

She looked down, and there were horses with leather armour and a whole throng of people in plate and mail and leathers—a small army had joined the fun and were slinging ropes and hooks around Simon's legs and tying them to the horses and then driving the horses off, so that at best the legs splayed and at worst they broke. Men and women with long pikes were batting at his many hands, severing the fingers and letting the weapons they held fall to the ground, where other soldiers were picking them, and the fingers, up and putting them in big baskets.

Emma was getting far too close to Simon's crotch, and the stench of it reminded her that she really did not want to go any nearer. She pulled the hook out, fell free for a second and then stabbed it into the thigh of one of his more human-looking legs. She took the sword from her right arm with her left hand and, as she hung from the fish-hook, slashed at the pulsing artery near the surface of the leg's pale skin, but all that gushed out was dark red silty dust like the bottom of a river that died before the start of Time.

It spilled out of him and drifted like smoke in the air, the smoke of something burned after it had rotted. And like smoke, after a while, it was gone.

Then that leg buckled at all of its ten knees, and suddenly she was hanging a few feet above the ground; she put her sword back where it belonged, pulled out the hook and dropped, landing catlike on all fours and springing up. A few feet away, a tall elegant woman in armour watched her with amusement.

The armour was solid and practical enough—but clearly not autonomous—and yet it was flattering and form-hugging to an extent that reminded her of...But it couldn't be.

The woman walked over to Emma and pulled her visor back. "Hi honey," the well-known voice said, and the mouth it came from was suddenly at hers, warm and wet and made of flesh. "Miss me?"

Oh, she had, it was true, but not any more. In her bones and her heart and her groin it was like a rush of water and high-arching violin strings and a hot summer breeze.

Emma had so many questions, but mostly she felt relief, and wrapped herself around her lover, for the first time feeling her breath on her cheek and the small hairs at the back of her neck under her fingers. But there would be time for this, and most of the questions, after Simon's slow destruction was entirely accomplished.

That seemed well under way, now. Brave people from both the new army and the garrison were clambering up his legs with axes and swords and chopping away at all his extra limbs, as close to his body as possible. For someone so fond of dismembering other beings and remodelling himself, Simon was not coping well with pain; his stolen voice was now just howls. He did not ask for mercy, and would certainly receive none.

Emma was surprised by how completely fine she felt about this. He had wanted to murder so many people, and he had comprehensively betrayed even his own allies. Though perhaps it would be worth keeping him around; he had, after all, had dealings with the ultimate enemy, and maybe could offer some clues.

She had more important things to think about now: Aserath for example. Not letting go of Caroline's hand, still drunk on the novelty of holding it for the first time, she walked back to the fortress and in at the now open doors; together they raced up the stairs to where Josette stood over Aserath, whose upper arm was now flaking away to white dust, as John Shallock's had in that Iraqi cell.

As they approached, Josette shook her head. Aserath was moaning gently, and Emma bent down to kiss her co-queen goodbye. As she bent, the armour whispered to her, "Which is more important to you? To keep my protection and company, or to save your friend?"

The answer was very simple. The armour flowed off her as she whispered, "My friend," and Emma took off the gloves and placed them on the flaking stump of Aserath's left arm. In a single fluid moment, the gloves became, not the armour, but a woman made of the same material, a woman who looked almost like Caroline, if Caroline were several inches shorter with stronger, more Mesopotamian features.

The woman who had been armour reached down and stroked Aserath's stump with a finger—as Emma, Josette and Caroline watched, the flesh grew back—briefly it was the same colour as the woman, but then faded back to Aserath's normal lush flesh.

The woman placed her finger on Aserath's eyes and lips, and the goddess slept; the woman turned to Emma and spoke.

"She will remember that there was pain, but will not remember the anguish or the fear. What is done with the Work, can be undone with the Work." She bowed to Caroline. "Hail and Farewell, sister and more than sister."

She turned to leave, but Emma put a hand on the woman's wrist. "When you were my armour, you never said who you were."

"For that, you must find Sof, and ask her."

Josette sighed. "But Sof is lost to all of us, even to Mara who loved her most."

The woman shrugged.

"Where are you going? I have so much to ask you," Emma pleaded.

"Into the dance of time and chance".

Years before, Emma had seen angels recede into a seemingly endless vista of space; this was not like that. The woman did not shrink or fade; she was gone and images of her were still there, and had been before she was gone. It was like the unfolding of a fan that vanished as it stretched, like the slowing of a film until you saw it frame by frame, like the rustle of cards as a conjuror shuffles them from hand to hand, like hands on a keyboard that move into blur.

Gone into time and chance.

Emma looked away, and it was as if the woman had never been there.

There were other things to do. The demolition of Simon was well underway without any help from the gods. His howling had ceased, which must be some sort of a sign. And so...

Emma took Caroline's hand firmly in hers, and then wrapped herself round her again and hugged and hugged as if the embrace would never stop, but it had to, because there were people coming out of the fortress door that her lover needed to meet.

"Caroline, you'll remember Josette—well, in the first place she's our boss and in the second..." And then she realized that her lover and her friend were talking to each other inside their heads—they had, after all, been talking for years, only now without any censorship.

No wonder Caroline looked so impressed and also so amused. Amused enough to forget how impressed she was and start teasing.

"I've heard a lot about you, recently, in your earlier life. Alex will really want to see you."

Josette looked genuinely excited. "Is he here?"

Emma realized, yet again, who they were talking about, and felt slightly miffed all over again, at being left out. Typical of Caroline, to be so much on first name terms that she wasn't even name-dropping him.

"Alex had always been here." Caroline was so enjoying being the one who knew the secret, just this once. "He came here early on, snuck in across the border from Hades when there still was a Hades. He decided that it was what you would want him to do. He's been freeing the damned—they call themselves the Wild Damned and have been running resistance up in the hills. If it weren't for the war, he was planning to challenge Lucifer. As it is, well, of course I told him how wonderful you are, Emma dearest, and he just trusted my judgement."

Emma knew that slightly predatory look; really it wouldn't have been any of her business. Caroline caught the implicit question, and pecked her on the cheek.

"You needn't fret dear. So very very gay."

Tsassiporah flew over from where they had been eating the eyes and filaments directly out of Simon's head, and looked quizzically at their mistress.

"Tsassie, this is Caroline. Caroline, this is Tsassiporah, child of the Bird and sibling of Jehovah's companion, Ghost. Tsassie used to be Lucifer's and is now sort of mine."

Emma noticed a small eyeball on the floor, and fed it to the bird. "Do be a love," she said, stroking their predatory beak, "and watch over Aserath until she wakes up."

As they walked down the staircase, they met Berthe coming up to look for Emma. More introductions, and what is the form for such moments?

"Berthe, this is Caroline, my lover, and Josette, my friend, whom I used to work for." Because clearly goddesses don't work for each other, just with. "This is Berthe von Rensler, the distinguished composer, who apparently I used to be. Shall I put you back into the flesh now? Sorry about earlier."

"Don't be silly, darlink. If we can't use each other like that, who can we? No, actually, not a body. I was thinking, we're mostly the same and if I snuggle into you, we'll just blend. I like the idea of dissolving into a goddess."

When Emma had peeked past a half-open door into Berthe's memories, she had seen a tiny portion of what passed into her now, soft and welcome as her own sigh. After a long tender momen it was done; and now she could speak German, knew a lot about archaeology and had a cello gigue in her head she was desperate to write down.

And so many more girls, so many welcoming witty mouths and lush thighs. Emma suddenly realized how chaste she had always been, and now was not.

"Oh god." Caroline picked up a hint from Emma's expression. "You're going to start composing, aren't you?"

"Only in my spare time, of which I have little."

But the next person they met, just at the door of the fortress, was

385

Judas, who was all business, all the future. For someone who had been paralyzed with guilt and shame and torment a few minutes before, he was almost irritatingly chipper.

"Emma, just the woman I was looking for. I was wondering, well, I'd like to go on clearing up my own messes and I really don't want to go back to Heaven any time soon. So, how would you feel if I take over your judging and social work duties for a while? You need time with your sweetheart, whom I see you've found."

He nodded politely to Caroline who grumbled, "She'll be too busy with bloody symphonies for me."

Josette hugged her brother. "I'm not ready to talk to the old fraud—so I'll keep you company for the moment. Aserath is going to want help putting things back together, and I've thought of several useful things we could build together."

The siblings went off into a huddle and Emma left them to it.

The two armies had piled the severed demon limbs into a vast tidy stack, on top of which they had placed what was left of Simon—the cylinder of his body, the gross phallus, his severed, blinded, still living head.

Emma and Caroline stood together, looking at it a moment. A young, very butch young man, with stylishly long hair and slightly protruding eyes, walked over and pecked Caroline on the cheek.

"You must be Emma," he gushed and flung his arms around her. "Caro's told me so much about you."

He offered her a pistol, the twin of the one Simon had used against Aserath. "Would you like to finish him?"

"Shouldn't we wait?"

Alexander laughed sardonically. "None of them will be out until it's done, except for Vretil. Tender consciences are what they deal in, all four of them, but someone has to be the butcher. Vretil won't do it, but it's his job to watch."

Emma could not quite bring herself to take the pistol—it was an unclean thing. Alexander laughed again. "He's your kill, but I don't mind giving the mercy stroke. If you can call annihilation mercy."

"Some think it so, but not Simon."

"He is a man that needs killing. And I know. I used to be one such myself, and even now…"

It was kind of the King of Macedon to offer to play headsman, but Emma was co-Queen and Judge of a larger realm even than he had known. She made a large thick red handkerchief out of the stuff of air, and wrapped it thickly about her hand before taking the gun that Alexander offered her.

She had not killed many men and this was the first time she had killed someone helpless in cold blood. Emma felt surprised at how little guilt she felt as she silently pressed the vile gun against Simon's ruined head and yanked at its stiff trigger. Again that vile noise; when the head was gone, she played the beam up and down the fragments until at the last Simon was white dust, that blew away as rapidly as the red dust that had bled from his many wounds.

Emma placed the gun on the ground and thought hard at it until it went away, somewhere locked inside time and chance where only she would ever be able to find it again.

She hoped a time when she might need it would never come.

Emma created another handkerchief and wiped her hands thoroughly, then looked round at the patiently waiting Caroline.

"There's one last thing. I have to do it, sooner or later. I'd rather not put it off, because I've got you back and I so want to know how you escaped Lucifer and found the Wild Damned, but it will have to wait, because there is a locked door in my memory palace, and Berthe was behind one like it and…"

Caroline hugged her. "I've so missed you gabbling at me when you're working something out. Is it safe? What you're doing?"

"I hope so, but Sof was Mara's sister and sweetie. Not incest, I don't think, some other relationship that I don't get—and she was married to Josette, back when. Aserath said nice to see us back together first time since the wedding. Something bad happened to her that no one is saying, or perhaps knows. And there is a door in my memory palace that I didn't put there."

"All right." Caroline kissed her cheek. "Be careful, is all I'll say. Sit down here, on the grass, and I'll hold your head, and whatever happens, it will be okay."

Emma closed her eyes, letting herself wander.

She was back in the memory palace, in the corridor she had no memory of building. The stack of files were still there, where she had laid them aside before the heavily locked door she had seen before, a door that looked as if it were wood panels over thick steel, and a padlock like a shield to hold it tight.

Beside it there were smaller doors she had not seen, and the open door that had been Berthe's.

One after another, the small doors flew open, and one after another, out walked young children.

When they saw each other, they reached out and took each other's hands, and danced around Emma before forming a line in front of her. They smiled at her in perfect trust and one after another they took her hand. She felt their short lives, dissolving into her like sweetness and with them moments, skipping and making daisy chains and licking honey from a spoon, the high points of those lives.

Emma walked up to the large locked door and set her hand to its principal padlock. A voice spoke to her from the lock, a voice she knew: Morgan's voice.

"If you are here, you know what you are doing, whoever you are. Beware: there is a reason for these locks. Do not destroy the door, because you may need it again. I hope you never find this door, but time and chance rule us all."

The lock sighed in Emma's hand, and then sprung open as if she had petted it and it knew her. The door opened slowly, as if giving a chance for second thoughts.

Emma looked inside.

A couch on which there lay, as if asleep, a woman whose features were as much hers as the armour's had been Caroline's. A strong resemblance and yet Mesopotamian, archaic...

She sat down beside the woman, reaching out to stroke her brow, and spoke tentatively. "Sof?"

The woman's eyes fluttered into wakefulness.

"Yes... I am Sof...." And then the eyes flew wide open, and she screamed.

Some Things About Roz Kaveney

She has been a professional writer since her twenties but is publishing her first novel *Rhapsody of Blood: Rituals* and her first collection of poetry, *Dialectic of the Flesh*, at the age of 63. Asked why, she says, "Well, I was quite busy."

Friends say it's hard to be out with Roz in Central London and not find yourself being randomly greeted by other people she knows. Some say this happens in New York, too, on the rare occasions when she goes there. This is because Roz's circle of acquaintance includes everyone from politicians to poets, art historians to dominatrixes, at least one serial killer to at least one Poet Laureate.

She helped negotiate changes to the law that helped trans people—Roz is a proud trans woman—change their legal status; she helped block a law that would have imposed stringent sexual censorship in UK bookstores.

She once rescued a flatmate from a Chicago mob hit.

She and Neil Gaiman once sold a two-book deal on the basis of a proposal they improvised in a meeting at which the publisher had turned their original idea down.

She discovered in the British Library an unknown verse play by a major Victorian poet; later, she told this story to a leading contemporary novelist, who based an award-winning novel on it.

She knows that British Intelligence has a file on her—she's seen the letter in which an Oxford don denounced her to them as a subversive. She does not know what the don meant...

She co-founded both Feminists against Censorship and The Midnight Rose Collective. Look them up.

She's contributed to reference books that vary from *The Cambridge Guide to Women Writing in English* to *The Encyclopaedia of Fantasy*.

She was deputy Chair of Liberty (The National Council for Civil Liberties), and active in the Oxford Union debating society, the Gay Liberation Front and Chain Reaction, a dyke SM disco she helped run in the 80s.

She's been on television talking about sex, alternate worlds and who should have won the Booker Prize in 1953 if it had existed then; she's been on radio talking about fan fiction and film music.

She was a contributor to the legendary Alan Moore anti-Clause 28 comic book AARGH! (Action Against Rampant Government Homophobia).

As a journalist, she's written about everything from the Alternative Miss World competition to the crimes of the Vatican.

Her acclaimed books on popular culture include *Reading The Vampire Slayer; From Alien To The Matrix; Teen Dreams;* and *Superheroes.*

"I was reared Catholic but got over it, was born male but got over it, stopped sleeping with boys about the time I stopped being one and am much happier than I was when I was younger."

She likes baroque opera, romantic string quartets, the music of Kurt Weill and Bruce Springsteen, the singing of Ella Fitzgerald, Ricki Lee Jones and Amanda Palmer.

She makes adequate chili, perfectly decent scrambled eggs, and a good cassoulet if she's got a couple of days.

She will write you a goodish sonnet in about five minutes if she's in the mood—sestinas usually take an hour.

When she grows up, she wants to be awesome.

For more about Roz, visit her Glamourous Rags website at:
glamourousrags.dymphna.net/index.html

CPSIA information can be obtained at www.ICGtesting.com
Printed in the USA
LVOW11s1814181114

414334LV00001B/118/P